D0205585

Mike Eller

Brent Ghelfi is the author of two other Volk novels, *The Venona Cable* and *Volk's Game*. *Volk's Game* was nominated by the International Thriller Writers for Best First Novel of 2007 and by *Mystery News* and *Deadly Pleasures* magazines for a Barry Award for Best Thriller. His novels have been translated into seven languages and optioned for film. He is currently working on the fourth novel in the Volk series.

Also by Brent Ghelfi

The Venona Cable

Volk's Game

Shadow of the Wolf

a novel

Brent Ghelfi

PICADOR

HENRY HOLT AND COMPANY

New York

For Al and Jan

SHADOW OF THE WOLF. Copyright © 2008 by Brent Ghelfi. All rights reserved. Printed in the United States of America. For information, address Picador, 175 Fifth Avenue, New York, N.Y. 10010.

www.picadorusa.com

Picador® is a U.S. registered trademark and is used by Henry Holt and Company under license from Pan Books Limited.

For information on Picador Reading Group Guides, please contact Picador.
E-mail: readinggroupguides@picadorusa.com

Designed by Meryl Sussman Levavi

ISBN 978-0-312-42928-7

First published in the United States as *Volk's Shadow* by Henry Holt and Company

First Picador Edition: February 2010

10 9 8 7 6 5 4 3 2 1

The star of death stood over us.
And Russia, guiltless, beloved, writhed
Under the crunch of bloodstained boots,
Under the wheels of Black Marias.

—Anna Akhmatova, *Requiem*

chapter 1

A man like me is not supposed to have doubts.

Especially not at a time like this, poised in the open fuselage of an Mi-24 assault helicopter, carving a tilted arc around a black square in the grid of lights on Moscow's south side. This is the worst time to be asking myself questions that can't be answered. But lately they're always there, corroding all those things I once believed so intensely. Defend the motherland, secure our southern flank, protect the innocents. Gripping a canvas strap to brace against the force of our turn, I whisper the words in a soundless incantation.

The AMERCO building rises from the darkness, a fiery, open wound torn midway up its south face. Smoke glows in chemical-pink wreaths against the night sky as the helicopter swoops, flares, drops to a hard landing. I leap out while the rotors are still thumping the air in a dying backbeat rhythm.

A policeman jumps in front of me. He shouts something about Chechen terrorists. The blast happened less than an hour ago, he yells, but I already know that and more. I circle my finger in the air impatiently, and he points the way to an improvised command center. Charging away from him toward the burnt skyline, I think that what he should have said is that the *first* blast is less than an hour old. More explosions might come, because at least two terrorists remain alive.

I am here to change that.

The General's orders, issued over a scrambled satellite phone, ricochet inside my mind. Do not delay. Do not negotiate. Attack. Dead hostages, destroyed property—whatever the costs, they will be less than the price of capitulation. Orders birthed by hard experience fighting a shadowy war against a faceless enemy. Orders that mean I don't have the luxury of doubt.

My path brings me within sight of the blown-out half of the sixth story of the targeted high-rise, the Moscow headquarters of an American oil company. Its southern side gapes like a screaming mouth, bent steel beams and metal studs for a tongue, belching smoke. The damage appears worse from here than it did from the helicopter.

Moving faster now, I rush past a staging area for the dead and wounded, set back about a hundred meters from the edge of the zone where rounds from the building might reach. Many of the wounded are missing pieces. Limbs, eyes, and, in the case of one shrieking boy, part of his jaw. Each step drives nails into my left foot—the foot that is not there—a phantom pain, the product of being this close to my old adversaries, entering a world of horror, knowing what is to come.

The millennium Moscow bombings in Pushkin Square left 150 dead, the takeover of the House of Culture Theatre 130, just two among so many others I can't bear to think of them all. The worst for me was the Beslan school massacre, during which 344 died, including 186 children. The architects of many such attacks are dead, some of them killed in operations memorialized by secret medals I've tossed into a cigar box, but others have risen to take their place.

The makeshift command post has been established in the first-floor lobby of an office building three blocks away from the one that was bombed. I cross a wide street emptied of traffic. Slam open the steel-and-glass door. A small group huddled around a folding metal table all turn to stare at me.

"Who's in command?" My voice sounds loud even to my own ears.

"Who wants to know?" Tall, thin, and spectacled, he looks like a haughty professor, although too young to be one. I know his kind at a glance. A staffer, privileged from birth by his family's social position in the old Soviet order. His uniform and red beret identify him as a special forces officer of the internal troops of the FSB—the principal successor of the KGB—but his kind can be found throughout Russia's military, political, and bureaucratic elites.

I throw off my overcoat so that he can see my rank on the tunic beneath. He turns his back to me.

"I'll get with you later, Colonel." He spits out the words as though he's trying to rid his mouth of a bad taste.

"Now."

He whirls to face me, lips twisted into a snarl. "You'll not speak again until I address you. Is that—"

And I am upon him, wrenching him onto the table. It collapses under his weight and the force of the blow. A laptop crashes to the floor with him as he smacks the marble facedown. I plant the heel of my combat boot on the back of his neck.

"Who is second in command?" I say, so softly that everyone in the room leans forward to hear me.

A florid-faced policeman snaps smartly to attention. "I am, sir. Inspector Barokov."

The FSB officer under my boot struggles to rise. Or to reach a gun. I pull my Sig, bend down, and crunch it against the side of his head to knock him out. Then nod to the inspector to go on.

Still saluting, he tries to draw himself straighter. "The Chechens took the AMERCO offices on the sixth floor. We didn't have time to contact them before a bomb blew. We're lucky the whole building didn't come down. We don't know how many are dead, and we can't get inside."

He waits for a response. I'm not surprised the building still stands. Its bones were erected during Stalin's heyday, when labor was forced at the end of a bayonet and buildings were made of steel, brick, and mortar laced with blood. I flick my right hand toward my brow. He drops his salute, but remains at attention.

"Two terrorists are left on the north side of the sixth floor with maybe ten hostages, depending on how many from the office are still alive."

"How do you know all that?"

"They released a hostage to communicate their demands."

I could not possibly care any less what the terrorists want. In my mind's eye I can see the General's granite features, like a craggy Neanderthal's, his heavy lips moving. *Do not negotiate.*

Barokov points with his chin to a woman sitting in a reception chair, doubled up with her hands cupping her face. She appears to be crying. All I can see of her is ash-blond hair and a soot-stained pantsuit with a long rip running down the sleeve. Another uniformed FSB officer, a lieutenant, stands stiffly beside her, but he does nothing to question my authority. He roughly jostles her shoulder to get her attention, and she looks up at him, then turns to face me. She has shell-shocked green eyes wet with tears. She's overwrought, nervously fingering a blue pendant swinging from a chain around her neck and looking back and forth from me to the officer.

"You heard what he said?" I ask her. "Two terrorists, ten hostages, sixth floor. That's correct?"

She glances at the officer. "Yes. There were two of them. Both on the sixth floor." Her Russian is bad, with a heavy American accent.

I turn away, gathering my thoughts. "Show me the building layout."

Inspector Barokov unrolls faded, tattered blueprints while others set the table upright and then stand aside, looking everywhere except down at the professorial FSB agent oozing blood onto the polished floor.

"They're here," he says, pointing to a wing of offices toward the middle of the building. "We might be able to get in here." His finger lands on a stairwell that I can see is accessible only by entering the building directly below where the terrorists are thought to be.

I grunt and pull the plans closer, searching for a likelier path, sliding my finger along the crinkled paper to an exterior door on the west side of the building. The portal is tucked beneath an overhang six floors below and roughly thirty-five meters from where the hostages are being held.

"That door will be locked," Barokov says. "And getting there will be a problem. But there are only two of them, so if you can make it inside, the stairs probably won't be guarded."

The lock doesn't bother me. But he's understating the difficulty of getting there. The path to the door will be a scramble through the terrorists' field of fire. The darkness might provide cover, but not if they have night-vision goggles, which they probably do. The American military hands them out in Iraq the way it handed out sticks of chewing gum in France after World War II. Except that in Iraq the goggles are then sold to the people trying to kill American soldiers—free enterprise as practiced by Iraqi insurgents.

I page through the plans to the structural sheets. The main building is twelve stories high. It narrows six stories up, the center column rising like a thick candle in the middle of a cake. The sixth-floor ceiling is dropped, with a crawl space above it. Less than one meter of clearance. I roll back several pages of plans to find the one I want, then consider for a moment, trying to burn the drawing into my mind like light onto a photographic plate.

Barokov clears his throat and steps back. The former hostage is still quietly crying. Back at the helicopter a team of five combat-hardened commandos awaits my orders, and the chatter in my radio, mostly confused shouts, tells me that a separate Vympel antiterrorism unit is deploying nearby. But I can hear the General's voice in my head, urging me forward. *Do not delay. Attack.*

I turn away from the group and radio my squad leader, talking in a low voice into my hand-cupped mouthpiece. Instruct him to deploy around the perimeter, storm the building at the first sound of fighting, save the hostages if he can, worry about me last. Then I set aside the radio and strip down to black paratrooper pants and tactical body armor over a long-sleeved, collarless shirt made of a body-hugging synthetic. Slide the Sig into a nylon holster. Adjust the knife hanging below the back of my neck. Take one last look at the plans, and then I'm out the door, where I wait for a moment while my eyes adjust to the pinkish gloom.

"Who the hell was that?" I hear Inspector Barokov say behind me.

Chunks of blasted concrete and scattered building materials offer the illusion of cover on my approach to the blasted AMERCO building. I avoid the islands of light where the fires still burn. Crouch, crawl, slither, and slide—all well-practiced maneuvers. Street fighting is in my blood from three years of little else in bombed-out Grozny and the surrounding villages. After Grozny I spent most of two years in the icy forests of Ingushetia and the snowcapped mountains of Dagestan. Right up to the moment of my surrender—and six long months in a *zindan*, a mud pit, where time was measured by the shivering intervals between torture sessions. Within minutes I make it to the smoking building, my back against a brick wall, sweating despite the chill air, but breathing easily. No gunshots, no shouts. Nothing.

The door is locked from the inside, the lock well made. I spend nearly ten minutes picking it by the light of flickering flames, probing with small metal tools, alert for a cry of discovery. When it finally tumbles, the mechanism sounds like a reverberating gong. I wait another minute, my breath fogging the air. Still nothing except for wailing sirens, crackling fires, and distant crowd-control instructions amplified by a megaphone. I wedge through the heavy door and close it gently behind me.

The stairwell seems as deserted as Barokov thought it would be. Another surprise, because I thought he had underestimated the danger here as well as on the approach to the building. Outside sounds are muted. A dull roar fills my ears, accompanied by popping flames that have grown louder, magnified as though the inside of the building has become a giant hearth. The steps are made of concrete edged with metal toe-kicks, the walls lined with tubular handrails slick from condensation.

I ascend the stairs slowly, quietly, pausing at each landing while the structure groans around me like the hull of a sinking ship. Reach the sixth floor and squeeze through another door into an abandoned hallway filled with smoke and drifting paper. Slide along a wall beneath portraits of smug executives to an oak door leading into the room we identified on the blueprints. Inside is a wide area partitioned into cubicles. I place a chair against the wall closest to where I think the hostages are being held, nudge aside a ceiling tile, and peer into the dark crawl space.

In the light of a handheld torch that barely penetrates the smoke, the heavy I-beams disappear into the grayish haze, crisscrossed every five meters or so by steel braces. Suspended below them is a strip-metal grid that holds fiberboard ceiling panels identical to the one I just removed.

I sheathe the torch. Hoist myself onto the top of the wall at the level of the drop-ceiling grid. Straddle a beam, gripping with my thighs for balance. Creep along the sweating steel, moving noiselessly, making good progress, the darkness so complete I can't even see across the span to the parallel girders I know run along both sides of the one I am on. I worm forward for about three minutes, counting each transverse brace to measure the distance, choking on unseen gusts of ashy air, blinking away particles of soot and dust. When I've covered thirty-five meters I think I am directly over the hostage room. Except for the muted snarl of popping flames on the other side of the building and the distant clamor of sirens, everything is deathly quiet. Too quiet if the hostages and their captors are below. Not even a murmur or rustle of movement comes to me.

And then an eruption of light from the beam across from me stabs my eyes.

"You're dead," says a muffled voice.

The shocking glare strikes so suddenly I lose my grip. I let myself fall, not in a planned dive or some other well-executed evasion, but just a clumsy tumble that takes me straight down through the flimsy ceiling tiles to crash onto a desk in the room below. All of the air blows from my body.

Five meters away the second terrorist, his vest bulging with explosives, mouth covered by a swath of black cloth, stares wide-eyed at me. The muzzle of his Kalashnikov droops uselessly as he struggles to process my sudden appearance. Above us, his partner fires blindly through what's left of the drop-ceiling beneath him. The stitching of bullets races toward his comrade and explodes his skull. All the while I lay writhing on the broken desk, helpless, while random bursts from the man on the beam spray more bullets. One or more slugs must strike the dead man's vest, because an explosion rips through the room.

When I was a boy assigned to the work farms I pretended to be a Stakhanovite, a shock worker like the famous miner who always exceeded the norms. On rare days off, I imagined I was Ilia Muromets, the legendary protector of the Russian people, battling invaders with my giant, gentle strength. But when things were really bad I tried to disappear, to detach from my body and float away. That's the sensation I have when the explosion hurls me through the air in a long, weightless tumble. Everything after that is a confused haze—searing pain, shouted curses, rough hands, a jolting ride.

I open my eyes to find a ring of faces staring down at me. "He's alive!" someone says, and they begin cheering. The red-faced police inspector Barokov drops to a knee next to me and probes my body for injuries, pausing when his hands encounter the rigidity of my prosthesis.

"Nothing appears to be broken," he announces. More cheering and clapping, but not enough to blot out the sirens or the crackle of flames that are now burning with renewed intensity. "You saved them!" another voice says.

I sit up and rest my elbows on my knees. I'm on a stretcher on the street outside the ruined building. I can't seem to draw a full breath. Everything hurts. My face feels as though it's been washed in acid. Wetness on my forehead turns out to be blood, which looks like chocolate syrup on the end of my fingers. The fabric of my shirt and pants has burned through in the places not covered by armor. Scorched flesh on my arms and legs triggers licks of pain. Standing is hard work.

"What happened?" I ask Barokov.

"Fifteen minutes after you left, the building blew again. We thought everyone was dead. Your men stormed in and found all ten hostages, alive. They'd been moved to the first floor, on the east side. They say the terrorist holding them vanished after the second explosion. Three of your men retrieved you after they rescued the hostages. The Vympel unit found parts of two dead terrorists."

Disturbing questions slosh around in my mind. Why did the terrorists bother to move the hostages away from the danger? If a third terrorist was guarding the hostages, how many more were there? And how did they know where to wait for me?

I stride off toward the improvised command post. No shuffle, no limp, nothing to reveal weakness except for the slight roll caused by the rebounding spring in my prosthesis. The inspector jogs beside me to keep up, weaving through rescue workers and soldiers, who are everywhere now. Eyes shining and wearing a broad smile, he claps me on the back like an old friend. "You're a hero!" The voices in the trailing crowd echo his sentiments, but they barely penetrate my consciousness.

We arrive at the command post, where I enter and shut the door on my admirers. Pull my overcoat back on. Wrap the clothes I removed earlier in my tunic and throw the bundle over my shoulder. Glance down at the forgotten FSB officer. He's curled up like a child, his face ghostly white against a canvas of pooled blood leaking through a makeshift wrap of torn cloth. I wonder why his lieutenant left him this way, then shake away the question and take a moment to gather myself.

The setting was urban, not rugged mountains the way it was in the past, but the attack bears familiar hallmarks. During the time he had me in the pit, Chechen rebel Abreg liked to talk about everything— philosophy, religion, global politics—so I have a window into how his mind works. He knows the psychological value of soft civilian targets, and he would argue that a strike such as this is a justified response to the devastation in Chechnya. But too many things don't add up. Why this building? Why trigger the bombs in the early evening, a bad time for a high body count in an office building? Why protect the hostages?

Inspector Barokov and the others are still waiting when I step back outside, probably so they can offer more unwarranted congratulations.

"What happened to the woman—the hostage?"

They exchange uneasy glances. The inspector's ruddy features appear even more flushed as he squirms under my gaze. He's short and roundish, but now he tries to stretch himself taller. "We don't know. She and the FSB lieutenant disappeared right after you left."

"Who is she?"

Barokov looks to his comrades for support that fails to come, takes a deep breath. "Everything happened very fast. She spoke English, very little Russian. The only person she talked to was the FSB man in there. The one you hit." His jaw hangs open for a moment, then snaps closed. "I'll take him to the triage area now, but we're not going to get any information out of him for a while."

"The hostage—did she work for AMERCO?"

"That's what she said."

"What happened after I left the command center?"

"Nothing. We waited."

"Did anybody talk about how I planned to get inside the building?"

A shadow ripples across his face. "We looked at the blueprints and guessed at some things." He shifts his weight from one leg to the other, then looks me full on. "Lots of people were talking on their cell phones. Everything was happening so fast, anyone could have—"

He steels himself, like a boy about to deliver bad news to his father. "I'm sorry, Colonel. I didn't think to lock everyone down."

✶

Five minutes later the ground falls away and I'm airborne through flurrying snow, arrowing north in the Mi-24 helicopter back toward the Kremlin to brief the General. During the bumpy ride a medic stitches my head then strips me down to the waist and applies salve to my burns. He's wasting his time. The pain is nothing to me, and I don't care about scars. These will only add to the road map of conflict already carved into my body—a decade of Russia's military hot spots memorialized in scar tissue.

My chronometer beeps. I was on the ground for less than an hour.

The General is waiting for me in his subterranean headquarters in the bowels of the Kremlin, so close to the Moscow River that the rock walls weep condensed moisture. A bare bulb hanging next to a soggy wooden beam throws more shadows than light. He sits behind his ebony desk without moving, seemingly carved there from stone himself while he appraises me from the dark hollows beneath his ridged brow.

"You've lost weight."

Six months have passed since the last time we saw each other in person, just after Valya hobbled away on crutches to be lost in the crowds at Sheremetevo-2 terminal. Since then my assignments have been routine: north to St. Petersburg to intercept a drug shipment and shepherd it over the border into Finland, east to Tokyo to eliminate a rogue ex-KGB agent selling secrets and lies, all of my international travel done under a diplomatic passport. Right now I smell like smoke and grilled flesh, and parts of me feel as if they're still on fire, so I'd prefer to end the inspection and get on to business, but the General, as always, plots his own course.

"You look like a half-starved wolf."

The passing months have roughened my edges instead of smoothing them as he might have hoped. Dislocated by the loss of Valya, my humanity is in regression, and I don't know what I can do to reverse the course.

After another moment he lowers his gaze to study photos of the bombing. "That was good work. You killed two terrorists. But we figure at least fifty civilians died in the first explosion. We'll know for sure later. They're still collecting the pieces."

"I'd be dead except for luck."

His head is still canted down. Resting his elbows on the desk, he applies a thumb to each temple, presses hard enough to make white orbs of skin around his thumbs, and massages in tight circles. "Luck?" He sounds distracted, as though the events at the AMERCO building happened weeks, not minutes, ago. "I doubt it."

He shuffles some papers on his desk. "Do you know Filip Lachek?"

"No."

"I've had dealings with him before. Like yours, his name suits his reputation."

Volk means wolf, of course; the General has always liked the idea that he commands a vicious animal. The root of the name *Lachek* means hunger.

"Lachek cleans up Putin's messes," he says. "Like you do for me. But Putin has become a god now that our oil is pumping rivers of money into his pockets." His tone is bitter. His features harden and darken, like magma solidifying into rock. "I missed out on that. I didn't act fast enough."

Putin has nationalized Russia's largest oil and gas companies, forcibly repurchasing assets and imprisoning those who disagree with his prices, his methods, or his politics. Through his control of petrochemicals, he now wields enough political and economic power to bring entire countries to their knees.

"I received a call from upstairs." He motions above his head, figuratively pointing through several meters of rock to the better-known buildings of the Kremlin. "Lachek wants the name of the colonel who took back the AMERCO building. Says it's urgent."

"Why?"

"I'm still trying to find that out, but along with everything else that's happening his inquiry doesn't bode well. I won't be able to put him off for long. You understand."

He means I will be on my own, that Lachek is beyond his ability to control. The General has been a father figure for me since the early '90s, when he plucked me from Isolator 5 prison, a bestial place where men fought for scraps of meat and a place to sleep. I was sixteen, barely holding on. He arranged my education and training and has managed my career ever since, often placing me in harm's way, but my debt to him can't be repaid. The idea that he won't help me troubles me only a little. I'm used to it. The fact that this latest attack—scores killed, a prominent high-rise destroyed—is only a part of what's bothering him concerns me far more.

"What *else* is happening?"

Ignoring my question, the General rustles two stapled pages from the pile in front of him and slides them across the desk to me. "Lachek is in his mid-fifties. Fought in Afghanistan, air force. Stationed in Singapore until a few years back. Wet work all over Southeast Asia—drug interdiction, antiterrorism—all clandestine, buried so deep even I'm not privy to the details. Since '03 he's been Putin's man here in Russia. One of them, anyway."

I crinkle the brief into the pocket of my overcoat, planning to read it later. Each movement rubs blistered skin against fabric. "I need names and background information of the hostages."

"Why?"

"I don't understand why they were moved to safety."

His icy gaze holds mine for several seconds. Then he scratches a note on a pad on the desk in front of him. "Give me a few hours."

"A woman was in the command center, claiming to be a hostage the terrorists had released." I try to draw a mental picture, but all I can conjure is a navy blue suit covered in soot and streaked blond hair draped over her hands cupping her face. "She gave bad information about how many of them were inside the building, and she disappeared before the second explosion. I think she also tipped them where to wait for me. According to a police inspector on-site, she's American."

Deep, parenthetical furrows on either side of his mouth draw tight and he lowers his head to stare at the table. His eyes are hidden beneath his cantilevered brow, so now it is my turn to appraise him.

The General commanded the notorious Fifty-eighth Army, responsible for the invasion and brutal occupation of Chechnya during the second war there. During my time with him I never glimpsed remorse or self-doubt. Once I saw him suffering and in pain, but even then no hint of deeper emotion escaped the leathery ridges of his heavy mask. Now he's a deputy cabinet minister, ostensibly reporting to the minister of defense, but in truth the only limit on his power is whether he has the resources to take it and hold it. His underground organization permeates military affairs, politics, business, and crime—or, more precisely, the soupy amalgam that passes for those things in the new Russia.

All of which is more astonishing because the General is a dwarf. The top of his oversized head reaches less than one and a half meters. In a culture that despises physical weakness, the titanic ambition that impelled his rise to power is beyond my reckoning.

He drums the knuckles of his left hand on the desk, apparently still thinking about the woman in the command center. "Terrorist recruits come from everywhere nowadays. Who knows, maybe she took on an American accent. Maybe you weren't set up at all, and they just had a man posted there."

I try to recall the sequence of events on the I-beam. Smoke-filled gloom stabbed by a laserlike beam of light, then, almost in the same instant: *You're dead*—spoken in a muffled voice, but one that comes back to me in flat, unaccented Russian as I replay the sound of it in my mind.

The General gets up and totters in his swaying gait to a humming freezer that sits on the stone floor near his desk. He pulls out a frosted bottle of vodka and pours liberally into a water glass, then returns to his desk, where he cradles the sweaty drink on his lap.

"Something's wrong here, Volk," he says in a tone that straightens my spine. "Too many things are happening, all too suddenly."

I say nothing, wary of the change in him.

"The call from Lachek is serious, I think, and . . ." His voice trails off.

Nearly a minute passes in silence while I mentally compile a list of all the things that might follow the word *and.* A red dot the size of a laser sight starts blinking on an electronic panel appended to a row of three phones on his credenza. He stares at it, transfixed, then makes a sound like a low growl.

"What do you know about the Imperial Easter eggs?" he says.

chapter 4

The General asked me about the Imperial eggs once before, right after Valya left. His interest in them comes as no surprise. But the timing of his question is so unexpected I can't think of an answer right away. He continues to look fixedly at the blinking red light, waiting me out.

"Only a little," I lie, wondering how this topic could possibly be more important than the terrorist attack.

"Fabergé produced fifty for Tsars Alexander III and Nicholas II, beginning in 1885. Five of them were thought lost during the revolution or during the troubled times that followed."

All of this I know, of course. Just as I know that the eggs are a priceless part of our cultural history, not spoils from conquests of Western countries or items purchased by the tsars from abroad.

The red light stops blinking.

The General sets his untouched drink aside, pulls an open book closer, and puts on a pair of reading glasses. "The Imperial eggs are 'elegant treasures so perfectly crafted that they elevated the jeweler's art to sublime heights.'" He removes his glasses and regards me levelly. "What do you suppose they're worth?"

I know from experience that he does not want to hear something idealistic about the eggs being invaluable. "Tens of millions. Each."

The red dot pulses again, seemingly more insistent this time.

"Six months ago I decided to find them." He contemplates the blinking light, addressing it instead of me, while I wonder who he used to search for the eggs. Under normal circumstances the job would have been mine to do, but I haven't been his top adjunct lately.

"Captain Dubinin was able to locate only one," he says, answering my unspoken question.

Captain Dubinin is another member of the General's handpicked cadre of shadow warriors, my more polished doppelganger, who apparently has become my replacement.

"He found the second ever made," the General says. "The Hen Egg with Sapphire Pendant. The pendant was missing." He locks his gaze onto mine. "The egg was stolen, just this afternoon."

"How?"

"Dubinin and his driver were moving it to the Kremlin Armory. It was in an armored case. The captain and his man were abducted and murdered somewhere between here and Vladimir after making an exchange, the egg for cash."

"Who had the egg?"

"Khanzad."

I know the name but not the man. Intelligence agents refer to him as "the false Chechen." Often photographed by Western journalists wearing a camouflaged uniform crisscrossed with bandoliers and studded with grenades, his spiked beard and hooked nose present a menacing appearance. In truth he is a Chechen from the Gunoi *teip*—clan—in northeast Chechnya, antiseparatist and pro-Kremlin when it suits him, a dealmaker willing to sell his soul. Valya's family was from a splinter sect of the same *teip*, thought by many to be the product of mixed marriages of Chechens and Russians. My nemesis, Abreg, sprang from the

Benoi *teip*, as did many of the other mountain fighters. To them a man like Khanzad, the false Chechen, is a traitor and a coward.

"How did Khanzad get the egg?"

"I don't know. Dubinin did the legwork on this. I've been—"

The General doesn't finish his sentence. I think the word on his lips was *distracted*, but he is not one to admit failure.

"Did Khanzad kill him?" I say.

"No. Khanzad made the sale, that's all. Killing is not his way. But he *is* a talker, so who knows how many he told about it."

I raise an eyebrow, but the General waves away my suspicions about the false Chechen. "We found the vehicle in a parking garage less than an hour ago, after receiving an anonymous call with a location. Two bodies stuffed in the trunk. The egg was missing."

"Not just bad luck? Wrong place and time?"

"No." His irises seem to flatten like a reptile's. "You'll see what I mean when you get there. Lieutenant Golko Kachan will take you." He stares at the blinking light as though it is menacing him.

I don't know a lieutenant named Golko Kachan. "I'd rather work alone."

"You don't have a choice, Colonel. You're going to need help with this, and I'll need regular updates."

"What's going on, sir?"

But he seems not to have heard the question. Instead of answering, he pins me with his reptilian gaze. "I don't know how or why, not yet at least, but Dubinin opened a door onto something big enough to catch the eye of the Kremlin. They think they've got me by the balls this time, and I'll be damned if I know why. Watch yourself, Volk."

✕

Soldiers lead me from the General's crying-stone room to a higher level. I lift the Lachek dossier from the overcoat, then return the military clothing and gear to the commissary. Take more stairs up to the infirmary, where a nurse inspects my burns. Her hands are less gentle than those of the male medic in the helicopter. When she's finished she hands me a tube of ointment. "Apply this several times a day. Maybe it will help with the scarring." She takes a last look at my seared flesh. "Or maybe not."

I limp back downstairs to a metal locker and drag on the same clothes I wore into the Kremlin earlier in the evening. Jeans, T-shirt, pullover, and a shoulder holster designed for my 9-millimeter Sig Sauer. Dried blood, scraps of flesh, and a tuft of hair are stuck to the barrel. I wipe down the pistol the best I can and holster it. Shrug into a worn leather jacket. Pull my Nokia from the pocket and thumb through the menu to see if I've missed any calls. I used to change the number compulsively, but I've left it the same for the past six months. The screen shows one voice mail and three missed calls from an unknown number, the first call coming three hours ago. I punch in the code to retrieve the message.

"Alexei, it's me," Valya says through a swarm of static.

The steel of the locker is cold against my palm when I brace myself against it. With my other hand I grind the phone into my ear to catch every syllable. It is the first time I've heard her voice in six months.

"Be careful—" Static breaks up her voice. "Alexei?" More popping static. "Abreg is killing soldiers—"

The message ends. I play it again and hear the same thing.

A sweaty lieutenant, overweight by ten kilos, enters the locker room and salutes smartly. One side of the front of his shirt is untucked. His hair is dark, nearly black, and thick, cresting over his forehead in ropy strands to form a wave held firmly in place with gel. Blue eyes squint above his surprisingly swarthy, chubby cheeks, one of them dimpled, one not. Perhaps he is from the southern regions, but who can tell these days. Post-Soviet Moscow is a bubbling stew of ethnicities.

"Lieutenant Golko Kachan, sir."

He looks as if he's about to say more, but I don't give him a chance. I flip up the collar of my jacket and march away, heading for the tunnel that runs under the Kremlin's Tainitskaya Tower, the secret tower, to the far bank of the Moscow River.

chapter 5

Golko drives north to the Khovrino district and steers through an intersection fired by pulsing neon from garishly lit casinos, restaurants, and shops. He parks next to a concrete garage adjacent to a residential high-rise and we climb three flights of stairs.

A black Mercedes sedan sits alone on the third level in a sawhorse-barricaded area fifteen meters square. All the other vehicles have been removed. Golko trots next to me, panting from the exertion of climbing and trying to keep up as I circle the car in a wide orbit. The hollow echoes from the tread of our boots are punctuated by splats of melted snow leaking through the joints of the concrete support ribs above us. Jaundiced lights cast wavering shadows.

As I pass through the barricades I ignore a saluting soldier who looks uncertain about my status. Several others are scattered about, stiffly holding rifles at port arms, cutting their eyes at me. I've heard whispers when they don't think I'm listening. The idea of a man like me—a military officer who works on the outside, doing the worst kind of things at the General's bidding—is the stuff of dark rumor to most Kremlin soldiers.

The Mercedes is parked crookedly on the line between two spaces. At first glance it looks like any other car with government plates, although a forensics kit sits on the oil-blotched concrete beside it. Completing my circle, I see a clot of dried mud near the trunk next to a set of skid marks made by dual tires.

"Who tipped us where to find the car?"

Golko squints at a spiral-bound notepad open in his gloved hand. The top page is already filled with writing. He finally looks up uncertainly. "No one knows, sir. It was a woman, that's all we can tell from the tape. The call came from a public phone."

"*How* was it found? What brought it to her attention? Did she see something strange? Did she see who left it here?"

"We don't know any of those things, sir."

"Stop calling me 'sir.' "

"Yes, sir." His cheeks bloom red when he realizes his mistake.

"Bag the mud and be sure to take a clear picture of the skid marks next to it."

He takes a few steps to the side to see what I'm talking about, then makes a note.

"What happened to the case they were carrying?"

"Gone."

"The bodies are in the trunk?"

He nods. "But not killed there, we think. Lots of blood on the bodies, but not so much in the trunk, and none in the passenger compartment."

I had my differences with Captain Dubinin. More than once he was prepared to let me die to achieve his objectives or, more accurately, the General's. But he wouldn't have become a member of the General's secret cadre unless he had thrived in the brutal war in the North Caucasus.

aning the captain would not have allowed his car to be hijacked with-
t a ferocious fight. Only trickery could account for his vehicle being
commandeered without bloodshed.

The lower third of the windows of the Mercedes is fogged on the
inside. "Are all of them in the trunk?"

Golko scrunches his fat cheeks and consults his little notepad.
"Both of them, yes."

"I mean all of their parts."

He squints at his notes again, then at me, looking thoroughly
confused.

I snap on a pair of surgical gloves from the forensics kit and open
the front passenger door. A smell like rotting fruit causes me to recoil,
the odor almost a physical presence that I have to push through to get
into the car.

The interior is pathologically clean, the way I would expect an
army vehicle to be, especially one under the General's command. The
carpeted front floor mats show lines from a vacuum machine, like freshly
cut fields of grass, but nothing else. Same thing in the back. The synthetic leather seats are spotless as well. If Dubinin and his man put up a
fight, it didn't happen in this car. Or else the car was meticulously cleaned
afterward.

The console between the front seats opens on the driver's side. I
pop the lid, but have to lean over with one hand holding the steering
wheel for balance to see what's inside. At first I can't make out what I'm
looking at, then the image appears like a slowly developing Polaroid.

A face. Or rather it is the skin from a face, rounded as if it still
wraps a skull but lacking the normal contours from cheekbones, forehead, nose, and chin. The flesh is mottled by a spackling of dried
blood, clumped where the skin has folded upon itself, curled up at the
edges. The bushy mustache that always seemed poised to jump from
the captain's upper lip like a furry rodent still resides under two holes
where his nostrils used to be. I don't need to see those green eyes glinting

their private smile to recognize the face that once belonged to the General's prized adjutant.

I raise my pant leg and pull a knife from the slot where it hides in my prosthesis. Use the tip to lift the sticky edge of skin. The underside is shiny with blood and gristle. Glistening beneath is an ivory oval the shape of a large egg—too crude by far to be one of the Imperial Easter eggs. This is a knickknack a tourist might buy.

I let the skin kiss back into place. I may be wrong, but judging by the amount of blood, I think somebody peeled off the captain's face while he was still alive.

Golko stares through the driver's side window. His swarthy cheeks have turned pale. "So that's what they did with it."

I back out of the Mercedes and pace slowly to the rear of the car, Golko in tow, trying to make sense of what I've just seen. "There's a manufactured egg under the face. Find out where it came from."

He scribbles on his pad, hand trembling.

At my command he keys the lock on the trunk, fumbling a bit. He averts his face when the lid swings up. I take his place and gaze into the compartment.

The cramped area holds two brutalized corpses. Naked. Entwined in a sadistic orgy of burned, carved, and peeled flesh. Dubinin's body with its faceless head is on top. His eyes are missing. They may be somewhere in the trunk with the rest of him, but I don't think so. The sockets aren't ragged the way they would be if his eyes had been gouged or hacked out; they're smooth, as though the orbs had been carefully scooped like melon balls by someone who wanted to save them. Dubinin's nipples and genitals are blackened where electrodes were attached to send jolts of electricity through his body. His wrists are encircled by livid ligature marks. The other man still has a face, his features distorted by the force of the bullet that blew away the back of his skull.

"Whoever did this left a message," Golko says hoarsely, apparently in command of his wits again. He points to the underside of the raised hood, which is streaked with finger-painted blood to form a series of numbers. Blood probably obtained from the palette of Dubinin's freshly skinned face. I have to bend my knees and cock my head to read it: *75859113323*.

The number, or code, or whatever it is, means nothing to me. My gaze drops back into the trunk. Empty as they are, Dubinin's eye sockets convey an accusing glare, begging for answers to all the questions going through my mind.

chapter 6

"Can you make sense of it?" I ask Golko.

He looks around the garage, then back at the numbers on the underside of the trunk lid, and screws his eyebrows together in concentration. "No."

"Talk to the General's encryption experts and tell me what you find out."

"Yes, sir."

"Do you have a camera?"

"Of course. Our forensics team will photograph the entire scene. The General wanted you to see it first."

The General's investigative resources would be laughably insufficient in any modern European or American city, but they are superior to those of the local authorities. The police in Russia functioned as political apparatchiks for far too long to have retained any real crime-solving expertise. Now they spend most of their time operating extortion and bribery rackets to supplement the pittance they're paid by the city government.

"Right now, on you, do you have a camera?" I say.

"No."

"Send a man downstairs to buy one at the market next door. The disposable kind."

Golko barks an order, and one of the soldiers hands his weapon to another and trots away down the stairs.

"Where did Dubinin live?"

"In the Kremlin arsenal barracks. He had his own room." Golko adds the last part with a hint of envy.

"Search it."

I take another turn around the Mercedes, trying a mental freefall to see if anything jars loose. The first thing that comes to mind is a story I was told years ago by a grieving mother, but I push that memory aside for the moment. The second is that Vladimir, the place where Dubinin traded Khanzad for the egg—an industrial city of almost a million people located just less than two hundred kilometers northeast of Moscow— would have been an easier place to hit him than on one of Moscow's crazed streets.

"Was Captain Dubinin coming directly from picking up the egg in Vladimir?"

Golko's chunky face goes blank, guileless. "What egg?"

"Don't pretend to be a fool, Lieutenant."

He swallows. "I don't know, sir. All I know is that he's been look-ing for the Imperial eggs for months, and he'd finally gotten a lead on one. I wasn't part of his assignment." He nudges an elbow in the direc-tion of the trunk. "The guy in there with him was."

"Okay. Was he coming directly from Vladimir, or did he make any stops here in Moscow?"

"We don't know where he got hit."

"Let's find out. Check—"

A voice squawks from Golko's radio. "Lieutenant! Cars are com-ing up the ramp—the police!"

The strident whoop of sirens sounds thunderously loud in the concrete confines of the parking garage. Two Moscow police cars screech up the ramp, tires smoking, their tops rippling with colored lights. The passenger door of the lead vehicle flies open before the car has stopped, and a police commander leaps out and aims a finger at Golko.

"What the fuck is going on here, Lieutenant?"

The commander is a stocky man with a perfectly round bald spot on the crown of his hatless head. His arms are too long for his body, extending almost to his bowed knees, and he tilts forward when he walks, like a baboon. He stalks toward the Mercedes, closer to Golko, aggressively invading the pudgy man's space.

Golko puffs out his chest. "I'm conducting this investigation. It doesn't involve the police."

The commander bulls past him. Peers into the open trunk, stares blankly as several seconds tick away, then suddenly turns ashen. He takes another moment to gather himself before wheeling on Golko.

"What in God's name happened here?"

Golko doesn't look to me for guidance. "These men were military, Fifty-eighth Army." He flips open a wallet-sized leather holder to show a badge and an identification card, which I can see from the insignia identifies him as a military investigator. "I've got jurisdiction."

"Bullshit! This is a fucking multiple homicide! In one of my goddamn districts! I'm not going to let you people cover this up."

I don't need to read too closely between the lines to know that the commander is not interested in justice. He represents parts of all three of Russia's incurable diseases: greed, corruption, and bureaucracy. No telling how much a crime scene this grotesque might net him in payoffs.

"You don't have a choice, Commander." Golko's tone carries a steely ring that surprises me.

The commander turns to the men who arrived with him in the police cars. "Cordon the area! And I want a medical examiner out here, now. Move!"

Golko shouts, "Elovich! Postnikov! Spalko!" His face is flushed, and he's sweating despite the cold. The soldiers snap to attention, awaiting orders, and the policemen freeze, all of us caught in a silent tableau.

Golko hesitates, just when he shouldn't. Five long seconds pass, then he startles when a car horn sounds in the distance.

The commander curls his lip into a sneer to signal victory. "Go on," he says to his men.

"No!" I take one step forward. The commander wheels to face me, but I address the soldiers. "You three, shoot every one of these men if they don't leave at once!"

Three of the soldiers unsling their rifles and take aim. From the way they move and their grim faces, I can tell that they are hardened veterans, not raw conscripts. The policemen stay perfectly still, looking to their superior for help.

"You wouldn't dare," the commander says, studying me with care. The cautious way he's holding himself tells me that he has noticed the same thing I have about how the soldiers handle their weapons.

"Roll the dice, Commander. See what happens."

He moves only his eyes, glaring at each soldier in turn. "Fucking Chechens," he says, dragging out the words. He intends the word *Chechens* as a slur, one used by many these days to refer to those who have returned from the war.

"On my order," I tell the soldier nearest me. "Shoot that fucking baboon in the kneecap."

The soldier shifts his aim. Boot leather creaks and a cop flinches at the sound. The commander growls something unintelligible under his breath. His feet are rooted to the ground but he's swaying, visibly torn about which way to go. Drops of water plink the concrete as the moment stretches to the breaking point. His gaze catches mine, holds briefly, wavers, falls away.

"Stand down!" he says through tightly drawn lips. As his men scramble to the safety of their vehicles, he says, "I know you now. Both of you!" He's pumping his fist so hard that his arm seems to shake his body, but his words don't carry any conviction. "This isn't over. Not by a long shot."

He retreats to his car without looking at me again, slams the door, and the cars peel away down the ramp.

When they're out of sight, Golko slumps and wipes the sweat from his eyes. I go to him and set my hand on his round shoulder, which feels rubbery with fat, but he's not trembling. Except for the moment of hesitation, the only sign of nerves he displayed during the confrontation was sweat.

"Are you really a military investigator?"

He nods.

"Why do you act like you've never seen a dead body before?"

"Only in pictures and at the morgue. I'm a lawyer. I investigate war crimes. Never been on a battlefield in my life."

"Battlefields don't always look the way you might expect them to."

"What's that supposed to mean?"

"It means that you're on one now, whether you know it or not."

chapter 7

I step away from Golko and scan the scene in the garage one last time to burn the impressions into my memory. "You've been busy, then."

"Huh?"

"Lots of war crimes to investigate."

"Yes—yes, I've been very busy."

Busy covering up, most likely. When things go badly the military does what it can to conceal what happened, aided by a sympathetic or even co-opted press and a public that has been taught to think of Chechens—and all the "blacks," as many refer to the people of the Caucasus—as lower life-forms.

"Do you ever *prosecute* any?"

Golko looks uncomfortable. The courtroom has become both a shield and a sword used by the Kremlin to protect its military assets and smite its enemies. Golko's services are no doubt used to pursue whatever objective most suits the Kremlin—or, in the case of the Fifty-eighth Army's many enterprises, the General.

"I do what I'm ordered to do," he answers finally.

"Nuremberg revisited?"

He flushes again. "Whichever side I'm on, I do the best job I can. What the hell would someone like you know about it anyway?"

I turn away to hide my face. I deserved his blast of anger. Golko has proven a sturdier sort than I first thought. "You're right, Lieutenant. My hands are a lot dirtier than yours."

The soldier dispatched earlier comes running up the stairs and hands me a green disposable camera. I snap a picture of the bloody numbers in the trunk, put the camera into the pocket of my jacket, and turn to face the military investigator.

"Move the Mercedes to a secure location where you can check it out for prints, fibers, hairs—whatever. You're not going to find anything useful, but it'll give you something to do. Then you can autopsy and dispose of the bodies properly. Nothing happened here. This is just where they dumped the car."

His eyes are narrowed to slits. He's still angry, but I think he's following me.

"Check the car's GPS and let me know exactly where Dubinin went while he was in Vladimir."

Our defense ministry built the Global Navigation Satellite System, called GLONASS, for military use, but the Mercedes probably has a more common GPS system. I doubt the General spent the money to change it, although he may have had the program disabled.

Golko makes another note.

"Get back to me about the egg in the car and the number in the trunk. And anything else you think is important." I give him my cell phone number. "And watch out for that police commander."

"You *wanted* to shoot him. He saw it in you. We all did."

I slap him on his rubbery back and head toward the stairs.

"The General says you're supposed to keep me informed, sir!" he shouts after me.

※

I take the steps fast, thinking of Captain Dubinin. He accepted the risk to himself as part of the job, as a feature of life in the General's elite corps. And I'm sure he died bravely, following orders right up to the awful end. But by the time I reach the bottom of the stairs the lump in my throat has turned to dread in the pit of my stomach.

I can't escape the idea that Dubinin's death is neither the beginning nor the end of something bigger than he was. The killer delivered a message in blood, and the kind of man who communicates that way doesn't stop—he has to be stopped. Worse yet is the memory the captain's glaring eye sockets have brought back to life, one of those echoes of war that won't fade no matter how hard I try to forget it.

The story was told to me almost four years ago by a mother whose face was inconsolable with grief. I was still a ward of the military hospital located on the grounds of Moscow's Zhukovsky air base, my left leg ending in a bandaged stump below my knee. But I needed to work then, no matter what the assignment. I wanted to feel useful, and I wanted to forget the things that had happened to me. So the General assigned me to a desk job answering questions for relatives of those killed fighting in Chechnya. Maybe it was his way of reminding me that I was one of the lucky ones.

"Why wouldn't anybody help me find my son?" she kept asking, searching my face with her prematurely aged eyes. "I begged. I wrote letters, even one to the separatist administration."

We were in an open hangar filled with dozens of desks pushed together and shoved against the walls. Each one was manned by someone whose job it was to record the stories so that somewhere another filing cabinet could be stuffed with reports that would never be read. Typewriters and keyboards clacked, phones rang, and radios blared, all merged with the din of many voices.

In front or to the side of each desk sat the people seeking answers—in my case a woman who was looking for a way to understand what had happened to her son, a boy who had gone missing in the war zone during the spring of '03. No letters, no news for months. According to his field commander, he had simply vanished.

"A doctor working in a hospital in Gudermes finally wrote back to me," she said, unconsciously rocking her upper body in the chair, sawing her lower lip between her teeth. "Look in Rostov, he told me. A special morgue is there, a place where they store bodies that haven't been identified."

She hacked phlegm into her handkerchief, trying to hide her face behind her hands. I looked away, unable to explain why we send our children to war without keeping fingerprints or dental records or DNA samples, or why we allow the unknown dead to pile up in the morgue in Rostov, a well-known repository of despair. Thin lines of sunlight slashed the tile beneath a window that looked out onto dirty snow. Dust motes swirled in the narrow shafts of light from between the blinds.

After a moment, she set aside her handkerchief. "It was summer when I went there," she said, so quietly that I had to scoot my chair closer to hear her. "Outside was hot, inside was cold. There were corpses everywhere—on slabs, in drawers, stacked on the floor of refrigerated cars. Missing heads, arms, legs."

She worked her lips and mouth as if she was trying to gather enough spit to talk.

"His body had decomposed. His fingers were gone—dogs, they told me. But some of what had been done to him was still . . ."

Her voice trailed away. The hanging folds of flesh on her face formed deep canyons and patches of shadow, like an old peasant woman in a painting by Repin. I glanced at her file. It said she was thirty-eight.

"His eyes were missing. Cut out. His ears and nose, chopped off. Lips sewn together with twine. I knew him only by a birthmark on his chest, like his father's."

I looked back at the particles of dust swirling in the sun, thinking that it would be easier to chart the course of each of them for the rest of time than to explain such evil.

She handed me a photograph, tears pooling in her eyes. But she didn't drop her gaze from mine. She held me captive in her well of pain, willing me to look at the picture. "He was a beautiful boy, can't you see? He had a kind heart. And he didn't deserve for something so terrible to happen to him down there."

It was a graduation photo, head and shoulders only. He was just as she described him, brown eyes and soft features. But what came to my mind at the moment, less than a month removed from that hellish zone, was that the beloved son she remembered may not have been the same person as the young man who fought and died in a dirty war in Chechnya.

✕

Outside the parking garage, in front of one of the neon-lit casinos, I hail a gypsy cab. As soon as I'm settled into the front seat I call Golko and tell him to check the files for the name of the mutilated son of the grieving mother. He seems surprised to hear from me so soon, and I imagine his pencil scratching a question mark onto his pad, but as soon as I finish telling him how the mother described the condition of her son's body he says, "Oh," and tells me he'll get right on it.

My driver likes to talk. He works for an aerospace firm. His wife thinks he spends too much time there. His teenage daughter dresses like a prostitute, just like the girl pop stars on the television. He shifts gears at the entrance to the M10 and glances at the butt of the Sig peeking from beneath my coat.

"Are you a policeman?"

I look out the window at a concrete jungle of apartment blocks. "Do you know why policemen always go in threes?"

"No."

"They specialize. One knows how to write. One knows how to read. And the third keeps an eye on the two dangerous intellectuals."

He laughs nervously, afraid to push for an answer to his question. But in a way I have answered it, at least in my own mind. I am more of a policeman than the baboonlike commander who confronted Golko. Unlike him, I will do whatever it takes to find out who killed Dubinin, and why.

chapter 8

My ride drops me in the central city, and I walk the last few blocks to Vadim's Café, on the edge of the Kitay-Gorod district, where I keep an office and, lately, a cot for a bed. The café is just a few blocks from the redbrick walls of the Kremlin, close to my old home in the loft but still far enough away to keep the ghosts at bay. I haven't slept in the high-ceilinged comfort of the loft since shortly after I said good-bye to Valya, when I realized that every square meter of the place was haunted by her memory.

It's just after midnight, although it feels as if far more than five hours have passed since I helicoptered into the aftermath of the first explosion at the AMERCO building. The streets are eerily quiet. Even the denizens of Moscow's night culture seem to have taken time off to decompress in the wake of another terrorist attack.

The café is closed, shut down early. I go in the back way via a narrow alley. Upturned chairs on top of the tables in the dining area poke spidery legs into the air. A cubbyhole tucked in a corner behind the

Formica counter provides Vadim a place to get away during busy times. It houses a cluttered desk, a wall-mounted rotary phone he seldom answers, and a locked, fireproof filing cabinet, all in an area too small for push-ups. I place the disposable camera on his desk with a note telling him to have the film developed by one of the techs at our porn operation.

When that's done I descend one flight of stairs to the basement. Black slate floor, shelves crammed with café sundries, and two rows of dusty slot machines lead to the wooden chair and table that serves as my office. The tabletop is almost always bare. When I need a computer or other office equipment I can use whatever I want in the state-of-the-art facilities at my warehouse.

Tonight a folded piece of yellow paper is taped to the back of the chair. Inside are two notes scrawled in Vadim's blocky handwriting. The first says simply, "Call Masha." Masha is an aging babushka, a fellow amputee who has become a friend and confidante like no other person in my life, save Valya. I visit her periodically, when the mood strikes. She has never called me before.

The second note says, "BM called, wants to see an important blues act." The words are followed by a Moscow-area phone number, probably one belonging to the American embassy.

Vadim would have no idea what the word *blues* means, but the note is clear enough to me. BM is Brock Matthews, an NSA operative based in the D.C. area, a man I've had dealings with before. Movie-star looks marred by a crooked nose and an indefinably tense demeanor. Naval Academy graduate, an American-style football quarterback for his school, he told me. Carrier pilot and veteran of the first Iraq war before becoming a member of America's intelligence services; probably a shadow warrior in Afghanistan and the second Iraq war as well, although the General's files don't go that deep. Matthews took me to see an unforgettable blues act—my first—one evening during a weeklong "joint intelligence exercise" between our two countries in '04, where neither side shared anything of value.

An urgent call from Matthews in the wake of a terrorist attack in

Moscow on an American target is not a complete surprise. Many people know to contact me here, although only Vadim knows that this is where I now live. The call from Masha is more disturbing, but the note doesn't say it's urgent, so I decide to wait until morning rather than awaken her now.

After a moment I put the yellow paper aside and go to a scarred-oak door that flanks the table. It opens onto my new home, little more than a closet with a drippy sink, military-issue cot, a hotplate, and a crude shower. All I really need, now that Valya is gone. A rope hangs from the ceiling, connecting to pull-down stairs that lead to an unused boiler room, my escape route in an emergency.

I researched the Imperial Easter eggs months ago, when the General first asked me about them, spurred by simple curiosity. The books I'd bought are lined up in a row under my cot. I open one to the page describing the Hen Egg with Sapphire Pendant and settle onto the cot with my back against the rough block wall. A picture of the document commissioning the production of the egg shows a handwritten note from a clerk that says, "Regarding the execution by the jeweller Fabergé of a hen made of gold and rose-cut diamonds picking a sapphire pendant egg out of a basket . . ." The hen and basket with the pendant would have been concealed in a larger egg, as was done with the contents of the other Imperial Easter eggs. Fabergé submitted a series of questions to the court minister, answered in pencil in the margin of the commission document. The last question was: "Should the pendant egg be removable or should it be firmly attached to the beak?" The answer: "It must be loose."

I park the book next to me on the cot, and waste no time wondering what the sapphire pendant might have looked like, because I am sure that I saw it five hours ago dangling from the neck of the woman who claimed to have been a hostage in the AMERCO building.

I pull the two-page summary of Filip Lachek's career from my pocket and study it. To someone like me its dry recitation of dates and postings reads like a nautical chart, graphically rendering hazardous shoals, treacherous currents, and disaster sites. Lachek has ridden the roughest seas of Soviet and Russian adventurism for longer than any man I know, except the General. Afghanistan, Iran, Turkey, Chechnya, and, later, Hong Kong, Bangkok, Singapore, Jakarta—the papers in my hand might as well be soggy with blood from the tales recorded by a thousand keystrokes. I fold the dossier, slip it into the book to mark the page about the Hen Egg, and return the book to its slot.

The stainless steel side of the hotplate works as a makeshift mirror for me to inspect the burns on my face. Singed eyebrows hover over bronze eyes blazing with their familiar ferocity. My nose and cheeks are slashed with crimson burns from the blast, the deeper ones already beginning to crust over.

I apply more salve to my face, then strip down and do the same for my arms and thighs. Detach my prosthesis, a wonder of titanium in carbon alloy with a rebounding spring, and rub my aching stump, absently feeling the abraded stitching of scars while considering the scene at the parking garage, trying to make sense of the numbers written in blood. The General's encryption experts may be needed to decipher it, but I don't think so. I suspect that the series of numbers was meant to be more obvious, at least to its intended recipients, just as the tortured bodies in the trunk were not subtle in any way.

By the time I turn off the lamp and lay faceup on the cot, I've still made no progress. I know only this much. Dubinin's murder was about more than an Imperial Easter egg. Whoever killed him that way knew him. They shared a past. I wonder how many others shared the same past and are doomed to meet the same fate as the captain.

chapter 9

Long periods of sleep elude me. The dead and dying haunt my dreams. During the years we were together, Valya would scoot next to me, her skin feverish under the blankets, as if the flame of passion—for life, for love, for the gift of being together—burned inside her. Her warmth narcotized me, helped to hold the ugly memories at bay. Now I'm lucky to get more than two or three hours uninterrupted by nightmares. This time I get four, so it's a good night.

The predawn streets are still quieter than usual. People must be staying home, fearing another attack. I ride the metro, then plod to a warehouse surrounded by spiking derricks and cranes on the banks of the Moscow River, the home of my porn and identity-theft operation. A youthful guard stands aside while I use a plastic key card to gain admittance. The inside is dark and still, strangely deserted. No movies are being shot, no video-feed performers are plying their trade, no pimply teenaged cyberpunks or sad babushkas are mining the Internet for identities to steal. I'm still standing near the entrance when I detect movement.

"Hello, Alexei," says Alla Anfimova, padding toward me from the darkness of the cavernous concrete-and-steel studio area. She's wearing a man's white T-shirt, which lifts to the top of her thighs and grazes her slender hips as she stretches her arms above her head, yawning.

Normally at this hour the studio would be brightly lit and thrumming with the activity of several shoots going on at once. Stage sets range from elaborate Egyptian palaces and East Indian harems down to nothing more than a thrown mattress with a blue sheet for a backdrop. Cables are taped to the concrete floor like captured snakes. Smaller rooms off the main area carry live-sex video feeds to the hard drives of voyeurs all over the world. Other partitioned areas in the warehouse are crowded with computer stations, usually manned by hackers capable of stealing the identity of a percentage of those foolish enough to buy our services through an unsecured payment processor.

Alla manages all these operations with a deceptively steely fist, every night performing a complicated logistical dance to choreograph performers, stage crews, film and computer equipment and operators, security, and finances. She's maybe thirty years old, a few years younger than I am, but I like to kid her that if she'd been born in London or Los Angeles she'd already be a famous movie mogul.

She finishes her stretch and regards me with sleep-dulled eyes that suddenly widen as I come closer. "You look like shit."

"Where is everyone?"

"Don't you listen to the news? Half of Moscow is burning. I heard they got the bad guys, though. What did you do to yourself?"

A steel door on the other side of the room leads to a long hallway lined with closed doors, behind which are miniature sets. Sometimes Alla lets the girls who work the rooms stay the night for a draw against the money they will make the next day or week or month. I keep going to the door all the way at the end of the long hallway, Alla not far behind.

"You alone?"

She scowls, pushes past me, and leads the way into her office. Her work area has been decorated with a soft touch. Cream carpet, mahogany furnishings, and an electric Kandinsky print, *Moscow I*—blues, oranges, yellow, pastel pink—on the wall behind her oversized desk. A set of closed double doors in the back opens onto her living quarters, but I've never been there. On the side away from her desk two overstuffed chairs face a leather couch across a coffee table. I take a seat in one of the chairs, so plush it threatens to suffocate me. She sits on the couch across from me and folds her long legs beneath her. The only light comes from the glimmering flame of a scented candle—mango and strawberries, it smells like—Alla's way of bringing a breath of spring to the coldest part of Moscow's winter.

Sometimes I forget how beautiful she is—highlighted blond hair, elegantly slanted eyes that sparkle like polished jade in the candlelight, model-thin, high and firm in the right places. I've seen her perform, live and on video. Some of the techs and girls call her "the Master," and I'm sure the nickname relates more to her skills as a posing porn queen than as the head of my multitentacled operation, although it shouldn't, because the latter set of talents is far more unique.

"I'm supposed to ignore that your face is covered with burns?"

I close my eyes and relax into the chair. For some reason I'm still tired.

"Vadim stopped by and asked me to develop some film."

Vadim is ghostlike. He was probably somewhere in the café when I wandered in a few hours ago and deposited the camera on his cluttered desk. She twists on the couch, reaches back to take a folder from her desk, and hands me a glossy photograph. It shows the underside of the Mercedes' open trunk lid and the bloody numbers 75859113323. Her taut expression tells me she's already looked at it.

"Does that mean anything to you?"

She shakes her head. "Whose blood?"

"Nobody you know."

"Did you put it there?"

"No."

She shifts her weight uneasily. "Maxim was asking about you."

"What does he want?"

"He gave a message to one of the girls. Mei."

Not a name I recognize, but that's no surprise. They come and go. "She works computers?"

"Cybersex. She's one of the prettiest. Small, but some men like that."

I pretend not to notice her potshot at my wasted love for Valya, who is waiflike, soft and strong at the same time, in the way that white-hot steel can be bent and shaped without losing its essential nature.

"What did Maxim say to her?"

"To tell me he's looking for you."

"That's all?"

"Wait." Then she's up and moving down the hallway before I have a chance to stop her. I'm sure Mei won't have anything to add. Just as I settle back into the chair my cell phone vibrates.

"It's me," says the General. "Filip Lachek has learned your name and that you're active military. I hear they're confused about how to track you down, but they'll figure it out soon enough."

Many government files purport to chronicle my life. One made available to the outside world says I was discharged from the Fifty-eighth Army as an invalid three and a half years ago with the rank of major, after I lost my foot, and lists a host of crimes I'm suspected of committing. The one Lachek has apparently gotten hold of contains the truth about my ongoing military status—including my rank and some of my activities during the past few years—which confirms that he is very high in the Kremlin's command structure.

"What about names and background information on the hostages?" I say.

"I gave the list to Golko."

"Did any jump out at you?"

"Marko Hutsul. Chairman of the oil and gas consortium Kombi-Oil. He could have been in the AMERCO building for a number of reasons—they're in the same business, after all—so that may or may not be significant. His was the only name I recognized."

Alla returns, towing a sleepy-eyed Asian girl with glossy, reddish-black hair that hangs to her waist. She stares at me, openly curious, while Alla cocks her head, apparently wondering who is on the other end of the phone.

"A woman called the American embassy," the General says. "Looking for help. She used one of the old numbers."

Back lines to the American embassy are rarely used anymore, new technology having made them obsolete. Nonetheless, the Americans routinely change the phone numbers, and the General—and probably others—just as methodically use English-speaking plants to answer the old ones, mining for nuggets of gold.

The message Brock Matthews left with Vadim immediately comes to mind. Except for the AMERCO link, I can't figure why or how the Americans are involved in this, but now that one more connection has appeared I'm sure that they are.

"Why does she need help?" I direct Alla and the girl toward the couch, but they remain standing.

"She claims that Russian agents abducted her and held her for several days before she escaped." He hesitates. "She insists that these same people killed a peace activist who was investigating a war crime supposedly committed near Starye Atagi."

Starye Atagi, located six miles outside the maw of the Argun valley, known as the Wolf Gates, is one of many Chechen villages devastated by war. Relentlessly purged, it was the home of one of the war's most notorious filtration points, where villagers were "processed"—detained, questioned, sometimes tortured, and often ransomed dead or alive. I intervened there and at other places when I could, but it was like trying to hold back an ocean of raw sewage with my bare hands. The General wasn't party to those atrocities, but he wasted little time trying to end the evil. "Besides," he once told me, "the extra money motivates the men."

"Lots of innocents were killed there." I keep my tone neutral, not wanting to reignite our old argument.

"She alleges that over two hundred were slaughtered indiscriminately, somewhere outside the filtration point. Not possible," he adds brusquely.

Of course it was possible. Men were shuttled all over Chechnya, often outside the chain of command. Rogue officers were everywhere, some of them going so far as to sell food, information, and weapons to the enemy. Almost anything was possible.

"How does this relate to Dubinin and the egg?"

"Dubinin was *alleged* to have been involved."

"Was he?"

"How can we commit crimes against vermin who blow up our women and children? Hide among civilians using their children as shields? Besides, the liberal press is all over Chechnya, painting Russia black and our enemies white. A secret like that couldn't be kept."

Those are the stock answers we always give when covering up another bloodbath. Not really answers at all, in other words. A painting springs to mind, one I saw years ago when I was taken as a boy to an exhibition at the Hermitage, but still knife-edged in my memory—a battlefield scene by Vereshchagin called *Surprise Attack.* I was mesmerized, so absorbed that I nearly sprang from my boots when one of my guards from the rehabilitation center, an ex-military man, clapped me on the back. He took nationalistic pride in the depiction of a nineteenth-century clash in Turkestan rendered in almost photographic detail. But the thing that captivated the child that was me was the unbridled savagery—not that of the Asiatic tribesmen, but rather the bloodlust of the Russians, so unlike the giant, gentle strength of my legendary hero, Ilia Muromets.

"Our operator must have said something to scare her," the General says. "Because she wouldn't say where she was. But we traced the call to a landline in a building in Kitay-Gorod. Find her, talk to her, figure out what's really going on." He gives me an address.

"What's her name?"

"She told the operator to call her Charlie."

chapter 10

After hanging up with the General I study the photo of the numbers for a moment, trying to guess their meaning in the new light of what he has told me. Then Alla clears her throat, reminding me that I'm still in her office with her and the girl.

"Who was that?" she says.

"Putin. He wants me to invest in an oil company."

"How many more does he plan to seize at the point of a gun?"

Just the attempt to make light at Putin's expense causes Alla to look around. Putin has earned a reputation for being everywhere at once, straddling the ocean, filling the sky, just like Stalin.

Alla puts one hand on each of the girl's shoulders and walks her forward until she is facing me.

"This is Mei," Alla says, and twirls her around as if she is on display.

She's light-skinned, likely from somewhere in northern China, slender but curvy. Thin cotton pajama bottoms with the waistband rolled

down stretch between her hipbones, leaving a two-centimeter gap between the elastic band and her flat belly below a cropped top. Shimmering black hair with red highlights swishes over a tattoo of a dragon on
her lower back, its wings frozen in flight to emphasize the curve of her
butt. Even sleep-tousled as she is, I can see how she would do well in
the video rooms or under the studio lights.

When she's made it all the way around to face me again, her gaze
catches mine. She seems amused by Alla's game of showing her off and
by my lingering appraisal, and at that moment I revise my opinion of
her, because the cool gleam peeking from the shade of her lashes warns
me that she's no fool.

"Maxim asked for me?"

"Not with your name," she says in broken Russian. "He told me to
pass along a message to the man in charge here. Alla says the message is
for you." Her smile reaches all the way up to her eyes, a good trick for a
sex worker.

"Why did Maxim go to her?" I ask Alla. "He knows how to contact me."

"Who knows why Maxim does anything?" Alla says.

Mei regards me silently until I query her by raising my chin.

"I was with him at the Savoy. He likes big parties and lots of girls."

Maxim is built like a giant ape, which causes most people to underestimate his intellect. The truth is that he has more brains than all
but a few of our most powerful oligarchs or politicians. Like many
driven men, his appetites match his ambition.

"What did he say?" I ask her.

"He wants your help."

Maxim never asks for help. He gives orders. I figure the true message must have gotten lost somewhere in Mei's muddled understanding
of Russian.

"Anything else?"

"He said to tell you oil is everything. Much more important than
food."

Tell *that* to a starving man. But the picture has just gotten murkier. AMERCO, Marko Hutsul and his company, Kombi-Oil—and now Maxim is sniffing the same confused ground. "What else?"

She shakes her head sadly, sticking out her lower lip. "I'm sorry my message is no good."

After sending the girl away, Alla says she's tired and heads into her room, pointedly shutting the door behind her. She doesn't like to hear me say that our relationship is best left at business.

I pull out the Nokia and punch the number for Lieutenant Golko. He answers after several rings with a sleepy hello.

"Golko, is each war crime investigation given a number?"

"Volk? Christ, what time is it?"

It's just past 5 A.M., less than ten hours after the first blast at the AMERCO building. The fact that I was able to wake him is another sign that Golko is a relative neophyte at the General's games. He can still sleep well.

"Yes or no?"

"Yes. Why?"

"How many digits?"

The chubby lieutenant doesn't answer right away. I picture him reaching for his notepad. "I thought of that, too, but it doesn't work. Our number has eleven digits. A war crimes investigation is given seven."

"Check the first and last seven digits against the records. If you don't get a hit, check every seven consecutive numbers. Look particularly for any alleged atrocity committed in the area around Starye Atagi. All the investigations are in a computer database, right?"

"Why Starye Atagi?"

"Let me worry about that."

"Look, Volk, I've already been through the database of defense ministry files. I've tried to connect the numbers to every investigation, complaint—there are thousands of those, most of which are ignored—disciplinary action, and anything else I could find. There's nothing there. But these files aren't comprehensive, and lots of crimes are alleged but never given a number."

No surprise in that. War crimes investigations are a low priority, one the Kremlin is unlikely to spend money to support. Maybe that's smart policy. What good can come of such things? But I think the alleged slaughter of two hundred noncombatants would earn its own file.

"Whoever dipped his fingers in Dubinin's blood and painted those numbers—or whoever ordered it done—had a reason. He *wants* us to figure it out."

I can hear him breathing heavily, but he doesn't say anything. The Nokia burns against my ear as I recall more of the rumors about the filtration point on the scorched earth outside Starye Atagi, headquartered on an abandoned farm that came to be known to the locals as the "poultry farm," one of the worst in all of Chechnya.

"Listen," Golko says. "I'm starting to think we're looking in the wrong place. What if the numbers relate to an interior ministry matter? Hell, whole villages were deported on their authority. I don't know how their numbering system works, but I bet I can figure it out if I can get a look at their archives."

Elite units from the FSB and the interior ministry were deployed throughout the Caucasus during both Chechen wars. Better trained and equipped than the mostly conscripted Russian army troops, many of the so-called flying detachments functioned as enforcers against the soft army of local civilians suspected of supporting the Chechen fighters. When on parade and dressed for show they wear red berets like the one the FSB agent had on when I took him down in the command center.

I step out of Alla's office, close the door behind me, and start down the hall.

"Yeah, I know," Golko says, misreading my silence. "How're we supposed to investigate *those* guys? But I think maybe that's where we could find our answer."

"Where are the archives located?"

He gives me the address as I pick my way over the taped cables in the deserted warehouse.

"Let's go look at those files."

"When?"

"Right now."

chapter 11

The interior ministry archives are located on the fifth floor of a Stalin-era building made of white limestone turned black by exhaust fumes. Dawn is still more than two hours away when we enter the lobby. Golko, looking harried, disheveled, and unhappy to be out at six o'clock on a cold morning, shows his identification to a uniformed guard in a red beret who doesn't bother to look at it. He waves us around a metal de-tector and buzzes us through a turnstile into the lobby. I pound up the stairs, the lieutenant chugging along behind me.

"What are we going to tell them?" he says. "We'll get nowhere with these people."

The fifth-floor landing lets onto another small lobby, this one empty. No windows and only one door. The door is made of metal, in-set with a frosted-glass panel over wire mesh. It's not locked.

Two men are on duty, both sitting on stools behind a wooden counter with a laminated top, watching a children's cartoon on a portable television. They wear interior troops uniforms with diagonal belts over their right shoulders hung with sidearms. The larger of the two stands and crosses his arms over his chest when Golko and I come through the door. The other, an officer, rises more slowly and gives us a look of mild contempt. Behind him are long crooked rows of files on bowed metal shelves.

"These aren't business hours."

He looks like a burrowing grub. Pale, almost hairless, so puffy that I think if I poked my finger into his cheek the impression would stay for a long time.

Golko flashes his identification again and requests to look through the files. "No bother to you," he says. "We'll see our own way around."

The officer slides a requisition form across the countertop. "Fill that out." He twists his heavy lips into a phony smile. "We'll contact you."

"How long will it be?"

"Probably never. These aren't army files."

"My credentials will check out."

The officer's smile widens. "Two months, then, if you're lucky. We're busy here, and sometimes requisitions get lost."

"We can't wait that long."

"Too bad." He leans forward, palms flat on the countertop, and blows garlic breath in Golko's face. "We have regulations to follow, army man."

Golko starts to negotiate some more, because entreaty is his way. But it is not mine.

The counter blocks their view as I reach down and slide my knife from its slot, holding it low in my left hand. With my right I draw the Sig and aim it at the guard's face. He responds with a slow blink. While he's still figuring things out, I haul back and drive the blade of the knife through the officer's puffy hand.

The blade cuts through sinew and bone and pounds deep into the wood with a wet thunk, pinning him to the counter. The sensation is like stabbing through a watermelon rind into a carving board. He shrieks, reflexively tries to pull away, and then screams even louder as the blade bites and holds fast.

"See what you can find," I tell Golko, and he haltingly backs away, his gaze locked on the officer's pinned hand.

"Shut up!" I tell the officer, but he keeps screeching, so I push the haft forward like a gearshift to give him a real reason to yowl. "Every time you make noise I'm going to do that again. Understand?"

"Yes! Yes!"

Blood wells up around the buried blade and spiderwebs around the ridges of his knuckles and corded tendons. More of it trickles down his chin from where he must have bitten his lip. He breathes in quick, shallow bursts, like a woman in labor. Golko heads down the first aisle, looking from a page in his notepad to numbers written on labels attached to the shelves, then he turns a corner. The sound of his heels carries during the short silences when the officer holds his breath between bursts.

"Both of you, toss your guns into the corner," I say, and they do, the officer struggling one-handed to unsnap his holster, trying not to move too much.

Golko's footfalls stop. Papers rustle, then he moves on again. A few minutes later a metal leg screeches when he moves one set of shelves to reach another. The officer buries his face in the crook of his free arm. His whole body is shuddering, but he stays mostly quiet. His comrade hides his face in his hands, not wanting to see or be seen. I move around the counter so that I'll have the door covered if somebody comes in. Cartoons are still playing on the TV. A new one starts. A cat is pummeled by a baby kangaroo that the cat thinks is an overgrown mouse.

Fifteen minutes later Golko returns to the front. He shakes his head gravely, and points to the computer. I touch the haft of the knife and the officer jumps as though he's been electrocuted, letting out a sound between a scream and a moan.

"What's the password?"

He rattles off a series of numbers and letters. Golko keys them in, then taps through several screens. "How are these organized?" he says without looking up.

"By year and file number," the officer answers breathlessly, before I have a chance to reach for the knife.

Golko keeps tapping for several more minutes. He writes a few notes on his pad. A shadow passes in front of the frosted panel in the door. I slip to one side, ready, but nobody enters. Five minutes later Golko shuts down the computer.

"Finished," he says.

"Pull the hard drive."

He stares at me for a moment, then reaches into his pocket for a knife attached to his keychain and uses the blade to unscrew the back of the computer case. He removes two more small screws to release the rectangular drive, then drops it into his pocket.

I put my hand over the officer's to hold it down while I pull out the knife. It can't be freed without some jiggling, so he gasps as the blade comes out, then he falls to the tiled floor, holding his injured hand against his chest.

"Wait for me on the street out front," I tell Golko.

"You can't kill them!" he hisses.

"Just go, Lieutenant."

He departs reluctantly, looking back over his shoulder. As soon as he's safely gone, I rip the cords out of the television and the computer case and tie both men by their wrists behind their backs, not sparing the officer when I tighten the knot.

"We won't talk anyway," he says, gritting his teeth. "It would be the end of our careers."

I give the bonds a last tug to make sure they're fast. They won't have to hold for long, just time enough for Golko and me to get out of the building.

✦

Outside the sky is still dark but the morning rush has begun. I lead Golko through the crowds to a fancy food market with tables in the back, and buy two cups of tea.

"What did you do to those men?" he says. His hands are shaking, but not, I think, from the cold.

"What did you find out?"

He hesitates, then pulls out his pad. I can see the numbers he copied from the trunk, *75859113323.* Each one is delineated by several lines. I suspect that he repeatedly traced over them as he tried to work out their meaning last night.

"Here's the way I figure it," he says. "The middle five digits represent a case file. We thought the center digit was a *one,* but it's not—it's a slash. So the inside marks were five-nine-slash-one-three. Usually a suffix, four digits to represent the month and year, would follow the case number—that's how all the other files were organized. But with this one we can safely assume the year was '03, because when I searched the '03 archives I found fifty-nine twelve and fourteen, but no thirteen. That file is gone."

"What about the computer?"

"All the electronic records had been deleted. But they missed two cross-references. The *contents* of those files had been deleted, too, but not the *names* of the files."

A man in khaki pants and a white shirt stops at our table and asks if we want breakfast. Behind him, at the entrance to the restaurant section of the market, are two uniformed men who stand out because of the red berets on their heads. They scan the place, say a few words to each other, then go back out onto the street. I shoo away the waiter just as Golko starts to order. He purses his lips and turns the page in his notepad.

"The first cross-reference was to a file called Starye Atagi." He looks up at me, waiting for my reaction to the news that my hunch was correct. Apparently the General hasn't mentioned the intercepted phone call from the woman who called herself Charlie. When I don't respond, he says, "I think that one was the master file for everything that happened at the village. Which means that the one we were looking for, fifty-nine-slash-thirteen, would have been one of many referenced under that name."

"I understand."

"The second cross-reference was to a Fifty-eighth Army corporal named Joseph Melnik."

I sit up straighter. "Now we're getting somewhere. If he was attached to the Fifty-eighth you can find out everything there is to know about him—"

Golko waves his pad in the air to stop me short. "I already looked at Melnik's file. Last night. According to our records, he never served anywhere near Starye Atagi."

"What made you look at his file?"

"I searched Dubinin's quarters, like you told me, and I found a couple of notes in his footlocker. Not my kind of notes. More like scratches. One of them was from a conversation he had with Khanzad, arranging the details of the sale and transfer of the egg. He wrote the name, Joseph Melnik, then drew squares around it."

"If Captain Dubinin was a note-taker, then he took *good* notes. You need to search again."

"Yes, *sir.*"

"Where does Melnik live?"

"Vladimir—the same place Dubinin and Khanzad agreed to exchange the egg for cash."

The drive to Vladimir will be two and a half hours each way. Not something I'm looking forward to, but Melnik's name showing up in two places is the first real lead we've gotten. First I need to see Masha, however. I don't want to wait any longer to find out why she called.

"Let's go talk to Melnik this afternoon."

He nods. "I found the memo from your interview with the woman whose son was in the Rostov morgue. The kid was a mechanic with the Forty-fifth Airborne Regiment."

"Ivashko," I suddenly recall, hearing his mother's voice in my head. "His name was Ivashko."

"That's right."

"Any connection to Starye Atagi?"

"Not that I remember. I'll look again."

"How about to Dubinin? Or Melnik?"

"No."

He takes a slow sip of tea, regarding me over the rim of the mug. "Let me show you something."

He turns his pad so that it faces me, then puts his index finger over the middle digits, so that three numbers show on each side.

"We know what the middle four numbers and the slash mean, right? That's our missing file, and it documents something that happened in the area of Starye Atagi."

"Go on."

"When you take those away, six digits remain. Turns out they're a soldier's ID. Guess whose?"

"Captain Dubinin's."

Silence. Then he nods, sadly. "The captain's ID number was seven-five-eight, three-two-three."

"Bring the General up to speed."

"Of course."

A strand of black hair has fallen down his forehead, like a bar between his blue eyes. At a high enough level in the military—or in politics, crime, and business—most Russians serve more than one master. Ambiguity, guile, and misdirection rule. Golko has played the role of helpful adjunct well. That could be all that he is, but I'll have to keep reminding myself that his loyalties might be divided. When I stand to leave he puts up a hand to stop me, looking uncomfortable.

"There's something else I have to tell you."

I wait for him to say more, watching him stir his tea.

"An FSB agent named Lachek died last night at Botkin Hospital. Blunt-force trauma to the head. The story going around is that an army commando laid him out with a pistol. His father, Filip Lachek, holds the highest Kremlin security clearance you can get." Golko lifts his face to stare at me. "He's looking for you."

chapter 12

On the walk to the metro after leaving Golko I keep seeing the same two cars, a blue Renault and a red Honda. Near the steps down to the train, three men wearing gray overalls and yellow rubber gloves lean casually against the hood of a dented Mercedes panel van. They studiously avoid looking at me as I walk past. Part of me is still geared up from the confrontation in the archives and from seeing the interior ministry troops at the market, so maybe my paranoia is misplaced. I'll deal with Lachek when I have to, but I can't imagine he's this close yet.

On the train ride to Masha's apartment I remember that I need to call Brock Matthews, but he can wait because I doubt he'll be anything but a bother; the Americans like to talk only when it benefits them. Instead I spend the time trying to arrange all the pieces in my head, searching for clarity.

The Nokia buzzes as soon as I'm back out on the street. I answer it with a grunt, assuming it's Golko.

"Hello, Alexei," Valya says through a swarm of static.

The emotion released by the sound of her voice is like a chemical bath of adrenaline and endorphins. "Valya."

"Why didn't you tell me how hard everything is with just one foot? I would have kept both of mine." Her musical laugh is symphonic, more pleasing to my ears than Tchaikovsky.

I step through the nearest door into a shop so that I can hear her more clearly. "Where are you?"

"Grozny."

"You're kidding."

So much time passes before she responds that I think the connection has been lost.

"I may not have a signal for long, Alexei, so listen. Abreg is targeting soldiers."

"Soldiers? He's blowing up buildings."

"I haven't heard anything about buildings. But I know he's killed at least three men in Chechnya, and now he's reaching into Russia. The story is that he ordered his men to take a knife to an ex-soldier's face and make it last for a long time."

"When?"

"I'm not sure. Several weeks ago."

I quickly make a whole lot of unpleasant connections. Ivashko, Dubinin, and this one, all killed and mutilated the same way. "Where?"

"Somewhere around Moscow."

"Do you know his name?"

"No."

Snow has started falling on the other side of the glass door. Two different men in red berets cruise past, heads moving from side to side like hounds on a trail.

"Why is Abreg targeting soldiers?"

"He's after the members of a unit that did terrible things to a group of civilians."

"Which unit?"

"Don't know."

"When and where?" I say, even though I think I already know.

"It could have been anywhere in Chechnya anytime during the past decade." Her tone is bitter, her anger palpable; I can almost see the smoldering fire in her eyes. "What building was blown up?" she says after a moment.

"The headquarters of an American oil company."

"Why would Abreg target a place like that?"

I remember thinking something similar just after the explosion. And as I consider the question again, another idea jumps into my mind, just as Valya gives voice to it.

"Are you thinking of Ryazan?" she says.

I cast my memory back to the days before my first deployment in '99, when Chechen separatists were blamed for a series of apartment bombings that killed three hundred people. The attacks became a rallying cry in the run-up to the second Chechen war, the war that Putin rode to power, although no terrorist group claimed credit and the official investigation was superficial. But questions surfaced later, after what became known as the Ryazan incident.

A night-owl resident of an apartment building in the city of Ryazan witnessed strangers placing heavily loaded sacks in the basement. He notified the local police. The men turned out to be FSB agents, and the bags contained hexogen—the same sophisticated explosive found at the scene of the apartment bombings—and a detonator. The FSB claimed the men were part of a civil defense exercise. Most people accepted the explanation, but the affair became fodder for conspiracy theorists, who claimed that Yeltsin enlisted the secret service to carry out another massacre in order to boost war fever. I don't know the truth of it, but not long after the apartments were bombed our tanks rolled into Chechnya.

I realize that I've been unconsciously shaking my head, and I find myself reading off the General's script that Russia can do no wrong. "The FSB dogs bite everyone, but even they would not stoop so low."

Valya snickers. "I'm glad you're such an optimist."

"What are you doing in Grozny?"

She doesn't answer right away. "I came back because I felt like I had abandoned . . . something. I'm not here to fight. The ones still fighting are fanatics, all of them. I'm trying to help the people from my *teip* who don't have food or a doctor or medicine for infection. I can't do much, but I feel more useful here than I did anywhere else." She hesitates. "And I've met some people working for unification," she says finally through the crackling hiss.

Attempts to unify the North Caucasus fell short during the '90s, when border disputes and blood feuds turned into internecine conflict fueled by Kremlin instigators. It is a silly, hopeless cause—just the kind to draw Valya.

"So we're both optimists."

"No," she says, laughing for real this time. "We're both crazy."

"Have you heard anything about where Abreg is hiding?"

"Speculation—always moving anyway—"

"You're breaking up!"

"I'll try to find out—"

"Be careful!"

But the phone has gone silent, and I don't think she heard me. Not that my warning would have changed anything. Valya will do whatever she sets her mind to.

I flip the Nokia closed and look around for the first time. I'm in a tailor's shop, the walls and tables lined with bolts of colored cloth and ribbons, small boxes filled with buttons and beads and trimmings set on a table in front of the stoop-shouldered proprietor. Behind him in a back room is another long table, this one lined with sewing machines operated by a row of seamstresses. He asks if he can help me with something, and I buy a swath of drab oilcloth and drape it over my shoulders to form a shapeless umbrella as I go back out to the street and the snowfall.

The red berets are nowhere in sight. I automatically go through a routine of doubling back, waiting on opposite corners, and frequent stops, making sure I don't drag an unwanted tail to Masha's apartment.

All the while grappling with the shocking news that Valya has returned to Chechnya, a place where she suffered terrible abuse, first at the hands of her incestuous father and his brothers and later at the end of ropes held by marauding bands of Russian and, worse for her, Chechen fighters from rival *teips*. Until we met, she said, she didn't know friend from foe, and so she fought everybody, making temporary alliances when she could.

I regain my senses and thumb through the Nokia's call log, but the number she called from didn't register. Maybe it was blocked; maybe it came from a satellite phone. Either way, I can't believe I just wasted the chance to talk to her about the things that really matter.

chapter 13

Masha lives on the ninth floor of a Khrushchev-era building with painted concrete floors, broken elevators, and rows of doors covered with sound-dampening blankets. Most of the tiny flats are inhabited by wrinkled babushkas who are forced to beg or sell trinkets to survive. Like me, Masha is an amputee, although her ancient wood-and-leather prosthetic foot is a far cry from the titanium-alloy marvel that mine is. Climbing the stairs, I wonder how she manages to do it several times every day, especially in her timeworn condition.

I have to wait a few moments after my knock for her to snick and rattle open the locks. She stands aside as I wedge into a flat not much bigger than my closet in the basement of Vadim's Café, although hers has a fold-out bed instead of a military-issue cot. A window on one wall faces shelves full of books on another. A small wicker chair, a sink, and a black-and-white TV with a foil-wrapped wire hanger antenna complete the furnishings.

"You should have told me when you were coming." Her voice is gravelly from a long life and too many unfiltered cigarettes. "I would have had something ready to eat."

"I've just eaten, Masha. Thank you anyway."

She's wearing a faded purple dress under a shawl so threadbare it is almost transparent, and clutching an afghan that must have been on her lap when I knocked. The boiler in her building is no match for Moscow's January blast. Her hair is long, frizzy, gone entirely to wintry whiteness; when she leaves the building to shop or visit, she tucks it under a colored scarf. Around her neck is a frayed leather necklace adorned with mysterious talismans.

For more than three years I have helped her to survive, giving her money to pay for the flat, for food, and for her own modest charities to aid others she knows are in need. I do the same in lesser measure for other aging widows of Russia's endless fighting and purging. Fueled by oil and gas revenues, Russia's new economy has generated more wealth for those who were already rich, and some of that money has escaped their clutches to find its way into the pocketbooks of a burgeoning upper-middle class, but many of our long-suffering elderly still miss the safety net of the Soviet state.

The blinds are drawn nearly closed, blocking most of the light from a wan morning sun just warm enough that it will soon turn Moscow's streets to slush, but she gasps when I step into the flickering cone of illumination cast by the television.

"What happened to your face?"

She reaches up and touches the burns. Despite the wrinkled dryness of age, her caressing hand feels soft. She gently pushes me back into the wicker chair and shuffles to the sink at my side, clicking on an overhead light. She fumbles water into a pot and puts it on her hotplate.

"I have medicine, Masha."

She opens a cabinet over the sink, studies the contents of several plastic baggies, then pours small piles of green, brown, and red herbs into a mortar made of speckled granite. I settle back into the chair. My body fits comfortably into a familiar depression shaped by many prior visits.

"The news says the terrorists struck again." She picks up a pestle and begins to grind the mixture of herbs into powder. "This will end. Just like all the other wars, this one will not last forever. But I'm afraid I won't live to see it."

I silently agree with her. The clash of cultures runs too wide and deep, each side sustained by a tortured vision of the god they claim to worship. The world has adapted to the new order, and a few, cunning and exploitive, have learned to enrich themselves from the chaos.

The shrill cry of the kettle startles me. Masha mixes some of the boiling water with the powder in a clay bowl, making a paste that she applies to the burns on my face. They've already been salved with enough balm to last a week, but I know better than to try to stop her.

She finishes with the medicine, settles on the edge of her bed, wraps the afghan around her legs, and goes to work knitting, hooks clicking rhythmically, dancing in and out of synch with the quieter ticking of the clock on the nightstand next to her.

"My friend has a granddaughter," she says. "Galina. A sweet girl, only twelve years old. Always laughing . . ."

The needles stall as her voice trails away. Her hands, splotched with age spots, settle into her lap. Her head stays bowed.

"Galina has been missing for nearly a week."

"Did she run away?"

She shakes her head vigorously. "No. The talk is that the body of another missing girl was found a month ago. Strangled and . . . abused. My friend is frightened out of her mind. She says that a boy from their old neighborhood came around before Galina disappeared. Semerko is his name. He was a soldier until recently."

"What about the police?"

"They can't find Galina *or* Semerko."

"What can I do that they can't?"

"I don't have anywhere else to turn," she says in a low, quiet voice. "I told my friend, I know a man. He gets things done that others can't.

Maybe he breaks the rules—maybe he breaks more than just the rules—but if he says he'll help, he will."

This is the first time Masha has acknowledged openly that she knows exactly what kind of person I am.

"Things like this usually end badly. If Semerko took her a week ago, it's probably over."

I didn't mean to sound so harsh. But I don't have time for fairy tales, and I can already envision the sad scene when I tell the girl's family a whitewashed version of the truth and watch their hopes shatter.

Masha's blue eyes are moist. "You think I don't know that she's probably already dead?"

I feel small enough to crawl under the door. I start to say something, but Masha hunches over her knitting again, and I close my mouth. Thinking back, I realize that when Valya left I disengaged in a way that I never had before. Even in Chechnya I distinguished predator from prey, and acted accordingly, and my willingness to help those who were worthy was one of the things that brought Valya and me together in the first place.

I look up to see Masha watching the emotions at work on my face. She points a needle at the shelves behind me. "I have pictures that might help you make up your mind."

Two unframed photos are lying flat on the shelf. I reach back and take them down. The top one shows an old woman hunched in a rocker, wrapped in so many blankets it is impossible to judge her size or shape. The skin of her face sags, and her white hair is so wispy that her freckled brown skull shows clearly beneath it. Behind and above her is a shrine on a makeshift shelf made from a board painted white. Thin church candles stand at each end of the board, stuck in a base of their own melted wax. Between them, plastic flowers frame a picture that I think is the same one as the second in my hand—a pretty girl in an over-the-shoulder pose that makes her appear very young.

Galina has laughing hazel eyes, curly brown hair, and skinny, little-girl legs poking from her flared polka-dot skirt. She looks nothing like

Valya, either now or as I imagine Valya would have looked at the same age. Galina is soft-brown innocence compared to Valya's smoky-white brilliance. And yet the association is impossible to resist.

I shut my eyes against the memories of the stories Valya has told me of her childhood. Stories I can't bear to recall, stories that make me feel helpless, powerless to prevent the spreading stain of evil. When I open my eyes again, Masha's gaze meets mine.

"Do whatever you have to do, Alexei. Please. Just find her."

I don't know how I'll be able to find one girl among Moscow's teeming millions. But I am not powerless, not this time.

"Why is Semerko a suspect?"

"Because he is a—" She breaks off, apparently trying to decide how to say what she thinks. "Semerko was never right, not even as a child. Then, in the army, he suffered from *dedovshchina,* bullying, and that made him worse."

I recall a time when I came upon such a scene during a reconnaissance, crossing a soggy field at night, hearing raised voices and shouts coming from an abandoned barn. Inside the barn a circle of lanterns swayed in the unsteady hands of drunken soldiers, most of them *kontraktniki,* contract soldiers, like modern-day pirates in their bandanas, wraparound sunglasses, camouflage jackets with the sleeves ripped off, and tattooed prison muscles. In the middle of the circle was a conscript with pimples and peach fuzz, trussed and gagged, wild-eyed, anticipating a kick, or the sizzle of a heated knife, or the crushing grip of needle-nose pliers—angry, confused, bored men can think of many ways to injure and degrade. He was Russian, and so one of their own, but he had done *something*—maybe it was a cross look, or a lisp—to make the mob believe he deserved these things. I saved him that night, but he was only one of many thousands over the years, and most of them received no succor.

Masha coughs. "Irina—Semerko's mother—told me he was beaten, maybe worse, and that he came back from the war as a devil."

"Will she know how to contact him?"

"Maybe not, but she might know something."

Masha puts her knitting aside and goes to the door, where she wraps her hair in a red scarf and takes a heavy coat from a hook. I stand and help her struggle into it.

It's 10 A.M. I'll have to call Golko and push back our trip to Vladimir.

chapter 14

Outside Masha's building the pale sun reaches hesitantly through the clouds, casting swatches of light among the darker shades. She leans into me, tired from struggling down the stairs, using my body as a shield against the wind. Sidewalks cleared of snow frame the small park between the buildings in her complex. The park is vacant beneath the empty branches of an enormous oak surrounded by sentinels of leafless silver birches. The walkway leads to a wider street choked with cars and trucks and scooters and bundled pedestrians. I don't spot any red berets.

We ride an escalator down to the metro and shove into a car without any available seats. A look from me causes a bald man with black tufts above each ear to give up his spot on the bench for Masha. I stand, holding the strap above her as the doors whoosh closed and the train begins rocking down the tracks.

Two stops later the train sways to a halt in the swanky Petrovsky district, and we climb back up to the street for a short walk. Wet snow begins to fall as the sun fails behind thickening clouds. Other than Masha's occasional "This way," we don't talk, but she presses against me as we're bumped by the morning crowd. She smells like spicy-sweet ginger. We reach an apartment building painted a light blue that appears faded, even though it's one of the mayor's modern architectural atrocities, only a few years old.

"Irina has money?"

She shakes her head against my chest. "Her daughter married into it."

The elevator whisks us up twelve stories to a short hallway with only one door. At Masha's knock a maid admits us into an enormous foyer and asks us to wait. Several minutes later, clicking heels signal the arrival of a woman with dyed red hair sprayed into the shape of a helmet.

Semerko's sister is older than he is by at least a decade. When he was born she would have been a young girl, probably living on the cusp of Soviet economic ruin. But the intervening years were good ones for her, and now more than age separates her from the brother who was poor enough to have been conscripted into the army.

"My mother is not allowed visitors here," she says coldly to Masha, refusing even to look at me.

Parquet tiles flow beneath her feet like liquid gold through double doors into what appears to be a sitting room. A door on our side opens to a powder bath, and from somewhere deep in the apartment comes the clinking of pots on a countertop. Masha and ten of her friends could live for a year on what it costs to rent such a flat for a month.

"We would like to see her now." I speak softly, in a tone she will recognize. This woman understands men like me. In fact, I would wager that her husband *is* such a man, because this much money in the new Russia was probably earned by force.

She still doesn't acknowledge me, just tightens the mask of her made-up face and motions for us to follow. She clacks over the golden floor to a hallway in the back and a room that was designed to be a walk-in closet. "Ten minutes. After that I will call security."

The closet houses a twin bed, a shaded lamp on a nightstand flaking gilded paint, and a hawk-faced woman watching a portable television. Irina fails to offer Masha a seat next to her on the bed, so I move a corner of the bedcover aside and clear a space for her to sit. Once she's settled I turn my attention back to Irina, who's trying to peer past me to see the TV screen.

"My name is Volk."

"He is my friend," Masha says. "He has questions about Semerko and Galina."

"Semerko had nothing to do with that girl." Irina's voice is cold like her daughter's, but more petulant than haughty. At the mention of her son's name she finally looks at me full on, her lips pinched together to form a beak.

"Where is he?" I say.

"Who knows where he went? South, maybe, back to the mountains. Not even the police can find him."

"Does he have a phone?"

She stares at me for a long time, gnawing absently on a yellow thumbnail. "Are you a military man?"

"Ex-military. Why?"

"The army led him to the devil, heroin. He has wasted away to nothing. Maybe he's already dead." Saliva seeps from the corner of her mouth where her teeth are working on the nail.

"Do you have a phone number? An address?"

"No. I don't care to see him. He has become one of those people who hates this country. A know-nothing."

"He knows war."

She pretends not to have heard. Her tongue, like a hoary gray caterpillar, wriggles out and licks the chewed bits of thumbnail. Just standing near this soulless woman as she demeans her child turns my blood cold.

"What did he do in the army?" I ask, mostly just to keep her talking.

"You think I know things like that?" The tongue mercifully disappears when she talks. "First they beat him, then they sent him to Chechnya and turned him into an animal. What he did there is not my concern."

"He is still your son," Masha says softly.

Irina shifts her weight and wipes her wet thumb on the blanket beneath her, but gives no answer.

"Are any of his things here?" I say.

At first she seems ready with an angry retort, but then she leans forward hungrily, her eyes as sharp as those of a predatory bird. "How much?"

"For what?"

"To look inside his footlocker."

I pull a banded roll of rubles from the pocket of my jacket. Count out three thousand, a little more than a hundred American dollars, and fan the notes in front of her eyes. She makes a grab for the cash, but I pull it away so quickly she nearly falls forward.

"Where?"

"The basement, in a storage area with the same number as the flat. I don't know the combination."

When we leave she's busy stuffing the fistful of notes into a hole in the bottom of her mattress, rushing to hide the money from her daughter. The maid sees us to the elevator. Masha shudders during the descent and I start to give her my jacket, thinking she's cold, but she shakes her head. "It's not that," she says.

The doors ding open and we exit onto cracked concrete, pooled in places with oily water. The air is cold and musty. Mechanical equipment is housed on one side, protected by a floor-to-ceiling chain-link fence, its gate secured with a combination padlock. Similar locks are attached to hasps on each of the dozen or so doors on the other side of the fence.

I find the door that corresponds to the flat of Semerko's rich sister.

One thump confirms that it's hollow, so I kick it open without bothering to pick the lock. Inside are dusty cardboard boxes, a broken chair, a child's bike, and stacks of shrink-wrapped white cartons labeled with the brand of a German computer-chip manufacturer. Now I know one of the ways her husband makes his money. At the very back is a metal footlocker, also locked, but easily cracked open with my knife.

The footlocker holds yellowing underwear, ripped jeans, khakis, a frayed sweater, four collared shirts and several logo-stamped T-shirts, and a fleece-lined parka, all neatly folded. A shoebox, containing rubber-banded Japanese trading cards that depict cartoon action figures and three pornographic magazines, records the transition from adolescent to teenager. Two dog-eared paperbacks, Tolstoy's *Hadji Murád* and Pasternak's *Doctor Zhivago,* sit on top of the box next to several music CDs.

"We are grave robbers," Masha whispers.

"You think Semerko is dead?"

"No. But the boy who owned these things is."

Looped in the back corner of the footlocker is a short length of climbing rope, orange with black stripes. I dangle it in the air, then slide it through my lightly closed fingers. It is sheathed in woven fibers that feel silky against my palm. When I tighten my grip and pull hard the rope stretches almost imperceptibly. It's slightly longer than a meter, maybe ten millimeters thick, cleanly cut at both ends. I wind it into a tight ring and put it into the pocket of my coat.

Beneath the rope is a glossy magazine for mountain climbers. A single page has been marked with a yellow paperclip. On one side of the page is a photo of a mountaineer decked out in the latest climbing gear, all available by mail order. On the other is a picture of a Dagestani mountain village coated in snow. A tumble of wooden and brick buildings appears to have been tossed at the base of a columnar minaret, the entire village lost and forgotten among colossal peaks and steeply falling valleys. The caption beneath the picture says it is called Tindi. I tear it out and fold it into an inner pocket of my jacket.

The elevator dings open and Semerko's sister charges into the basement, trailed by a uniformed security guard.

"Leave that alone!"

Still sifting, at the bottom of the footlocker I find an article cut from the *Novaya Gazeta* newspaper—which I slide unnoticed into my pocket next to the glossy magazine page—and a picture in a cheap metal frame that's already coming apart at one corner. The photo shows a young man standing on the wooden platform of a train depot, wearing a dress uniform and a tentative smile. Self-conscious and proud at the same time, half-turned away from the camera's gaze, but still standing ramrod straight as he had so recently been trained to do. Taking a last look inside the footlocker, I decide that Masha is right. The boy who treasured these things is gone. I also believe that the mother who locked the image of her son in this hidden place bears a measure of responsibility for the sins of the man he came to be.

"I said, leave my things alone!"

I roll the magazine into a tight tube and turn to face the two of them, putting Masha behind me. The guard reminds me of a slack-jawed version of the baboonlike police commander: all the same viciousness, but without the brains to channel it into a lucrative career.

"When was your brother last here?" I say.

She narrows her eyes. "Go away!"

"Answer my question."

Without looking at the guard, she commands, "Arrest them!"

He unslots his nightstick, scratched and dented from much use, and twirls it to the side of his body, smiling with anticipation as he moves closer. He opens his mouth as though he's about to give a warning, then suddenly swings the club in a long arc toward my skull. I step inside his swing and ram the end of the rolled-up magazine into his Adam's apple. The force of it knocks him backward off his feet. He lands heavily as the nightstick clatters away behind me. He lies paralyzed for several seconds, face turning blue, eyes rolled back. Then he grabs his throat and starts gagging for air.

Semerko's sister stares down at her fallen man. All I can see is the shiny red dome of her helmet of hair.

"When was Semerko last here?"

She raises her bitter gaze to look into my face. "You think I want to protect *Semerko*? Eight days ago. That's the last time I saw him. I haven't the slightest idea where he went. Now get out!"

I ask Masha for her cigarette lighter, then tell her to wait for me in the lobby. She nods and walks slowly past the sister and around the guard, who is curled into a fetal ball now, both hands around his throat, but he appears to be breathing.

As soon as the elevator doors close, I start pulling the shrink-wrapped cartons out of the storage room, forming a pile on the wet concrete.

"What are you doing?" The sister's face has been Botoxed into a tight mask, but her fear is plain to see.

I toss Semerko's clothes on top of the pile for kindling, then set fire to one of his T-shirts, holding it away from my body by the sleeve. Her face turns ashen.

"Stop! Wait a minute!"

I throw the flaming shirt onto the pile. The whole lot begins to smolder. Brown-ringed holes form and expand in the plastic that wraps the cartons.

"I have an old address! Put out the fire and I'll give it to you." She takes a crumpled envelope from one of her pockets and stands holding it.

A thick cloud of smoke rises as the first flame grips a carton and pops to life.

"Makhachkala!" she says, flinging the envelope toward me. It flutters to the concrete near my feet.

I pick it up and turn it in my hands. It's empty, dirty the way it would be if it had gone through the post, with a return address in Makhachkala written in the corner. I don't think she's lying, not anymore. Makhachkala is the capital of Dagestan, and that connects with the picture of Tindi. I shoulder past her and push through the panic hardware on the metal door leading to the stairs, just as the fire sprinklers cut loose and the alarms start whooping. Before the door swings closed behind me, I catch a glimpse of her desperately pulling away the burning clothes in a wasted effort to save what she can of the contraband.

✄

Masha remains silent during the walk back to the metro. I help her down the steps, and she rests her head on my chest after we have boarded. As the train lurches down the tracks I take out the newspaper clipping. The article is dated October 13, almost three months ago. It describes a fire on the outer west side of the city, near Victory Park. A former Russian army corporal and his two-year-old son were killed. The tragedy was blamed on faulty wiring. I could ask Golko to check the records and confirm it for me, but I don't need to see a file to know in my gut that the dead man was Semerko's former superior, and that he had probably instigated *dedovshchina* against the young conscript.

The train begins to slow. Masha presses harder against me, her head down. All I can see is the top of her red scarf.

"Next you'll talk to the police in District Thirty," she says conclusively.

"Later today," I promise, thinking that the AMERCO building is in District 30, and remembering the florid-faced inspector named Barokov who owes me a favor.

chapter 15

NSA agent Brock Matthews is waiting for me at Vadim's Café when I arrive that afternoon, a blast of cold air accompanying me inside. Smatterings of diners sit near the front, a few of them at the long communal table in the center of the room, but Matthews occupies a table in the back, facing the door. He acts as though he's glad to see me, smiling as I approach, rising to his full height of about two meters—athletic, all hard planes and angles. Just as he did when I met him in D.C., he has a tight way of holding himself, as if anticipating a threat. He's wearing a tailored black suit without a tie over an open-collared white shirt. His smile reveals large, white teeth set in an angular jaw, giving him a somewhat horsy appearance.

His smile vanishes as I draw near.

"What the fuck happened to your face?" he says in English.

"The outdoor grill at my dacha's been acting up. What can I do for you, Matthews?"

"Your new tan wouldn't have anything to do with the fracas at the AMERCO building, I don't suppose?"

American intelligence has improved in the years since 9/11. Even so, I'm surprised they've already connected me to what happened there. Maybe he's just guessing. I scrape back a chair, and we sit at the same time, facing each other across a scarred wooden table set with two paper place mats, white napkins, mismatched knives and forks. Matthews has pushed his place setting aside and drawn a ceramic bowl of stuffed olives closer.

"One thing we gotta respect," he says, plucking an olive and popping it into his mouth. "You guys don't fuck around. It was the talk of the whole department. The Delta guys are jealous. Wish they could go in fast like that, just start slaughtering bad guys. After Haditha, it's like we have to notify a goddamn military judge before we shoot back at a guy blowing AK rounds at us. Who sets that policy anyway—Putin?"

The diner is loud, and the other patrons are far enough away that I don't think we can be overheard, even if someone within earshot speaks English. Still, I'm uneasy with the topic.

"I'm not privy to things like that, Matthews."

"Putin," he says thoughtfully, as though he didn't hear me. "Now there's a study. He's got oil for blood. It's all he seems to care about, ever since he closed Transneft's pipes for a day and brought Europe to its knees. Short run that stuff might work, but when are you guys going to figure out that nationalizing the country's resources is a good way to go broke?"

"You know a better way?"

"Sure. Answer's right in front of you. America, Britain, Japan, now even India—the list is endless. Hell, the Chinese are going to beat you to it if you don't get your shit together."

"Sorry I asked."

"Know what we call this country now? Putin, Inc. Capitalism sucked through the filter of a police state. You get the worst of both worlds."

"You like the part about slaughtering bad guys without having to answer all those annoying questions, but you're upset we don't have a free press?"

He holds out a hand and laughs a little, as if we're not really discussing anything important. "At least neither of us is as bad as Islam's right wing. Tell them they're not peace-loving and they'll kill you. How's that for hypocrisy?"

"Your message said you had something important to talk about."

"Yeah, Putin. Do you work with the guy? Because you should see our file on that fucker."

I don't understand why he insists on discussing Putin so much. We've reached the end of the lunch hour, but the restaurant is still noisy. Rattling dishes, raised voices, clinking flatware. The lines of mortar between the bricks in the wall behind him form a disjointed pattern that fails to resolve in my mind.

Matthews leans forward on the table to bring his face closer to mine, suddenly serious. "I know how much you hate to tell me anything about what it is you do exactly, but just answer that."

"I don't work for Putin."

He gives a slight nod and tosses another olive into his mouth.

"General Nemstov and Putin," he says, munching. "What's up with those two?"

"I have no idea."

"Word's out that Putin's got a hard-on for him because the General's been selling black-market arms to Iran, maybe other countries, too. Putin figures that shit'll come back, either to Chechnya to kill Russians or because of political fallout at the United Nations. Not that anything ever happens at the UN."

Selling weapons to potential enemies of Russia is a terrible idea. That's one thing on which I agree with Putin. But I'm not about to give Matthews the satisfaction of knowing how I feel about the General's side business.

He absently pushes the bowl of olives away, then slides it back.

"Your General's got a nice little racket going. Strong-arming the mafia, collecting protection money from crooked businessmen, trading black market art—I suppose it's good work if you can get it."

I make a show of checking my watch.

"All right, then." He seems satisfied, although I can't figure out what he thinks he has learned. Maybe now he can check those things off a list he keeps on a desk somewhere back at the American embassy. *Talk to Volk about Putin, done. Tell him we're on to the General, done.* He repositions his chair and stretches his legs. "Let me tell you a story."

He stares past me for a moment, as if considering how best to say what's on his mind, an act I don't buy.

"There's an American senator from the Pacific Northwest. Three-term guy, the right family connections, all the big Senate committees, including foreign relations, and a decorated military vet. Solid. West Coast liberal, but not over the top, not a political bomb-thrower. Electable, in other words—and still young enough to have a couple of shots at the top job. We'll leave him nameless for now. I don't think you care about that anyway. Suffice it to say he's got lots of clout in D.C."

Matthews eyes me quizzically. I find his description of the senator's politics amusing. To me the differences between American politicians are insignificant, and mostly rhetorical; damn near every one of them voted to bomb Iraq until the sand turned to glass, all the while condemning Russia for invading Chechnya. One thing I understand well, however, is power. The senator he's describing certainly has that in abundance.

Whatever Matthews reads in my face causes him to shrug.

"The senator's got a daughter. More likely, he *had* a daughter, but I'll get to that in a second. Mid-twenties. East Coast education—Vassar. Dated movie stars, had her picture splashed all over the tabloids and a couple of fashion magazines. About a year ago she's in Paris during one of those demonstrations, the kind where they protest everything, someone lobs a Molotov cocktail through a storefront window, riot police fire water cannons, a few loudmouths get arrested."

He waves his fingers in the air dismissively. Chews on another olive and gazes over my shoulder, contemplating the view of the café and the street outside. I don't need to worry about my back, not with Vadim lurking somewhere about. Vadim would fight to his last breath if need be, although it's still not the same as when Valya was my guardian angel. She protected me with a fury that not even Vadim can match.

"She hooks up in Paris with the leader of a group called Peace Now," Matthews says. "A Singaporean named Ravi Kho, real trouble-making piece of shit. Like a rock star in those circles, goes by just Ravi. She becomes an activist—antiwar, antiglobalization, antimultinational, pro–World Court and United Nations. You know the type. Or maybe you don't. The important thing is she quit the party-girl circuit.

"Daddy pulled some strings, and she joined the UN with a bullshit title, special attaché or some crap like that. Supposed to be a cushy gig, but she didn't want it that way. Spent time in Darfur, of all places. What a shithole. Then about six months ago she went to Singapore, probably to hook up with Ravi. She was working with a UN aid group in Malaysia when a couple of Aussie relief workers were beheaded. Truth is, the Aussies saw some things—and some people—they weren't supposed to see. You want my opinion, they were intel ops all the way, not a couple of peaceniks. They knew the score. Just like you and me, right, Volk?"

Matthews is probably a tough, brave man. He's probably flown air strikes against outgunned military opponents, maybe even pulled a trigger in a Falluja back alley, but he's never been on the short side of the power ledger. So he is not like me in ways that matter.

"Anyway, the senator's daughter was in the thick of it. She met the terrorists, a Jemaah Islamiya splinter group. Got to see the heads come off up close and personal. Probably not what Daddy figured on when he signed her up. You ever see something like that, Volk?"

The things I have seen, and done, are locked down inside, and best left there.

"Yeah, you have. And worse."

His gaze meets mine for a moment.

"They let her go. Probably because of her relationship with Ravi Kho, but who knows what motivates those people. How do you get something to drink in this place?"

On my signal Vadim materializes with a teakettle so quickly that Matthews startles upright in his chair. "Does this guy understand English?"

"Don't worry, he's deaf."

Vadim is far from deaf. Lasting nearly ten years in an Arkhangelsk work camp requires all the tools for survival, including the ability to fade into the background and know everything without appearing to show interest in anything. His skeletal frame and swarthy Gypsy looks fool the uninitiated into thinking he's less capable than he is. Many Russians think of his kind as inherently inferior, an attitude bordering on racism that permeates many of our policies.

Matthews seems undecided for a moment, then nods, seeming to accept the lie, maybe for the same reason many Russians underestimate the man.

"Got anything stronger?" he says, watching Vadim, who is far too clever for such a simple trick.

I wait until Vadim has me in his line of sight before saying in Russian, "Bring a bottle of vodka."

Matthews leans back, long legs stretched in front of him again. "Where was I?"

"You were telling me about the senator's daughter and Ravi Kho."

He nods. "Turns out Ravi may have been feeding the Jemaah Islamiya boys information he got from her, classified stuff she could get her hands on by throwing her father's name around. See, right after they let her go the group's raids became *more* daring. They blew another nightclub, this one just outside Jakarta, like what happened in Bali. They launched a busload of tourists off a cliff near Bandung. We worked to get that one reported as an accident, but it damn sure wasn't. Point is, no matter what we did, they seemed ahead of us all the time."

Vadim returns carrying a tray with a bottle of toxic bar vodka in a bucket of ice and two shot glasses. Matthews waits until Vadim is looking at him before he says, "Got any gin, a little tonic maybe?"

Vadim pretends not to understand and walks away. I fill our glasses, raise mine in an obligatory toast, say "To America," and knock it down. Matthews lifts his drink, shoots it, then winces at the harshness of the alcohol. As soon as his glass hits the table I pour us both another round, then return the green bottle to the bucket of ice.

"She has a history of helping terrorists?"

"No. She was being used, but I don't think she knew it. She still puts Ravi up on a pedestal. To be honest with you, we think she's a total whack job. Last week she took a razor blade to her wrists. The blade went deep, a lot deeper than it would have if the whole thing was just an attention-getter. That tells you what we're dealing with here."

He regards the vodka sourly, takes a sip, which is not how it should be drunk, and sets it aside gently, as if it might explode.

"Right around the time Jemaah Islamiya upped the ante, Ravi's Internet postings became more militant. Bad enough that he made a big blip on our radar screen. Then he went to Chechnya. He wanted to expose the atrocities committed there, according to his Web site. Un-fucking-believable how the Web has enabled these bastards.

"Not long after he got to Chechnya, Ravi starts making noise about a really nasty piece of business. Two hundred Chechens supposedly marched away from a filtration point—tortured, raped, whatever—and then killed. Sometime during the winter of '03. Maybe you were there." He grins at me, but it is a halfhearted stab at humor, because his eyes betray how edgy he feels.

I prefer to wait him out, say nothing while he keeps feeding me information, but the bad feeling in my chest is starting to metastasize into an ugly realization in full bloom.

"Where was this supposed to have happened?"

"Starye Atagi."

chapter 16

I hold myself still, trying not to show any reaction to the name of the village. Vadim glides past our table carrying a tray loaded with black bread and bowls of steaming cabbage soup while Matthews tracks him with his eyes and begins talking again.

"Seriously, can you imagine just how bad that would look in the world press? Not that we care. We'd love to take the attention off so-called American atrocities for a change."

I pound down another shot, not even bothering with a toast. The peppery liquid coils like a cold snake down my throat and catches fire in my belly.

"Anyway, Ravi starts making noise about it. Tells the media he's got irrefutable proof. Lucky for you guys, the only paper that reported it was a liberal Moscow rag no one pays any attention to. Like you said, that's one good thing Putin's done, he's gotten a tight rein on the press over here."

I'd said nothing of the sort, but he can believe what he wishes.

He's right about Putin's control of the press. Businessmen with close Kremlin ties have been buying up television and newspaper outlets like trinkets. Matthews makes wet circles on the table with his glass while a father herds his son past us and into the back restroom.

"Twelve days ago," he continues, "Ravi disappears. Couple of days after that, he turns up dead outside of Moscow with a bullet parked in his skull. The coroner called it a suicide. That's when the senator's daughter started playing with razor blades." He kills the last of his vodka and plunks the glass upside down on the table. "Don't pour me any more of that shit."

He drags a rawboned hand down his face. We sit in silence wrapped by the white noise of the café as he apparently tries to decide how to finish his story.

The vodka Vadim brought to us is called *palenka,* a rotgut concoction often made in homemade distilleries. The drink, along with Matthews's reference to the General's extortion racket, takes me back to a time when Valya and I confronted a gangster named Yakov, a man who had cobbled together a consortium of *palenka* distilleries in the Urals by force after the collapse of the Soviet Union.

He worked out of a two-story office in Yekaterinburg. On a day when we knew he was inside, we overpowered two guards in the otherwise empty first-floor lobby. I left Valya posted just inside the doorway, an Uzi in the crook of her right arm with its open metal butt resting on her hip, and headed up the stairs.

Yakov was in a back room at the head of a table ringed with five of his lieutenants, tilted back in his chair with papers scattered in front of him. One of the men saw me coming and jumped up, gripping the butt of a pistol tucked into the waistband of his jeans, but he was too late. My Browning was already aimed at Yakov's face. I walked to the end of the table, within a meter of him, then stepped to one side and put my back against a wall so he had to twist his chair around to see me.

"I'm Volk."

"So?" He had piggish eyes set in a face layered with folds of fat. Despite the gun almost touching his nose, he showed no fear.

"With the Fifty-eighth Army."

He looked confused. I was not merely another hoodlum out to make a name for himself, not an outraged farmer whose land his trucks were churning to muck just to cut off a few miles of road, not a cuckolded husband seeking revenge.

"The Fifty-eighth is staffed in Vladikavkaz," he said warily.

I thumbed back the hammer, in no mood to explain that two thousand kilometers were not nearly enough to protect him.

"I know this man, boss." The voice came from one of the men seated at the table, his face marked by a jagged scar that plowed down his cheek from a point just below his left eye to his upper lip. I recognized him as a former staffer from the North Caucasus Military District. "He's the one I've been telling you about. The assassin who's always with the Chechen girl."

Yakov stiffened. It is one thing to face an unknown rival, even one with military connections, but another to contend with someone like me. Still, backing down in front of his men was hard to do. The weight of the decision warred on his features.

"Boss, the girl is *always* with him."

Yakov looked quickly toward the door, then stared down the implacable barrel of the Browning. Several seconds ticked by before he melted into his chair. "How much?"

I told him that, and I explained how the pickups would work, and I itemized the consequences for him if he failed to deliver. Looking back upon it, I realize that he was one of the first to feel the muscled tentacles of the General's Fifty-eighth Army, flexing, strangling him in their sticky embrace.

The memory of Yakov and his *palenka* consortium has gone through my mind in an instant while Matthews stares into space, apparently still trying to decide how much of his story to tell, how much truth to mix in with the lies.

"Listen," he says. "I'm trusting you on this, Volk. The senator's daughter went missing five days ago. There's an awful lot of heat on us to find her, fast. Problem is, we think Putin might've had something to do with it. In fact, we're pretty damn sure he did."

"Why Putin?"

"Because one of his main men for Southeast Asia started asking about her just before she disappeared, a guy named Filip Lachek. You know him?"

I maintain eye contact without changing expression. Hearing the name Starye Atagi again so soon after it first came up has prepared me for more surprises, but Lachek's name has landed like a sucker punch.

"No."

"Heard of him?"

"No."

One of the servers drops a tray behind me, glass, cutlery, and crockery crashing to the slate floor. Neither Matthews nor I react.

"Lachek was an air force guy, like your father," Matthews says casually, his gaze tightly focused on mine. "Served right around the same time, too."

My father disappeared shortly after I was born. During my childhood, as I was passed like chattel from one work farm to another, I often wondered about his fate. Later, I thought about it less. Lots of Red Army officers were purged during the Soviet years.

"We think Lachek killed Ravi Kho," Matthews says, as though he'd never mentioned my father. "No loss—who's going to miss another rabble-rouser like that? But the daughter of an American senator? Different fucking issue entirely. If Lachek's involved in her disappearance, everything changes."

His expression seems to flatten into something harder, unyielding. "We're looking for an angle here, Volk. We can't go public, and we can't go directly to Putin, not until we know more. We've got to work our way around the edges, peel back a few layers. That's where you come in."

"What's in it for me?"

He smiles again, because this is a language he understands well. "Information? Something—or someone—you want to know about?"

"My father is ancient history. I don't care what happened to him." But even as I say the words I realize that I do.

Matthews stands up and adjusts his jacket. Rights the upturned glass in front of him, grabs the neck of the vodka bottle, and twists it a few times in the slush. Yanks the bottle out of the bucket and holds it dripping in his left hand.

"One of our operatives spotted a colleague of yours in Grozny a few days ago," he says, switching to perfect Russian with a Petersburg accent. He sweeps his gaze over my head, taking in the crowd. "Beautiful young woman who walks with a limp. We've been trying to figure out whether she's on the right side or not. Who the hell knows a terrorist from a civilian in a place like Grozny?"

Fear for Valya squeezes my heart to a stop.

He pours a shot, lifts it toward me, and knocks it back. Fast, the way a Russian would. No grimace. He slides the bottle back into the bucket, rattles the empty glass onto the table, and tosses another olive into his mouth like a peanut, grinning around it as he chews.

"Someday soon we'll have to answer that question. Is she a terrorist? Complicated country, Chechnya. Hell, it's a pretty complicated world nowadays. Just like you did at the AMERCO building, sometimes we think it's better to shoot first, worry about truth and justice later."

My blood has turned colder than the slush in the bucket on the table. Matthews keeps looking at me with his horsey smile, waiting me out.

"I'll ask around about the senator's daughter. What's her name?"

"Charlene Thomas," he says. "Everyone calls her Charlie."

chapter 17

After Matthews leaves I wander down to my office in the basement and collapse into a chair. Visions of Valya shimmer in my mind, too many to catalog. A porcelain-doll tsarina with white hair and big eyes and a lithe form so kinetically charged she seems to be in motion even standing still.

And then a memory erupts, one of agonizing pain and grainy darkness etched by tracers of green and red, then everything suddenly lit white-hot by an exploding illumination flare. Silhouetted in the electrifying incandescence above me is Valya, holding her Kalashnikov aloft in both raised arms, frozen in the glare like a leopard in mid-leap.

"Everybody fucking dies!"

Even now, more than four years later, the recollection is powerful enough to start my heart racing.

I retrieve the Lachek dossier from my room, find a pencil—rough with teeth marks from Vadim holding it in his mouth—and form a column on the back of the first page. Write *Starye Atagi, Ivashko, Dubinin/Egg,*

Melnik, Khanzad with plenty of space between each name. After studying it for a moment, I put *Abreg?* at the end of the list.

Drawing a line to form a second column, I write *AMERCO, Lachek, Kombi-Oil, Marko Hutsul.* I hesitate for a moment before adding *Matthews/Charlie/Ravi.* I underline Charlie's name, and make a line connecting it to Starye Atagi, since, according to the General, she mentioned the village. Then, remembering what the Chinese girl told me in Alla's office, I add the name *Maxim.* I consider whether to write Abreg's name here, too, but decide against it, thinking that this line of inquiry feels too big, too complex, like giants wrestling with their feet planted on both sides of the continent. It seems beyond his scope—and mine as well.

And as I'm thinking those thoughts I recall the cool gleam in the eyes of the Chinese girl. *Oil is everything,* she said. Cursing myself for not having seen beneath her surface beauty, I realize that the canny glint I took for hooker cynicism might have been something else entirely— and suddenly a different way of looking at the names in the second column occurs to me. *Russia, America, China.* I draw a circle around them. Next to the circle I write *Oil.*

On the last third of the page I write *Galina/Semerko/ Dagestan/Tindi,* thinking about the over-the-shoulder smiling girl and the boy's things buried in the basement. A single life hangs in the balance here, but it feels no less important than what I've written before. I finger the length of climbing rope and the envelope in my pocket, and tap my pencil from one column to the next, one, two, three, making leaden dots like holes in a gun range target.

I call Golko.

"When do we leave for Vladimir?" he says by way of greeting.

"Later tonight. I need you to research a Singaporean named Ravi Kho. He died less than two weeks ago somewhere around Moscow. Find out how. Look for links to Abreg or any other terrorist. Do it fast and call me."

I settle in to wait for his return call. The back of my chair is straight, unyielding, uncomfortable. Like the blocky table, it was made from oak and iron-hard maple, mortised at all the joints, sturdily built long ago by gulag prisoners. Its curved wooden arms have been worn to a sheen by the rubbing of countless elbows, glassily smooth except in the places where the wood has been gouged into jagged craters and canyons filled with ink like river water—casual marks, for the most part, likely made by bored bureaucrats serving their Soviet masters, literally and figuratively marking time. The time before lunch or the day's end or, perhaps, the time before the next purge—the heart-stopping boom of a gloved fist pounding your door, announcing the arrival of the secret police and the beginning of the rest of your life.

During the Stalin years the process of the purges was refined, reduced to mechanical, impersonal routines that made you less than a human being from the moment of your arrest on some absurd charge. You were dragged away in front of your coworkers or, worse, your anguished family. Stuffed into the caged rear of a Black Maria, a paddy wagon crowded with other doomed souls. Bounced in an awful ride to the bowels of the Lubyanka or one of many other prisons, where you were photographed, stripped, and searched, fingers probing every orifice. Deposited in a bare cell of brick and steel to stand naked in five centimeters of freezing water, taken out for questioning at varying intervals. Sooner or later, depending on how much you could tolerate, you signed the inevitable confession. Because the Soviets never arrested anyone who was not guilty.

Confession signed, guilt confirmed, you were transported by rail in a hellish Stolypin boxcar north through the tundra and taiga, occasionally given scraps of food and a cupful of water, maybe a bucket for a toilet to be shared by thirty people crammed into a rolling prison cell wrapped in barbed wire and steel mesh. Then, finally, weeks or months later, if you managed to survive the trip, you arrived at the camp where you would live out your days in hard labor, always cold, always on the ragged edge of starvation.

My father disappeared late in the life of the gulag, not long after my mother died as I clawed out of the womb. As a military man, he might have been picked up anywhere—from a barrack, a base, or on the street—or he might have been killed outright in any one of dozens of Cold War theaters. I once found the name S. Volkovoy among the records of the political prisoners of a camp in Kolyma during the winter of 1979, but that probably meant nothing because Volkovoy is a common name.

All of these unproductive thoughts stream through my mind at a subconscious level as I consider the implications of what Matthews has told me. The one that overrides all others is that the North Caucasus is one of the most dangerous places in the world—a remorseless amalgam of warlords, tribal leaders, political appointees and their apparatchiks, *mafiya* thugs. If Valya is in Grozny, she has placed herself squarely in the crosshairs.

Golko calls back. "Ravi Kho was the former leader of Peace Now, a subversive group based in Singapore. He was in Grozny until recently, spouting all the separatist propaganda. And, yes, he was rumored to have met with both Khanzad and Abreg. Did you know Abreg used to be a journalist? Now he's a cripple."

I can picture Abreg now, hunchbacked and twisted, leaning on his gnarled cane as he stared down at me from the top of the pit. I look down at my missing left foot and conduct a quick mental inventory of my wrecked psyche. Many of us are crippled in different ways.

"What about Ravi?" I say.

"He was found dead of a self-inflicted gunshot wound to the head at a private residence near Suzdal twelve days ago."

Suzdal, set in the meadows on the winding banks of the Kamenka River, is a former medieval capital, its skyline a sea of domes and cupolas, less than a thirty-minute drive north of Vladimir.

"Whose dacha?"

"Well, that's the strange part. I—look, it seemed as though you didn't like me talking about him before."

"Who?"

"Filip Lachek," he says. "Ravi Kho's body was found on the grounds of a country estate owned by Filip Lachek."

I turn over my notes and study the typewritten pages of the dossier. Nothing has changed. Military, secret service, clandestine operations—Lachek is a rabid Kremlin dog on a very long leash.

"Volk?" Golko says after a minute.

"Did anyone give a reason why Ravi supposedly decided to kill himself?"

"No note, nothing. A single shot through the roof of his mouth with a .32-caliber pistol."

I realize that I've been unconsciously digging my fingernail into one of the craters in the arm of the chair.

"The M.E. figured out what kind of knife was used to kill Dubinin," he says.

"A *kinzhal*."

He doesn't say anything for a few beats. "Yes, a *kinzhal*, the Caucasus dagger. How did you know that?"

Because Valya told me Abreg was killing soldiers. "Because I'm gifted."

He snorts. "Ever seen one?"

I have, just as the blade was about to lay me open, wielded by a man the size of a chimpanzee who came closer to killing me than all but a few others.

Golko waits for an answer, then says, "Big knife. We also found prints left in the blood on the trunk lid of the Mercedes."

Prints will lead nowhere.

"No matches yet," he says. "Captain Dubinin had foreign tissue under his fingernails. We'll be able to make a DNA match if we have a suspect. That would make for a certain conviction. Even civilian tribunals love DNA."

A suspect has absolutely no chance of making it to trial. Why does

Golko think I'm here? "Did the General give you the list of the hostages from the AMERCO building?"

"I've got it in front of me."

"Check out Marko Hutsul, the chairman of Kombi-Oil."

"Why?"

"Because I want to understand why Chechen terrorists would let him and nine others live."

"They wouldn't, not unless they had to."

"Exactly." Maybe Golko is catching on.

"No, I mean they must not have had time to do anything after the second explosion. According to the reports I've seen, your squad and a Vympel antiterrorist unit stormed the building immediately."

Guess not. "Whoever was guarding them had time to empty a magazine into ten hostages," I say dryly. "Pick me up on the east side of Red Square at midnight. We'll go to Vladimir and find Melnik."

I end the call, pull on my jacket, and head up the stairs. I think the missing daughter of a United States senator has a pendant that belongs to the Russian people. And she might have answers about why soldiers are suddenly dying for something that happened near the Chechen village of Starye Atagi. So I'm going to pay her a visit right now.

chapter 18

The Kitay-Gorod district is a tightly packed warren of twisting streets, baroque churches, dead-end alleys, and bustling commerce, hard east of Red Square on the north side of the Moscow River. Old Moscow's trading and financial center, the district is crowded, claustrophobic, sweaty in summer, and now, in the dead of winter, cloaked in snow and ice. Exhaust fumes threaten to choke me as I shoulder my way through the throngs.

The address the General gave me for Charlene Thomas—before we knew she was a U.S. senator's daughter—leads to an ancient, three-story brick structure on a street running diagonally away from Lubyanskaya Square. The building is tucked so far behind a wide hotel that its entrance is nearly invisible from the street. It hosts a pharmacy and an electronics store on the ground level and residential flats on the top two.

I quickly pick the outside lock on the residential doorway and slip into a cramped stairwell. Kick a bloodstained syringe skittering into a corner beneath a pay phone hung crookedly on the wall next to two rows of mailboxes, fifteen to a row, no names, just numbers. This must be the place where Charlie made the call traced by the General.

I go up to the second floor and cruise a hallway so narrow my shoulders barely fit, past green wooden doors, each with a number spray-painted on the bricks next to it. Empty bottles and wet fast-food wrappers are piled into a corner, giving off the sharp tang of urine. I take the stairs to the third floor. Same thing here, although the smell is less bad.

American rock music pumps from the flat at the end of the hall— lots of guitars, a marshal beat that vibrates the walls. I draw the Sig, stand to one side of the door, and knock. The door is opened by a man in a dirty undershirt, his white gut squeezing out the bottom of it. The music thumps my chest, much louder now. Over his shoulder I can see his wife or girlfriend washing dishes in the kitchen with a thumb-sucking child holding on to one of her thick knees. I hide the Sig along the side of my leg. "What do you want?" he shouts over the music, and I tell him sorry, wrong flat, and go back down the stairs to wait across the street.

The dinner crowd rushes past. Streetlights paint the dirty snow with waxen luminance. Younger shoppers frequent the electronics store; the pharmacy caters to all ages, shapes, and sizes. I cruise around the building, looking up at the framed lights on the upper two floors, most of them flickering from the glow of televisions. An old man is pressing his forehead against one of the windows. He sees me and blows a cloud of cigarette smoke that curls around his head in the shape of a hood. Taped to a window two over from the old man's is the symbol for peace, a circle cut by three lines. Second floor, three in from the corner.

I'm back up the stairs in seconds. The door third from the end is number 28. Silverware clinks on the other side, along with low voices from a radio or TV. I stand to one side and knock, three quick, polite taps. The clinking stops.

"Who is it?" The voice belongs to a young woman who speaks lousy Russian with an American accent. It is the voice I remember from last night.

I pivot and jackknife my boot into the door next to the knob. The old wood splinters and the door gives, but it fails to spring all the way open, held in place by a short chain. A panicked scream greets me as I ram my shoulder into the door to break the chain and lunge inside, drawing the Sig, crouching low.

The tiny vestibule opens onto two rooms—a pocket kitchen and a combo bedroom-living area. The supposed hostage from the AMERCO building, the woman with ash-blond hair, stands petrified in the kitchen. Then she scrambles back, trying to escape, but she has nowhere to go. I drive three steps forward, clutch the fabric of her top with my left hand, and yank her down just as she yells, "Wait!" She thumps the floor with a whoosh of expelled air. I point the Sig around the flat, searching for other targets. Aluminum dining table set with a half-eaten hard-boiled egg, a plastic bottle of *kvas,* and one glass; a portable television turned to a news station; an unmade, built-in bed, walled in on three sides; an empty bathroom. No people.

From flat on her back, Charlie grunts as she launches a kick at my groin. I block it with my thigh, but it still hurts. She aims another kick, but I punt her in the head with the toe of my left boot, trying for a glancing blow. She makes a sound like a jukebox when the plug is pulled, a fading groan, then her whole body goes slack. I have no feeling in that foot, only the sensations telegraphed from my prosthesis to my knee, so I may have kicked her too hard. The hit I delivered last night to the younger Lachek is proof enough that my touch is suspect.

Just in case she had protection, I rush to stand with my back against the wall next to the hinged side of the broken door, but nothing happens. I check the hallway. The other doors on this level are still closed, so I don't think anybody heard my crashing entrance. Or if they did they don't care.

I go back into Charlie's flat and push the door as far closed as it will go in its shattered state. Drag a chair in front of it and prop it beneath the knob so that no one else can come in as easily as I did, and lift Charlie onto the bed.

A sapphire egg pendant with a silver cross of diamonds nestles in the pale hollow of her throat. I bounce it in my cupped hand, feeling its surprising weight, then jerk it free of its gold chain and shove it into the pocket of my leather jacket next to Semerko's rope.

Charlie's purse—Prada, black with silver fittings—rests on the kitchen counter next to a toaster with a glass door. Inside is her phone, a flat rectangle with a keypad underneath the display screen. The display lights up when I press the center button, but requires a password, so I set it aside.

Her wallet holds just over eleven thousand rubles, a fistful of credit cards, and three hundred crisp American dollars. Charlie's Washington state driver's license lists her as five-seven, a hundred thirty-five pounds. In the picture she wears her hair cut short in the back, longer in the front so that it frames her tanned face. Her tan clashes incongruously with Moscow's gray January, visible through a tiny kitchen window hanging over the dinette, dark clouds and snowflakes illuminated by the streetlights below. She has sea-green eyes and parted lips, revealing startlingly white teeth. One of the front ones overlaps the other ever so slightly.

She moans and twists on the bed, beginning to regain consciousness. She looks different now. The tan is gone. Her closed eyes have dark rings around them. Her hair is longer and her face thinner. A trickle of blood jags down her temple where I kicked her. She's wearing tight jeans low on her hips and a clinging cashmere sweater. The sleeves of the sweater have ridden up on her wrists, revealing the edges of white bandages.

She groans and sits up, holding the side of her head. Her eyes widen when she sees the blood on her hand. "You had no right to hit me!" she says in English, petulantly.

A round is already in the chamber of the Sig, but I pull back the slide for show, and for the sound it makes, then I aim the barrel at her right foot. "What were you doing in the command center last night?" I say, also in English.

She tries to tuck her foot underneath her left leg. If the bandages are any indication, she's not afraid to die, but she apparently doesn't like the idea of being shot to rags first.

"I was being held by the man you hit on the head." She says the words as though that is something I should already know. Just from her tone my opinion of the senator's daughter drops several notches. She is not an enlightened Athena fighting for justice, except perhaps when it suits her to don the mantle. She's a self-absorbed child, so wrapped up in her own situation that she expects everyone else to already be familiar with it.

"By Lachek?"

"I don't know his name."

"Why were you being held?"

"I don't know that either."

I gesture impatiently with the Sig. "Get to it, Charlie. What happened?"

She doesn't seem surprised that I know her name. She eyes the gun and hurries to answer. "I was picked up a few days ago. That man—Lachek?—and another kept me in a country house. I have no idea where. Yesterday they drove me to the city. The building was already on fire when we got there. Lachek told me to pretend to have been a hostage and he told me what to say, just that and nothing more. My Russian is bad, so it wasn't hard to keep quiet."

"How did you get away?"

"The other man—the one next to me when you came in—led me out of the building as soon as you left. He was talking on his phone, and he kept jerking my arm so hard I thought it would come out of the socket. I kept pulling back, because we weren't going *away* from the burning building. He was leading me right *toward* it. What are you doing?"

I've already taken one step closer to her, in an almost unconscious reaction to what she just said, and now I take another, bumping the bed. I prop a knee on the mattress and dangle the barrel of the Sig near her wide eyes.

"Don't lie to me, Charlie."

"I'm *not* lying!" She pouts her lip. A long time ago the look might have been charming; on a woman in her mid-twenties it is puerile.

"What was he saying on the phone?"

"I wasn't listening! I was trying to keep up while he was dragging me. Sirens were going off all around us. People were screaming. Everything was dark except for the fire."

"Where did he take you?"

"To the side of the building."

"Which side?"

She gives me a helpless look. "I don't know directions in this city."

"What happened?"

"He talked some more on his phone, and then we waited, maybe ten minutes or so. Then there was a huge explosion. Until you're close to something like that, you just don't have any idea how awful it is. It was like a giant hand shoved me into the wall. I hurt my head." She holds her hair away from the side of her face to show me a fresh scrape, barely noticeable.

"And the man guarding you?"

"He was down. Not dead, at least I don't think so, but hurt. I ran."

I step back from the bed. The part about being abducted jibes with what Matthews told me, and with Charlie's failed phone call to what she thought was the American embassy. And the man who was with Lachek might explain how those inside the AMERCO building knew I was coming—he could have called or radioed them. All of which takes me to a place I don't want to go. It is one thing to toy with the idea of government involvement, quite another to confront hard evidence. If FSB interior ministry troops orchestrated the AMERCO explosion, then I am on perilous ground.

I contemplate the senator's daughter. "How long was the drive into Moscow from where you were being held?"

"Two or three hours. I'm not sure."

About the distance to Moscow from Lachek's country estate in Suzdal, I figure. "Where did you get the pendant?"

She reaches a hand to her throat. Her eyes widen when it comes up empty. "It was a gift from my boyfriend. I want it back."

"Why did Lachek let you keep it?"

"He didn't plan to. First he took it, then he put it back around my neck." She shudders. "He said to keep it warm for him."

I hold up her phone. "Password?"

"*Charlie* and the number *one*," she says reluctantly, eyeing the Sig, and I key it in with my thumb, then scroll down to an icon labeled "Pics & Videos" and tap the screen to open it.

The first folder, not labeled, contains several shots of an Asian man I assume is Ravi. He has unlined features darkened by an intense expression bordering on fanaticism—something about the sharp angle formed by his eyebrows, I think.

"I can get you money if you let me go," she says.

Most Americans and, especially now, more and more Russians seem to think everything comes down to that. Maybe they're right that cash is the new Russian orthodoxy.

Another unlabeled folder opens with pictures of Charlie in various stages of undress, along with a thirty-second video recorded from above while she gives the cameraman a blowjob. I keep it running to the end just in case something meaningful was hidden in the file.

"Having fun?" she says scornfully. "Pervert."

I don't bother to tell her that Alla shoots five per night that are infinitely better. "Ravi Kho?"

"Aren't you told the names of the people you kill, Mister—what's your name?"

I navigate back to the main picture menu. "I didn't kill him."

"Then one of your government friends did."

Several other files, named "Singapore," "Paris," and "Girlfriends" might be worth looking into later, but I scroll to the last folder, unnamed, which opens on a picture of the Hen Egg, just as it was described in the commission document copied into the book under my cot. A silver stand holds a pearled egg with a luminescent glow, opened to reveal its golden innards. A hen made of gold, encrusted with white diamonds to mark the outlines of feathers and rose-cut diamonds for eyes, has been set in front of a gold leaf basket. The basket holds the sapphire pendant that's now in my pocket.

All of that was arranged on cloth, green with two stripes, one white and one red, overlaid with a circular design that's hard to make out in the photo. But I don't need to see it to know that inside the circle is a dark wolf under a full moon. The egg and all of its pieces were arrayed on the Chechen rebel flag.

chapter 19

The first thing that goes through my mind is that Khanzad would not have displayed the egg, or any other prize, on the rebel flag unless it suited his need of the moment to pretend to be a ferocious freedom fighter. I think the flag means Khanzad was trying to fool someone stupid enough to believe his posturing. Maybe someone like Ravi, or maybe only Ravi's naive American girlfriend.

I grab a metal chair from the dinette and swing it around so that I can straddle it, facing Charlie. She shifts uncomfortably under my scrutiny and picks at the loose edge of the bandage on her left wrist.

"Why didn't you go to the American embassy after you escaped last night?"

"I wasn't sure how to get there, and I was afraid. I came here because I knew it was safe. Then I called, I used a special number, and the person I talked to told me to go to the square and wait, she said somebody would come, but—"

"What?"

"It just didn't sound right."

The General's operator could have inadvertently tipped Charlie in any number of ways. It might have been as simple as a misplaced word or a strange turn of phrase.

"Why the peace symbol in the window?"

She looks surprised, then heart-struck, inconsolably sad. "Is one there? Ravi must have put it up before he . . ." She looks away. "This was our getaway place."

I mentally count the number of emotions she has displayed in the short time I've been with her. Fear, self-pity, insolence, surprise, grief—she's a psychologist's wet dream, a mental train wreck with a rich daddy to pay the bills.

"The newspapers say Ravi killed himself."

"That's a lie!"

"Maybe you're right. Anybody could have killed him. Selling secrets to Jemaah Islamiya terrorists put a big target on his back."

Charlie's face boils bright red, and she comes off the bed and charges me, flailing with her fists. Without standing I stiff-arm the top of her head, grab a fistful of hair, and twist her to the floor, where she kicks out and tries to rake her fingernails across my face. She manages to slash open a freshly scabbed burn on my neck before I can slam my heel into her solar plexus so hard that her ribs seem to wrap around my ankle. I gather both of her hands into one of mine and hoist them over her head, silently vowing to start carrying those plastic zip-tie cuffs everyone is so fond of using now. Chalk up another emotion for her analyst to consider: blind rage.

She struggles for air, mouth opening and closing. Her face turns purple before she's able to suck in a first shallow breath, then another until she is gasping. I release her hands and she uses them to cover her face and curls into a ball.

"You bastard," she says quietly. Her eyes are closed, face still red, and the artery in her neck pulses rapidly. "You're all evil. You destroy all the good things. Grind men like Ravi into hamburger under your boots. Nothing ever changes."

Brave words, however fatalistic they might be. She has surprised me again, this time with a buried kernel of serious thought. Maybe this is a hint of the Charlie that was meant to be, or the residue of what she was when she was with Ravi. I look away from her. The window at the far end of the flat has darkened even more, signaling another onslaught of snow. This is turning into one of the coldest Januarys in recent memory. Which means the north will be particularly frigid—good news for those who wish to hide the horrors of the gulag. Once every few years someone discovers a mass grave from that era, but for the most part the northern permafrost conceals the bodies, keeps them safely tucked away in blankets of icy soil that shroud decades of lies.

I'm not sure why I'm thinking these things. Like the distant memory of the father I knew only as a chimera, they keep blading their way into my brain at the wrong times.

I refocus. "Why do *you* think they killed Ravi, Charlie?"

Tears leak between her fingers. She mumbles a few words I don't entirely catch, something about wishing she were dead. Melodramatic, the kind of thing you might hear in an American movie, so I repeat the question more harshly.

"Ravi was going to expose your army of murdering animals in Chechnya—killers and rapists destroying homes and villages." She's still hiding behind her hands. "How many stories have to be told before people will listen?"

The twenty-first century echo of Stalin's purges—forced relocations, death squads, filtration points, torture, slave trafficking—is not lost on me. I witnessed some of those things, but because I nearly always fought alone or in small groups my exposure to the worst of it was limited. Only lately, since Valya left, have I begun to consider whether I might have been one of the oppressors perpetuating those horrors rather than a loyal soldier fighting for my homeland. Such thoughts are hard to face.

"Ravi was an idealist," Charlie says. She's still on her back on the floor. She drops her hands away from her face in a resigned way. "He kept telling me and anyone else who would listen, 'I need proof.' And he got it. He got a video that not even the slimiest, slickest weasel in your government could deny. A video! You can't lie about that!"

She stays flat on her back, almost panting with emotion.

"And then they killed him like a dog," she whispers.

"Where's the video now, Charlie?"

The senator's daughter swipes at a stray tear. Her lower lip trembles, but when she tries to firm it she succeeds only in appearing more helpless. She squirms away from my chair and sits up with her head between her knees. She's shaking, but not only from fear and loss, I realize. She's enraged again.

"I have no idea where that goddamned thing is, but if I had it, every frame would be splashed all over the Internet. Fuck you! Fuck all of you."

Her anger is wasted on me. Ravi wasn't nearly as innocent as she believes. And I am certain that, whatever the video depicts—whatever flash point in the maelstrom is illuminated by its frames—it will show only a small part of the whole. Good and evil are not so easily distinguished.

I believe her that she doesn't know where the video is. But the pieces of the puzzle she has supplied are beginning to fall into place for me. If it exists, such a video would damn more than just those shown on it. In some ways, it would indict the culture that spawned the crimes it records. Fairly or unfairly, it would be used as an international bludgeon against Russia. And it would be used by a man like Abreg to target the soldiers depicted in it. *Abreg is killing soldiers,* Valya said, and now I know why, and how he has been determining which ones deserve his wrath.

"Have you seen it?" I ask Charlie.

"No. Ravi told me it was shot with a handheld camera, maybe a cell phone—all short scenes stuck together. Twenty-nine minutes of Dante's hell, he said."

"Who made it?"

"I have no idea. Ravi didn't either, at least I don't think he did. He was very secretive about it, at first, and he was here and I was still in Singapore and . . . I didn't ask enough questions. I wish I had."

"How did he get the video?"

"He said it was given to him by a man with a conscience."

"A conscience? What does that mean?"

"That's all he said. I don't know what he meant by it."

"Who did Ravi talk to in Chechnya? Who did he meet with there?"

I think in her current state she would defy me if she thought it might help Ravi, but it won't, and I can almost see her come to that realization.

"Khanzad," she says. "Ravi was working for peace with a freedom fighter named Khanzad."

chapter 20

One viewing of the video and Khanzad would have understood the value of what he had in his possession. Air strikes against his rivals in the Caucasus, assassinations, money wired into a Swiss account—the owner of such a video could demand those things and more.

Charlie cups both hands on her cheeks and pulls them back to wipe away the wetness. "I know what you're thinking, and it's not true. Khanzad didn't kill Ravi. The Russians did."

As ignorant as she is of the politics of Chechnya she can't be expected to understand that one might be the same as the other. Whatever Khanzad promised Ravi was a lie.

"Tell me about the Hen Egg, Charlie."

"What? Jesus, are you kidding me? What difference does a fucking golden egg make now?" She motions toward her phone. "Ravi sent a picture. He knew I liked things like that."

"Where did he get it?"

She sucks in a deep breath and releases it in trembling flutters. "I asked but he wouldn't say." She touches her temple, smearing the blood there into the shape of a folded maple leaf. Then she hiccups and struggles to her feet and stands swaying for a moment, not looking at me. "I really need to clean up."

I check the bathroom again, this time for weapons or a way out. It's small enough to brush your teeth and wash your face while sitting on the toilet—which would have to be done sideways, facing the sink and tub, because there isn't enough room for a person's knees in front of the bowl. A toiletry bag rattles with a bottle of prescription pills while I search it, finding only the usual assortment of items. The room has no windows and nothing that can be used as a weapon, at least not by Charlie. At my nod she slips past me and closes the door. Water hisses in the shower.

I take a few minutes to consider what I've learned from Charlie. Then I call Golko, tell him where I am, and instruct him to send two men right away to pick her up. If Matthews wants her as badly as he seems to, then she's too valuable to lose. And just as I think that, I notice steam leaking from beneath the bathroom door. I pound on the door and rattle the knob.

"Charlie?"

The idea, the possibility of what she might have done, comes to me all at once. I kick open the door and rip back the plastic curtain. It comes down, rod and all.

Clouds of steam boil around Charlie's sprawled form. She's still wearing all her clothes, her thin wrists wrapped in bandages. Frothy white foam bubbles from her mouth. Her eyes are open, glassy.

I grab her slick body under the arms and hoist her onto my shoulders. Her head bangs the jamb as I carry her from the bathroom to dump her faceup on the bed. I put one hand on top of the other just below her sternum and pump, again and again, until a frothy mixture of foam and milky fluid braided with red borscht and brown *kvas* oozes from her mouth. I probe her throat with my fingers to dislodge anything that might be stuck there. Once I'm sure the airway is clear I pump some more until she's breathing on her own, then roll her onto her side and go into the bathroom.

The pill bottle is empty. The label says it originally contained thirty OxyContin in 80 milligram doses. No telling how many she took.

When I return to the bed her pupils have contracted to pinhead-sized dots. Her skin is cold and clammy. Suddenly she retches violently and pukes more cloudy fluid ribboned with reddish-brown that smells like beets, not blood. She draws her knees toward her chest, breathing fast and shallow. I find a dirty glass in the sink, fill it with water, and try to make her drink it as I cradle her head in my lap. Most of it slops from her mouth, but some makes it down her throat. I press a hand under her left breast. The beat is fast but steady.

With nothing to do but wait, I peel back the bandage on her left forearm. Two jagged scars crosshatched with black stitches like railroad ties run vertically from the base of her palm toward the crook of her elbow. Some people fight for life. Others crave oblivion.

Charlie is unconscious but breathing well when Golko's men, two of the soldiers from the parking garage, arrive. They've donned civilian clothes, but with their hair clipped down to shadows darkening their skulls and the stiff way they hold their shoulders, they might as well be in uniform. I take the peace symbol from the window. Drawn on a square not much bigger than my hand, the back was made to peel away and stick to a smooth surface, but the wax paper is still in place. I fold it into Charlie's jeans pocket, wrap her in the blanket from the bed, and they carry her out between them as though she is sick or drunk. She will become a resident of one of the General's cells beneath the Kremlin, a bargaining chip to be played when the time is right.

After they leave I stand in the middle of the room and look around one last time, but I don't notice anything important. I have three hours before meeting Golko for the drive to Vladimir. Enough time to see Barokov and ask some more questions about the explosion at the AMERCO building. And maybe help save someone who's worth saving. Charlie may have given up on her life, but Galina might still have a chance to live hers.

chapter 21

The District 30 police station is made of unevenly settled slump block that gives it the appearance of a crumbling ruin. Inside, the air is hot and close. A desk sergeant parked on a high stool behind a counter and a sliding-glass partition doesn't bother to open the glass when I ask for Inspector Barokov, just talks right through it in a loud voice.

"Who are you?"

His side of the countertop is cluttered with the wreckage of his last meal and curled report forms that appear not to have been disturbed since perestroika.

"Tell him it's his friend with the missing left foot."

That's the best I was able to come up with on my way here. My name won't mean a thing, and I can't say I'm the colonel that Barokov met last night, not here in the open. I figure he'll remember the surprising feel of my prosthesis when he was checking me for injuries after the building exploded for the second time. The sergeant elevates to peer over the counter through the glass, his belly hanging between his knees like an uncomfortable sack of meal, then settles back again, looking disappointed. The only thing to see is the boot that fits over my false limb.

"You're not missing anything."

"It's an old joke."

He knits his eyebrows, probably trying to decide whether he's being made fun of, then hauls himself off the stool and lumbers toward the back, leaving me to wait in the receiving area.

The station is falling apart for want of repairs it won't get anytime soon. Its white walls are trimmed in green paint cracked like a dried lake bed. The boiler downstairs gasps and thunks, fighting a holding action against Moscow's January freeze. Condensation drips from the overhead pipes, and more moisture wicks from the corners of the ceiling, where radiating brown stains that look like tree rings mark the advance and retreat of past incursions.

A disheveled, thirtysomething American with a diamond stud sparkling in his left ear argues with a police officer in English. "The hotel has my passport and visa. Here, call them." He tries to give the deadpan cop the key card to his room. Instead of taking it, the cop shoves an open statute book at him. It's in Cyrillic, so the tourist has no way of reading what it says about the requirement that identification papers be carried at all times. But he pretends to do just that, staring uselessly at the book instead of using his head to figure out the obvious way past his problem, which is a payoff. He looks up from the book. "I'm going to contact the American embassy."

I translate for the cop.

"Good. They can come see how broken-down this place is. Maybe give us money to fix it." He glances at the tourist. "Fucking idiot."

The fat sergeant returns and jerks his thumb toward the metal door. "All the way back."

The door leads to an antechamber, empty except for a desk missing its drawers that sits facing an unoccupied holding cell with floor-to-ceiling bars and a built-in concrete bench. Another door, made of fractured wood with a hole where the doorknob should be, hangs halfway open. I walk through it into the squad room. Three cops occupy tables as old as mine, typing, talking on an ancient black rotary-dial phone, and handwriting notes on a form. Two others stand together in conversation off to one side. The place stinks of stale cigarette smoke, mold, and men who go too long between showers. They stop what they're doing to stare as I walk between the desks to the back, where Barokov waits in a miniature office. I close the door behind me and settle into a listing roller chair, my knees bumping the front of his desk.

He's wearing a rumpled brown suit, possibly the same one he had on last night, and, sitting as he is, seems even rounder than I remember.

"You look different, *Colonel*," he says, eyeing my civilian clothes.

"You're no fool, Barokov. Figure it out."

He nods thoughtfully, studying me. "Just what every Russian fears," he murmurs. "The first man through the door. A killer in the night."

I liked Barokov from the start, when he stepped forward after I delivered the blow that killed Filip Lachek's son. That may be why his words, as justified as they are, cut more deeply than they should.

"Yes," I say quietly. "The first to kill. And the first to die."

He blinks twice, quickly, as though I've slapped him, and then appears to consider my words. "True enough." He leans back, composing his features into an expression approaching friendliness, and crosses one leg over the other. "Your face looks bad. How's the rest of you?"

"The woman in the command center last night, blond hair, navy blue suit."

"What about her?"

"You tell me. Did anything about her strike you as odd?"

He frowns. "She was bedraggled, smoky, upset—almost incoherent. Nothing unusual about that, considering. Why?"

"Did her demeanor change when Lachek arrived?"

"Lachek was already in the room with her when I got there. He beat everyone to the scene, had everything set up, including the blueprints. I don't know how he managed to do it so quickly."

That part of Charlie's story checks out. She and Lachek arrived at the scene together.

"What are you suggesting, Colonel?" Barokov says.

But I don't have the time or the desire to speculate with him. I change course. "A girl in your district has gone missing."

His sudden stillness tells me I've struck a chord. "Who?"

"Galina Cheslava."

"Why are you interested in that?"

"It's personal," I say, which is likely to make him believe my interest is anything but.

From the look on his face, Barokov wants to tell me not to interfere in police business. But a Moscow police inspector has to defer to an army colonel, even one without any definable authority. Or especially one such as that.

"She's only been missing for a few days. Lots of twelve-year-old girls run away."

"What about the girl who disappeared a month ago?"

His expressionless face contemplates me. "Murdered," he says flatly. "By an extremely violent pedophile. The crime scene was a horror show. Lots of DNA that didn't belong to the victim, but nothing to match it against. Why are you interested in this?"

"I'm a friend of Galina's mother. I'd like to save Galina from—what was the murdered girl's name?"

"Tanya."

"I'd like to save Galina from Tanya's fate."

He picks up a paperbound code book and absently riffles its curled pages with his thumb. "Your uniform last night said Fifty-eighth Army."

"So?"

The last pages snap closed. He spins the book to thump back onto his desk and rises wearily to his feet. "I don't have time for this shit."

"What are you talking about?"

"Listen, I owe you—we all owe you—for what you did last night. But I'm not going to let you cover anything up. If that army kid had anything to do with either of those two girls then he's going down, I don't care who gets a black eye."

"Semerko?"

He huffs around his desk, squeezes past me, and yanks open the door. "This conversation is over."

I stand. "Listen to me, Barokov. I'm not trying to cover up for the Fifty-eighth or protect Semerko. Not unless he's innocent."

We're so close he has to crane his neck to look me in the eye. His breath smells like fast-food chicken and fried potatoes. "He's not."

"Then why didn't you arrest him when you had the chance?"

"Because I couldn't find him. And because I don't arrest people without proof, Colonel, as strange as that concept may be to you."

"Maybe I can help if you let me look at the file."

"You can't."

I reach into my pocket and slowly pull on the orange and black rope. It slithers out like a coral snake, sinuously unwinding until the end drops nearly to the floor. His eyes track its movements as though he's been hypnotized.

"Where did you get that?"

"I'll tell you where after I've seen the file. And I *will* see the file, even if I have to tear your office apart to find it."

He studies me, nostrils flaring, but he had sufficient demonstration of my proclivity for sudden violence last night, and the rope seems to have convinced him. He turns to a stubby metal cabinet flanking his desk and quickly locates a thick accordion file and a manila folder. "The smaller file is the one for Galina Cheslava, the missing girl. The bottom one is Tanya. Start there."

He shoves the stack into my hands.

"Try to keep your dinner down."

chapter 22

I settle into a chair at the table in the squad room. The accordion file—Tanya's murder book—bulges ten centimeters thick. Front and back it is covered with scribbled names, numbers, and cryptic notes, along with doodles of a cat with pointy ears that morphs into a horned devil holding a trident. Inside are summaries of witness interviews, a hand-written timeline, notes about the location and condition of the body made on a diagram of the area where she was found, sketches of the surrounding alleys and streets marked to show possible routes and places where a witness might have seen something, forensics reports, and Tanya's medical history.

I didn't eat dinner, but rising bile burns in my throat as I page through the contents, starting with the when, where, and how.

Tanya turned thirteen on December 12, almost a month ago. She went missing the next day. Her body was found two weeks later, dumped outside a housing unit about ten blocks from here. She was strangled with a garrote made from a meter of orange and black climbing rope 10.5 millimeters thick, constructed with an interior core protected by a woven exterior sheath for maximum strength, durability, and flexibility—all of the manufacturer's specifications are in the file.

An envelope contains the crime scene photos. Tanya's blanched, diminutive form looks like a marble sculpture chiseled after a giant had taken her in his hand, crushed her, and flung her to the ground. She's naked, crumpled on her side in a patch of wet dirt, cords of rope looped on each side of her head like rabbit ears. The middle part of the colorful rope is buried in the soft flesh of her neck. Her head is twisted to one side at an impossible angle. The M.E.'s notes posit that the killer snapped her neck postmortem.

One leg is bent at the knee and wrenched to the side. The other one sticks out at nearly a ninety-degree angle, as if she is halfway to doing a split. Her pallid skin is covered with dark glyphs that make it look as if someone scrawled all over her nude body with a brown crayon. Deep cuts, according to the report. Grainy splotches like ink blots mark where she was beaten long enough before her death for bruises to form. An autopsy photo shows a bite mark below her left nipple, done hard enough to break skin, and another, shallower one, on her neck over the carotid artery. Both bites left matchable impressions, according to the M.E.'s notes.

Some of the men in the squad room pretend to work while they surreptitiously watch me comb through the contents of the murder book. I put my hand over my eyes to block the fluorescent glare from above. An hour in, Barokov pokes his head from his door and asks if I need anything, but I wave him off and plow through the file again. I try to let my eyes bounce over the worst of it, but by the time I've finished the gory essence of Tanya's murder has made a slimy reconnaissance into my memory, readying a place for permanent residence.

I set it aside and reach for the manila folder.

Galina was reported missing a week ago. Her mother provided Barokov with a list of friends and relatives, medical information, and places Galina was known to go—school, one of her girlfriend's homes, a store that sells video games, a local mall—along with pictures, one of them the same as the picture in Masha's flat of Galina smiling coquettishly over her shoulder. Barokov and another cop canvassed the area and interviewed potential witnesses, along with her relatives, friends, and neighbors. Acting on statements that Semerko had been "hanging around" and "acting strangely" and "saying crazy things," and a hysterical accusation by Galina's mother that Semerko "stole" her daughter, Barokov searched for Semerko without finding him. He interviewed Semerko's mother and sister on January 7, four days ago, and he searched the sister's apartment. Just as they had done with me, they denied knowing where he was, although his mother said that he might have gone to the Caucasus. They also told Barokov that they didn't have any of Semerko's possessions, which explains why Barokov missed the footlocker in the basement.

If Semerko killed Tanya, as I am now almost certain he did, and abducted Galina, which seems likely, then Galina is one week into a nightmare beyond imagining. Unless Semerko is on the move, looking for safer ground. Maybe then she is being spared the worst of it until he finds a new lair.

I continue to study the photo of Tanya's abused form long after several of the cops in the squad room have begun a murmur heard on the edges of my consciousness. Then I replace the contents of both files and take them into Barokov's office. He hangs up the phone when I walk in.

"We're checking to make sure the rope matches," he says. "But it sure looks like it does. That son of a bitch."

"Any idea where he might have gone?"

"South, his mother said. That's a lot of territory."

I hand him the page from the magazine that shows the snow-covered Dagestani mountain village of Tindi. "Maybe he took Galina on a trip. Posing as brother and sister, something like that."

Barokov examines the picture, chewing on the inside of his lip with a worried look on his face. "Where'd you get this?"

"The same place where I got the rope." I tell him where to find the footlocker, not bothering to mention that I've already burned half of its contents. He calls in two of his men and instructs them to pick it up, then he settles back into his chair, studying the picture of the village some more.

"He could go there easily enough. Shit, he might not even have had to pretend to be her brother. Sometimes those questions never get asked. I can make a few calls, but what am I supposed to do with someone in the southern highlands? That place is postnuclear, you know?" Apparently remembering who he's talking to, he looks up at me quickly. "Yeah, I suppose you know all about that."

Looking at the envelope I got from Semerko's sister, I scribble the address in Makhachkala and my cell number on the outside of Tanya's murder file, next to the devil-and-trident doodle, and push it across his desk. "Pick up Semerko's trail there."

"How did you get this?"

"I don't think he's there anymore. I'm betting he's gone to the mountains. But whoever *is* there might be able to give you something else to go on."

He absently runs an index finger over the address. His left eye tics under the weight of his worry. "Sorry I questioned your motives, Colonel. I hope you don't doubt our commitment to finding this animal."

I don't know whether better police work would have spared Galina. That's a question he'll have to answer—and live with—by himself. I already have enough of my own.

Thinking of Valya, who would make it her mission to find Galina if given the chance, I tell him, "Find out what you can from the address, then call me. If you can get me close I'll find him. And if the girl is still alive, I'll find her, too."

I head back through the squad room and the broken door. The diamond-studded tourist is sitting in the holding cell, arms folded, shivering. A knobby-kneed prostitute has been thrown in the cell with him. She's arguing with a cop about getting picked up. Why her and not others? How much to be cut loose? The cops didn't pinch her just for hooking. My guess is one of them has been eyeing her. Bail will be a night spent servicing him and his friends at the station, which explains the impatient looks I was getting a few minutes ago. I doubt Barokov will participate, but you never know.

"How much money are you carrying?" I say to the tourist in English.

"Huh?"

"You want out, yes?"

"Hell, yes! Look, I wasn't doing anything—"

"When the policeman comes back, give him four hundred American dollars. Then this will be over." Less would do it, but the cops need money, too, and their curious ethic is not to steal it outright, at least not from a man like him; it has to come at them in the form of a courteous gift accompanied by a wink, or at least a thank you.

"No shit?"

But he's talking to my back, because I'm gone, through the dilapidated lobby and into the night, where snow is falling in fat flakes. Golko and I won't be able to make Vladimir in two and a half hours. Not in this weather, even in light traffic. I finger the pendant in my pocket, satiny smooth except for the diamond facets in the shape of an orthodox cross. Before meeting Golko I need to make a quick stop to store my prize. It's not the Imperial egg itself, but the pendant is a start, a jeweled marker on the path to answers.

chapter 23

I ride the metro to the stop nearest Masha's building. The air in her flat is thick and sweet with the smell of tea. A kettle burbles on the hotplate. The only illumination comes from a floor lamp in the corner that's been covered with an ochre cloth, coating the room like linseed oil on an old painting. I settle into the familiar embrace of the wicker chair and pull the pendant out of my pocket, staring at it as I wonder what kind of journey it has made through the world. Who else has admired it, touched it, felt its weight around her neck?

Masha hands me a pottered mug of tea. "Is it real?"

I place it in her palm. She rocks her hand to feel its weight, studying it the way an astronomer peers through a telescope at a distant galaxy. Her palm is the color of nutmeg, so pebbled with wrinkles that the blue sphere seems to be resting on a bed of wet sand.

"What am I supposed to do with this?"

"Hold it for me. I'll come back for it when I can."

Still looking at the pendant, she fingers one of the carved figurines on her necklace. It is a woman in a flowing robe, head bowed. Mokosh, goddess of moist Mother Earth. Mother Russia.

"Have you found out anything about Galina?"

"I've learned a little." I consider how much to tell her, but she is not one to be patronized. "The other girl you heard about who disappeared—Tanya was her name. It looks like Semerko killed her about a month ago."

"Oh, no."

"You know how these people work? The patterns?"

"I watch television."

"Okay. Semerko held Tanya for about two weeks before he killed her. Nobody suspected him until later, so he had time and he probably used a place he had already picked out and prepared. That means there's a good chance he didn't kill Galina right away either. But with her it was different. Her family raised a stink and the police focused on him immediately, so he had to run. He might have taken her south."

Masha doesn't say anything. I suspect she's considering how much, if anything, to tell Galina's mother, and I don't envy her the task. While she's doing that, I think of Semerko, gone to the high ground with his latest victim. This makes me think of Valya, of her unbridled courage to wander the Caucasus among her enemies in search of something good. And finally my thoughts shift to Abreg, stretching his claws north to kill soldiers. Everything points to the same place.

"I'm going to have to go back to the mountains, Masha. Soon, I think."

She stares at me just as intently as she studied the pendant. Her eyes are the lightest of blue with pinpricks of white that look like stars. "You're afraid."

"Yes. I'm afraid."

chapter 24

Upon leaving Masha's flat I walk back to the metro under storm clouds that push like snarling faces into the light from the street lamps. The station is steaming hot after the bone-chilling cold of the Moscow night. A man on crutches, one leg so badly mangled he's forced to drag it behind him as if it's a dead dog on a leash, lurches along the platform among the people waiting for the train. Holding a woolen cap upside down, he asks the waiting passengers for money.

"War veteran," he announces.

He looks familiar in the way a part of the urban scenery seems to have always been there when you notice it for the first time. Most of the passengers avoid eye contact with him. A boy about five years old stares open-mouthed at his dangling leg. The boy's mother turns his face away with a hushed whisper, but he continues to peek beneath the folds of her coat. "I'm hungry," the beggar says. A scrawny teen, both eyebrows riveted with a row of silver studs and his lower lip sporting another one, gives the beggar a shove that nearly topples him.

The Nokia buzzes.

"Colonel?" Barokov says.

"Go ahead."

"I need to talk to you some more, but not on the phone."

"Then it will have to wait."

The digital clock counting down the time to the next train says fifteen seconds.

"I've been thinking," he says.

In my mind's eye I can see him in his rumpled suit in his cramped office, the weight of his concern contracting his forehead into fat cornrows of flesh.

"You've got ten seconds before I lose the signal."

"Something was wrong last night. The more I think about it, the surer I am. But I can't say, not over a cell phone."

The train hisses to a stop. "Five seconds, Inspector."

"Ryazan," he whispers. "FSB men with explosives and a detonator, you know the story. Could that have happened at AMERCO? "Is that possible?""

※

I end the call and step into the train. Settle onto a plastic bench seat that runs the length of the car and rest the back of my head against the window. The beggar drags in behind me. As he approaches, I scoot across the bench, pushing against an annoyed woman next to me to make room for him. Sitting is a production because he has to swing his useless leg in an ungainly way and hop on one foot until his butt is poised over the seat and he can drop onto it.

"Thanks, my friend." He swipes a dirty, gloved hand under his nose. "Been a long day. Shit—long year." He laughs wetly. "Lately, there's more money, less mercy."

The young thug who pushed him earlier eyeballs me from across the aisle. I think he's just curious about why I'm talking to the bum, but then he spreads his hands in front of his chest and lifts his shoulders in a what-about-me? gesture, pantomimes a blowjob, and mouths *five hundred*. Five hundred rubles is a bit less than twenty American dollars.

"How'd it happen?" I ask the beggar.

"Took a bullet in my ass during a recon in Vedeno," he says, referring to a hellish zone in Chechnya made worse because it was the birthplace of a now-dead terrorist leader. "Cut the sciatic nerve. Too high up to get rid of the pain in my leg even if I chop the damn thing off. So I keep it, drag it around. I'm not sure why. Sentimental, I guess."

I point at the money in his hat. "How much is yours?"

"None. My handler takes it all, gives me back a bag with a slice of meat, stale bread, and a bottle of vodka this big." He holds his thumb and index finger about eight centimeters apart. "All that for twelve fucking hours of this shit." His wry smile reveals a graveyard of yellow, crooked teeth. "What a deal."

His situation isn't unusual. The mafia runs strings of disabled soldiers and broken-down babushkas as beggars, each of them taking in as much as fifteen hundred rubles a day from their forced labor.

"Who's your handler?" I ask, and he names a small-time hood who reports a long way up the chain of power to Maxim, the mafia kingpin.

The train rocks to a stop. I press five thousand rubles into his hand. The crust worked into the fabric of his glove crackles. "This is for you, not him."

He gives me a grateful nod just as my phone buzzes an incoming call from an unknown number. I charge up the stairs to make sure I don't lose the signal.

"Valya?" I hold my breath.

"That's better," she says into a clear line. She sounds as if she's standing three feet away, and I wish she were. "I have a new phone—one of my own, not one I borrowed. You want the number?"

Outside the station, the storm clouds suddenly seem less brooding. I tromp off toward St. Basil's to meet Golko. "Sure," I say, matching her breezy tone. "Maybe I'll call you sometime."

"Hah! And maybe I'll be too busy to answer."

I memorize the number as she recites it. "You're in Chechnya?" I say, but what I'm thinking is that I'm a coward, still too afraid to talk to her about the way I feel. About how much I need her.

"Vladikavkaz now," she says.

Vladikavkaz, the capital of North Ossetia, lies in the shadows of Mount Kazbek, one of the giants of the southern range. The city began as one in a line of garrisons built by Peter the Great, and has often been used as a base of operations by tsars and general secretaries. Its name means "to rule the Caucasus," a misnomer if ever there was one.

"We're looking for a Red Crescent cargo container loaded with an influenza vaccine," she says. "The local mafia stole it."

Pity the thief if Valya finds him. "The people you're with are working for unification?"

"Some of them, some of the time. I know, it's hopeless. Everybody hates everybody. But it can't hurt to try."

I don't even consider arguing. Valya understands how futile that cause is. The region has been shredded by history. Over five million souls strewn over seven autonomous republics: Adygea, Karachai-Cherkessia, Kabardino-Balkaria, North Ossetia, Ingushetia, Chechnya, Dagestan. For centuries it was a labyrinth of tribes, clans, and sects without end, dozens of languages and dialects, shifting borders, blood feuds—fighting one another, fighting the Cossacks, fighting the tsars. And then came seven decades of the Soviet Union's iron fist: maps drawn deliberately by Lenin to promote conflict; deportation to the Central Asian steppe under Stalin's brutal policy of *likvidatsia*—liquidation.

After all of that, the region imploded again when the Soviet grip released. The power structure vanished. Economies disintegrated. Old vendettas reignited, borders lost meaning—many remembered and sought to enforce the ancient tribal borders—tribes split, the power balance tipped, and then the crescent and the cross tangled like bloody vines when we invaded Chechnya and razed Grozny, as if that would be the *end* of anything.

The overwhelming scale of the problem would appeal to Valya, not deter her.

"Many of them hate you, Valya. They remember." And so do I. Parts of it, at least. *Everybody fucking dies!*

"Some do," she says dismissively. "None of it matters anyway because Abreg refuses to listen to reason from his own people. He wants to fight the Russians *and* the old wars between the *teips.*"

"You've *talked* to him?"

"One of the men here did." Her tone is solemn. "He said that Abreg has a list of soldiers he intends to kill. And now he's working with a man in Moscow, someone powerful."

Lachek, I think, but I don't say his name out loud. Lachek and many other powerful men in Russia fight the mere suggestion of unity, some because they don't want an independent region on our southern flank, others because they'll lose the income they derive from the simmering conflict there. Men like Abreg fight the idea on general principles, unwilling to unite with the leaders of other tribes that theirs have been fighting for centuries. Lachek and Abreg maybe, just might, hold their noses and crawl into a smelly bed with each other in a temporary alliance.

"The country is beyond redemption," I say.

"I don't think so. Most people just want the fighting to end."

"I meant Russia."

She hesitates, surprised, I think. Several seconds pass while she works it out. "Don't cross the line that separates hope from despair, Alexei."

I'm halfway across Red Square, treading over the same bricks where ICBMs rolled in parade past Soviet dignitaries lined up on the steps next to Lenin's tomb. The domes of St. Basil's glow like a burning crown above the Place of Skulls, where more than three hundred years ago Peter the Great executed the Streltsy revolutionaries who conspired to put his exiled sister, Sophia Alexeyevna, on the throne. Russia can't escape her past.

I tell her about the AMERCO building and Lachek, Dubinin and the egg and the video, Galina and Semerko. By the time I'm finished I'm standing in the shadow of the cathedral, twenty paces from an idling Mercedes like the one that held Dubinin's body. Through the clouds of steam billowing around the black car I can see Golko behind the wheel, impatiently drumming his fingers.

"There have always been rumors about Starye Atagi," she says. "And if Abreg has a video he would use it to identify the people he wants to kill."

"I was thinking the same thing."

"But I would have heard if he was the one behind the explosion. He hasn't claimed credit. No one from here has."

Golko taps the horn and I hold out my hand to tell him to wait. The connection is so good I can hear Valya breathing.

"What can I do to help, Alexei?"

Her simple question makes me turn my back on the Mercedes, just in case Golko can see the emotion washing over my face. I would do anything for her, of course, and in her ageless wisdom I'm sure she knows as much, but to hear her say she is willing to do the same for me is enough to tighten my throat. The moon breaks from behind the clouds and bathes the square in an icy glow like white frosting, and for a moment I can see the beauty here again.

"I'm sorry for . . . I never should have pushed you away, Valya."

I can hear the wet clicks in her mouth when she swallows. "Even when I'm in a crowd I'm lonely without you, Alexei. You understand?"

Unable to force out any words, I nod as though she can see me.

"You have help there, right?" she says. "The General, and the chubby lieutenant, and the worried inspector?"

"Yes."

"I can be in Makhachkala by tomorrow afternoon," she says. The Dagestani capital city is on the edge of the Caspian, about two hundred dangerous kilometers through Chechnya from Vladikavkaz, but she sounds untroubled. "Tell me the address. I'll go there and learn what I can. And if Semerko is there with the girl, I'll take care of him."

The way she says it sends a chill up my spine. In a case like this one, Valya's hardened sense of justice might be even more severe than mine.

I pull out the envelope and read out the address. "Thank you, Valya. I— I— Well, thanks."

She laughs at me. "Check your phone. I'll send you a present."

chapter 25

As soon as I climb inside the Mercedes Golko chirps the tires pulling away, steering toward Vladimir 180 kilometers to the northeast. I try to set aside my conversation with Valya and concentrate on Melnik, the man whose name appeared in Dubinin's notes and was cross-referenced in the missing war crimes file.

"I've got big news," Golko says.

"Uh-huh," I say, still thinking about Valya.

My response makes him testy. "Who was that on the phone?"

"My stockbroker. He says I'm too heavy into oil and gas."

He huffs. "Sure. You talked for ten minutes and you were already half an hour late."

"My alarm didn't go off. We all have to sleep sometime, Golko."

He takes a small blue light from the dash, sets it to flash, and reaches out the window to stick it on the roof of the Mercedes, negotiating each intersection with reckless abandon. The light is called a *migalka*. It allows him to use a special lane on certain roads and break the traffic rules on all the others. *Migalka* lights are reserved for the political and monied elite—men like the General and Lachek—and are usually arrogantly abused in a way that slows down the thousands of others trying to use the same roads.

"Where do you live, anyway?" he says.

"I keep a suite at the Ararat Hyatt, but spend most of my time at my country estate."

He purses his lips. "If you don't want to tell me, just say so."

"I don't want to tell you. Okay, what's the latest?"

"I briefed the General. He said to tell you he needs more. He said, quote, tell Volk I need a hook into these people, unquote. What's that mean?"

It means Lachek or somebody else in the Kremlin has him dead in their sights because they're going to pin him with whatever happened at Starye Atagi—and maybe other things as well—unless he can figure out a way to leverage them.

"I don't know what it means," I say.

He runs a red light, cuts off a bus, and accelerates onto the M7. Once we're in the fast lane he hands me several yellow pages filled with handwriting. "Dubinin's notes," he says. "You were right, he took good ones. He kept them in a hidden compartment in his footlocker. I didn't find it the first time. Who writes things down on paper anymore?"

I shuffle through the pages, once quickly, then more slowly. All the entries seem to relate to the Hen Egg. Interview summaries, quotes from research sources, snippets of his supposition—the whole of it neatly organized. No names that I recognize other than the ones we already know about, including the name Joseph Melnik with squares drawn around it.

"Tell me the gist of it," I say, interested to hear if he has a different view than mine.

"The tsars kept the Hen Egg in St. Petersburg's Anichkov Palace until the revolution," he says, weaving expertly around the few cars too slow to move out of the way of the blue light. "Kerensky's provisional government confiscated it when they seized power in 1917. They took it to the Kremlin Armory, but just a few years later, it was gone. All that everyone knows. The rest is speculation."

"Pretty informed speculation, it looks like."

"Maybe. During the civil war years the Chechens united under Sheik Uzun Haji in a holy war against the White forces of the tsar. All that was fine, from the point of view of the Bolsheviks. But when they tried to reassert Russian power after the revolution, it got ugly. The Reds had already suffered massacres, famine, disease, drought. They didn't have the resources—men, matériel, cash—to fight a protracted war in the Caucasus. Then the Chechen autonomous region was established in 1922, the same year the Soviet Union was formed."

Golko seems to like giving me a history lesson. The snow is letting up, the road less crowded. He turns off the windshield wipers, powers down his window, admitting an icy blast of air, and takes down the *migalka*.

"Dubinin thinks they made a trade," I say, to keep him going.

"It looks that way. One of his sources said the Bolsheviks paid off the leaders of the Chechen resistance with the promise of autonomy, as illusory as *that* turned out to be. And, because the Bolsheviks despised everything to do with the tsars, they also bought off the warlords with some of the Romanov's treasures, including the eggs."

Golko steers around a long-haul trailer. "Dubinin tracked the Hen Egg through Sheik Haji, the man the Bolsheviks needed to appease to end the fighting in the Caucasus. Interviews with the surviving relatives of one of Haji's wartime comrades led him to a trading firm in Tbilisi that advertised a piece described as—" He waves his hand toward the notes.

"As 'a golden egg containing a gold hen encrusted with diamonds and a sapphire pendant with a diamond cross,' according to his note," I say.

"Right. The egg went from Tbilisi to an investor in Warsaw, a man named Zuckerman. Zuckerman died in the ghetto uprising. The trail died with him. Dubinin found references to the egg made by black-market dealers right here in Moscow as recently as a few years ago, and he discovered a Web page with a picture of the Alexander III Commemorative Egg—another of the eggs lost during the revolution—but those leads went nowhere. Then Dubinin got the call from Khanzad that he had the egg."

If I had to guess I would say that an anonymous soldier pocketed the egg when the Red Army stormed through Warsaw in the waning months of World War II. After that it probably gathered dust in a drawer for several decades until an enterprising son or daughter rediscovered it and tried to sell it. Somewhere along the chain of buyers, Khanzad came to possess it.

I take Charlie's phone out of my pocket and start thumbing through the picture icons.

"According to the coroner," Golko says, concentrating on the road, "Dubinin probably died of blood loss, but they stuck him with the *kinzhal* just to be sure. The thing was twenty-seven centimeters long! The driver was killed with the dagger, too, then they put a bullet through his skull."

In Stalin's camps, the winter harvest of dead bodies would be stacked like cordwood onto sleds. Before they were hauled off for dumping into pre-dug graves a guard would skewer each frozen head with a *szompol*—a thick wire sharpened to a point and attached to a wooden dowel for a handle—to ensure that no one left the camp alive. The driver's bullet was similar to a *szompol*. One final act of butchery to be absolutely sure nobody lived to tell the tale.

Golko grimaces. "Some men carry a *kinzhal* with a smaller knife tucked into a special sheath in the scabbard. The smaller knives are good for skinning."

Charlie had lots of pictures and several videos in her phone, but except for the photo of the egg none of them appear to have anything to do with the things I care about. Hundreds of contacts, filed alphabetically. Ravi is listed under his given name only. Lots of Virginia and D.C.

area numbers and addresses, many others in Milan, Madrid, Paris, Singapore, Hong Kong, Beijing, Los Angeles, Athens—an international potpourri that evinces Charlie's globe-trotting lifestyle. It is a far cry from where she is now, in a cell beneath the Kremlin.

"Want to hear what else the M.E. said they did to Dubinin?" Golko says.

"Hooked him up to a power source and fired a few thousand volts of electricity through his balls. Took their time scooping out his eyes. Peeled flesh. Am I missing anything important?"

"No," he says.

All the text messages—assuming Charlie used that feature—have been deleted.

Golko shifts his weight and tugs at the bunched fabric in the area of his crotch. "Whose phone?"

The call log ends several days ago, which coincides with Charlie's abduction. The number of one of the last incoming calls looks familiar, but it doesn't show up as a name, meaning it doesn't correspond to one of her contacts. Her default Web page is Google. The feature that automatically saves browsing history has been disabled.

I navigate back to Ravi's name on the list of contacts and hit a tab on the screen that says "Details." It opens onto a new screen that has the same contact information, formatted differently, but also a memo pad for electronic notes. A Moscow number is listed. It is the same as the familiar-looking number on the incoming call list.

I hit the button to dial it.

"Northern Lights Escorts," says a woman in a smooth, professional voice.

I hang up. Thumb a lever on the door so that my seat whirs down to offer a low-angle view through the passenger window. The night has become cold and clear. Silver birch trees whip by so fast they seem like a frosty smear below a velvet sky. I close my eyes.

"I thought you said you just woke up?"

"I need lots of sleep."

I didn't recognize the number to my own escort operation because I never dial it. The only person I talk to there is Alla, and I always go by the warehouse or call her on her cell phone, although lately I haven't done either as often as I should.

"What did you find out about the egg hidden under Dubinin's face mask?" I say.

"A factory in the Urals mass-produces that brand and distributes them through hundreds of knickknack vendors in Moscow and other cities. Just like you thought, nothing to trace."

The Nokia buzzes a blocked call. I answer anyway, because I have too many feelers out now to ignore calls.

"Goddamn it, Volk, two fucking days I been trying to reach you." Maxim Abdullaev's voice is so deep it seems to vibrate the phone in my hand. "The Chinese bitch said she gave you the message personally."

I haven't talked to him in months, but the Azeri kingpin addresses me in a familiar way, as if we'd just finished another phone call an hour before. I glance at Golko, who pretends to have all his attention focused on the road, but his ears seem to swivel toward sound like a cat's when he's listening extra hard.

"She said you needed help," I tell Maxim. "You never need help. I figured the message was bullshit."

"Not bullshit," Maxim says. "I got an opportunity for you. Come to the Swissôtel before dawn."

He hangs up before I have a chance to protest.

"What kind of man never needs help?" Golko asks.

"One with nothing to lose."

"Or one who is very powerful."

The Nokia vibrates to tell me I have an incoming message. It's a picture sent from the phone number Valya gave me. I angle the tiny screen away from Golko and open it.

chapter 26

Even at night Vladimir is shrouded in a blanket of industrial haze. Glowing particles swirl in the floodlights strung along the top of a chainlink fence that marks the perimeter of a power plant on the way into the city. Smokestacks spew noxious vapors over the M7 as we pull off the freeway onto a wide thoroughfare that's nearly deserted at 3 A.M.

We drive for a while, past a bus depot and a train station with an empty platform, and make a few turns. Golko consults the onboard navigation system, grunts, and reverses course. We wind around blocks of residential buildings, then through a stoplight already turned red at a lifeless intersection. Just past the intersection Golko says, "There it is," and turns the wheels suddenly.

The undercarriage of the Mercedes scrapes the gutter as we bounce into an alley leading to a back lot behind a large building. He parks next to a high wall made of smooth stucco adorned with graffiti and kills the engine. The only light comes from a single spotlight some fifty meters away, aimed at a fenced-in storage lot filled with car bodies stacked three and four high.

Golko checks his notes then points to a narrow rectangular dwelling sided with aluminum on the bottom and clapboard on the top. "Melnik lives in the top unit."

The upper half looks as if it was an afterthought, haphazardly stacked on top of something that was already there, the whole thing pressed up against the graffitied wall of a machine parts shop. Rickety wooden steps crawl along the aluminum to a landing the size of a crow's nest. We get out of the car. When I draw the Sig, Golko stops mid-stretch, eyes widening.

"Watch my back," I tell him. "Nobody likes to be woken up at three in the morning."

The steps are slick with thinly layered ice that crackles underfoot as I make my way up to the landing to pound on a hollow metal door. Nothing happens, so I bang harder. Still no response. I squat to see the lock in the dim light. It appears to be brand-new. From directly below the landing comes the familiar ratcheting slide of a shotgun. I instinctively clench my knees.

"Who's there?" It is a man's voice, reedy and raw from sleep. "Get down right now—"

"Drop the weapon!" Golko screams, and I brace myself for a load of buckshot, but nothing happens.

I lean over the railing without putting any weight on it. Golko has a pistol pressed against the balding skull of a man dressed in pajama bottoms and a sleeveless red undershirt. As I clatter down the stairs, Golko relieves him of a worn 20-gauge shotgun, good only for killing birds. The door to the lower unit is open. A woman's frightened face pulls quickly back into the darkened interior when I look toward the door.

"Cut him loose, Lieutenant."

Golko is sweating in the chill air. "What?"

I gently push his pistol down, take the shotgun away from the man, and eject three shells before handing it back to him, empty. "You live here?"

He nods jerkily.

I point toward the open door of his house. "Don't go inside, but tell your wife not to worry. We're police."

He stiffens. Now he's even more frightened.

"We're not here for you. Tell her."

He steps over to the door and says something, then closes it behind him. "What do you want?" He has a week's stubble on his thin cheeks and an eyetooth with a gold inlay that flashes when it catches some of the light illuminating the graveyard of cars.

"You own this place?"

"Uh-huh."

"You rent the top to Joseph Melnik?"

He squints at me. "The police already know all that."

I look over his shoulder, and he chances a quick glance back, then snaps his head around to me when he sees the pistol still in Golko's hand.

"Yeah, Melnik used to rent from me, until he turned up dead. He still owes me money, and now I can't rent the place because the cops"— he looks from me back to Golko—"the *real* cops won't let me fix it."

Golko raises his eyebrows at the news that Melnik is dead.

"How did Melnik die?" I say.

"Murdered." The landlord shivers in the cold night air.

"When?"

"He disappeared from here about a month ago. They found his body a few weeks back."

"How was he killed?"

He picks nervously at the crust in the corner of his eye. "One of the cops told me it looked like someone put his face in a dicer. Why won't they let me clean up the mess? I need to rent the place."

"What kind of mess, blood?"

"Nah, he died somewhere else. A couple of days after the police were here, though, someone broke in and . . . well, they were looking for something. My wife and me, we'd gone to Moscow. Good thing, I guess. When we came back the upstairs door was busted open. Looked like someone had tossed a grenade inside."

We follow him up the stairs to the swaying landing, which groans to protest the weight of all three of us. Golko's gun is still out and I draw mine, not knowing what to expect. The landlord opens the door, goes inside, and pulls a chain. Light bathes a room that looks worse than his description of it. Upended and shattered furniture, shredded mattress, tossed shelves. The bed frame looks like a metal skeleton. All the way around the walls the gypsum board was cut away to open up the wall cavities, leaving a dusting of white talc over everything. A nail juts out from one of the exposed studs facing the spot where Melnik's bed used to be.

Golko shows the landlord an old army photo of Melnik, confirming that he was the former tenant of this place, while I search through the rubble and find an icon, a thin sheet of wood crudely painted on one side.

"Who ran the investigation?" I say.

"A woman inspector," the landlord says. "Olga. I'm surprised the stairs survived."

Golko starts to work his phone to track her down.

While he talks I examine the icon, lightly running my finger along the painted side, a rendering of Christ descending into hell. A sticker on the back says it's a copy from Vologda, late fifteenth century. It would have been the last thing Melnik saw each night before he went to sleep, something to terrify a guilty conscience.

"Inspector Olga Paraskova investigated Melnik's murder," Golko says, and dials another number.

The drawer from the fractured nightstand has spilled onto the floor beneath a foil-backed strip of yellow insulation. Inside the drawer is a Bible, thicker at the edges; I suspect it has lain open more often than closed, probably when Melnik fell asleep reading it. The pages are thin as onionskin, their outer edges fuzzy from much handling.

The landlord is watching me. "Melnik was a churchgoing man," he says, and for the first time I think that maybe I can detect a breath of sympathy for his former tenant.

"She says to stop by the station at a decent hour," Golko says, holding the phone away from his face with his thumb over the hole in the mouthpiece.

I rehang the icon, carefully using the stud as a plumb line to make sure it rests straight.

"Tell her she has fifteen minutes."

chapter 27

Golko pilots the Mercedes back toward the train and bus stations we passed on the way into town. We pull to a stop in front of a cinder-block building as badly in need of repair as the police station in Moscow, and he kills the engine.

We crunch through frozen puddles to a cement slab covered by a wooden overhang. Stamp our boots free of ice, blowing steam. The lobby welcomes us with curled linoleum, cracked plaster walls flaking the same ubiquitous green paint that coats so many government buildings, and a glass-enclosed cubicle for a desk sergeant, if one was on duty. The station even has the same musty smell as the one in District 30 where Barokov plies his trade. We shed our coats, but keep them folded over our arms instead of hanging them on the hooks that line the wall. As deserted as the station seems, coats left untended might still disappear.

"Hello?" Golko calls.

I brush past him, stride through the area with the holding cell, open the door to the squad room, and bump into a woman the size of a Shetland pony. Even her brownish hair hangs like a mane, partially hiding her face.

"Who're you?" Her voice is almost as deep as Maxim's. She's working a cud of gum that turns her breath into a wall of sweetness.

"Volk." I jerk my thumb over my shoulder. "That's Golko. We're here to talk about the Melnik murder. Let's get to it."

"I don't like being pulled out of bed in the middle of the night."

"Just a moment, please," Golko says. He steps in front of me and flashes his ID, smiling, clumsily trying to offset my rough ways. "I'm Military Investigator Golko Kachan. We'd like to look over the file, ask a few questions. We appreciate your cooperation, and we're sorry to have bothered you."

"What about him?" She jabs a thumb the size of a tree stump at me and blows a pink bubble that pops between us.

"You know what I am, Ms. Paraskova."

She considers me for a moment, then grins with half her mouth. "Yeah, I suppose I do." She's not wearing makeup, so her eyes seem small, almost invisible in her doughy cheeks, but by their light I would guess that she's enjoying the moment. "Come on, then, let's get it over with." She leads the way into the squad room, which is empty except for a middle-aged cop with old-man eyes. "Take a break, Dabro," she tells him, and he puts on a stained blue overcoat and a woolen cap with earflaps and leaves us alone. Olga settles her bulk into a chair behind a table and gestures in front of her. "Grab a seat." The metal feet of the chairs screech against the tile floor when we draw them close.

"Melnik," she says to me, all but ignoring Golko. "Ex–Russian Army corporal, Chechnya veteran. Found his body dumped in a warehouse near the tracks. He'd been stabbed in the heart with a knife big enough to kill a bear, but only after he had his eyes popped out and face hacked up. It would have been a lot better for him if it had happened the other way around. Far as we could find out, no one hated him enough to kill him, let alone dance the tip of a knife all over his face. In fact, people that knew him said the guy spent every free moment in church. Who would want to kill him?"

She pauses and studies my face. "Am I telling you anything new here, Volk?"

"Were his eyes left at the scene?"

"No."

"How did the killer get them out of his head?"

Olga chews her gum and contemplates me curiously. "We aren't sure. They weren't poked or hacked out—there were no holes in the back of the socket. It looked like someone took his time to keep them whole, a trophy hunter maybe. The optic nerves were cut cleanly."

Golko looks at me and writes something on his notepad, like a reporter.

Olga swipes aside a lock of her mane with the edge of her hand so that her gaze meets mine cleanly. "Maybe this'll get you. You're my second strange visitor in a month to ask about him."

"Who was the other?"

"Lachek." She pops another bubble.

Golko stiffens and stops writing.

"Old or young?" I say.

"Old. Looked like the Grim Reaper. You guys have any idea who you're dealing with here?"

I don't need to ask Olga whether she told Lachek everything. She did, because she had no other choice, just as she has no choice now except to talk to me.

"What did he want?"

"The file. Just took it and left, no questions, nothing."

"What?" Golko says.

"He informed me the investigation is now a matter of state security and removed me from the case, effective immediately."

Suddenly, I am desperate to see the contents of that file.

"Yeah, I thought that would get your attention," Olga says. "And you're gonna love this next part. Melnik rented space on the north side of the city. The day after Lachek took the file from me, Melnik's landlord called to tell me the place has been trashed. A real thorough job. I wonder what the cadaver was looking for?"

Golko is tapping his heel hard enough to vibrate his entire body. I put a hand on his sleeve to stop him. "We've already been there."

"Well, then, here's something else for you to think about, Volk," Olga says. "Lachek looked at me the way a rotten kid looks at a kitten he's about to toast in a microwave oven. I can see that you're a mean one, but this guy Lachek, well . . . Watch yourself, man."

"Christ," Golko says under his breath. Half-moon sweat stains show under his arms. The squad room is hot, but not that hot.

Olga regards me quizzically, apparently interested to observe my reaction to whatever she's going to say next. "So, naturally, after that I was even more interested in this guy Melnik, and I made it my business to keep asking questions. One day about a week ago I was out at the place where they dumped the body. Just sniffing around, talking to people, doing nothing, really. The operations manager has an office in front with big windows that overlook the warehouse floor. It's so he can keep tabs on everyone, but that means he's in a fishbowl, too. Two people were in there talking to him. Asians, a man and a woman. Both young. I didn't get a good look at him, but she was a knockout. Long black hair, body shaped just right."

Olga eyes me, leaning back. Her chair issues a submissive bleat of protest.

"You probably think I lean that way, but I don't. I like men, for whatever that's worth. You're too skinny for my taste. And him?" She nods toward Golko. "He's too fat. I like mine somewhere in the middle."

"Who were they?" Golko sounds irritated.

Olga holds my gaze for another moment, then turns slowly to face him. "They were driving away by the time I got around front, but they told the manager they were interested in buying the place."

I thumb back through the picture icon on Charlie's phone to the image of Ravi's intense face, wishing I had a picture of Mei to show her as well. "Him?"

She studies it for a moment, then hands the phone back to me. "I can't say for sure, Volk. I never got a clear look."

"What kind of warehouse was Melnik's body found in?"

"What do you mean 'what kind'? A big, open building filled with lots of boxes. High ceilings, forklifts."

"What do they store there?"

"Knickknacks. Chess sets, painted boxes, *matryoshka* dolls, fake eggs. The cheap crap they sell at all the tourist stalls."

We sit in silence while I absorb this information. I don't know what's going through Golko's mind. He's never met Mei, so he can't know about that possible link, but I'm sure he's made the connection with the egg under Dubinin's face. At my direction, he notes the address of the warehouse, which Olga recites from memory.

"Was he killed there?"

"No. Not enough blood on the floor for what was done to him. We never did find the place where he was killed."

"Who owns the warehouse?"

"I don't remember. I recall there was one company at the top of an alphabet soup of partnerships, corporations, and trusts, but the chart we made was in the file Lachek took."

"Do you remember the names of any of the principals?"

She sweeps the mane of hair out of her eyes. "Sorry. This had the earmarks of a body dump. We didn't think the warehouse led anywhere, so we didn't spend a whole lot of time working it, and none of the names jumped off the page into my memory. My partner might remember."

"Call him."

"Her." She glances at a wall clock. "How about if I wait a few hours?"

"Take us to the warehouse."

Golko stiffens. "It's almost four in the morning!"

Olga creaks back her chair, stands up, and lumbers into one of the offices at the other end of the squad room. She returns in seconds, wielding a sledgehammer like a mace. "I'm game."

"What's that for?" Golko says.

She swings the handle onto her shoulder with a grunt. "Some people just don't listen."

chapter 28

Channeled-steel skin wraps the warehouse, which along the roofline is lower in the middle, like a headless body shrugging. It hunches at the end of an unlighted street near the railroad tracks. Golko crackles the Mercedes over patches of gravel and dirt to one side of the darkened front office, where Olga directs him to park in front of a roll-up door secured by a padlock. A sign announces the name of a distribution company. Golko dutifully writes it down, but I'm pretty sure it doesn't matter. We're looking for a company higher up on a chart, a parent of a parent.

We climb out and Olga plods over to the roll-up, holding the sledgehammer loosely by her side. As soon as she's close enough she swings it overhead and clobbers the padlock. Sparks fly and the entire building booms a metallic echo as the lock breaks open. She slips it off the hasp and rattles up the door. Except for some boxes stacked near one side of the entrance, I can't see anything inside the dark space.

"He was supposed to leave a lockbox so I could get inside whenever I needed to," she says. "I knew he wouldn't listen."

"Who?" I say.

"The manager. I can arrange for you to talk to him if you want."

"Why the lockbox?"

She chomps her gum, looking at me without expression. "My file may be gone, but this damn case is a long way from over."

She leads the way inside. Walks to a round post and hits a bank of switches, all at once. A dull hum fills the air and arc lights hanging in cylindrical steel cones from the high ceiling pop into life.

Two columns march the long way from one end of the building to the other. The empty space between them, about twenty meters wide, has colored lines painted on the floor. The area along one side and the back wall contains cardboard boxes with the names and addresses of Moscow-area vendors stenciled in black on the side of each one. The boxes are stacked halfway to the underside of a mezzanine that runs along three walls, except for a strip of space in the back where there's another roll-up door set in a bay wide enough for a forklift. A few random boxes are stacked haphazardly on the metal grid deck of the mezzanine. The storage area along the other wall is empty. The sizzling arc lights make the air metallic, electric, as if each swirling dust particle is individually charged.

"They're not very busy."

"I've been here ten times, at least," Olga says. "I've never seen more than half the floor space used. Look at this." She walks over to a stack of boxes and taps one that has a black line drawn on its side. "I made that mark a week ago, and the damn thing's still here."

She motions us to follow her to the back wall. Her shoulders roll like a soldier's with each heavy step. When we reach a spot below the mezzanine near the bay door she lifts a box off the stack and hands it to Golko. "Here's where they found him," she says, thumping another one on top of the first before he can protest. We form an impromptu line and soon clear the area.

"Nothing," Golko says.

I squat for a closer look. Smooth concrete bisected by a painted line that was once blue but has now faded to gray. A smudged stain, cloudy, nearly invisible, seems to float beneath the surface of the concrete.

"You said he didn't bleed here."

"The warehouse was shut down for a week, so it was a while before he was found. He burst like a rotten melon when they tried to move him." She blows up a pink bubble until it pops. "Part of him left here in a mop bucket."

Whoever dumped the body probably knew the warehouse was going to be closed. They may have worked here, or lived in the area. I voice these thoughts.

"Maybe," she says. "We interviewed all of the employees and we canvassed the area for witnesses. A few of the workers had criminal records, nothing serious, and none of them knew Melnik as far as we could tell. I could give you more if I had the file, but . . ." She raises her broad shoulders.

"Was the body covered?"

"Nope. Naked, pasty, hacked up, bloated. Then he busted open and it got even worse."

"How did the killer get the body into the building?"

"Broke the lock up front, just like we did."

"What's behind here?" I say, banging the metal roll-up.

"Loading dock."

The door is locked on the outside, so we retrace our steps through the warehouse and out the front and crunch across the gravel amid clouds formed by our own breath. The back area is weakly lit by a lone floodlight mounted high on the exterior wall. A concrete apron separates the loading dock from a strip of asphalt that stops just short of the terminus of a rail spur, leaving a ribbon of muddy snow beneath the branches of a flat-topped cedar tree. Four box trucks are lined up along the concrete apron, gray with narrow horizontal stripes, red and yellow, running from the cab back along the cargo box. All of them have dual rear tires.

"Did you check the trucks for signs they were used to move a body?"

Olga pops a bubble, stares at me for a few chews, then says, "What makes you think the body was brought in from back here? I told you the lock up front was busted. This lock wasn't."

"Nobody wants to carry a dead body for any longer than they have to. If they came in through the front, they would have dumped it there."

"You've hauled lots of dead bodies around, have you?" She holds up her hand between us like the blade of a bulldozer. "Never mind. I don't want to know. The answer is, my partner probably looked inside the trucks, but I doubt she tore them apart or got on her knees in the back with a magnifying glass or did illumination tests. We could check the pictures in the file if you can get Lachek to let you have a peek. Do you know what you're suggesting?"

"Yes."

"What's he suggesting?" Golko says.

"That the killer didn't need to break the lock," Olga replies, still looking at me. "He had a key."

"Oh, come on, Volk," Golko says.

"Do me a favor," I tell Olga. "Take pictures of the rear tires and send them to Golko. He'll compare them with a picture we took last night in a parking garage."

"All right," Olga says.

"You got an evidence bag on you?"

"Why?"

"I want some mud."

She stares at me for a moment, working something out in her mind, then reaches into the pocket of her overcoat, pulls out a wrapped sandwich, peels off the clear plastic, and hands it to me. She holds up her sandwich—processed meat, lettuce, and leaking yellow mustard. "Want half?"

"Thanks, no."

She swallows her gum and takes a bite that makes a quarter of the sandwich disappear. I walk across the asphalt to the muddy ribbon of earth near the rail spur, squat, and pry loose a chunk of earth. "He's crazy," I hear her tell Golko through the food in her mouth while I'm bagging my prize. Once I have it I walk to the other side of the tracks, away from them, and call Alla.

"Yes, Alexei," she says alertly. She's probably in the middle of a multitude of issues. A lighting problem here, a whiny actor there, a computer glitch in the back room, it could be anything. The early morning hours are often her busiest.

"Who can dial out using the number for Northern Lights?"

"The front desk has six lines. It's not watched all the time, so anyone in the building could have called from there. When was the call made?"

"Six-thirty P.M. on the ninth, almost three days ago."

"We have a video camera monitoring the desk, but the tape restarts every forty-eight hours. I can print a list of all the calls."

A record of outgoing calls won't add anything; I already know one was made from there to Charlie's phone. What I don't know is who made it, and why, although I have a suspicion.

"Use the building logs to make a list of everyone in the building at that time."

"Twenty minutes," she says, and hangs up.

When I rejoin them, Olga's sandwich is long gone. Golko is making another note on his pad. "We have an investigator who's trained in palynology," he says, taking the plastic-wrapped mud from me as we go back to the car. "He might be able to match the pollen fingerprint with the mud we found next to Dubinin's car. No good in court, but it might be a step in the right direction."

The results won't tell me very much that I don't already know or suspect. I mostly wanted to get away for a few minutes to make the call to Alla. I'm beginning to trust Golko, but not that much.

When we reach the car Olga takes a chunk of bubble gum from her pocket, removes the wrapper using her teeth on one end and a practiced pull on the other, and begins chomping. Golko starts the engine and cranks up the heater, which proceeds to blow cold air. On the drive back to the station house tiny needles of ice force him to run the windshield wiper, and he keeps glancing in the rearview mirror.

"What is it?"

"A Mercedes panel van. I saw it when we drove to the warehouse, too."

I recall the three men wearing gray overalls and yellow rubber gloves, carefully not looking at me as I walked by. Maybe my imagination wasn't so overactive after all.

From the back seat Olga holds up Golko's blue *migalka* light. "Pull it over. I'll see what's up."

"No," I say. "We'll see if they follow us back to Moscow."

"It's gone now anyway," Golko says.

I rip a page from Golko's notepad, write my phone number on it, and hand it to Olga. "Call me if your partner remembers the name of the company that owns that warehouse."

At the station, she reaches over the seat and shakes my hand. Her grip is warm and strong, and the corners of her eyes crinkle with humor.

"Stay away from whoever took a blowtorch to your face, Volk."

I try not to smile, but one may slip past.

A frigid blast of predawn wind swoops into the Mercedes as she opens the back door and climbs out, carrying her sledgehammer. She slams the door and starts across the parking lot toward the dilapidated building. Then she suddenly about-faces and motions for me to open the window. I hit the button and it slides down, crackling its skin of frost.

"Watching you walk around that warehouse, Volk, I made a decision." She leans an elbow on the door and blows a bubble in my face.

"What's that?"

"You're not too skinny."

She gives me a playful cuff on the shoulder that feels like a wallop from the sledgehammer and bursts out laughing. She's still chuckling as we pull away. And, despite myself, I'm laughing with her.

"I'm glad you're enjoying yourself, *sir*," Golko says, but he's laughing, too.

We're back on the M7 when my cell buzzes. I answer and Alla says, "Fifty-two."

"Read them."

She does. I recognize two of the names. Hers and Mei's. A trip to Vladimir and a phone call to the daughter of an American senator—Mei's been busy.

"Does that help?"

"Maybe. Thanks, Alla."

I power back the seat. Close my eyes and concentrate, mentally reviewing the columns I made on the back of Lachek's dossier, looking for patterns. Several lines of inquiry are entwined like battling snakes in a living, fanged Gordian knot. Like Alexander, I'll have to cut through it with a sword rather than try to unravel the whole mess.

The General started Dubinin searching for the Imperial Easter eggs, an inquiry that eventually led Dubinin to Khanzad, Melnik, the Hen Egg, and—somehow—the video. Dubinin tried to trade, but he ended up on the butcher's block, the egg and the video gone, two cryptic clues left behind. The number written in his blood leads back to the purged file about Starye Atagi and points an accusing finger at Dubinin himself. The egg under his face led here, to this obscure warehouse, although I don't know why.

Ivashko, Melnik, Dubinin. I say the names under my breath like a litany, convinced they were killed in the same signature manner on the orders of the same man—Abreg—for the same reason: a heinous war crime at Starye Atagi. Worse, I think the deaths will keep piling up, because now Abreg is using the video to identify targets, and he won't stop until the job is finished.

Within hours of Dubinin's abduction and murder the AMERCO building exploded in flames. The younger Lachek, a special forces officer of the interior troops of the FSB, was at the command center almost before it happened. Another officer, the one who helped Lachek abduct Charlie, radioed the men inside the building to warn them I was coming. I can't say whether the explosion was orchestrated by a faction of the FSB or by men acting out of their own private interests, but either way I don't believe it was a coincidence that Marko Hutsul, the chairman of Kombi-Oil, was among the hostages who were spared.

All of which has drawn the attention of the Americans and, apparently, the Chinese. Saving the senator's daughter may be part of what motivates Matthews and his handlers, but I think the stakes are higher. Looking back on my conversation with Matthews, I see the subtexts more clearly, thinly coded messages that I believe he intended me to receive: Putin and Lachek, oil, terrorism, and criminal syndicates.

And, of course, I still have the third column on my chart to deal with. Somewhere in the south is Galina, captive but maybe not yet damaged beyond repair. Maybe being on the run has kept Semerko from doing his worst to her.

I squeeze my eyes closed until all I can see is blackness, and then fuzzy orange spots that float away like dissolving balloons. I'm hoping for insight, but my imagination fails, because the only mental vision I can conjure is that of radiant, ethereal Valya, the one from the picture she sent me earlier. An impressionistic, pale blur of curved cheekbones and enormous gray eyes glowing as if fired from the inside by a white-hot forge.

✳

I wake up. The road ahead is black. Golko is looking at me, his worried face lit by the dashboard lights. "What did you say?" I ask.

"I said, the van is back."

chapter 29

We're forty minutes outside of Vladimir, Golko tells me. The M7 is quiet, lined on both sides by birches and scrub brush. His eyes keep jumping back and forth from the road to the rearview mirror.

"You're sure?" I say.

"I recognize the configuration of the front lights. It's fallen back again."

A few minutes later he grunts to say the lights have returned. Looking out the rear window I see two glowing orbs.

"Notice how one of the headlamps is dimmer than the other?" he says.

"In a few minutes, turn on your emergency blinkers and slow down. Hug the side of the road until we come to a service lane, then pull off and drive slowly. I'm going to jump out. Keep rolling for another hundred meters or so, then stop." I tap his holstered sidearm, a Makarov. "Do you know how to shoot that thing?"

"It's been a long time." He adjusts his grip on the wheel, then wipes his palms one at a time on his pant leg.

I pull out his pistol, pop the eight-round magazine to check the load, then slide it back into place. "This will do. Put it in your lap. Pretend to be talking to someone on your cell phone. If anybody gets close to the car, shoot them in the belly. No warning, no hesitation."

"Maybe we should just see what they want."

"Sure. We can talk about it over tea and cake."

I arrange my jacket into a roundish lump over the headrest. On my signal Golko hits the flashers, slows, and eases off the M7 onto a service road. The two-lane strip of asphalt is slightly elevated. On my side it drops off at a shallow angle into a snow-filled gully. I can't get out here because the snow will show my tracks. The lights from the cars on the M7 disappear among the thick stand of trees behind us.

"Are they following?" I say, looking ahead for a likely spot.

"They're about a kilometer back. I'm sorry, Colonel, but I have to protest. I think it's a bad idea to get off the main road. There's safety in numbers. Nobody will do anything in plain sight of other motorists."

Golko may be minutes away from catching a bullet with his teeth, so I figure he's entitled to an explanation. "If these are Lachek's people, they would shoot us on the Novy Arbat if it suited them. We need to fight them on our terms, on ground we choose."

"I still think we need to make sure they're a threat before we do anything rash."

"Uh-huh." Too late I've remembered why I don't take time to explain things. I detach the interior light and toss it on the floorboard. Ahead of us, the cone from our headlamps catches a dark patch where run-off from earlier in the day has cleared an area of snow. "I'll go there," I say, pointing. "Ease off the gas, but don't touch the brake until I'm out."

I open the door, wait for an instant to judge the speed, then roll out onto the dirt, letting my momentum carry me down into the gully. My shoulder breaks through ice into a thin trickle of water at the bottom. I jump up fast. Slip among the trees, flitting between them parallel to the road, following behind Golko as he eases the car to a stop.

The white panel van stops about half a kilometer away, then slowly closes the gap. Two people are in the cab. The van has no side windows behind the front door, so I can't see how many others are inside. The driver pulls up across from me, about twenty meters behind Golko, who has his phone to his ear, his head bobbing as if he is deep in a conversation. The lump from my jacket looks like the head and shoulders of a passenger.

I creep along the gully, then approach from the blind side just as both doors open and the driver and a passenger step out. I can't see the driver, but I can hear his boots crunching against the pavement. Probably at least one more is still inside.

The passenger carries an MP5 submachine gun, holding it against his chest. His attention is focused on the parked Mercedes. My foot slips on gravel, and when he turns toward the sound I crush the back of his skull with the butt of the Sig. I make a grab for the MP5, but it jerks out of my grasp and skitters into the gully as he falls.

Turning, I fire a blind pattern of five shots into the body of the van, holding the Sig chest high, spacing each bullet as I circle around to the back. The sound is like rolling thunder. The driver shouts a question, unsure what's happening, whether his partner is still alive. I drop to the road and crawl beneath the undercarriage. Only the driver's ankles and feet are visible. He's shuffling with his back to the radiator grille of the van, trying to reach his fallen comrade. I shoot him in the foot. He screams and falls forward in a heap. I pump three more rounds into him. Change magazines. Roll out from under the van, staying down on my elbows and knees.

Golko is out of the Mercedes. He's holding the Makarov with two hands in front of his body, bent at the waist, approaching the van. The windshield explodes above me as a shot rings out, and he spins and falls. I reach up with the Sig until it's pointed through the open door into the cab and cut loose five rounds.

A sudden silence follows the cracking roar of gunshots. Golko is curled up in a heap on the road. I crawl to the back of the van and open the rear doors, careful to stand to one side. The cargo area is empty, both sides perforated by holes from my blind shots. The third man of the team is twisted behind the driver's seat, mouth and eyes open, wearing a bib made from the blood pumping from his torn throat.

By the time I reach Golko he's already sitting up, examining his left arm, the sleeve dark with blood. I cut it away to reveal a puckered groove.

"It just grazed you."

"Yeah," he says, looking over my shoulder at the bodies.

I use one part of his sleeve for a bandage, wrap the rest of it around his arm, and tie it off. Now that the adrenaline rush is gone the night is cold. The whoosh of cars on the M7 sounds loud.

"That'll hold you until you're back at the Kremlin."

I walk back to the van and drag the driver and passenger into the cargo area behind their partner. All three of them are dressed in casual clothes, their heavy jackets strewn over the bench seat in the back. I find cash and photo IDs. I pocket the IDs to give to Golko, but I'm sure they'll lead nowhere. Scattered on the steel deck are enough guns to fight a small war. Stuffed into the back corner are the gray overalls and yellow gloves the men were wearing when I saw them in Moscow.

✸

Golko mutters and jumps in his sleep while I drive the rest of the way into the city. I wake him up outside the Ararat Hyatt. He looks at the hotel, then at the dashboard clock.

"It's eight in the morning. You don't really have a suite here, do you?"

"Get yourself bandaged up, then find out why Lachek was interested in Melnik's murder."

He starts to rub his eyes, winces. "I've been thinking about Lachek and the interior ministry connection. Maybe he's not the top of the food chain. Maybe we're dealing with someone a whole lot higher."

"I don't think it goes much higher."

"When we were in the archives I looked through more than a dozen files before I finally figured out the numbering system. Know what name I kept seeing? Constantine."

Constantine was a legendary Cold Warrior who outlasted Stalin and several of his successors. Often invoked, the name has become symbolic, representing hidden power in the Kremlin, used when real names can't be. It still conjures feelings of dread, even in me.

"Constantine is long dead. Don't waste your time chasing ghosts. Find out what you can about the warehouse back there. Who owns it, the name of the company that makes the eggs they distribute—do what you're trained to do, investigate. Unless you think the warehouse and the egg wrapped with Dubinin's face are a coincidence."

"I'm not sure what to think about that."

"Good, keep an open mind. Meet me for a late lunch at Vadim's Café in Kitay-Gorod. You can give me a progress report."

He looks down at his bloody arm. "That was awful, what happened to those guys."

"There are probably ten more just like them looking for us right now. Any one of them would shove a knife down your throat at six and then go to his kid's piano recital at seven. You better start sleeping with that pistol under your pillow."

chapter 30

Getting to the thirty-four-story Swissôtel Krasnye from the Ararat is a long tramp on ice-clad sidewalks, but I figure the walk and the chill will help clear my head for a meeting with mafia boss turned oligarch Maxim Abdullaev. Unpredictable, cunning, rapacious, Maxim is the quintessential carnivore. I'll need to be on guard.

Olga calls when I'm halfway there.

"Talked to my partner." She pops a bubble into the phone. "She's got a better memory than I do. The company at the top of the food chain that owns that warehouse is called Kombi-Oil. That help?"

"Maybe." Kombi-Oil again. Marko Hutsul's company lurks around every corner, it seems.

The Swissôtel heaves into view, rising like a lit sword off the eastern tip of Kremlin Island between the Moscow River and the Obvodny Channel. A passing diesel blows fumes in my face and splashes cold water on my pants.

Olga pops another bubble. "Great talking to you, Volk. You're a hell of a conversationalist." She disconnects.

I cross the Moscow River and approach the entrance to the hotel. Men from two of Maxim's omnipresent rings of security check me out, one team outside the building and the other in the hallway when I get off the elevator on the thirty-fourth floor. A black-suited bodyguard finally leads me to an oversized suite.

Maxim presides at the head of a rectangular table. The arms of his Herman Miller office chair have been pushed out so far they're pointing away from each other. He appears to be exploding from the chair's embrace.

My best guess is that he pushes a hundred and forty kilos after a big meal. Coarse salt-and-pepper hair bristles like wire from his swarthy skin. His eyes are gray and violent under bushy brows, roiling like the stormy Caspian Sea at the hard edge of land in his hometown of Baku. Valya used to say that he reminded her of an *almasty,* an abominable snowman, a characterization that would fit perfectly if such monsters were blessed with a raging intelligence.

Eight well-dressed men sit around the table with him, squirming, twirling pencils, staring down at yellow legal pads on the tabletop. Most of them have the sharp, well-groomed look of Moscow's new capitalists— former Communist bureaucrats turned suddenly wealthy. Others have the bearing of ex-military men, their pasts hidden from the untrained eye beneath designer suits and a corporate demeanor. But wealth has its price, one aspect of which is that the closer they move to the locus of power the more dangerous life becomes. One word from Maxim and these men would face horrors they have only imagined—or only ordered done to others.

Maxim stares them all down, looking disgusted. The silence hangs palpably, like the noxious fumes that cover the city of Vladimir.

"Get the fuck out." Maxim's voice is so cavernously deep it sounds like the rumble of a distant tank. His minions nearly knock one another over in their rush to leave. All of them studiously avoid looking at me, which is a smart thing to do. Keen observation skills and a long memory are bad things to bring to a meeting with Maxim.

When they're gone, Maxim sends away his bodyguard and gestures for me to sit. I plant my ass on the edge of the table and look around. All the wood in the modern room is bird's-eye maple polished to a high gloss. The walls and ceiling are cream with cinnamon accents; modish niches lend them depth. The windows offer panoramic views of the city, which Maxim ignores.

"I fucked up, Volk."

I shift my weight to take pressure off my stump.

"I thought food was the key—grain, livestock, produce. Not anymore." He shakes his head like a bull elephant just before it charges. "Energy is."

Through the services of a key Kremlin administrator, a fellow Azeri, Maxim has held Moscow's food markets in his crushing grip for over a decade. His empire also includes arms trafficking, selling and transporting people across international borders, and trading in drugs, pornography, and, more recently, black market art. The last time I worked with him we stole a long-lost Leonardo from the catacombs of the Hermitage museum. His greed and my hubris led to Valya losing her left foot in a Prague prison.

"Putin." Maxim spits the name like a guttural curse. His chair grates in its housing as he rotates it to stare out the window while he talks. But I still don't think he's admiring the view; his gaze is focused inward. "That fucking troll has gone from a KGB bootlicker to the second coming of Stalin. Backs down entire countries just by closing the pipes. And now he puts his friends in high places so he has a soft place to land and pull strings when he stops playing politics."

A jewel-handled dagger magically appears in his meaty palm and begins to twirl. I still don't understand why I'm here, although I have an idea. Someone needs to die, or to be persuaded the hard way. The doubts that displaced me on my bumpy ride down to the AMERCO building are still chewing at the edges of my consciousness, coming closer to the center of things, altering the way I look at the world. I'm tired of doing everything by force. I *won't* do something like that just to help him make more money.

"Everything is changing again." He spins the knife. "The government says, okay, we don't care anymore how you got it. Fly straight, scratch our backs, you can keep it. Don't and we'll take it away from you with our new law."

The Putin-controlled Duma gave the central government sweeping powers to confiscate the property of "extremists," a word that means whatever the government wants it to mean on a case-by-case basis. Stalin took what he wanted through brute force. In the new Russia expropriation is done under the camouflage of law. Civil rights and media groups screamed the loudest when the law was passed, fearing it would be used to silence opposition politicians and the press. *Mafiya* capitalists like Maxim probably never even knew the legislation existed until the Kremlin started bludgeoning them with it. The most important things have a way of sneaking up on you and staving in your skull when you least expect it.

"The food markets are open now," he says. "Drugs, guns, and gambling, there's still money to be made, but there's more competition. The big money comes harder. I need to go legit."

"I can't help you with that."

He stares at me as though I've just puked on his new alligator-skin shoes. "What are you working on now?"

"Nothing. Another project."

He whirls the dagger like a drumstick, looking at it instead of me while he gives me a chance to reconsider.

And then it dawns on me that I've been a fool. The big Azeri has his fingers in every pot. He knows everything, including why a man like Marko Hutsul would be a seeming captive in the bomb-blasted AMERCO building and why Hutsul's giant of a company, Kombi-Oil, is playing around on the fringes with a ratty warehouse in Vladimir.

"You've heard of Kombi-Oil?" I say.

He frowns, not bothering to answer such a stupid question.

"This is personal. There's no money in it."

"No money?" His laugh comes from somewhere deep inside, a low rumble like an earthquake. The dagger twinkles and disappears. "Okay, no money."

"What's so funny?"

"Kombi-Oil owns enough oil and gas to power the world for years. And it's got minority interests in electrical grids, refineries, petrol stations, and pipes—you get the picture? How the fuck do you think oil moves?"

Putin's got oil for blood, Matthews said to me. *He can bring Europe to its knees just by telling Transneft to shut down the pipes.* I heard him, but the message he intended to deliver went over my head.

"Any pipeline in particular?" I say.

"Lots. Three from the Caspian Sea oil fields. The one to the north shoots up into Ukraine. The one in the middle goes to the Black Sea. The southern pipe ends at the Mediterranean."

He picks his teeth with a thickly ridged thumbnail, which he keeps filed to a point for close fighting, although I can't imagine anyone who would be willing to fight him hand-to-hand.

"What's going on, Volk?"

"The northern route—"

"Not very big, maybe a hundred thousand barrels a day. It needs expanding, and it needs more electrical grids and refining capacity. That means there's lots of money to be made even before more oil flows."

"Where does it go?"

"From my town, Baku, northeast through Dagestan, Chechnya, Ingushetia . . . You need me to go on?"

The point is clear enough. After it leaves Azerbaijan and until it reaches Ukraine, the path of that pipeline runs through Russian territory—much of it in the disputed Caucasus, but Russian nevertheless, and not likely to become independent any time soon.

"What about the other two?"

"From Baku to the Black Sea and to the Mediterranean, but no part of them touches Russian soil. Not routes favored by the Kremlin."

The big Azeri locks his gaze on mine. It feels like I'm staring into the depths of a furnace, so burning is his passion.

"There's more," he says. "Lot's more. The U.S., Europe, and Georgia want to build a pipe under the Caspian to deliver Kazak and Turkmen gas to Europe. Russia wants to pipe it through Russian territory, and is willing to pay almost anything to make that happen. A nuclear power plant in Kazakhstan. A joint Kazakh-Russian uranium enrichment center in Siberia."

Maxim settles deeper into his chair and watches me process this information, staring at me from beneath his tangled brows. He almost looks sad.

"Why do you think they send men like you to fight in the mountains, Volk?"

chapter 31

Maxim scrutinizes me with crocodile eyes, almost as if he can see the path of my thoughts as I try to dovetail what he has just told me with what I know. Brock Matthews represents the American government, at least one faction of it. Lachek, I think, is acting in a private capacity, as is Maxim—two different strains of the same breed of men who are still, after all these years, engaged in the primitive accumulation of post-Soviet capital. How many others are involved?

"Let's take a walk." Still looking at me as though he is gauging my reaction, he bellows, "Mei!"

The sleepy Asian girl whose smile reaches all the way to her eyes emerges from an open doorway and pads toward us. She's wearing a hotel bathrobe and nothing else that I can see, but her effort to stay in character is wasted on me. Not only because she was the one asking questions at the Kombi-Oil warehouse and calling Charlie from the front desk of my escort service, but also because I've never known Maxim to keep the same girl for more than a night. Just as he shifts his place of business frequently, he changes girls for the same reason. The fact that she's here means she's not just another prostitute.

Her gaze finds mine with the same cool gleam I noticed before.

"Call down to the guards and tell them I'm going for a walk," Maxim tells her. If he is disappointed by my lack of reaction to Mei, it fails to show.

He leads the way out and we cross the bridge to chug along the embankment on the edge of the Moscow River, the big man huffing like a steam engine, his bodyguards trailing some distance behind us like freight cars. The cold and wind turn his face red, but he seems happier to be outside.

"In a hundred years we'll kill each other for different reasons," he says. "But only one kind of world politics matters right now. Petropolitics. The pipes are the asshole of the oil and gas world. Shut them down, how long you think everything else keeps going? And just wait until the crazies in Iran start aiming suicide boats at Persian Gulf tankers."

He stops just before we reach Red Square. One of his men rushes toward us with a cup. Maxim pops off the lid, slugs half the boiling brew inside, and loudly smacks his lips.

"Not *just* the Caspian or Kazakhstan or Turkmenistan, Volk. Siberia, too. China and Japan want more. So does the U.S. Which way does the Kremlin go with new pipes? Maybe both ways, but everyone will have to pay to play."

The Chinese are going to beat you to it. Matthews again, but I don't think he was delivering a message when he said that. I suspect he was projecting America's fear of a Russo-Sino alliance. They wonder: Will Russia turn to Asia or Europe? I don't think anyone has the answer to that question. Our cultural identity is so hybridized that sometimes we have no identity at all.

Maxim tried to tell me once through Mei, and now he's told me again today: Oil is the key. It is his path to legitimacy. Everything else is secondary. "How long have you been involved?"

"Years. I told you, food is not enough. Baku is my town. I can control the Caspian. And I have power—influence—in lots of other places. Guerrillas in the Caucasus, opium farmers in Afghanistan. I sell weapons to the mullahs in Iran, distribute wheat all through the federation, deliver drugs to Moscow and Petersburg. I don't have as much leverage as the Kremlin, but enough to get my piece. Now is my turn at the oil table."

He's looking at me without really seeing me. I think he's picturing the faces of those he is able to persuade or conscript to become allies to pursue peace or make war. He's seeing trade routes, distribution patterns, cornered markets, negotiated settlements of long-running disputes. He is, I realize suddenly, disturbingly, seeing the world through a prism of a different size and order of power than I had believed him capable of using.

"Who bombed the AMERCO building?" I say.

"That's your job. You let me know when you find out."

"Who told you it was my job?"

He kills the last of his coffee, not bothering to answer. A bus whooshes to the curb near us, its brakes howling in protest. Farther up the sidewalk a man bumps into one of Maxim's bodyguards, stumbles, starts to say something ugly, then snaps his jaw shut and hurries on.

"*Why* was it bombed?"

Maxim tosses his cup into the river. We watch it twist and skitter with the current before being caught in a whirling eddy. He huffs out a cloud of vapor once, twice. "When you figure that out, come see me and we'll talk more politics," he says, then he lumbers away along the embankment, building a good head of steam while his men hurry along behind him.

I dial my private number for the General, who answers without saying anything because, who knows, maybe I'm in pieces in a torture chamber, and a guy with a bloody saw in one hand is speed-dialing with the other.

"We need to talk about Marko Hutsul and Kombi-Oil," I say.

chapter 32

A female staff officer who looks only slightly younger than Masha leads me down the steps beneath the Kremlin Arsenal. Marble, tile, and then river rock, the topography progressively worsens, slowing her already careful steps. The final twenty meters is a cavelike passageway that ends at the General's weathered door. At her knock I'm admitted into the room made of crying stone.

He's behind the ebony desk, bathed in bluish light cast by an array of computer screens. The rest of the room is dark. The door thuds shut behind me, then seals itself tight with a sound like sucking air, reminding me of the technology hidden behind the primitive facade of the General's command center. He keeps rapping keys while I stand and wait. Now that the door has blocked the light from the corridor, he seems suspended in a nimbus of radiance that makes me feel as if I'm gazing up at him from the bottom of a well.

He finishes on the keyboard, flicks a switch that suddenly illuminates the room in the light from the naked bulb above my head, and points me to the chair in front of his desk.

"The police found three bodies in a van near the M7," he says, adjusting his cuffs. "Probably a drug hit, they're saying."

"How's Charlie?"

He motions over his shoulder in the direction of a cell block he maintains in his warren of tunnels beneath the Kremlin. "They tell me she's deranged. The Americans have ratcheted up the pressure to find her. The one making the most noise is the agent you worked with in Washington. Matthews. He says they're going public in a few days."

"Let them. We should keep her, just in case we can put her to use."

He doesn't bother to answer. He understands the power of leverage better than I do. "Golko briefed me," he says. "Now fill in the blanks."

I reel off my progress report, hitting all the important points. Nothing moves on his face while I talk, but when I mention Kombi-Oil and its ownership of the warehouse where Melnik's body was found his eyes seem to glimmer and he taps something into his computer. When my report is done, he hands me a folder.

"Marko Hutsul's file. You'll recognize the type of man he is."

"How well do you know him?"

"He never served on the front lines," he says with the contempt of someone who did. "His appointments were political. We attended many of the same briefings, argued once over the deployment of an armored division into the Caucasus. I can't put much more flesh to the bones you have there." He gestures toward the file.

A soft chime sounds. The General presses a key on his computer and the door at the back of his chamber hums open. The frail staffer who led me here takes a careful step inside and hands him a folder about two centimeters thick. On closer inspection she seems a bit younger than I thought, maybe early fifties; her stooped posture makes her look like a walking question mark and adds years to her appearance. The General glances into the folder while she backs out of the room, then slides it to me the same way he did the Hutsul dossier.

"That's what I've been able to find so far on Kombi-Oil. Most of it is publicly available, but some of the financial information is not. In addition to owning huge chunks of our oil and gas reserves, it owns six refineries, hundreds of kilometers of oil and gas pipelines, and a sales network of petrol stations located in eighteen Russian regions."

"Does AMERCO share any interests with Kombi-Oil?"

He shakes his head. "Not as far as I can tell."

"What about the Chinese?"

He recaptures his computer mouse, taps on the keys while eyeing the closest monitor, and frowns. "No interest in Kombi-Oil."

"What is it?"

I can tell by the changing play of light on his face that the General is speed-reading through different windows. Several minutes pass that way.

"The energy ministry says China National Petroleum Corporation might be offered twenty percent of the main oil assets of Yukos, which owns seventeen percent of our reserves."

"At what price?"

"This doesn't say. But it could be one hell of a consolation."

"What would be in it for the Kremlin?"

"Another huge market for our oil and gas. A counterbalance to American power. Assurance that Russia will continue to be a hub for energy routes. A lever to use in the future if China steps out of line."

The General drags each word out. He's still flipping windows on his main computer, each click of his mouse marking a new one until he lands on something that causes him to pause for a long time.

"The police inspector in Vladimir—Olga?—was right. Kombi-Oil controls the distribution company that owns and operates the warehouse there, among others."

The General's face glows blue, then chrome-white, then blue again. He reads something on the screen, and then the light flickers back to whiteness as his eyes pinball from corner to corner. His gaze finally settles near the top of the screen.

"What did you say they shipped from the Vladimir warehouse?"

"Wooden and ivory eggs, lacquered boxes, chess sets, things like that."

"How big can that business be?"

"I don't follow."

"Did the warehouse look busy?"

"Half empty, unguarded, damn near falling apart. And it was shut down for a week at the time Melnik's body was dumped."

He nods toward the computer screen. "One of Kombi-Oil's segment reports breaks out its distribution operations. They own that warehouse and five others. You have to do some digging, but when you get down to it, the operation has annual revenue of almost a billion American dollars."

"That's a lot of knickknacks."

"That's a lot of free cash in somebody's pockets."

He pushes himself away from the screen and regards me steadily for several heartbeats, then picks up the phone and whispers into it. After he hangs up he says, "Bank records. We should have an answer within a few minutes."

The General makes more phone calls while I start reading through the files he gave me. I can't make out the topic of his calls. I can hear his side of the conversations, of course, but he talks mostly in monosyllables that tell me nothing meaningful.

Hutsul got his start in October 1993 as a major general in charge of a tank battalion, called to action when Yeltsin ordered the 125-millimeter guns turned on the opposition legislators from the Supreme Soviet who were barricaded in the White House parliament building. One of the prizes Hutsul earned for his role in the affair was a seat on the board of Kombi-Oil.

The General ends his latest call. "Wait here," he says, and then leaves through the door at the back of his office. I stare at the door for several seconds after he's gone, wondering how he intends to use what we've learned, then open his file on Kombi-Oil.

Like many of Russia's largest private concerns, Kombi-Oil had insignificant assets in the early '90s, when it was formed, but grew quickly as its principals followed a familiar pattern. Gather assets, preferably former state-owned holdings, through force or political power. Bribe political and administrative officials to ensure favorable treatment: clear supply lines, duty-free exchanges, no regulation of such niceties as worker safety, quality, or accurate weights and measures. Pay off law enforcement to arrest real or potential competitors. Within a few years Kombi-Oil owned chunks of Siberian and Caspian oil and gas reserves and a sprawling distribution network. All of this takes several pages to document and explain. It's only when I read the last page of the file that the final piece of the puzzle drops into place for me.

In addition to Hutsul, Kombi-Oil has eight sitting directors. One of them is Filip Lachek.

I remember Valya's comment that Abreg was working with a powerful man at the Kremlin. I still don't understand *why* he did it, but Abreg clearly meant to set up Kombi-Oil and his sometime partners Lachek and Hutsul when he ordered the egg to be planted under Dubinin's face. The egg pointed to the warehouse, a dilapidated front for siphoning money into the pockets of two directors at the expense of their partners. And the egg served its purpose, because now Lachek and Hutsul are in the General's crosshairs.

An hour passes before the General returns. He seems contemplative, but I can't read anything more than that from his bearing or expression. "We're on to something here," he says. "I'll know more in a day or two and get back to you."

Just as I start to retort—to tell him that this is about Russia's future, not political gamesmanship—a light starts blinking on the bank of phones in front of him, the same one that disturbed him the last time I was here. He snatches the receiver, but says nothing. This time his irises don't flatten into their reptilian glare, but his tightened grip on the receiver reveals the tension he feels. He hangs up within seconds.

"That's it for now, Colonel. I'll get back to you."

I stand. My body feels like one big corded muscle. The voice inside my head is screaming. Doubt has turned into certainty that ideals count for nothing.

"This is *all* dirty, sir. Those soldiers did something awful, and damned if it wasn't recorded somewhere. I can't tell you how many others are in line for the same treatment, but for sure more are going to die. And you can guess at the rest. AMERCO, Kombi-Oil, China National Petroleum Company. They're all wrapped up in this, every goddamn one of them, and probably others, too. You know what I think?"

He leans back to contemplate the soggy beam above him. "Tell me."

"Russia is for sale."

chapter 33

When I leave the General's lair my cell phone begins to blink. Two messages. The calls didn't come through because microwave signals won't penetrate the rock and whatever additional security devices the General has installed. I punch in the password.

"Barokov here, Colonel. We need to talk."

The second message is from Alla. "The police were here. Let me know if I can help, okay?"

I stand on the south side of the Moscow River and watch the meridian sun peek through a gap in the dark clouds and send golden shafts off the dome of the Ivan the Great Bell Tower. I gather myself. I need to forget about fanciful notions of right and wrong, focus on survival. I need to find Lachek and kill him before he kills me.

The Nokia buzzes. The caller ID shows Valya's number.

"Hey," she says. A public address announcer blares in the background, reporting the arrival of a train from Khasavyurt. "We missed Semerko, but he was here in Makhachkala less than forty-eight hours ago."

"We?"

"Some of my friends are helping. One of them is close to Abreg." She whispers the last part, and I picture her cupping one hand around the phone.

"Did Semerko have Galina with him?"

"Three *men* were in the apartment at the address you gave me." Her voice drips scorn. "Wahhabis, like the Black Arab," she says, referring to a malignant Saudi mercenary, now dead. "They talk not of independence but of jihad, of changing Chechen culture from *adat* to radical Sharia. None of them wanted to help me find an innocent girl."

Adat, the Chechens' long-standing social code governing relations between children and parents, husbands and wives, friends and enemies, is fast becoming a casualty of war, losing its place to the religious body of laws and rules in the Sharia.

"So?"

"So I convinced them."

Valya is an expert at finding and exploiting weakness. And in a case like this, with Galina's life at stake, she would have been ruthlessly efficient.

"They stopped posturing and started talking very quickly," she says. "I separated them to make sure the stories matched. Semerko has taken Galina to Tindi, just as you suspected. I'm on my way there right now. My phone probably won't work."

The PA blares another message, but I can't make out the words. I'm thinking that what I've asked her to do is acutely dangerous. She was already at risk, and now I've added to it. I'd better talk to Barokov and find out if he's learned anything new.

"Be careful, Valya."

"Yeah, yeah," she says. "You be careful."

✶

Inspector Barokov must have several crumpled brown suits, because that's what he's wearing again when I enter his undersized office. I bump my knees taking a seat across from his desk. It's dark outside, the storm clouds having drowned the sun, and drafty in the station. The squad room is empty except for a cop who's asleep with his head in his arms at one of the tables.

Barokov leaves the door open to provide the illusion of space. A shoulder holster snugging a Glock with a worn leather grip is slung over the back of his cracked-leather chair. A picture in a gilded frame shows him standing outside the Moscow Circus, one arm around the waist of a woman a head taller than he is and his hand resting proudly on the shoulder of a boy with ruddy cheeks like his own. He seems happy in the picture, which I failed to notice my first time here, but he's upset now.

"I've been trying to reach you ever since we were cut off last night."

We weren't cut off. I hung up on him because I don't like the answer to his question about Ryazan, and I don't know what I'm going to be able to do about it anyway. "You shouldn't buy into the leftist propaganda about the apartment bombings," I say, dismissing his concerns in the usual way.

He holds my gaze steadily for a couple of seconds, then drops his eyes when I don't look away. "That's not what I want to talk about anyway. I need your help."

He shakes a sheet of fax paper free from a stack on his desk and holds it out at arm's length to read from it. "Semerko and his younger 'sister' passed through the train station at Makhachkala at 4:35 P.M. on January ninth. Three days ago. He showed his papers, but of course nobody bothered to check out his story about the girl."

Barokov sets the oily page back on his desk, but he doesn't say anything more. He just waits, looking at me with wide eyes as though he expects something. I'm wary of saying anything about Valya, not because I don't trust him, but rather because I don't trust the people he might tell. And I'm disappointed, because my hope that he might have uncovered something useful was wasted. Valya has made far more progress than he has.

"So?"

"You know people there, don't you? You served in the region."

"I don't know any policemen."

He picks up a paperweight shaped like a pyramid and turns it in his palm. "I'm not getting any cooperation down there," he says, talking quietly, looking down at the paperweight. "I've made phone calls, e-mailed and faxed inquiries and requests, sent pictures of Galina and Semerko. I'm ashamed to say that I haven't been able to find anyone who cares enough to give me any more than lip service."

When he finally looks up at me his eyes are filled with embarrassment and sadness for the failings of his profession. The Soviets turned family, friends, and neighbors into informants. Everybody watched everybody. Most fearsome were the self-righteous, the small-minded, the bitter—all those seeking to resolve petty grievances with whispered words, true or false, words that caused enormous hardship for their enemies. They were the most efficient police force in the world. When the institutionalized rigidity of Soviet life vanished suddenly, as if a chunk of the country had fallen off the earth, we had no frame of reference. Crime was everywhere, and the police were lousy investigators, the courts terrible arbiters, the prisons poorly equipped to deal with real criminals. Corruption and incompetence filled the yawing gap, and men like Barokov feel the shame of it.

He drops the paperweight with a bang and leans over his desk on his fists. "We have a serial killer on our hands, Colonel. Our own Rostov Ripper, and *he* got more than fifty before they caught up with him. I think to myself, this kid Semerko, he's just starting, but what he did to the dead girl, Tanya, was the worst I've ever seen. I can't sleep nights I'm so goddamned afraid for Galina. I keep thinking everyone I pass on the street has blood on his hands."

He's trembling from repressed emotion. His left shoulder and cheek twitch with every word.

"Then you gave me the section of climbing rope, out of the blue, and guess what, it's a dead match. Same manufacturer, same brand, same dye lot—just a different piece cut from the same length of cord. And your hunch that Semerko went south paid off. I've got a clean line of sight on him, but there's no money to send me to Dagestan and the local authorities won't get out of a chair unless they're paid. They want blood money! *These* are police?"

Barokov reaches over his desk and clamps my arm just above the elbow, breathing hard. "You've got resources, Colonel. Go down there and find that girl!"

My respect for him has increased threefold, enough that I decide he's worthy of information. "I have someone in the area," I say, sure that by now Valya is on her way to Tindi, long gone from Makhachkala. "She's doing what she can. If she finds Galina and needs my help, I'll be there."

"Really?"

I have to go. I can't bear to look at his newly hopeful face. He follows me outside the station, and I stop at a place on the sidewalk where the shadow of the building hides his features. Just to our right a grate spews warm air over a gathering outside of a liquor store. Cigarette haze mingles with auto exhaust to foul the air. A blue American sedan with a grille like a baleen whale's mouth plates is double-parked across the street, its idling engine belching clouds of steam. Traffic eddies around it in clots separated by jaywalking pedestrians.

Barokov pulls a pack of Sobranies cigarettes from his pocket, jiggles one loose, and dangles it from his lips while he applies the flame. "Who is this person you know?"

How do I answer a question like that? Valya is my friend, my lover, my confidante, my guardian angel; she is a refugee, a fighter, a woman who becomes stronger in adversity.

"A friend," I say.

He blows a smoke ring and we watch it break apart in the hazy light. "This fucking city," he says. "This country. Maybe the old ways were better."

"Time does funny things to our memories, Inspector."

✶

After I take a short nap, Vadim feeds Golko and me an early dinner of borscht and toasted black bread with white cheese and salami. Golko's arm is so heavily bandaged it looks as if it were ripped off and then reattached. I raise my eyebrows and he says, "The doctor told me two centimeters to the right and I would have lost it," in a defensive tone. While I'm eating, he sets out two computer-generated maps, each scarred by a jagged red line.

"These show the movements of the Mercedes during the last day Dubinin used it." He holds up a sheaf of documents. "These give us places and times."

I stuff a spoonful of hot borscht into my mouth and nod to tell him I understand.

"This one shows that Dubinin went from Moscow to Vladimir. This one"—he puts the second map on top of the first—"is larger scale, and it shows his movements within the city of Vladimir." His chubby index finger crinkles the second map when it lands. "The car was parked here for over an hour."

My hand, loaded with bread, stacked cheese, and salami, stops halfway to my mouth. I grab the sheaf of papers from his hand and search through them to find the street address, just to confirm what I already suspect. Golko's chewed fingernail has landed on the terminus of the rail spur where the warehouse is located. We won't need pollen fingerprints from the mud or pictures of dual tires to confirm that Dubinin met his fate there.

Golko stuffs a broken-off chunk of black bread into his mouth and chews thoughtfully. "If Olga's partner hadn't remembered the name, we might never have connected Kombi-Oil to that warehouse. That has to be *part* of what Lachek was trying to cover up when he took Melnik's murder file."

He takes a sip of tea. The group at the communal table in the center of the room guffaws. When one of them stands to make a toast his chair topples backward and the others laugh even louder.

"What do you think Lachek was looking for in Melnik's apartment?"

"The video," I say, thinking of Melnik's careworn Bible and the icon that was the last thing he saw before going to bed. "Charlie told me a man with a conscience gave it to Ravi, and I think that man was Melnik. Have we come across anybody who fits that description better than he does?"

"No."

I remember the names I wrote in columns when I was trying to organize things in my mind. I placed Lachek in the one labeled *AMERCO*, and he belongs there, but he also is a part of the column headed *Starye Atagi*. The man is thoroughly dangerous.

"Remember what I told you about Lachek and his men," I remind Golko.

He nods, and wipes a film of sweat off his forehead. While he's gathering his things together, I receive a text message from the General telling me to come to his headquarters.

chapter 34

The walking question mark leads me back to the General's office and closes the heavy door behind her as she leaves. He finishes with something on the computer, shuts it down, and regards me inscrutably.

"Of course Russia is for sale," he says, as if our earlier conversation had never ended. "Everything is for sale. You need to worry about the things you can control."

His anxious, temple-pressing demeanor is gone, replaced by the more familiar confidence. I wonder how much is enough for him? How many millions of rubles, dollars, euros, or pounds cached in an electronic account in a Swiss bank will it take to satisfy him?

I was wrong to think of Lachek and Maxim as different strains of the same breed. They're different animals entirely, because Maxim has evolved. And so has the General. The dogfight for post-Soviet capital, first won by men like Hutsul and Lachek, has turned into a sophisticated reallocation of critical industries and assets back into the hands of an all-powerful state controlled by a cynical few. Guns and bullets have given way to laws, regulations, court orders, well-crafted business plans, and complex legal maneuvering. The rules have changed, but I've seen all this before, and I have no interest in watching it play out again.

My chronometer beeps. Seven P.M. Forty-eight hours ago I was on a sweating beam in the hearth of the burning AMERCO building. My face hurts, and I'm tired. Not sleep-tired, but a bone-weary ache that makes me feel rudderless, drifting without meaning toward—what? And as quickly as the question comes to mind the answer follows. The General is right. I need to worry about the things I can control. The things I really care about.

No more soldiers should die for whatever happened at Starye Atagi. Those in charge deserve that fate, maybe, but not the conscripts. Chechnya was an acid trip through the inferno. Professional soldier, conscript, it didn't matter—sanity was the first thing to go. The men killing those soldiers are not fit to judge them.

Galina should live. She should not become another nameless victim of Moscow's toxic violence. A metaphorical image comes to mind: Moscow burning, just as it did on the day Napoleon took his prize, robbing him of his victory, symbolically portending the future of a city captured in the flaming embrace of change. Maybe Valya and I, together, can pull Galina out of the fire.

And Valya—wherever she is, whatever she needs, I'll be there for her.

Those are the things that matter now.

The General has been studying me. I'm sure that he thinks he knows me as well as I thought I knew him. What I need is a bit of convincing. He pulls his chair closer to the table and repeats his admonition.

"Worry about what you can control, Colonel."

"Which is?"

"Two gigabytes. Two fucking gigs."

"The video? *That's* what you care about?"

"It happened when the Chechens had you in the pit. A flying detachment of interior ministry troops seized a group of rebels." He talks slowly, gauging my reaction. "Damn near two hundred, a third of them women, some of them children. This was shortly after we suffered terrible losses in—"

"Bullshit! Don't say that! This wasn't a bunch of hotheads getting revenge."

"Think about that place and time, Volk! Rebels hid among families. Twelve-year-olds killing with Kalashnikovs they can barely carry. I'm not telling you our people were right, I'm just saying this is *not* one-dimensional. Who had time to discriminate between combatants and civilians?"

"They weren't taken in a fight. They were rounded up at a filtration point."

"You know this to be true how? Because liars like Abreg and Ravi Kho and his spoiled American girlfriend say so?"

"Because so many people are willing to kill for it. General, we've seen this before at the filtration points—smaller in scale, maybe, but the same damn thing."

He goes through his routine of massaging his temples with the pads of his thumbs, kneading the skin into whiteness, eyes closed. I don't think it was an act when he did it before, but it is now. He radiates an emotion more akin to excitement than dread.

And then something else occurs to me. Dubinin was regular army, just like Melnik and the boy in the Rostov morgue, and he was killed the way he was killed for the same reason they were. His assignment to a special detachment of interior ministry troops would have been noted in the General's file, no matter how it was classified.

"You knew about Starye Atagi. You knew Dubinin was there."

"I knew about his posting. I didn't pay attention to all the rumors about what happened there."

He looks away, and I realize that Dubinin's duplicity is deeply disturbing to him. Not in the way a father is disappointed by a son, but because of the vulnerability it suggests in his organization.

"What did happen there?"

"They lost control. Slaughtered them all. It went on for almost two days before the last one died." The words seem to resound even after he stops talking, as if they, like the deeds they describe, refuse to be silenced.

"You've seen the video?"

"I talked to someone who saw part of it."

"An interior ministry detachment wouldn't have fallen under your command, General. This isn't your fight."

"I know that, goddamn it! You think this is about *me*?"

He hops off his chair and paces. He appears agitated to the point of distraction. But the false note remains, an indefinable sense that wicks poisonously into my mind. Almost as if the corners of his mouth are turned up in a smile of victory.

"Those stupid fucks gave our enemies enough ammunition to destroy us. The Western media, the hand-wringers at the UN, the breakaway republics—not to mention Chechen scum like Abreg. This is *not* something we can allow in the public eye."

"It's on video. Probably *digital* video. The thing could have been copied a million times and we wouldn't be able to tell one way or the other. I can't believe it hasn't already been spread all over the Internet."

His jaw muscles ripple the skin below his cauliflower ears, the only visible sign that he doesn't like having to argue with me. "If we can get a copy of it, we can control what happens. In the meantime, we have no choice except to negotiate."

"With who?"

"Abreg is making demands, through an intermediary."

"Of course." I say this matter-of-factly, because a downward trajectory this steep can end only in the worst possible landing. "And he's using Khanzad as his go-between."

"That's right."

He regards me with a bright-eyed look, like a teacher waiting to see if his star pupil understands the lesson. "Put the rest of it together, Volk. What do you see?"

The story is granular, nuanced, layered by time and colored by motives both noble and base. But stripped to its essentials, I think I know the gist of what happened to both the egg and the video.

chapter 35

After the revolution, the Hen Egg landed in Chechnya. Maybe Dubinin got it right that the Bolsheviks made a trade to appease the rebels on their southern border, but how it got there is no longer important. What is important is that Khanzad acquired it, whether by purchase, theft, or trickery, the means don't really matter.

He put it on the market and connected with Dubinin.

At the same time, Melnik was living his guilt-ridden existence in Vladimir. The former soldier with a penchant for making movies was spending his postwar days in prayer, seeking remission that never seemed to come. Melnik probably started his secular attempt at absolution with an Internet search for an organization that would help him put his video to its best use. His electronic queries bumped into Ravi Kho, a supposed peacenik who had just posted a high-profile Web entry that he was going to "expose the atrocities" in Chechnya. Ravi must have seemed like the perfect person to bring the video to light—an outsider with no political or economic ax to grind.

Melnik gave Ravi the exposé of a lifetime. Ravi, either because he had been seduced or because he had his own agenda, handed the video over to Khanzad. And Khanzad betrayed them both. He sold it to the highest bidder—or to the man he feared the most, which amounts to the same thing. Khanzad sold it to Abreg.

"Khanzad set the whole thing up," I say to the General, because how much simpler can it be said than that? "He sold Abreg the video *and* information about where to find Melnik and Dubinin. And then he sold Dubinin the egg and a copy of the video, and Abreg got those, too, when he killed Dubinin."

The thick flesh around the General's mouth settles into a look of satisfaction. "That's what I think, although I'm not sure how the girl, Charlie, ended up with the pendant."

"My guess is that Ravi figured out that he'd been betrayed. I'll bet he stole the pendant and sent it to her. Probably at the same time he e-mailed her Khanzad's picture of the egg."

"What about Lachek? Why was he in Vladimir stealing a police file and searching Melnik's apartment?"

"Lachek was at Starye Atagi. He had to be. He was covering up, just like he was when he quarantined file fifty-nine thirteen."

"No. He's too old, and he was in Asia in '03." The General settles back into his chair. "Think about it for a minute."

It takes me a whole lot less than a minute to make the connection. "His son. The punk I smacked on the head, he was there, and Lachek was trying to protect him."

The General nods. "Lachek is all over this thing like a bad smell on a dead fish. As a director of Kombi-Oil he also has a stake in our other little project. Oil. But that's my part. You concentrate on the video. Go get it, and if you can bring back the egg at the same time, all the better."

"Why doesn't Abreg go public with the video?"

"Because he's smart enough to realize it's more valuable as a negotiating tool."

"What does he want?"

"Money. Withdrawal of all Russian troops from Chechnya. Political assurances of independence, and concrete steps to make it happen within two years. We'll pay, so long as the amount is not unreasonable. We'll wire money anywhere he wants. The last two conditions are out of the question."

"This is bullshit. A copy of the video will be all over the Web the day after we pay him off."

"I already told you, we have a way around that. Let me worry about it."

"Withdrawal and independence? What makes Abreg think it's worth so much?"

"Because he is a fool who overestimates his hand."

I remember Abreg talking to me in the pit—philosophy, religion, politics, economics. He may have been wrong about many things, but not foolishly so.

The General leans back in his chair. "He wants you to pick it up. He'll put it into your hand, no other."

My stomach lurches and starts my heart racing toward my throat. I'm responding like one of Pavlov's dogs, except I'm reacting to remembered pain. The General's cold eyes measure me, like two blocks of green ice balancing on a scale. I meet his stare.

"When?"

chapter 36

An hour after finishing with the General I'm back in my basement home, gathering the things I'll need for a trip to the mountains. At least two days from now, the General told me. Two days or two minutes, I want to be ready. Valya's new phone rings without answer. I thumb through the Fabergé book and reread the pages of Lachek's dossier without really seeing the pictures or the words. Throw them aside and waste another minute with the phone pressed against my ear hoping that on this ring, or maybe the next, she'll answer.

I leave the café, still roiled by the General's plan and not in the mood to talk to Vadim. The evening sky is cooking-pot black streaked with crimson runnels where the lights from the city bleed into the clouds. With nowhere else to go for the moment I stop at Stolovaya Thirteen, a broken-tile, fifty-rubles-a-meal cafeteria on the grounds of a central Moscow market beginning to empty itself of drooping babushkas toting their baskets home after another hard day. As soon as I finish eating I dial Alla.

"I need to talk to Mei," I say. The General wants me to back off, but I'd still like to get another angle on the Chinese side of the oil equation.

"She's no Valya, Alexei."

"Not for that."

"I was kidding, foolish man. Valya can be half a world away, and she's still attached to your hip. I know it, everyone knows it. Mei's not here."

"What about later?"

"She's not on the schedule. Sometimes she comes in anyway, for extra money, but she'd be here already if she was planning to work a shift tonight. Try Zona. Once in a while she works there."

The sounds of the cafeteria are muted to a comfortable buzz. The warm air smells of grilled lamb, fried onions, and baked bread. I don't have anything else to say, but I really don't want to hang up either.

"You got my message about the police?" she says.

"Yes."

"Another one came by today asking about you. Nothing I can't handle. I just thought you might want to know."

"Thank you, Alla."

"Business is good. Lots of money in your account. How long since you took any out?"

Six months. I still have enough cash stuffed into a duffel bag to last for several years the way I've been living. "A long time," I tell her.

During the last months my human contact has been at a remove, as if I were sheathed in rubber. Now that I'm back in touch with Valya I seem to be able to feel things again, a strange sensation. Alla's tone gives me the impression that she can sense the change in me, and I want to keep the conversation going, even the parts when we're not saying anything.

"Are you all right?" she says.

"I'm fine. How are you doing?"

The sound of her laughter tinkles in my ear. "Is this really you, Alexei?"

A frumpy woman picks up my tray, quickly pockets her tip, and hurries off in case I change my mind.

"Don't worry about me," Alla says. "I love my job. And I can do more, you know."

"Yes, you can. We need to talk about that. Someday soon."

"Maybe then we can talk more about what you *really* do. Maybe you'll let me help you with some things."

So talented, so capable, Alla is a unique blend of abilities. "I think that's a good idea."

"I'd like that."

She sounds young. Spirited in a way I have never heard her before. Strange how so few words can work such magic.

"Good-bye, Alla."

" 'Bye, Alexei." Then she gives another happy little laugh and hangs up.

Zona nightclub has room for more than a thousand patrons in its five stories. The theme here is prison chic: camp guards and patrol dogs greet guests from a watchtower behind coiled concertina wire; massive doors, iron bars, inmate cells, and waiters wearing convict garb complete the motif inside. All of this is artfully mixed with a dance floor with changing levels, a rotating bar, strobe lights firing beams of blues, reds, and greens, and a transparent floor stocked with live white rats under the glass.

On the fifth level is a VIP room. Dark, with muted spotlights pointing to the ceiling, the music still loud but not overwhelming, a roomy scatter of tables, private dancers grinding away, lots of staff circulating with food, alcohol, drugs—whatever those rich enough to afford this room desire. A prison-guard bouncer takes my measure and lets me be while I look around.

Three Asian men occupy a corner table. One of them has a club dancer on his lap. The other two are engaged in an animated conversation while several girls pretend to hang on their every word, but then all the men look up toward the high ceiling and stop talking.

Dancing in a lowering cage is Mei. She's wearing a tiny gold

G-string and bra combo. Eyes half closed, she rotates and sways, liquid in the tsunami of sound from the weapons-grade speakers, lost in the narcotic spell of the music and the rhythms of her own body. Her dragon tattoo undulates with each sinuous movement, glowing fiery red and orange, a living thing beneath her skin. I use the distraction to study the men some more, confirming my initial impression. When the song ends, the cage rises on nearly invisible wires until it disappears into the smoky gloom of the high ceiling, only to reappear seconds later holding another gyrating prisoner, this one naked except for some yellow paint in the shape of a bikini. Conversations resume.

I follow the curved wall to a set of metal stairs and wait on a landing. A few minutes later Mei glides down, wearing a black topcoat over jeans. She's looking into her Gucci bag and doesn't see me until I'm at her shoulder, matching her steps down the stairs. Her gait falters.

"Taking a break, Mei?"

She swivels her head to look around me, then checks the stairs behind her. Grabs my hand and hurries me down to a unisex bathroom on the next level, into a stall with a clear glass door that frosts opaque when she locks it behind us. She opens her coat to reveal a tight, thin T-shirt, crushes her body against mine, and looks up at me with all the sincerity of a porn star.

"I didn't expect to see you here, baby."

"Why are we hiding?"

Her face is still flushed from the cage, and her body and hands are warm where they touch me. "I have customers. They can't see me with you."

"You looked like you were leaving."

"Only taking a break."

I catch her hands in mine and shove her backward until I have her pinned against the marble wall. "Who are your customers?"

The gleam in her amber eyes is no longer coolly amused. "Just another party of men. Same as always."

"Asian men."

"So?"

I put my mouth next to her ear. Her sprayed-on fragrance smells like orange blossoms. "I think they're Chinese state security, Sixth Bureau," I whisper, and ever so slightly she stiffens in my embrace. "Just like you are."

I pull my head back until our noses are touching. Her eyes are closed now. It feels as though her body has melded into mine. I haven't held a woman this close for a long time. Someone bangs the door of the stall and shouts to hurry up.

"Why is Sixth Bureau here?" I prompt her.

"I don't know anything about state security." Her hands have somehow escaped my grip. One of them finds its way under my shirt.

A moment later I recapture it and hoist both of them over her head. I no longer have her pinned, but she's still glued to me anyway, moving her hips the way she did when she was dancing. More banging on the door. I squeeze her wrists. She moans, her hot breath in my face.

"This isn't going to work, Mei. Why are you here?"

No answer. Her eyes remain closed. Her Gucci bag dangles from her shoulder. Still jammed against her, I reach inside, fumble around, and remove a Soviet-made PSM, a slim weapon built for concealment. I let it fall back into the bag disgustedly.

"Maxim knows everything," she whispers. "Things will be better for me if you hear it from him."

We stay like that for several beats of her heart, then I peel her away and step back.

"What do *you* know?"

"I told you the first time. Oil is everything."

"What does that mean?"

She doesn't reply, just stares up at me, resolute. I could take a knife to her and she might talk, but I don't think so, and I'm not prepared to do that anyway, not about this. I bang open the door. The man standing there goes wide-eyed and says, "Oh, sorry," then stumbles backward as I shove past him.

chapter 37

My breath fogs the air on the street outside the nightclub. I stand there for a moment, getting eyeballed by club security in the form of a phony prison guard and his watchdog, a real-enough German shepherd. It's after midnight, but people in the intelligence profession are nocturnal, like bats, snakes, and scorpions. Decision made, I head for the American embassy. The time has come for another confrontation with Brock Matthews. I think he'll be more truthful now that I have Charlie.

Too many night crawlers clog the sidewalk along the main road, so I decide to take backstreets. As I cut through a narrow alley I speed-dial Vadim, who answers with a grunt. "I need the phone number for the American. Matthews. It's on your note in my office." A clunk in my ear tells me that he's dropped the receiver to go downstairs.

I reach a slightly wider street, deserted except for a beggar cocooned in blankets up to his nose who approaches slowly, peering at me through bottle-thick glasses, and a kid who snarls by on a moped. The rumble of a powerful engine makes me look over my shoulder. The

American sedan with the baleen grille emerges from the alley and creeps toward me. I quicken my pace, cautious, feeling an adrenaline buzz. I've stirred up so many serpents they may have to form a conga line, and all of them want me dead. I drift to the edge of the sidewalk closest to a brick commercial building. Slide my hand under my jacket and grip the Sig.

A cab appears at the mouth of a cross street in front of me just as a motorcycle rips around the opposite corner, engine roaring. I snatch a glance over my shoulder. The sedan has closed the gap, still idling along, now less than twenty meters away. The cab noses into the street in front of the motorcycle, forcing the rider to brake so suddenly that he has to lay the bike down and slide, sparks flying. The big engine of the sedan suddenly revs into a throaty growl.

"Ready?" Vadim says in my ear, just before I drop the phone.

The sedan swerves violently, jumps the curb, and barrels straight at me, its toothy grille aimed at my chest.

All in one motion I draw the Sig and go airborne, barely clearing the onrushing chrome maw, and bounce across the hood, rolling as I go. I crash into the windshield just before the car slams into the wall. The safety glass gives with a dull crunch but doesn't shatter. The recoil lands me on one knee on the hood, my other leg braced behind me and my arms extended, aiming the Sig with both hands. The driver goggles at me through the cobwebbed safety glass. I pump two rounds into his shocked face, the windshield falling into the front seat in one piece so I can clearly see the passenger raising his Uzi to cut me in half. I snap two bullets into him, then spin onto my back and fire blindly between my knees.

Glass explodes from a storefront. Nobody there. I whip around and take aim at the taxi parked in the street, angled haphazardly, its doors winged open. My next two shots blow out its windows.

The motorcyclist is racing away from his smoking bike, a pistol at the end of one of his pumping arms. I twist awkwardly on my back on the hood, line up, and squeeze off one shot, then another before I cut him down. That leaves just one round in the ten-shot Sig. I tear another magazine from my belt as I scan the area for more targets.

Just as I'm about to pop the empty magazine I'm startled by a clink of metal behind me, inside the car. I turn to find myself staring into the bore of an Uzi that peeks over the front seat. I drill my last round through the seat just as the Uzi jets flame. Hot slugs scorch my cheek as they rip past. I drop the extra clip just as the machine gun falls away, then a head pops up and down again, like a jack-in-the-box. *Two* men in the back seat!

I ditch the empty Sig, claw madly at my prosthesis to draw the knife, and plunge through the front window. Land hard on the shattered windshield and the dead driver. Swarm over the back of the seat, leading with the knife, slashing wildly. The blade bites into flesh.

"Stop him! Shoot him!" someone shouts behind me.

Something punches my thigh. I keep chopping with the knife, stabbing it again and again into both of the men in the back seat. One of them screams and thrashes as he tries to ward off the blade. The other was probably already dead from my last bullet. Blood flies in arcing, twisting ribbons.

Another sharp blow lands high on the back of my neck, and everything seems to slow. The knife feels as heavy as a dumbbell, impossible to swing. Hands tug at my shoulders and arms. Voices shout, scream, but I can't make out any words. I kick at my new attackers, but the leaden press of bodies in the close confines of the car and my own ebbing consciousness weaken the blow. I have just enough of my wits left to wonder, *How many of these fuckers are there?*

chapter 38

Everything is still dark when I come to. A cyclone roars in my skull. My hands and feet are too heavy to move. No, not too heavy—shackled with metal clamps attached to the thick, wooden arms and legs of a bulky chair. My head throbs as if I've been sandbagged, but as my memory returns I realize that I must have been put down by a tranquilizer. Drugs are better than a bullet. Somebody paid a heavy price to capture me alive. I figure I got as many as five, maybe more, depending on whether anyone was in the cab when I fired into it. Not worth getting my face skinned off, but a high body count is better than nothing. Maybe it's the drugs, but somehow even the thought of what is probably in store for me can't keep me from nodding into oblivion again.

The jangle of keys awakens me. Lifting my head is an act of will. The metal door of my cell crashes open, admitting a shaft of artificial light. Nothing else happens for a moment. My eyes adjust enough to make out the brightly lit doorway and the dingy plaster walls around it. Steps boom from the hallway outside. A thin shape bisects the light, a slash of darkness in the glow. An overhead bulb bursts on.

A cadaverous man with a face like the blade of an ax drops his hand from the light switch and stalks inside, trailed by a slope-shouldered lackey with a bandaged head. Ax-face looks like a bag of bones in a charcoal suit. He stops a few feet in front of me so I can see him clearly while he regards me as if I were a dirty toilet. The resemblance to his son is startling. The main differences being his rabidly bright eyes and the way he moves, like loosely connected parts that tighten spasmodically just as each lurching step threatens to tear apart the whole, jerky and sinuous at the same time. Filip Lachek's son may have tried to adopt his father's poses, but he failed to match the sheer grotesquery of the original.

"This is Volk?" Lachek's voice is pitched abnormally high, keening like a blade trying to cut stone. Tar stains mar all of his teeth except for one upper canine, which is long and white, an ageless crown.

"Alexei Volkovoy," says the bandaged man, reading from a document in a folder. A photo ID tag clipped to his belt says his name is Edorskai, and only then do I recognize the blanketed beggar from the street where I was abducted, probably the leader, smart enough to let the others die until he had a clear shot with the tranquilizer gun. His thick glasses reflect the light as he turns a page, concentrating all of his attention on the dossier, not on Lachek, as though he is afraid to be caught in the blast zone of Lachek's rage.

"Orphaned from birth. Served time in prison as a minor, records later expunged by military order. Moscow Military Academy and two years' special operations training at Balashikha-two, then attached to the Fifty-eighth Army. Supposedly discharged with the rank of major after losing a foot in Ingushetia, but now he carries the rank of colonel. One year of diplomatic training. Speaks English with an American accent. Plays at being a mobster, sometimes functions as one of Maxim Abdullaev's dogs between projects for General Nemstov."

Lachek curls his lip at the sound of Maxim's name.

Edorskai claps the folder shut and shifts his weight away from Lachek, almost cringing. "Witnesses at the AMERCO bombing say he pistol-whipped your son for no cause."

Lachek approaches me executioner-slow, talons my pinned forearms and lowers his face close to mine. His sour breath smells as if something is rotting inside of him. A perfectly repugnant, old-man stink, an odor of decay that captures the essence of who he is—all the curdled malevolence that was used to poison the world for decades. The fetid stench tells me something else as well: Lachek is dying from the inside out. Somehow I am absolutely sure of that. He's staked naked to an anthill with nothing to lose.

"Do you know . . ." he rasps, dragging out each word, "do you have *any* fucking idea the things I am going to do to you?"

Edorskai hovers near the edge of my vision. His complexion has turned ashen. Reflected fluorescent light paints the lenses of his glasses a glowing white, like sun-struck quartz.

"Your son." I say the words just as slowly as Lachek did, staring into his wildly dilated pupils. "Your son was human excrement. But he was still the best thing that ever came out of you."

I expect fury. What I get is much worse. He smiles. Blows more of his rancid breath into my face, sticks out his purplish tongue, and licks my cheek.

My head jerks away involuntarily and smacks the high back of the chair so hard that my vision flares. He licks me again. This time his tongue slimes a wet path over my lips and nostrils. I finally regain my senses enough to launch a head butt at the pocked wedge of his nose, but he pulls away in time.

The grinning death mask of his face hangs over me, just out of reach. Saliva tickles down my cheek. My nose and mouth are chill with it. I wipe off what I can on my shoulders.

"My son . . ." He hesitates, and in that momentary pause I think I see all the disappointment he felt watching the boy become a man, then his expression reverts back to something obscene. "He was my only son," he says hoarsely. "And you took him away from me. Pain will come. Unimaginable pain. But so will worse things. I like to break men like you. I will reduce you to something that won't even remember the man you used to be."

"I've been there, Lachek. You'll kill me before I break."

He rattles a cough in my face. The foul wetness of his mucus spackles my skin. "How many times do you think I've heard the same pathetic garbage? Everybody is strong at first. Even your father was strong for a few days."

Lachek was an air force guy, like your father . . .

"My father was a hero," I say, because that is what I've always wanted to believe.

"He was a traitor and a coward. I've read his confession. Believe me, you'll experience much, much worse than he did."

He stands erect again, staring, so much malice packed so tightly he seems ready to explode from the pressure. A rush of blood swamps my mind, drowning me in a child's anger and pain, exactly as I'm sure he intended.

"You killed my son like a dog," he says. "And you ruined years of planning. I'm going to make this last forever."

He has destroyed so many in this way that he expects a predictable reaction. Rage, defiance, or, at the other end of the spectrum, terror. The serene expression I plaster on my face is not one of the usual standards. So he pulls out his trump card, stepping back toward the door with a wet smile.

"This doesn't end here, Volk. While I'm working on you I have a man in Dagestan with his nose to the ground. He knows the territory, has friends everywhere. And when he finds your one-legged bitch I'm going to bring her here. I'm going to tear her apart."

I don't twitch. I don't allow the serenity of my expression to dip in the slightest. But Lachek can smell the fear on me the same way I could smell the presence of death in him. He shapes his mouth into an *O* and circles his tongue along the edges of his lips.

"Spend some time thinking about that," he says in a husky voice.

chapter 39

Lachek leaves, but his scent fouls the air behind him. Edorskai, his FSB puppet, barks orders at two uniformed prison guards who come in from the hallway. They cover me with submachine guns while he prepares a syringe.

"Diprivan, Volk." He sticks the needle into a vial filled with a milky liquid and draws back the plunger. "I'm going to knock your ass out. No way will I give you another shot at me. I saw what you did to those poor bastards on the street."

"Who does Lachek have in Dagestan?"

He stops what he's doing for long enough to give me an incredulous stare. "You're going to leave here in pieces. I wouldn't be worried about anything else besides that."

When the syringe is loaded he approaches me cautiously, although I'm securely locked into the chair. Standing well back, he stabs my thigh like a striking snake. He injects the drug and then jerks away so quickly that the tip of the needle breaks off in the muscle and a stream of liquid follows the arc of the broken hypodermic in his fist.

"You're going to wish you had a whole lot more of this stuff, Volk. Trust me, the best time you have left is the time you're passed out."

The drug begins to act within seconds. The world wobbles and turns fuzzy. Edorskai says something to the soldiers, but I can't make out what. One of them inches close and jabs the barrel of his gun into my ribs while Edorskai watches from a distance through his glowing white lenses. When I don't react to the prodding, he edges to my side and says quietly, "His son was just like him. You did the world a goddamn favor." He pulls his face away to make sure I'm still cognizant, then leans back in and says in a dreamlike whisper, "Lachek's man in Dagestan is named Khanzad."

※

I awaken in a windowless stone shaft so cramped that my body is wedged upright against the rough walls. My prosthesis is gone. The feeling is akin to losing a live limb. My right leg is bent crookedly beneath me in a way that doesn't provide support, so my unprotected stump and naked back are grinding into jagged granite.

Pushing against the walls with my hands and elbows, I raise my body like a gymnast working the rings and reposition my right leg so that I can reach the bottom of the pit with my foot. Minutes pass before it's able to take my weight and I can straighten my leg. When I do, the motion tears the skin on my back, but I keep pushing until I'm in a half squat, canted back at an angle that takes the pressure off my stump. All my weight is concentrated on my foot and, with my body stuffed into the tight space, on my knee and back against the sides of the pit, everything joined in an agonizing symphony of pain. My best hope is to hold the position long enough for numbness to set in.

I looked into such a shaft once before, from above, when I was sent to interrogate a prisoner in the cavelike warrens of the lowest levels of the Lubyanka after the Moscow theater crisis in '02. One terrorist survived the gas, although that was never reported, and he had been crammed into one of several holes like this to soften him up. They're like a chimney, less than a meter across, capped by a solid iron lid that allows no light in when it's closed. Some are square. This one is circular—a rough tube of icy stone. My right leg is ankle-deep in freezing muck at the bottom of the shaft. Fetid air forces me to breathe through my mouth.

The Diprivan is holding some of the pain at bay, I think, but I doubt it will last much longer. Worse, claustrophobia chokes me. Not just the jammed confines of the pit, but also the squeezing grip of fear crushing my viscera. Lachek was right, Khanzad will find Valya. They both come from the Gunoi *teip,* and their circles overlap in countless ways. He will know how to find her. It might take time, but Khanzad will find her. The man is a walking plague. He will know how to find Valya . . .

I have to think of other things. I'll suffocate if I don't.

I force my thoughts in another direction, mentally wandering through faded memories. Starting with the father I never knew. I couldn't tell if Lachek was lying about his fate, but however he died I have no way of knowing whether he would have been a father worth having. To me he is like a drawing made with a few bold strokes on white paper, a minimalist image created more by its absence of detail. As a child I longed for an ideal, not flesh and blood, and eventually the empty space was filled by another family, headed by the General.

Maybe that was the wrong family. That's what a rebel fighter once told me—a brave woman close to death. As I recall her words my mind replaces the iciness of the pit with the bitter cold of a glacier in mountainous Dagestan.

chapter 40

I was chugging uphill on the smooth open flow of a Dagestani glacier, a wide tongue of ice and snow spilled down the steep side of a mountain, slogging through four inches of fresh powder, crunching with every other step through the hardpack below. Three thousand meters high, wearing all-white camouflage gear—even the assault rifle slung across my back was painted a blotchy gray and white. My breath ballooned in front of me and hung tinkling in the air as I charged through it, knees pumping high, plowing across the snowfield toward the leading edge of a craggy moraine, where a bulk of dark granite jutted from the snow at a forty-five-degree angle, like the broken bow of a breaching submarine.

Twenty meters away. A lifetime too far.

White puffs erupted just in front of me. Cracking drumbeats of rifle and machine-gun fire seemed to come hours later. I kicked into my highest gear, my legs pistoning madly, knowing I had to disappear or die right there. More white geysers jumped into the air all around me.

Something tugged at the sleeve of my jacket, burned like a branding iron as it passed through.

Five meters to the big outcrop . . . three—

I dived headlong behind a jut of rock and made myself small, my legs on fire from the effort of climbing. Then I flipped onto my stomach and cranked out a few rounds, just to slow them down. Sucked in a few heaving gasps of thin air to quiet the pounding in my ears. Scuttled to my left behind bigger rocks and wriggled deeper into the snow. Then peered through the scope, tracking along the jumbled ice to the ridgeline below the half-kilometer field I had just crossed, and then over to the flanks, where more glacial cracks and scattered deposits of rock provided concealment. Nothing moved.

Drying sweat froze me in an icy sheath. I scrambled to another spot and pressed my back against the stone wall of the outcrop so I could see the rest of the moraine studding up the mountain. Twenty meters away was another outcropping, separated from the one I stood behind by a three-meter split between two deposits of granite. This column of rocks appeared to offer an elevated perch that overlooked my present position, but from where I was I couldn't be sure, and I could see no obvious way to get there without leaving telltale tracks. I scanned the ragged line of stones leading away from my hideaway and found a possible route—a narrow bridge of broken slabs that ended at the split. But the scramble to make it there would be tough and, once there, I might not be able to leap across the gap.

I made another sweep with the scope. Still nothing. Just as I started to pull my eye away a plume of smoke from an RPG launcher appeared behind the cracked ice on my right flank. I hugged the rock face, but the concussion of the burst slammed my head against a sharp edge. Blood poured from my forehead down my cheek, warming icy skin. Several drops of it pocked the snow with crimson. I set my rifle aside. Removed my left glove, pulled out a combat knife, and sliced the heel of my palm cleanly, so the wound could be more easily sewn together later. Then I squeezed my wrist like a tube of toothpaste until the snow all around was bright red. I wiped more blood onto the collar of my snowsuit. Another quick check through the scope showed a flash of movement among the broken ice. As I had expected, the rebel patrol was picking their way up the slope, flanking me.

I stripped off the white suit to my long underwear, packed it with snow, tore off my boots, crampons and all, and stuffed the leg cuffs into the boot tops. Then I arranged the lumpy mass into a shape that resembled a bloody dead man.

I made a quick scan of the rock face as I slung the assault rifle. Leapt as high as I could, caught a three-centimeter ledge with my fingertips, chinned up, and hooked one socked foot on a shaky toehold. From there, clinging like a spider to a wall, I clawed straight up for three meters to a wider ledge. Another explosion blew snow and a hail of rock fragments on me. With the launch of each RPG, all six or seven of them would be charging farther up the mountainside. I lunged up and hooked on to another shelf. My freezing toes slipped and I had to scrabble to keep my grip. Finally, I was able to snag a sharp rock and swing my legs enough to catch my foot on a gnarl of scrub brush and lever myself up and over.

On top of the massive outcrop, plates of upthrust granite made the path to the split resemble the spine of a stegosaurus. Screened from below by the side of the mountain, I wobbled along the ice-slick rocks, arms out to keep my balance. A few shivering minutes later I faced the cleft—almost three meters across at its narrowest. Another RPG blast pounded my recent hideaway.

No chance for a running start. I squatted, then exploded into the air, hung weightless for a sickening moment, then slammed against the unyielding granite on the other side of the chasm. I held there for a while, quivering and breathless, before I was able to catch a heel on the edge and haul myself over the top.

Once there I lay on my back, panting, listening to the rebels stomping around below, very close now. Another grenade cracked the air, mushrooming snow, then one more. Shouted instructions, followed by an argument in a dialect I couldn't follow. But the gist of it was clear enough. A long time had passed since I had fired at them; I was probably dead or badly wounded. But no one wanted to charge into the crosshairs if they guessed wrong.

I used the time to take up a prone position behind a funneled rock formation that made a natural embrasure. Below me, my bloody snowsuit was bunched from the concussion of the grenades, but in the heat of battle I thought it would pass for a body. Excited voices boomed in loud disagreement, amplified by the rocky defile.

An arm appeared at a corner of rock and looped a pull-action grenade into my former hideout. I kept my face buried in the snow as the explosion wasted itself against the rock face and shivered the air above me. Another tossed grenade, then four rebels charged around the outcropping, shouting, firing wildly with a mishmash of weapons—two Kalashnikovs, a bolt-action rifle, and even a pistol. When they spotted my discarded snowsuit, they riddled it with bullets, whooping war cries and screaming curses.

A cold, stony silence followed the cacophony of sound. Clouds of smoke billowed. One of the rebels called out to her comrades, while another fighter approached the bloody suit, which now appeared to be a headless man shot to pieces. I couldn't hear what she said, but the others must have believed the area was clear, because two more of them crept around the rocks and into my former hiding place. Too late the woman shouted at them to go back.

I went to work first on those closest to the edge of the outcrop. The assault rifle spit a hissing band of steel that cut through their close ranks like a scythe. I made one pass, slammed in a fresh magazine, then raked back in the other direction until all of them were down in the blood-spattered snow. I replaced the magazine. Finished the two still moving with carefully placed single shots until only one was still alive— the woman who had led the charge.

She was slowly dragging herself with one arm, laboring to reach a rifle lying half buried in the snow a meter away. Nothing below her waist worked anymore. I scrambled down from my lookout and approached her, keeping a wary eye on the others in case one of them was pretending to be dead. When I drew close to her I picked up the rifle and tossed it away.

Her irises were islands of ceramic brown, the whites showing all around in an expression that was equal parts shock, resignation, and hatred. Blood seeped onto the snow from her lower back through a ragged smock made of white sheets, now mostly red. One arm was trapped beneath her. I checked the others, but nobody was left alive. A pistol had fallen into the snow near the woman—a Makarov. I popped the magazine, emptied it except for one round that I racked into the chamber, and half-buried the gun in the snow just beyond her reach. She would be able to get to it, but only after more hard work when I was safely away. My snowsuit was in rags, but the remnants were better than nothing, so I climbed back into it.

"Abreg will kill you," she said in Russian. She lay still now except for the tremors of shock.

I pulled on one of my boots. "Maybe."

"Why can't you leave our people alone?"

When ready to go, I squatted beside her. "The ghosts of the innocents blown to bits in Pushkin Square won't let me."

"Red Army Day, 1944 . . . you know that date, don't you? Stalin deported . . . every Chechen and Ingush to central Asia and Siberia. For collaborating with the Nazis, he said. Even you . . . you can't believe *that* was anything more than pretext."

Her face had lost all color except for a webbing of blue veins under her left eye.

"New Year's, 1995 . . ." she said. "Russian armored columns assaulted Grozny and eventually killed . . . over a hundred thousand people. Most of them civilians, some ethnic Russians. I could give you a dozen more examples. And *we* are the terrorists? A uniform . . . makes you right?"

Red from the label of a pack of cigarettes peeked from an unbuttoned pocket on the sleeve of her jacket. I removed the pack, shook out a cigarette for her to take with her free hand, and lit it using one of several wooden matches stuck under the plastic wrapper of the pack. She tugged deeply. A growing patch of red snow seemed to be drowning her plaited black hair.

I placed another cigarette and match in the palm of her good hand, then returned the pack to her pocket. She should be able to light the match with her thumb.

"What did you used to be?" I said.

"Teacher." Her lips twisted bitterly as she exhaled a cloud of smoke. "I taught history . . . to children who had no future."

Exhaustion from the running battle and the cold crept through every corner of my body. I thought of Valya and the others, waiting for me, wondering where I was. But they weren't in danger now. I would get back to them soon enough.

"You want me to do it?"

She shook her head no.

I climbed to my feet, both of them bloody and painful but still strong and sure, the fate of the left one almost a year away, and glanced at the Makarov budding from the snow. "You'll be able to reach it?"

She nodded. Closed her eyes. "Why can't you just go home? Leave us in peace."

"The army is my home."

"How sad." Her eyes remained closed, as if to ward off something evil. "Can't you see what . . . what you're doing to the people of this place? Can't you just open your mind for one second . . . and truly *see*?"

I turned away and took off around the outcropping, following the rubble of the moraine into a valley carved by an ancient creep of ice. I would have to stay off the skyline and work the scree-covered terrain for concealment to avoid more patrols. About four hours to reach Valya, I figured, unless I was forced to hide out somewhere along the way.

In not much longer than the time it takes to finish a cigarette, the crack of a single shot echoed off the steep walls of the valley behind me.

chapter 41

The incident on the glacier-capped mountain happened sometime during my last year of fighting. I know that because Valya was so much on
my mind at the time. Episodes like that one have merged into a blurry
tapestry where time has collapsed in on itself, measured only by the
peak moments of violence when fear and adrenaline scored my memory
the deepest. I recall the events now because the shivering chill of my
claustrophobic cell reminds me of the bone-freezing cold during my
long trek back to our camp in the remains of the bloody snowsuit. And
because, if I could go back and talk to her today, I would try to explain
to the dying teacher that we don't choose the family we're born into.

 I'm not sure how long I've been in this hole. More than a day, I
think, maybe all of two, with no food or water. Licking the wet walls
leaves a disgusting gaminess in my mouth. The air is so thick with the
reek of excrement, from me and from previous inhabitants, that I can almost chew it. Something else seems to squirm in the ooze, but in the
darkness I can't see any of the things that share this space with me.

A hollow, scraping sound comes from above, someone sliding the iron grate above me. I'm so cramped I can't even look up. But my time in the pit has finally ended, and I'm grateful for that. Whatever Lachek has planned for me will at least be different, and I won't let it last for very long.

I'll need just one moment of distraction. A slip, a straying gaze, a vulnerable finger to grip, snap, and relieve of a weapon—almost any opening will do. Then I'll take down as many as I can, and if the worst comes to pass I'll turn the gun, or the knife, or whatever comes to my hand, on myself. I know the end game. My tolerance for pain is high, but nobody's is high enough. Dying quickly is infinitely preferable to the alternative.

Bright light fills the pit, even brighter than the shaft that impaled me on the I-beam in the AMERCO building. Something strikes my head. I flinch from the sharp pain and reach for it instinctively. It's one of the metal fittings on a leather harness that flops onto my shoulders.

"Put your head and arms through the loop."

I must be even more addled than I believed possible, because the voice seems familiar. I do as I've been told, creakily, like a man made of rusted iron, even more slowly than I really need to, because the perception of weakness is my ally. The process takes several minutes while I listen to the grumble of voices above me. The leather loop cinches under my arms as I make the jerky ascent, bumping and scraping against the jagged sides of the pit, and then quick, rough hands claw it loose and deposit me on the cold tile.

I pucker my eyes against the pain of the light. Several wavering forms swim in the harsh glare above me. One of them detaches from the others and looms over me, looking down from a great height.

"For fuck's sake, Volk, you look terrible," Brock Matthews says.

chapter 42

Two men dressed like orderlies load me on a stretcher and carry me away. Matthews strolls alongside while another man trails us beyond my vision, the sound of his footfalls the only clue to his presence.

"You found the girl," Matthews says.

"What girl?" The time in the pit has so dulled my senses that for a moment I really can't think of who he's talking about. My mouth is so gummy I can hardly make my tongue work.

"The senator's daughter."

I don't think he knows that I found her. He's guessing. "Where's Lachek? Skinning a puppy?"

We reach an elevator. Its doors ding open and our little group gets in and rides up several stories to a hallway that takes us to a gleaming medical ward. Matthews stands aside while the two orderlies lift me onto a gurney and deliver me to a male nurse who's hairier than Maxim and nearly as big. He scrubs me down roughly, first with soap and water, then with a sterilizing solution that causes my eyes to tear up, followed by plain water again before he pats me dry.

"How long was I in there?" I say to Matthews.

"Today's the fifteenth." He checks his watch. "Almost five in the afternoon. When did they stick you in there?"

More than two and a half days—lost. I wonder if Valya is safe, and if she has found Galina. I wonder whether this is part of what Lachek has planned for me or if someone has truly intervened.

A doctor who looks old enough to have treated Stalin jabs an IV needle into my forearm and starts a drip. Sticks electrodes all over me and attaches wires that lead to a handheld computer. When it begins to hum, he sets it aside and rubs a burning gel into the gash on my knee and the lacerations on my back. Inspects my burns from the AMERCO explosion without comment and then slathers ointment on them with a gloved hand.

"Where's my foot?"

The ancient doctor ignores me. He fiddles with a dial on the IV tube. Claps a blood pressure cuff around my other arm and listens to my pulse, the diaphragm of the stethoscope cold against the crook of my elbow. He notes something on a chart. Uses the stethoscope on my chest and listens for a moment.

"We'll get your foot for you, Volk," Matthews says. "But first we need to find Charlie." He's standing to one side. I would have to strain if I wanted to see him.

"I can't help you with only one leg."

"Help us or go back to Lachek. Your choice."

The doctor attaches a pulse oximeter to the end of my finger. Scribbles on the chart again. Sticks a probe into my ear. Checks my pupils with a small flashlight. Makes more notes. Stabs a needle into my shoulder.

"What's an NSA operative doing in the Lubyanka?"

Matthews doesn't answer. Just waits in the corner off to the side while the doctor methodically checks me over for broken bones, pressing my ribs, working my arms and legs, pulling back my lips to check my teeth. This must be the *before* picture. I still can't see who else is in the room with us.

The doctor uses forceps to remove the splinter of the needle Edorskai left in my thigh. I had forgotten it. He regards it without interest for a moment before flinging it into a silver waste bucket. Then he turns away to read a paper printout from his handheld device, nods once, rips off the sticky leads he attached earlier, gathers his equipment, and leaves.

Matthews moves close to me. He's wearing too much of a spicy cologne. "What about Charlie, Volk?"

"How did you talk me out of Lachek's clutches?"

Just as he seems about to respond harshly, he thinks better of it. He looks behind him and then steps aside as another figure approaches my gurney, moving without haste.

Thinning gray hair parted on the left. Sad eyes that droop at the corners, webbed by worry lines. Dentures or caps for teeth, straight and white. A nose that's been broken more than once, probably a long time ago, because although he may have been a featherweight brawler at one time I would label him a thinker now. He's wearing a rumpled, coffee-colored suit that's a size too large and a frayed white shirt. His open collar exposes a wattled neck that looks hollow beneath chevrons of hanging skin.

"Do you know who I am, Colonel?" He talks in a whispery rasp that sounds painful, as though metal shavings are ripping apart his throat.

"Yes," I say, because I do, although we've never met and until a moment ago I assumed he was dead. Legend says that his vocal cords were fried by liquid fire when he was captured during a Sino-Soviet border clash in the late '60s and someone forced his head back and poured flaming brandy down his throat.

The name Constantine is common enough. Standing alone, without the companionship of a patronymic or surname, however, the appellation conjures something that's more myth than man. Constantine occupied—

occupies, I mentally correct myself—a post in our government somewhere in the rarefied air where rank and political appointments are meaningless. He has outlasted premiers and presidents from Stalin to Putin.

I recall again the scene of missiles rolling in parade through Red Square past Soviet dignitaries standing on the steps next to Lenin's tomb. Somewhere in that tableau is a nondescript man hovering near the shoulder of the most powerful politician, within earshot of the commanders of air, naval, and ground forces, a whisper away from the head of the secret police—Beria, Andropov, Putin—a place where he has resided for nearly half a century, always in the eye of the political storm.

He says, "I need you to tell this man where Charlene Thomas is being held."

"I'm not going to say a word about her until I'm sure Valya Novaskaya is safe. Safe from you, from the Americans, from everybody."

Matthews shifts his weight. Constantine changes his expression not at all, just thrusts out his chin to open a pathway for his words. "As long as you cooperate, we won't harm her. But we cannot guarantee her safety. She puts herself in danger."

"What's that supposed to mean?"

"She is south, in the cauldron. Some of the people she's with are members of the failed confederation. They're negotiating with warlords, opposition and friendly governments, military commanders—anybody who will listen to them—and she is in the middle of it."

Constantine's expression is flat, without judgment, like an indifferent god's. He might have just told me that Valya was spending her time restoring a painting at the Pushkin Museum of Fine Arts. Nevertheless, I don't believe his act.

Lachek is ass-deep in the cesspool of the explosion at the AMERCO building, the video, and the egg. He is an operative, executing stratagems developed by others, and he has grown rich and mighty doing it. But I was wrong to think he was the powerful man Valya was referring to when she said that Abreg was rumored to have made a strategic alliance. Constantine is that man.

Constantine occupies an international stage. From deep in the background he pushes colored pins into maps that show existing and proposed refineries, power grids, and pipelines; adds and subtracts the names on a chart showing political appointments, including those of the Russian regional government in Chechnya; negotiates missile treaties with NATO, China, and North Korea. He probably has some self-laudatory strategic objective in mind to rationalize what he has done, but Constantine is the one who has crawled into bed with Russia's enemies in the Caucasus. I know it as surely as if he had told me himself.

"Charlene Thomas?" he prompts.

I tell them the address of the dingy flat in Kitay-Gorod where I found Charlie, less than a kilometer from where we are now, knowing they'll find nobody there but trying to buy time. Matthews makes a call on his cell phone and holds an urgent conversation with his back to us. Constantine watches him for a moment, then he lifts a hand to his throat as if to adjust a nonexistent tie.

"I understand you have made inquiries at the interior ministry archives, and that you have been questioning our Chinese friends. Stop."

"So I'm done here?"

He clears his throat with a sound like gravel being drawn through a flex-steel hose. "I have use for you."

"General Nemstov commands me."

"Not anymore."

The depth of the emptiness I feel at the thought the General might be dead surprises me.

"The General has not been relieved," he says, as though reading my mind. "You are on loan."

"To you or him?" I point at Matthews, who's still busy on his phone.

Constantine juts his chin again to unlock the mangled pipe in his neck. "Why do you think the AMERCO building was attacked?"

"Because Abreg is an animal."

The vellumlike skin of his face crinkles, conveying a sense of disappointment without a change of expression. "Rise above your station, Colonel."

"Meaning you want me to buy into the psychobabble about terrorists' motives?"

"Look deeper. Ask yourself, why this *particular* building? Why *now*?"

"Save me the trouble." I'm playing dumb because I'm unsure what he knows about AMERCO, Kombi-Oil, the egg, and the video—all that the General and I have talked about. The General is many things, some of them wicked, but I trust him far more than the specter standing before me.

"You know enough to reach your own conclusions."

He raises his hand toward his throat. I think the gesture is an unconscious acknowledgment of pain, real or remembered. He studies me in a way that few men have, comfortable enough with silence that he doesn't need to fill it with words. His long look reminds me of the one the General gave me when I stood shivering before him in the yard at Isolator-5.

"Money and oil," he says. "Those things are not unimportant. People like your *mafiya* friend Maxim, and your patron, the General, will always kill for them. But they are not the things that drive men like us, Volk. We exist to protect this country."

Noble words, but I think they amount to just another brick in his wall of lies sealed with the mortar of half-truths. He knows me, or he thinks he does. He's probably seen every one of the dozens of psych profiles I've been administered since childhood. The man revealed by those psychological renderings cares little about oil, money, or political power, or even the prospect of Russia's international prestige destroyed by the raw footage of a wartime atrocity. That man is driven by a visceral need to protect his country and her people. But all those profiles mapped the mind of a man who never suffered from doubt. That man has ceased to exist.

Matthews ends his call, pockets his phone, and moves to Constantine's side.

"What are we protecting the country from?" I say. "The outcry if the Starye Atagi video lands on the world stage?"

Constantine swallows with difficulty. "The video? That, too, is important, but it is manageable, no matter what happens. We have far bigger concerns. Tell him, Mr. Matthews."

Matthews looks from Constantine to me. He seems even more tightly wound than usual.

"December 18, 2006," he recites. "Eighteen containers loaded with three hundred and twenty-six kilos of enriched uranium that had been used to fuel an East German research reactor left Dresden on an Ilyushin seventy-six cargo plane bound for the Podolsk processing center. Two hundred and sixty-eight kilos were *highly* enriched—weapons grade. Every gram was weighed and cataloged. Each piece of uranium was placed into stainless steel tubes, then those containers were packed in transport casks with walls about two inches thick."

He pauses to give me time to absorb that, his gaze penetrating as he searches for the cues that tell him I understand the significance of what I'm hearing.

"Highly enriched uranium," he repeats. "Good for bomb making. Once in Podolsk, all of it was supposed to be mixed with low-grade uranium so it wouldn't be a proliferation risk."

I remember reading about the transfer, the largest of many made as part of a joint U.S.-Russian program designed to keep nuclear materials out of the hands of terrorists.

"So?"

"Abreg tried to hijack three casks. Fifty kilos, enough to make a bomb big enough to 'deter the Russian animal.' "

"No fucking way."

"You're right, he failed." Matthews puts his fists in his pockets and pulls his jacket tight. "But not for lack of planning or ingenuity. Oil for food was the tip of an iceberg of corruption, Volk. When it ended, many people needed to supplement their income. Abreg knew this. He cultivated more contacts than you want to imagine, and he damn near pulled it off. You would be surprised how easily. False journal entries, phony manifests, bribes to people who are paid next to nothing—suddenly three drums never existed. If it had worked, nothing would have been missing on either end of the transfer. How do the people with ledger books and computerized inventories account for a figment?"

"But it didn't work?"

"No," Constantine rasps. He puts on a shapeless overcoat, heavy and blotchy, worn by time, rain, and snow. "Not this time."

He lets those words hang in the air. He's manipulating me, working off the old psych profiles, but his ploy succeeds, because the prospect of weapons-grade nuclear material in the hands of a man like Abreg is enough to start my heart racing.

"The essence of your mission has not changed, Colonel," Constantine whispers. "The mountains still beckon. Abreg is calling for you. No one else but you, he says. He also wants the American girl, for protection. He knows her through her terrorist boyfriend, Ravi Kho, and he thinks nobody will drop missiles on him as long as she's near. So you will go, just as you and the General had planned, and Charlene Thomas and Mr. Matthews will go with you. We will not"—he struggles to swallow—"we will *not* lose track of her."

The meaning of that is not lost on me, nor is the opportunity it presents. I need to call the General as soon as I can get a phone. "On whose authority am I acting?"

He works his chin and neck again. "Proceed the way you always do. Use your wits. Do whatever must be done."

"What about the Americans?"

He glances at Matthews. "They are here to help." He says this as only a Russian can, without irony. "Work together."

And then he's out the door and gone without a sound.

chapter 43

Matthews checks his phone for a message and immediately flips it closed. Disappointment flashes across his face, then disappears just as quickly. "How old is that guy?" His voice sounds loud after Constantine's hoarse whisper.

"Where's Lachek?"

"No idea." He glances at the doorway through which Constantine just left. "Man, that fossil can still bite. I've never seen so many people trying to please someone so fast."

I sit up on the gurney, joints cracking, a dull ache throbbing through my whole body. "How did you connect with him?"

Matthews sticks his hands into the pockets of his jacket and wings it open with an elaborate shrug. "My boss says to meet someone at Lubyanskaya Square. Constantine shows up, and we march across the street and in here like he owns the place, which from the looks of things he does."

"Where's my foot?"

"The doc went to get it."

"You ever heard of a guy named Marko Hutsul?"

The skin around his eyes tightens. "That's right, you don't know, do you?"

"Someone forgot to drop a newspaper into my hole. Know what?"

"Marko Hutsul ate three bullets yesterday in Kiev."

The doctor returns, carrying my prosthesis, so clean it must have been autoclaved, along with my laundered clothes, all of which he dumps on the gurney next to me.

"Like room service at the National, Doc," I say, checking for the knife and attaching my foot.

Just when I'm convinced he's a master at ignoring me he gives me a level stare. "You're healthy. Probably live to be a hundred, unless somebody kills you first. I'm taking odds on the latter."

Matthews chuckles. "You make friends wherever you go, huh, Volk?"

The doctor leaves, and I finish dressing, the shoulder holster last before my coat. "My gun?"

Matthews pulls my Sig from the pocket of his overcoat and expertly spins it around to present it butt first. The weight tells me it's been reloaded after I emptied it during the firefight, but I check the magazine to be sure, then slot the weapon in the holster under my arm.

He hands me my cell phone, spare magazine, and my usual roll of bills wrapped by a rubber band. The cell is charged and the magazine full.

"You carry lots of cash. You should be more careful. Moscow is a dangerous place."

I pocket everything except the phone. He watches while I dial, and I can still feel his gaze when I turn my back on him, willing Valya to answer, but her phone rings without end. I end the call.

"I have to talk to someone here before we go."

"You can't go after Lachek now."

"Not him. An FSB agent named Edorskai."

228 / Brent Ghelfi

"Why?"

"I need to arrange for someone to watch my dog while we're away."

"Fuck you," he says, but he unclips his phone and thumbs in a long series of numbers. Murmurs into the mouthpiece briefly, then closes the phone. A few minutes later a man in a suit leads us down several flights and through a door to a hallway bathed in fluorescent light. We march past a procession of offices fit for lawyers or accountants, surreal after the hellish conditions in the pit below us. The trip takes longer than it should because my body feels disjointed, as though the impulses from my mind to my limbs are on a split-second delay.

We're left alone in a conference room. Matthews leans against a wall. I do the same.

"If this is a revenge thing, forget it," he says a few minutes later.

"It's not revenge."

Lachek is going to have to wait. If I get the chance I'm going to take my time with him. First I'm going to find out what he really knows about my father, and then I'm going to make him suffer. He thinks whatever is eating him up from the inside is the worst thing that can happen to him. I intend to show him how wrong he is. Right now, however, I have to make sure the dog chasing Valya is called off the hunt.

Matthews makes a call, then another. I think he's inquiring about the search for Charlie. While he's talking, I speed-dial the General.

"Constantine wants to send Charlie to the mountains with me," I whisper when he answers.

He grunts, indicating that he already knows.

I picture Charlie's wounded forearm, puckered, jagged scars running vertically from the base of her palm toward the crook of her elbow, stitches still in place. A doctor will be able to restitch her skin using the original holes, so the wound won't look fresh. "Rig a transmitter. Only you and I can know the frequency. Implant it in her forearm beneath the razor cuts. Then give her up to the Americans."

The General grunts again, this time in a satisfied way, and disconnects.

A few minutes later, Matthews finishes his latest call and snaps his cell phone closed. "She's not there, goddamn it." He strides closer to me, jaws clenched. "My people say the place looks like it was raided. What do you know about that?"

I return his hard stare. "She'll turn up."

"How do you know?" he says, then he backs away as the door opens suddenly.

Edorskai is escorted inside by the same two guards who covered me while he shot Diprivan into my thigh. How quickly our roles have reversed. He looks around the room for allies. His gaze slides past Matthews without seeming to recognize him.

"Listen, Volk, I have nothing against you." As the words tumble out he lifts his hands, palms up like a beggar, imploring me to believe him. "Lachek says boo, I jump. So do about a thousand other guys. It was just my turn in the box."

"Tell me about Lachek and Khanzad."

"What?" At first he seems genuinely puzzled, then his eyeballs go up and down as though he's clicking a computer mouse to find a stored memory. "I don't have anything to do with—"

My expression stops him. The two guards stand at attention, blocking the door, carefully not hearing a thing. They will park a bullet in Edorskai's skull at a word from me, just as they would have blown a round through mine if he had ordered it before. Matthews leans against the wall and picks a thumbnail, seemingly absorbed in the task, but I saw his eyes narrow when he heard the false Chechen's name.

"Look," Edorskai says. "Everyone knows that Khanzad rolls over for money. The guy's for sale. I can't tell you how many times Lachek has bartered with him. All I know is he figured out you have someone there you care about and he sicced Khanzad on her."

"Call him off."

He makes a huffing sound and holds out his palms again. "I can't do that. I don't even have a way to get in touch with the guy. Everything went through Lachek, and he's gone. He got the word from the old man and he was out of here so fast nobody saw him leave."

Matthews believes him, apparently; he straightens as though he's ready to go, and jerks on his jacket to make it sit right on his shoulders. The tension seems to drain from the guards.

Maybe I'm not thinking clearly. I'm still in pain, still trying to recover from the psychic roller coaster of the pit. One minute I was staring an awful death in the face, the next I'm here, a conscript in Constantine's manipulative shadow war. Whether I'm disoriented or not, however, I think Edorskai knows more than he's telling me.

I take two casual steps closer to him, gently catch his wrist and twist it behind him with one hand, then slam the back of his elbow with the heel of my other hand. His joint pops out. He screams. His knees buckle, but I'm still holding his wrist so all his weight falls on the dislocated joint, and his scream turns into an agonized bellow.

"Jesus Christ, Volk!" Matthews rushes over but I stop him with a look. The guards jerk back to attention, eyes forward.

I press the heel of my hand against Edorskai's unhinged elbow and he shrieks some more until I release the pressure slightly. "Where is Lachek?" I have to shout into his ear so that he can hear me through the sound of his own screams.

"East! He'll go to Asia!"

"Where in Asia?"

"I don't fucking know!"

I apply more pressure. It's like raising the volume on Satan's stereo. "Where is Khanzad?" I shout.

"I can get a number! I have it on my phone! In my office!"

I nod to one of the guards and he rushes out of the room. I release Edorskai's twisted arm and he crumples to the floor, sobbing loudly. He's still whimpering when the guard returns minutes later and places his phone in his good hand. He scrolls through the menu, then reads out the twelve digits for a satellite phone while I key them into the Nokia. Someone answers in a guttural dialect.

"Get me Khanzad."

A minute passes in silence broken only by Edorskai's wet breathing.

"Who's this?" says a voice in Russian.

"Volk. If you hurt Valya Novaskaya I'll carve you up."

"Volk!" Khanzad says as though we're long-lost friends. "Just the man I've been wanting to talk to. Do you want to buy an Imperial egg? Mint condition, except it's missing a pendant."

"Do not hurt Valya," I say slowly, emphasizing each word.

"It seems we have many mutual acquaintances," he says in the same genial tone. "One of them calls himself Abreg. The lone outlaw, that name means, did you know that? A man to be admired and feared. He is to have a meeting with you, I'm told. But he would feel much safer if he had a bit of security. So I've been trying to arrange something with Valya. I have my sights on her, so to speak."

I turn my back on the room and lean my forehead against the wall.

"Suddenly you're not so talkative," Khanzad says genially. "Don't worry, I won't harm her. After all, we're from the same village."

And he hangs up.

chapter 44

Matthews and I leave the Lubyanka through a back door tucked next to a heavily guarded portal big enough to drive a truck through, closed during off hours by enormous steel doors that protect the place like the portcullis of a fortress. No snow. The night is clear and cold, with a wind that works through the seams in our clothes like the frostbitten fingers of a witch. My bones ache from the chilled, cramped confines of the pit.

"What the fuck was that all about?" Matthews says.

I call Valya again. No answer.

"Charlie will be out soon," I say. "Have you arranged transportation to Tindi?"

"You've had her the entire time?" When I don't respond he says, "We can leave on two hours' notice."

We're crossing Lubyanskaya Square near the inscribed Solovetsky stone slab, on our way to Vadim's Café, when my cell phone vibrates. I don't recognize the number, but answer anyway.

"Where have you been, Volk?" Barokov says in a tone that sounds more distraught than irritated.

"Why?"

"We got a problem at a warehouse. Your warehouse."

Matthews eyes me. I turn away. "What kind of problem?"

"We found a body," Barokov says. "It's . . . well, we need you here."

✴

Throbbing lights, red and blue mixed with pulsing yellow, wash the high walls of my warehouse. I snap police tape and tear free from the grip of a cop who grabs my arm, ignoring his offended "Hey!" Jostle past a medical crew that appears to have nothing to do and muscle my way into a circle of talking heads just outside the main entrance. Barokov stops mid-sentence when he sees me.

"Volk—"

"What happened here?"

"Wait a second, calm down—"

Shouldering him roughly aside, I bull through the crowd to the metal door, which stands ajar, guarded by a cop as wide as he is tall. When he makes a grab for me, I catch his arm, jerk him closer, and pile-drive my fist into his belly. He drops away as I gather steam into the white blare of studio spots that light a stage set to look like a Roman bath. Nobody's here. I hurry past more empty sets, through the side door and down the hallway lined with webcam rooms, all the way to the end, where two more cops guard the door of Alla's office. One of them draws his automatic while the other talks on the radio, and just as I arrive he claps a hand on his partner's gun, relaying a message that causes them both to stand aside before I have to pummel them.

I charge through the doorway.

Cream carpet, mahogany furniture, the Kandinsky print—blues, oranges, yellow, and a pastel pink the color of watered-down blood. Just like the blood splashed on the wall in feathery arcs.

The plush couch and chairs and coffee table in front of her desk have been pushed aside to make room for Alla's sprawled form. I drop to my knees at her side, plunging them into pooled blood, captivated by the sightless gaze of her sea-green eyes. I can't breathe. A lump the size of a hand grenade in my throat dissolves into something that feels like ground glass and acid.

Someone crouches beside me. "I'm sorry, Colonel," says a voice from far away. Barokov, showing his humanity.

Mango and strawberries. The fragrance of Alla's still warm candles makes me want to weep for the loss. For the utter waste. But I'm too emotionally drained. I don't even have the capacity for such a simple act as that. And I can't bear to look at her, certainly not as closely as I would have to if I was investigating her death. But an investigation would be a wasted effort. I know who killed her. I just don't know how bad he made it for her.

"Was she . . . ?"

Barokov avoids my eyes. "We won't know for sure until after the autopsy." He stands tall now, his habit when he delivers bad news. "But from the look of things, yes."

"Okay," I say into a wellspring of pain so deep I can't see my way out of it. "Okay, I get it."

"What?" Barokov says. "I couldn't hear you."

After a while, Barokov turns away from me and starts hollering orders at the herd of cops gathered in the hall outside the door. My vision clears. I'm kneeling in more of Alla's blood. The patterns of it on the floor map the progress of her losing battle with her killer. Matthews stands silently in the doorway wearing a bleak expression, overcoat across his arm, hands buried in the pockets of his jacket. This may be the first unguarded moment he's had in my presence—certainly the only one of mine in his—and for the first time I don't dislike him for his smug American certitude, a gift purchased with the blood of the generations who came before him. Because he's here now, by choice, one of those men who are the first to die, and he may even be my ally, which means he is likely to be dead soon.

"Lachek did this," I say to him, my voice echoing strangely in my head. Pulling myself to my feet is harder now than it was after the explosion in the AMERCO building blew me into the air.

Barokov is looking at me. "You know who killed her?"

"The person who did this wanted revenge against me. His name is Filip Lachek. You can't touch him."

One of the cops who had been guarding the door trots into the room and starts talking excitedly. While Barokov tends to him I locate Maxim's number in the call history of the Nokia and punch the button to dial, hoping it's one he's still using. Someone answers without saying anything.

"It's Volk," I say.

"You're not dead." Maxim's voice is so deep that the inflection rarely changes, but if I wasn't so sure that he is bereft of all emotion, I would describe his tone as relieved.

"I'm ready for my lesson in politics."

His breathing sounds like a train huffing up a long grade. His mind is fast, but apparently he has lots of decisions to make about me. Barokov stands on the other side of Alla's splayed body, still issuing orders. Matthews is watching me.

"I'm at the Baltschug Kempinski," Maxim says finally. "Bring your American friend."

He ends the call.

"Who was that?" Barokov says. "And who is this person Filip Lachek you say I can't touch?"

I return the Nokia to the pocket of my jacket and regard him. He wears the familiar earnest look that seems to be so much a part of him. "Just stay out of my way, Inspector. I'm not following the rules on this."

I shove past him, dodge Matthews, and charge off down the long hallway.

"I don't think you ever follow the rules, Volk!" Barokov yells at my back.

I stride past the stage sets, stiff-arm the coded metal door, and step into the cold outside. Stop there for a moment with my hands on my knees, dizzy, a loud buzzing in my ears. Then I start walking. As I go, I try to imagine that I'm carrying Alla's smell of spring with me, lodged deep inside my mind, but the truth is that I'm leaving it behind forever, and with every step my grief turns to fury.

chapter 45

The Baltschug Kempinski lies across the Moscow River to the south of the Kremlin, yellow with white trim, manned by greatcoated doormen wearing spotless gloves and professional smiles that freeze at the sight of me: bloodstained pants, pallor from two grim days in the hole, feral blaze in my eyes. They stand aside without a word as I barrel past and enter the lobby, where two of Maxim's bodyguards await. The guards lead me into a coat-check room and are in the middle of a weapons search when Matthews joins me.

"Do you know who we're here to see?" I ask him in English as they spread his legs and raise his arms.

"Maxim Abdullaev. Azeri mob. Food distribution, arms, drugs, prostitution. Soon to be the part owner of Kombi-Oil, one of the world's largest privately held energy consortiums."

He stands like a crucified man while one of the goons pats him down ankles to armpits and the other one wands him with a metal detector. They relieve him of a Beretta, a switchblade, and some finely crafted lock-picking tools hidden in a fancy gold pen. Along with our two lumbering escorts, we get into the elevator for the ride to the penthouse suite.

"How did Maxim get a piece of Kombi-Oil?" I ask. "Three shots to Hutsul's head?"

"I'm sorry about the woman back there," he says.

"Yeah." I concentrate on the numbers lighting above the elevator door.

"We got Charlie," he says.

"Uh-huh."

"Maxim formed a new joint venture group that bought into Kombi-Oil's action," he says, finally getting around to my question. "His new group is called Avisopor. I've never seen an organization move so damned fast in my life—like fucking General Electric."

I'm struck by the ironic name of Maxim's new prize. Forged *avisos*, promissory notes, were used by ethnic mafia groups, including the Chechen and Azeri mafias, to siphon billions of Soviet rubles from the Central Bank in the early '90s. They bribed Russian bank officials, then traded the worthless *avisos* for cash that quickly disappeared into the ether of wire transfers and tax-haven banks. The architects of these schemes were called *vosdushniki,* or "air men," who could create money out of nothing.

"Who are the members?" I don't need him to answer. I think I already know.

"Let's just say it has an international flavor."

"America? China?" And no doubt two major Russian players, at least: Maxim and the General are going to join Constantine, who I'm almost certain already had his part wired together a long time ago. For all his talk about the noble goals that drive him, Constantine has been in the oil mix from the beginning and is just now deciding who else to deal into the game. None of that matters to me. I want to protect Valya, avenge Alla, and catch Semerko before he ruins Galina. And I need to stop Abreg from ever acquiring enough uranium to kill even more Russians than he already has. Let the others have their oil and their money.

Matthews says nothing more as we finish the elevator ride. The bodyguards lead us into another of Maxim's lavish suites, this one with wide views of the Kremlin, the Moscow River, and the Cathedral of the Assumption. The big Azeri makes us wait in the main room for several minutes, probably while he listens to a translation of what we just said in the elevator. When Maxim rolls into the room, Matthews sucks a quick breath, emitting a slight whistle that I would have missed if I wasn't standing right next to him. The sight of the man tends to do that to the uninitiated, even those who have seen him in pictures.

Maxim clips a Partagas as Mei floats out of the room he just came from, wearing a gray suit that makes her look like a banker. She flicks a lighter that jets blue flame, which the giant bends toward to puff the cigar to life.

"General Electric?" Maxim says to no one in particular. "I like that."

Matthews doesn't react to the news of Maxim eavesdropping on us. He probably guessed as much.

"America and Russia fight Islam while the fucking Chinese conquer the world," Maxim says, inspecting the ash of his Partagas appreciatively. "But they're finally getting smart."

He offers us both a cigar and a cutter but not seats. I decline the cigar. Mei lights Matthews's when it's ready. Then she walks over to stand near me and says quietly, "I'm sorry about Alla. We knew you were in danger, but not her."

"You understand the politics now, Volk?" Maxim says from across the room.

"Some, but not all."

Another puff, then he flicks ash onto the carpet. "You tell him, America," he says to Matthews, who has found himself an ashtray.

Matthews takes a moment to consider his words.

"The Americans and Chinese want—*need*—guaranteed access to Russia's oil and gas. Europe, too, but most of the infrastructure is already there. Lots of production-sharing agreements were signed in the early years, but not enough. Rampant corruption, the Kremlin's fear of giving away the riches of the motherland, the *chinovniki*—the bureaucrats—all that and more has been standing in the way. We kept thinking things would change once Putin tightened his grip on things over here, and they did, but not in the way we expected. The Russian energy sector operates under a new model, now, one predicated on total state control."

Matthews draws on his cigar. I realize that he is higher in the food chain of American intelligence than I had thought.

"We need a new framework. The private sector—companies like Kombi-Oil, as it's recently been reconstituted—needs to play a key role developing resources and infrastructure. The Kremlin has to ensure investment stability and recognize property rights."

The room has filled with smoke. Mei glides to a couch near one of the windows and sits with her legs crossed, one knee on top of the other, looking down at St. Basil's. Maxim growls, eager for Matthews to get on with the story.

"The Kremlin wants to deal," he says abruptly. "It wants into the WTO. It wants support for how it handles breakaway republics. And it wants America to stop expanding NATO and stop parking missiles and missile defense systems on Russia's borders."

"Relations have gone bad," Matthews says, talking faster now. "Iraq, Iran, North Korea, Venezuela, South Georgia, Ukraine, Poland—lots of territory for disagreement between us. Putin hates America's unilateralism and wants Russia to be a counterweight in the world. We hate Putin's insistence on sending weapons and nuclear technology to psychotics and dictators. Then came the AMERCO explosion."

He pauses. Narrows his eyes.

"Some people thought America could be intimidated, but the effect was the opposite. We knew who had targeted AMERCO—and it wasn't the goddamn Chechens—and we figured out who had abducted Charlie, even if we didn't know where to find her. That gave us leverage to force the Kremlin's hand, and to show Constantine why he could make better partners than the ones he had. Suddenly, they *wanted* to negotiate. But there's only so much oil. If we're in, others get squeezed out. In this case, a faction led by Hutsul, Lachek, and some of the other owners of Kombi-Oil."

I don't have the complete picture, but I can see enough of it to guess what happened next. AMERCO, China National Petroleum Company, and Avisopor, Maxim's new company, were allowed in, while the old guard members of Kombi-Oil were kicked out. The perfect play for the Kremlin—strategic partners gained at the cost of expendable players. Like a rich man dumping his first wife for a platinum version twenty years younger.

Maxim points the red tip of his cigar at me. "You get it now?"

"Lachek's group blew the AMERCO building?"

"Him and Hutsul," Maxim says matter-of-factly, as though Russians blowing up Russians is perfectly natural. "To make the Americans back down."

"Like Ryazan."

"Close enough," Matthews says. "Lachek planned it, and Hutsul—he had access to AMERCO's offices—planted the bombs."

"Who killed Hutsul?" I say.

Maxim angles his gaze toward Matthews, who blows out a stream of smoke that rises in a curled cloud over his head. "We can't let people blow up our buildings and kill American citizens without retaliating," Matthews says.

"Uh-huh. Don't you have a saying about unintended consequences?"

"You're going to sing in *that* choir? Give me a break."

Maxim grunts. "People respect power," he says, ending the argument. "America is finally learning that lesson." He jerks his head toward the door behind him. "Follow me, Volk."

He leads me through the door he and Mei had emerged from earlier. The room was intended to be a bedroom, but most of the furniture has been replaced with a bank of computer monitors on a long table. Several screens show charts and stock scrolls from markets that could be anywhere in the world. Two men busily key data while another one watches the projection from several cameras on a divided screen, and as we come in he clicks a mouse to enlarge a view of the room we just left, where Matthews is now sitting on the couch and talking to Mei. We continue on to an adjoining bedroom and Maxim shuts the door behind me.

"How long have you been working with the Chinese?" I say.

"A year. Hard for the last three months, when I realized I needed a big partner. Lots of politics and economics go into deciding where to put new pipes."

He joined forces with the Chinese about the time Mei came to Moscow.

Confirming the direction of my thoughts, Maxim says, "They approached me through the woman. I am weak that way. You too."

"I don't have that weakness."

"For one woman you do."

I gaze out the window at a barge hauling coal up the Moscow River.

"Oil, politics, money—you don't care about that bullshit," Maxim says matter-of-factly.

I turn back to face him. "No, I don't."

"But you can help us settle things in the mountains. You're good at that, the best."

The General, Constantine, Maxim—and, in his own way and for different reasons, Barokov—all telling me to go to the same place.

"I heard about Alla," Maxim says.

I don't respond, just look over his shoulder at a pastel watercolor of a girl and boy sitting in a boat on a pond.

"Who did it?"

"Lachek."

He nods. "You need help?"

Alla will be laid out on cold stainless steel in the coroner's office by now, ready for the saw. "Yes. I need you to find him for me. I'll do the rest."

He regards the end of his cigar grimly, then flicks the ash onto the carpet. "Done."

chapter 46

The road we take toward the village of Tindi is little more than twin ruts that crawl along the base of the high mountains—Allah's mountains, jagged peaks and carved valleys thrown into deep shadow by the angle of the morning sun. Home to highlanders, known as *gortsy,* as varied as any people on earth, speaking a babel of languages but sharing a thousand years of warrior culture. The multipurpose truck we were assigned last night in Khankala, a military base on the eastern edge of Grozny, is a six-wheeled Ural-4324-49 painted camouflage gray and green. Twelve tons of groaning metal, patched and primer-coated in places, rusted in others. Its passage tears the mist that clings to the ground all around us, leaving a livid wound in our wake.

The back compartment holds slatted-steel benches bearing only remnants of torn foam padding and bolted into a grooved steel deck, upon which Matthews has fallen asleep at my feet, half covering a rust-colored stain that might be dried blood. A canvas tarp stretched over a metal frame does nothing to keep the cold from biting. Charlie huddles under filthy military-issue blankets on the bench across from me, shivering, propped against a metal tank sloshing with extra diesel fuel.

A hole cut in the back of the cab lets us see ahead through the smeared front windshield, where the brooding massifs of the Caucasus loom. Our driver is a wiry Russian from Nazran clenching a cold pipe in his teeth. He wears a cap with an orange oriole on the front. Next to him on the bench seat is our guide, a bearded mountain man clothed in an Astrakhan fur hat with earflaps and a sergeant's greatcoat with the patches of its former owner ripped off the shoulders.

Three hours into the drive we roll out of the flatland and into the first ridges of the mountains. One after another false summits appear and then fall behind us as we wind higher on switchbacks so tight the driver needs the reverse gear to negotiate them. Bare rocks and scrub brush give way to oak, hornbeam, beech, birch, and pine, and still we serpentine upward in a haze of eye-watering exhaust fumes. Patches of snow fill the spaces between the trees, white on brindled brown and black.

The engine coughs, misses a few beats, and then grumbles at a lower pitch as the driver downshifts to grind up a particularly steep section. Icy wind buffets the canopy, and the terrain gradually becomes whiter, the snow spreading like a slow stain on the ground. More twisting turns take us into sodden clouds like dropped curtains, and the world closes in around us.

Ten hours have passed since Matthews and I left Maxim at the Baltschug Kempinski. We went to the café to pick up my things and then met a car at the American embassy and sped to Moscow's Zhukovsky air base. Charlie was already there, as demanded by Abreg. We hopped a Sixty-first Air Army Il-76 cargo plane to Budennovsk, a town in the Stavropol region of southern Russia best known as the place where Chechen rebels stormed police and administrative buildings and herded more than 1,500 prisoners into the hospital building. Six days later a cease-fire was negotiated—a capitulation unprecedented in the history of the Soviet state and the Russian Federation—

and the terrorists were allowed to escape. The first Chechen war ended when peace accords were signed in August 1996 at Khasavyurt, a name that came to symbolize Russian weakness, at least in the minds of many in the Kremlin.

From Budennovsk we loaded into a Mi-8 transport helicopter and then watched the ground pass beneath our feet through old bullet holes, small rings of silver framing snippet views of the flowing brown landscape as we thumped our way to the Khankala base. There, after a meal of mutton stacked in rice, we boarded our six-wheeled truck and headed south and east, skirting Vedeno, the birthplace of many terrorists and a crossroad in the battle for Chechnya, and eventually worked our way into the mountains and the wet clouds.

Morning dissolves into afternoon. Charlie falls asleep, her head bouncing against Matthews's shoulder as the truck heaves and lurches like a ship in rough seas. After more countless turns a crystalline village rears into view. The flat-roofed wooden and brick buildings look like the discarded toy blocks of a child clinging to the steep mountainside, sucked into the snow. A minaret powers up out of the shimmering whiteness and into the pale blue sky—a russet column capped with a polished-steel dome that gleams in the sunlight.

We bounce along the outskirts of the village, a tooth-jarring slog around a hodgepodge of sheds, lean-tos, and huts from which bundled people emerge to stare curiously. Our route takes us higher, until we are above the village center, looking down into crowded courtyards, every part of them used for something—chickens, goats, milk cows, a broken-down mare; covered garden plots with trestles holding barren vines; windblown laundry; outhouses sprouting crooked vent pipes.

The driver throws an uncertain look back at me as the muezzin's cry rides the thin air, a lyrical chant that evokes ages past and ages to come. Our guide raises his hand and says, "Halt," in guttural Russian. He clambers out and prepares to pray while the rest of us remain seated in the truck, godless interlopers.

A donkey drifts past, long ears drooping sadly, and my thoughts seem to wander along with the beast, figuratively traveling over a land defiled by war, among people forever scarred by generations of suffering. Abused by Russia and, most cruelly, by their own, by men like the swaggering brigand Khanzad, full of smooth lies as he treacherously jumps from one side to the other to fatten his bank account.

And then another image pops into my mind, this one unbidden and unwelcome: Abreg, hovering over me on the edge of the pit, wavering and indistinct.

My fingers tingle and I tuck them beneath my legs, worried that Matthews might see them trembling, but he's busy with his own thoughts. I glance at Charlie. She's awake now, sitting with her knees pulled to her chest and her arms wrapped around them, gazing at the back of the canopy as if it is a silver screen showing a motion picture only she can see.

A small part of me hurts for her, but I can't afford to act on sympathy. Abreg is far too wily to be killed in a direct confrontation. I'll need to use deception and misdirection. I'll need a Trojan horse.

When the prayers end, we trundle across more rutted roads for nearly an hour before our guide signals a halt. A boy on a shaggy pony approaches us. He looks about fourteen. The side of his face is networked with puckered scars. He wears an AK-47 slung from one shoulder and a cartridge belt with grenades clipped to it over the other.

He talks to our guide in a dialect I don't understand. Both of them use their hands, pointing and motioning. When their conversation ends the boy rides to the rear of the truck, lifts the tarp, and carefully inspects the interior. His taut gaze falls upon Charlie, hesitates, then sweeps past her to stop on Matthews, who stares unflinchingly back at him. Then the boy turns to me, his look flat and cruel—demented. When he lets the flap fall back into place, the temperature seems to drop several degrees.

"Oh, God," Charlie cries.

The truck lurches ahead, zigzagging up more switchbacks.

Matthews lights two cigarettes and offers one to Charlie. Her hand shakes so much that she has trouble bringing it to her mouth. He talks to her quietly for a few minutes, then he takes off a glove and strokes her hair with his rawboned hand, calming her, and she leans into him with her eyes closed. Senator's daughter, socialite, sometime activist, she is far removed from anything she's known before.

Charlie's not trembling as much a few minutes later. Matthews murmurs something reassuring, and then, with one hand brushing the overhead support frame for balance, he crosses the truck bed to sit next to me. I keep my voice low so that she can't hear.

"All of that stuff you fed me about Charlie and Jemaah Islamiya and Ravi Kho was bullshit. Ravi was Chinese intelligence." I say this not because it has just occurred to me, but rather because looking at Charlie brings the magnitude of her folly into clear focus. She mourns a man who used her almost as badly as we are using her.

Matthews lets his head fall back against the canvas and closes his eyes. "Yeah, Ravi was being worked by Sixth Bureau. She still has no clue. She thinks Lachek wasted him because of the video, and that might have been part of it, because Ravi was using Khanzad and the video to leverage Lachek, but the fact is that Lachek had lots of reasons to kill him. They had history, those two."

We're both silent for a few miles, swaying with the rhythm of our ride, but he keeps fidgeting. Finally he gives up the fight for sleep and lights another cigarette, sucking it halfway to the filter.

"This is a generational problem, Volk," he says on the exhale. "Just like what we have in Afghanistan and Iraq. That kid back there will never know anything except how to fight and how to hate. Unless something changes soon, neither will his children. And they won't even understand why."

I remember thinking something similar in Masha's flat. How long ago was that? Four days, I think. Maybe five. The hours in the Lubyanka hole warped my sense of time. I haven't been able to raise Valya to warn her about Khanzad, and now it's too late anyway. He either has her or he doesn't. I'm sick with worry.

"This isn't new," I say. "The highlanders haven't known anything except fighting for a thousand years."

But even as I say the words I know that I've evaded the point. The children of the Chechen wars are refugees in their own land. They represent the beginning of a new cycle, not a continuation of what began long ago. A downward spiral that won't end until something cataclysmic disrupts it.

"Maybe that's why we're both getting our asses kicked by a bunch of hunter-gatherers," Matthews says, and stubs out the butt of his cigarette on the steel plate beneath our feet.

An hour later, in the half-light of dusk, the truck groans to a stop facing a dilapidated structure that, from the outside, appears to be no more than a large shack. The crude building rests on a foundation of gray bricks stacked in intervals around its perimeter, allowing some of the cold to bleed off below. An elevated porch overhung by a slat-board roof sleeved with tin and ice leads to an opening covered with hanging animal hide. Curled planks along the muddy street offer a dry path to other neglected huts, all of them listing, dun-colored, collapsing one framing timber at a time.

When the engine dies a shocking silence fills the space its racket previously occupied, a silence almost profound after the long rumble we've just completed. Then other sounds begin to permeate—cackling hens, a barking dog, wind-driven metal banging on wood. The outside air is bitter. The time required to negotiate the switchbacks was misleading, we are only about ten kilometers above and to the east of the town, parts of which are visible through the bare branches of the trees between two craggy spurs of rock. We're standing, stretching, trying to get our bearings after the long ride when the scarred boy on the pony clops slowly around the building. His AK-47 rests casually across the saddle. Following him is a gaunt old man with a patchy beard who rides a mangy horse.

"Go with Yusup," the boy says in Russian. "All except for you." His bottomless eyes shift to me. The barrel of the rifle seems to drift of its own accord to point at my chest.

"This wasn't part of the deal, Volk," Matthews says, talking under his breath so that Charlie can't hear him. "They promised we could stay together."

Our driver, who had been leaning against the fender of the truck near the ticking motor, straightens stiffly and raises his hands. Our guide pulls a revolver from his pocket and stands with his feet well apart, holding it on us. He's still wearing the Astrakhan hat and the stolen greatcoat, but he doesn't look so ridiculous now that we're in his world.

"Right now we're probably on the wrong end of about twenty guns," I tell Matthews.

He looks about, but there's nothing to see except the ramshackle buildings dripping ice and a scabrous mongrel pissing in the muddy street. The dog finishes its business and approaches the truck, sniffing the tires.

"What's the plan?" Matthews says.

"Let's see if they kill me. If they do, I don't care what happens after that. If they don't, they probably won't kill you either."

"You're such a fucking comedian, Volk." But he says this without animus, under his breath. "I always said I wouldn't go easy. Never could understand the poor bastards with their hands tied behind their back and a bullet in their skull. Guess I was wrong."

He sidles closer to Charlie and whispers something to her. She begins to cry silent tears. He gestures to the old man, Yusup, who reins his horse around and leads them away. Matthews puts his arm over Charlie's shoulders and talks to her as they wobble along the planks around a chicken coop. Just before they disappear behind a pile of broken bricks she looks back at me, her face a portrait of despair.

The boy dismounts. He leaves the reins dangling and points with the rifle, ordering me to lead the way up to the elevated porch. I stand there while he pats me down, ankle to crotch, roughly, far more thoroughly than Maxim's bodyguards. It takes him a few minutes to figure out the knife in my prosthesis and work the catch to release it. He turns it in his hand, then slides it under his belt beneath his coat.

Another man approaches from the direction Matthews and Charlie went. He wears a biblical beard so thick and black it appears to be an extension of his chin. A rebel-green headband tops his leathery face. His obsidian eyes burn from hatred so all-consuming I'm surprised he doesn't burst into flame.

He runs a handheld metal detector over every inch of me. It chirps at one of my coat pockets. He searches there, digging with a hand that's almost black with grime, but finds nothing. When he wands the detector over the same spot again, it remains silent. My prosthesis starts the device screaming, and he squats to feel every part of my foot, then gestures for me to remove it and inspects it minutely while I rest my fingertips on a splintered rail for balance. His probing fingers curl and dig into the slot for the knife, then he grunts at the boy, who respectfully pulls the blade out of his pocket and hands it over. The blade shines dully while he tests its weight and balance and strums the pad of his thumb over the tip, unimpressed. My knife is no match for the long *kinzhal* attached to a scabbard at his waist. He gives my knife back to the boy, returns my prosthesis to me, and leaves as I'm putting it back on.

As soon as he's rounded the corner of the building, the boy rakes my face with the sight on the end of his rifle barrel, casually, a quick flick of his wrist that rips a gash below my eye. Blood trickles warmly down my cheek. The boy watches its progress, his eyes gleaming. Under his breath he says, "You're going to die, Russian pig," and then he prods me through the hanging animal-hide doorway.

chapter 48

Someone grunts when I stumble into the smoky gloom of the shack, and something pounds the wooden floor with a sound like kettledrums, but at first I can't see a thing. Incense, lantern oil, sizzling mutton, and smoke from a poorly ventilated fire blend into an aroma that seems as old as time; the room might have smelled the same in any century of the last twenty. As my eyes begin to adjust I see that the smoke comes from a potbellied stove in the middle of the room. A long table lit with flickering tallow candles and an oil lamp dominates the area to my right. An array of oddly shaped bottles, most without labels, clutters the shelves behind the table, casting gold, silver, and blue reflections from the flames. The other walls are covered with thick wool rugs.

The boy shoves me from behind and I take several steps forward. To my left is a knee-high, circular table covered with the hide of a Caucasian *tur,* a wild goat. Resting on the tabletop are a World War II–era Lugar, an unsheathed knife, and plates filled with strips of meat and flat bread.

Another boy of about fourteen, his face unscarred but still unmistakably the twin of the one behind me, sits on the round edge of the table closest to me. He too wears a green headband. His crossed legs cradle an AK-47. Next to him is a man who looks so similar he must be the father of the twins. They both glare at me with expressions so filled with malevolence that I'm sure we have a past, although I don't recall either of them. Maybe I am merely a representation of all the things they hate in this world.

Something moves near my feet—a man dressed in army-issue fatigues lies on his back, drumming his heels on the wood floor. A rope wraps his arms against his body like thread around a spool. A clear plastic bag sheathes his head like a giant condom. His mouth is gagged. The area around his nose snuffs in and out as he labors to breathe through a pencil-sized hole; the harder he inhales, the tighter the plastic molds to his face and blocks his air supply. Deep-set, panicked eyes roll in the chalky smear of his face beneath the plastic. No one except me pays him the slightest attention.

And then neither do I, suddenly, as a gust of frigid wind pushes through the hide-covered doorway and the candles flare. All my attention jumps to the third man sitting at the low table and my blood boils, fight or flight.

"The spider," Abreg says, "has only to wait, and the fly will come to him."

He makes no threatening gesture. The light from the guttering candles dims as the wind dies, but my eyes have adjusted to the darkness so I can see him more clearly now. He's wearing a blousy, oversized jacket that billows shapelessly around his seated form, except at the back where his humped spine tents the fabric. Thin wrists stick out from the sleeves, his fingers long and bent, one hand curled around the handle of the same gnarled cane he used to lean on when he stared down at me in the pit. Dark, shaggy hair hides all of his features except for his hooked nose and his eyes, the right one as black and shiny as I remember it.

I take two steps forward, deliberately, and pick up the knife from the table. Abreg holds up his right hand, and nobody makes a move to stop me. He simply observes me, expressionless, his confident calm no doubt reinforced by the presence of the boy who stands behind me, covering me with his Kalashnikov. But the boy alone couldn't stop me, not before I'd killed Abreg. The only thing that stays my hand is the fear that, through Khanzad, he has Valya.

The knife has a hollow handle with a compass fitted into the butt. It will unscrew so that wooden matches, string, and other small survival tools can be stored inside. Abreg watches indifferently while I kneel next to the bound man on the floor, who is rail-thin, his body wasted by drugs or malnutrition, and slit the plastic to enlarge the breathing hole. He wuffs in a huge snort of air. Snot sprays when he clears his nasal passages for another breath. While everyone watches him dispassionately, but almost as if they are curious to see whether he lives or dies, I slip the knife into the pocket of my coat and stand.

The boy and his father look up from the man on the floor and study me the way a hungry man eyes a pig roasting on a spit. Abreg waits patiently for my response, wearing the same serene expression he used when I was in his clutches the last time.

"Sometimes," I tell him, "the fly is not a fly, and the spider dies."

I say this while staring into Abreg's left eye, the milky-white, bottomless one, trying to separate the man in front of me from my memory of the man I knew before. He drops his gaze to the bound man, who is still greedily sucking air.

"That is just like you, Volkovoy. Acting without thinking. You should ask yourself, is this man worth saving? Is he my friend or my enemy? You see the uniform, what's left of it anyway, and the program in your mind drives you. All trace of independent thinking flushed down the sewer of Balashikha-two. Such a waste."

I've unscrewed the butt of the knife in my pocket. "No one deserves to die that way," I say, although the truth is that if the man on the floor is Semerko—as I suspect—he does deserve an awful death, but not before he tells me where to find Galina. As I'm talking, I tear off a magnetic homing beacon that looks like a porcelain button sewn onto the inner flap of my pocket.

Abreg leans forward with a motion that's more like a spasm than an intentional act. The simple movement clenches his face with pain. "What shit! How many men have died slowly so that you could learn some bit of information that would be outdated within hours?"

"I never find amusement in the suffering of others." I use my finger to push the beacon into the hollow handle of the knife past the other small implements inside, then screw the top on again, all done easily enough with one hand.

"You think I do? You think I like what I've become?" Fluid leaks from his dead left eye, slides down his face, and gathers at the corner of his mouth. "Remember, Volkovoy, I never did anything to you except talk."

In a former life when he had a different name, before the first Chechen war, Abreg wrote a newspaper column for one of Grozny's daily papers. He advocated a separatist position, but his writings were not strident or militant, not really even anti-Russian, or so it seems from the columns preserved in his file. One intelligence expert wrote a report suggesting that Abreg devolved into violence when "hail"—incoming fire from a Katyusha multiple rocket launcher—obliterated his home, killed his wife and child, and left him a deformed wreck in Grozny's Hospital Number 4 in the midst of raging epidemics of cholera, diphtheria, hepatitis, and dysentery. All of that matters little now, though, because who hasn't suffered?

"You had others do your dirty work for you."

"I kept you alive!" he thunders, springing halfway from his cross-legged position. The sudden movement makes him grunt, and he drops back into place. The father and son both reach out to him, looking concerned, but he waves them off.

I gesture to the bound soldier. "His name is Semerko?"

"You know him?"

"What happened to the girl that was with him?"

"Russian children are more important than Chechen children? Your bombers level entire villages without remorse, but you'll go to the ends of the earth to find one little girl from Moscow? You see how something like that makes me angry?"

"Not angry enough to harm the girl."

A vertical line forms between his snarled brows. "You think you know me so well?" He aims the end of his cane at my face. "I'll wrap her face in plastic and kill her the same way I kill him. And I won't feel a thing. How would you like to watch a movie, Volkovoy? See what your people do when they think no one will find out. Ten girls just like the one from Moscow—ten of the *blacks,* isn't that what they call us?— killed in worse ways than that. And their mothers and fathers and brothers, too, no one was spared! Watch this, and tell me why I should spare any of you."

He reaches painfully into his jacket pocket and holds up a silvery mobile drive, about one centimeter by four, then tosses it at me like a coin so that I have to pluck it out of the air. Made of matted metal, the top of the drive slides off to expose the male connection to a computer port.

"Starye Atagi was an abomination," he says.

I put the drive—the General's "two fucking gigs"—into my pocket next to the knife. "No copies?" I ask, even though I already know the answer.

He snorts. "Of course there are copies. You people paid for nothing."

Semerko thrashes on the floor, struggling for more air, but only humming sounds escape the gag. Behind me the door flaps open, admitting another icy draft. The bearded man clumps in and hands Abreg two tracking devices similar to the one I just placed in the knife. One of them would have been on Matthews, the other attached to the undercarriage of the Ural truck.

"You think we're fools, Volkovoy?"

"How many of the soldiers in the video have you already killed?"

"Five that we found here in Chechnya. One of the survivors recognized the first one at a checkpoint outside of Chiri-Yurt. We captured him when he went to use the latrine. He led us to the others. We thought the trail had gone cold, then we got a lead on the man who made the movie, and now we'll be able to find the rest. Like your friend the captain. Your *tovarish*." My comrade. "They'll all die."

"So this never ends?"

Abreg's lower back seizes, and his face contracts into a rictus of pain, but he doesn't answer right away. The father of the twins glares at me. I slip a hand into my pocket again and finger the knife.

"*Now* you want things to end?" Abreg says, his face still twisted.

"What about the egg?"

"A trinket from the tsars? Is that what's important to you?"

Abreg climbs to his feet. He looms over the table with his unbuttoned jacket winged out, looking like a vulture as it bounces to a landing near its prey. The boy sitting at the table stands with him and aims the barrel of his rifle at Semerko's gaping face and pretends to pull the trigger. Abreg snaps something in a Chechen dialect, and the twin lowers his rifle, looking chastened.

"Let's take a ride," Abreg says to me as he adjusts a woolen cap over his skull and the tops of his ears. "Let's go fill a freshly dug grave."

chapter 49

Abreg walks slightly stooped, like a jerky marionette, as if his mind is dragging his body along piecemeal in a tragic parody of the beggar pulling his dead leg through Moscow's metro tunnels. We leave the shanty out the back, and he slowly leads the way to an American-made four-wheel drive with a silver bucking bronco logo on its tailgate. When the vehicle was new the back of it was enclosed, but the rear half of the roof was chopped a long time ago, judging by the rust stains, so now it looks like a pickup truck with seats bolted onto the bed.

The twins and their father follow us, cradling their weapons like swaddled babes. They sit in the last row of seats in the truck bed, behind Abreg and me. The bearded man who searched me throws the bound Semerko at their feet and gets into the front next to the driver, who steers over humped ridges and through hidden valleys in frosted air that cuts to the bone. Nearly three hours into our drive the truck fishtails around a curve and churns to a stop in a clearing. Bathed in the glow of our headlights are seven horses, blowing steam and stamping, their reins clutched in the hand of another young fighter. Six of the horses are saddled for riders; the last one carries a packsaddle.

"Cold ride ahead, Volkovoy," Abreg says.

He struggles to climb down from the open bed, helped by two of his men, who handle him gently, like a son would an aged father. I join him in the clearing, still covered by the two boys, who are experienced enough to keep several meters between their guns and me. The bearded man loads Semerko on the packsaddle facedown, like a sack of meal, then cruelly jerks the straps in a way that leaves him twisted in a sideways bow. The ride will be unremitting agony for Semerko.

"And now I'm afraid I must ask you to return the knife." Abreg holds out his hand.

I take the knife from my pocket and hand it to him, handle first.

He arches his brows. "No denial? No argument?" He shakes the handle next to his ear, pursing his lips while he pretends to listen closely. "Maybe a little gift here for me?" He unscrews the compass top and empties the contents into his hand—a plastic tube of matches, tiny tweezers, needle and thread. He probes the handle with his long finger and fishes out the homing device, feigning surprise at the sight of it in his cupped palm. "My, my," he says. "Have others fallen so easily?"

The answer is yes, that was how it was done in some cases, but the last such mission I was involved in was not as easy as it was later made to sound. A Russian agent carried the beacon implanted under the skin of his scrotum, and he called the missiles down upon himself when he was close enough to put the rebel leader inside the blast zone. Russian heroes are rarely acknowledged, even posthumously.

Abreg tosses the beacon into a snowdrift. "There. Now your people can blow up some trees, watch the fireworks from the comfort of your control center. Where is that, anyway? Vladikavkaz? Rostov? Mozdok? What does it feel like to have the power of God to rain death upon innocent people?" After regarding me for a moment, he gestures toward the horses. "Come."

His man helps him onto a sorrel with a white blaze between its eyes. Sitting in the saddle, Abreg seems whole again for an instant, as if the power of the animal's quivering muscles has been transferred to his wasted frame, but then the horse makes an unexpected jump forward and he winces. He calms the horse by patting its neck. Pulls a Mosin-Nagant rifle from a scabbard hanging from the saddle, lays it across his lap, and works the bolt to check the load. The gnarled cane goes into the scabbard.

Urged by the scarred twin, I mount a wild-eyed roan gelding that dances and snorts as I settle into the saddle. The other twin hands off his weapon, jumps aboard behind me, and ties my hands behind my back with a thin rope, careful to tighten it under my gloves. I flex the muscles of my wrists as much as possible while he works, and as soon as he's finished I start rolling my hands to loosen the bonds, trying to gain enough circulation that I don't lose hands or fingers to frostbite. One of the men lights an old-fashioned lantern, and we trail him single file into the dark tree line, Abreg right behind the lantern bearer, then me followed by the others, how many I can't tell for sure, but at least six.

Powdery snow begins to fall, barely more than a frosty mist. I'm dressed for cold weather, and I keep working hard on the rope, but even so my hands quickly grow numb. Soon we're traversing just below a ridgeline—I can tell that much from the angle of the ground—but with no stars to guide me I don't know our direction of travel. Hours pass. We keep climbing steadily.

"Has time changed your perspective, Volkovoy?" Abreg's voice rides the wind back to me. "Do you understand the futility of what was done in Chechnya?"

Starlight leaks through a break in the clouds, shining dully on the barrel of Abreg's rifle and, when I turn to look behind us, on other rifles and the thicker tubes and warheads of RPGs. One side of our narrow path falls away into inky darkness.

"A man like me doesn't suffer from doubt, Abreg."

The roan bobs his head and snorts. The stars disappear again as the clouds thicken, but not before I see Abreg twist his head to look at me.

"Are you lying to me or yourself?"

Ahead of us is a diffuse blob of yellow—the lead rider, pulled up, waiting for the column to close ranks.

"Do you remember our talk?" This time Abreg speaks without looking back. A pillar of condensation, lit by the light from the lantern, rises above his head. "The last one, before your foot?"

My last conversation with Abreg had covered this same ground—justice in Chechnya—although I don't remember much of it because I was consumed by ravenous hunger and pain and because so much happened just afterward. Something about him not really being the person he was meant to be, and how Russians were destroying humanity. His usual propaganda, in other words.

"No."

We ride along, brushing past pine boughs loaded with fresh snow, winding ghostlike, higher, always higher. We cover nearly a kilometer before he speaks again. "What were you before the war?"

He already knows this. He knows things about me that I wouldn't even tell Valya. Drugs and torture will make the strongest man talk like a drunken schoolgirl. But talking is a good distraction from the cold, so I answer anyway.

"A prisoner in Isolator 5."

"How old were you?"

My roan sneezes a blast of wet air. Pale moonlight blinks through the storm clouds, momentarily throwing the serrated edges of a mountain ridge into sharply defined relief.

"Nobody is ever old enough for that place."

"What was your crime?"

"Too many to list."

"Lots of Cargo 200 in your wake, Volkovoy," he says, using the Russian Army euphemism for dead bodies that need to be hauled away.

The man leading our caravan reins to a stop and consults a map by the light of his lantern. Another rider, the father of the twins, I think, trots his horse past us, and the two of them consult in a whispered conversation, dark shapes in the mist, framed in umber, a scene that might have played out a thousand years ago.

"The boys," Abreg says, gesturing behind us while he's still facing forward, watching the men trying to decide our course. "They're twins. I knew their mother before all this . . . before all the fighting." His humped back alters his silhouette, turning him into a shrouded goblin. "I'm responsible for them now. Maybe I have failed them, but I don't think things would have turned out differently even if I had made other choices."

A third man joins the first two in front of us. They cluster around the map and whisper some more.

"We can't use radios or phones here," Abreg says. "The drones are everywhere these days, and they triangulate the signals very quickly. But then you know all about that, don't you?"

A gust of wind routes a blade of wet snow down the neck of my jacket.

"One of the twins was captured, once, the one with the scars. It was at a checkpoint near Chiri-Yurt. Did you know any of the men there? They threw the boy into the back of a Kamaz and took him to a filtration camp. Tied him to a post and beat him with plastic cola bottles filled with water. After a few days of this they ransomed him for three thousand rubles.

"His cousin was not so lucky. On him they used an old phone to crank electricity through his body. When they tired of watching him bounce, they gutted him like a hog. His body went for four thousand rubles. The price increased because the soldiers knew how much anguish his family would suffer if the proper funeral rites weren't observed."

The conference ahead of us breaks up. We slog on for several more hours. Two fingers on my left hand no longer seem to be a part of me, much like my lost foot. Still we meander higher through the darkness, stopping only occasionally, just long enough for the lead men to get their bearings.

"Do you go to church, Volkovoy?"

"No."

"You know about the Russian church? The liturgy, hours of it, with all the chants and songs? Was it Chekhov who described it so beautifully in 'Easter Night'?"

A freshening wind brings with it the smell of wood smoke.

"Russians pray with their eyes open so they can become a part of the icon. I'm told the icon possesses spiritual power. It animates the believers and shows them a pathway to the holy. So can you understand why some of our people believe that the worst thing they can do to a Russian is to cut out his eyes?"

The horses lunge through a snowbank.

"Do you believe that, Abreg? Are you so foolish and superstitious?"

His reply is lost in the shifting wind.

"What?" I say, almost shouting.

"I said, this is not me. Do you remember when I told you that? This is not me."

I don't know what he's talking about. One by one, the horses squat on their haunches and slide down a rocky slope that descends into a gully, then gather themselves for the explosive leaps that propel them up and over the top on the other side. That brings us to a wide, snow-filled meadow illuminated by a flickering circle of firelight. When we're closer the flames resolve into handheld torches, a necklace of them, trembling higher into the blackness of the night above a thin band of ivory that promises the dawn.

"Do you remember me telling you that before?" Abreg says. Now that we're off the narrow trail he has pulled his sorrel next to my roan so that we're riding knee to knee. His profile is as rugged as the mountains, but his good eye and his lips are pulled down with weariness.

"Telling me what?"

"Your people have done this, Volkovoy. They have turned me into something I'm not supposed to be." He kicks the sorrel forward and then wheels to face me, hunched in the saddle. Places his right hand over his heart and thumps his chest three times. "This is not me. I'm not supposed to be a man who burns people alive."

chapter 50

More than two dozen armed men stand in the circle, which breaks at our approach to allow us to walk our horses to the rim of a pit encircled by mounded dirt. The hole is seven or eight meters across and about five deep, filled nearly to the top with a great pile of logs, branches, and brush, enough fuel for an enormous bonfire.

Dawn's light dims the torches. Another column of riders appears at the edge of the meadow, a group of about fifteen. They snake through thinning silver birches glowing on one side from the horizontal rays of the breaking sun. Several of the riders in the middle of the group slump as though they're wounded.

"Men are for sale, Volkovoy," Abreg says.

"What does that mean?"

"I almost had my hands on three barrels of highly enriched uranium. H-E-U." He drags out the letters, delivering each one like a punch, but I already heard this from Matthews so his words come as no surprise. "It was being moved for processing, so that it was no longer a *proliferation risk.* Such masters of the language, those United Nations bureaucrats."

Abreg slides his cane from the scabbard and slots the Mosin-Nagant rifle into its place. His man hurries over to help him off the horse, but instead of dismounting Abreg remains seated, looking into the pit.

"It's when they move the stuff that it's most vulnerable—the in-between times, when something is neither here nor there. Things disappear. Magicians do it all the time. I once saw a magic show in Grozny, a few months before your people razed it to the ground. A magic man made an elephant disappear." He snaps his fingers. "It was gone."

He bows his head. "Gone like my Zamira. And my son. He was six, Volkovoy. He loved the magic." His head is still cast down so I can't see his face. "How old is the girl you're looking for?"

"Twelve."

When he finally looks up his good eye, the black one, is without tears. It is as if the moment of remembrance about his wife and child has vanished like the elephant, unseen but still present.

"With fifty kilos of HEU I could build a bomb just like the one the Americans dropped on Hiroshima. One that could be parked in a garage near Red Square or delivered in a cargo container to the Winter Palace. A few hundred kilos, that's all the whole thing would weigh."

Ten of the approaching horsemen carry Kalashnikovs pointed toward the sky. The other five men ride with their hands tied behind their back, like mine. One of them wears a ragged black greatcoat and has bone-white features under thinning gray hair blown wildly out of place. Older by years than the rest of his men, the former officer appears dazed, disoriented by time and place.

Abreg nods to his man with the biblical beard and the green rebel headband. Now, in the dawn's light beneath a faultless sky, I can see that he was the one who led our pack through the mountains in the night. He picks up a battered can the size of a small suitcase and douses the woodpile with kerosene. The can gurgles as it empties, spraying fuel until the branches and twigs of the giant tinderbox are glazed with it. Overhead, the morning sky is like the bottom of a giant pewter bowl, and the sheltered meadow is as still as a cemetery. The doomed men slump in their saddles. Either they don't understand what's about to happen or they're too beaten to care, at least until the moment when Abreg's soldiers drag them off their horses.

As though awakening from a ghastly dream, the officer in the greatcoat cries, "No! Have mercy!" and the others begin shouting at once, begging to be spared. The scarred twin releases Semerko's straps and drags him off the packsaddle to the edge of the pit. The officer keeps crying "Mercy!" over and over again, like a litany. I brace myself for someone to pull me out of my saddle, but no one does.

The fighters throw the men onto the pile, one by one. They crash through several layers of the bramble until they hang suspended—all except one man who is so heavy that he keeps jerking through the maze until he lands on an enormous log at the bottom. A broken branch runs through the meatiest part of Semerko's thin leg. He cries beneath the plastic that still covers his face. He looks like a ten-year-old boy who fell out of his tree house—like the boy who once played with the Japanese trading cards now locked away in his footlocker.

"I wouldn't blow the bomb," Abreg says. "Not as long as we were left in peace. I would take pictures. I would tell the world I have it. But all I want is a deterrent."

"The Russians, the Americans—*nobody* will allow you to come that close again. Can't you see that?"

"I've had a target on my back for a long time, Volkovoy. I'll survive. But if I don't, someone else will take my place. And that's bad for you, because whoever it is will be far worse than I am."

The bearded fighter stands on the edge of the pit, pointing and laughing, evil in full bloom. The twins and their father join him, along with several others, watching as he sprays kerosene directly onto the prisoners.

"These men"—Abreg motions toward the doomed Russians below us—"these men are guilty. They are murderers, rapists, torturers. No redemption. No absolution."

"What about me? Isn't that why you insisted I come? To make your bonfire that much brighter?"

He twists the sorrel around. "You still don't understand, do you? I told you, I spared you before for as long as I could, and I'm going to spare you again."

"Why?"

"Because you still have a chance."

"So do they."

"No, they don't," he hisses. "You won't think so either once you see the video."

"Then kill them quickly."

Abreg regards me silently while his sorrel prances backward, the clink of its harness adding a musical note to the cries for clemency. He starts to say something, clears his throat, and looks away. The edge of the sun flares over a serrated mountain ridge in the east. When he looks up, one lone snowflake floats in an eddy of cold air and lodges on an eyelash. He blinks it away.

"I'm not sure how much longer I can keep control," he says quietly, angling his head toward the bearded fighter with obsidian eyes. "The Wahhabis hold power almost everywhere now, stealing the hearts of our young. Some of them aren't even Chechen. They're not fighting for independence. They're fighting *ghazawat,* a holy war."

His horse dances to one side, snorts, and shakes its mane. More snowflakes zigzag down. Drifting dispatches from the heavens that land like cold pinpricks. Abreg draws a deep breath, but says nothing, just absently twists the handle of his cane.

Then he shouts an order in a harsh dialect. The bearded man roars, railing at the injustice of it. He grabs a torch and swings it as if he's about to throw it into the pit. Several of the men surround him and hold him back with their hands against his chest even as he continues to spit angry words. The twins and their father jabber excitedly among themselves, then with the others. Abreg gazes into the distance. The quarrel might as well be happening ten kilometers away.

Just when the outcome seems certain, the mood shifts. I don't know how Abreg's spell is broken, but suddenly all those restraining the bearded man drop their hands and stand aside. He whirls the torch above his head in a fiery loop and hurls it above the pit, where it hangs for an instant, then plummets. With a great *wumf,* a banner of flames explodes skyward, crackling more than five meters into the air, black smoke spiraling from the tip. The roar of the inferno fails to contain the animal screams of the burning men.

The roan backs away from the fire, and I knee it around so that the heat strikes my back instead of my face. Abreg has done the same thing with his sorrel. His mouth hangs open as if he is trying to take in more air. Behind us, one of the twins cackles and someone else shouts in a mocking tone. Abreg's gaze catches mine, then it falters and he looks down.

As the flames continue to crackle and pop, the bearded man mounts his horse and prances closer to us. When he looks at me the orange flames are reflected in his eyes, performing an insane dance, and I can see that he's thinking that I should be down in the pit with the others. He angles the barrel of his Kalashnikov toward my belly, looking at me without blinking, then fires a burst into the air, wheeling his mount in a tight circle. Soon he's joined by his supporters in a triumphant dervish of gunfire and celebration.

"I might not be able to save you this time, Volkovoy," Abreg says.

chapter 51

By the time we get back to Abreg's ice-clad shack of wood and tin I'm so cold that my whole body shakes uncontrollably. The return trip seemed to take longer than the outbound one. Every time we stopped I wondered if it was the last time for me. The worst was when Abreg rode off the trail with the bearded Wahhabi and I could hear the angry sound of their voices in the distance. Both men were tense when they returned. Abreg stayed near me for the rest of the ride, resting his hand on the stock of his rifle, but he said nothing. The round-trip journey took about a day, so night has fallen as we unload. My hands are still tied. Two fingers on my left hand have not regained feeling.

Abreg exchanges harsh words with the father of the twins, both of them gesturing at me. I limp to the back of the shack and lean against a splintered gray beam under the watchful eye of the scar-faced boy. Abreg finishes his argument, and gestures for me to follow him inside, where the same warm smells of incense, smoke, and mutton pervade.

Different men are seated around the table. They regard me with hostility as Abreg leads me past the shiny bottles of gold and silver, out through the hide-covered entrance, and onto the porch. The boy takes station behind me. A sliver of night sky shows in a half-meter fracture where the porch roof has pulled away from the rest of the building, clear and cold and prickled with lights, one of which, a satellite, moves among the others like a slowly falling star.

"I think this is the last time we will see each other, Volkovoy," Abreg says. His hunched back is to me, so I can't see his face.

"Why did you bring me here?"

"I don't know anymore. In the beginning I thought to kill you. Then I thought, maybe not, maybe this time I will finally be able to stare into the eyes of my enemy and find . . . something to take away, something to help me make sense of things." He shakes his head sharply, like the bridled sorrel. "It was a foolish thing to hope for."

Off in the distance I hear a churning cough and then a low rumble as a cold motor turns over and begins warming up. His cane clacks against wood as he stoops his way down the steps and onto the warped wooden planks in front of the shack. When he turns to face me his features are still distorted from the pain caused by each jolting step.

"The girl you were asking about, Galina. Khanzad has her. He gave us Semerko, but he kept her. He thought she would bring a good price, either from you or someone else. He also has your precious egg."

"Khanzad is a plague."

Abreg fixes me with his black and white stare. I don't know which eye to look at, but as always my gaze seems to be drawn to the dead, white one.

"So kill him."

And then he turns and hobbles away, moving with great care, his gnarled cane rattling against the mud-set planks. He looks back once, but his face is in shadow and whatever he means to convey is lost in darkness.

After he disappears, the scarred twin marches me up the road that Matthews and the others took the night before. As soon as we round the bend past the chicken coop the boy drills me in the kidney with the butt of his AK. The blow drops me to my knees. I throw myself forward and roll onto my back to avoid the swiping barrel, then launch a kick just as he lunges at me, hoping to hook his ankle and use my other boot to crush his kneecap, but my reflexes are shot. My heel catches him on the thigh and he spins, dropping the rifle.

While he scrabbles to try to recover it I clip the side of his head with my knee, then jump on his back and ram my elbow into his head, trying to knock him out, but with my hands tied I don't have enough leverage to deliver a powerful blow.

A sharp whistle cuts the night air. The gaunt old man, Yusup, stands outside a low-slung hut, holding a sulfurous lantern and a rifle. The boy is lying in the muck, bleeding from his nose and mouth. I kick his rifle out of reach. He takes a long time getting up. When he's finally back on his feet he stands in place, wobbling, until I nudge him toward the light from Yusup's lantern. He has recovered enough to be muttering curses when we get there. Yusup says a few harsh words and dismisses him with an impatient wave of his arm.

Once he's out of sight, Yusup stands studying me like a botanist observing a new genus of plant. He reminds me of a slightly older version of Vadim. Lean, all tendons and bone, slightly slumped. So many of his front teeth are missing that his chin seems to be too close to his nose. Webbed wrinkles and a scar deep enough to hold a matchstick upright hover above his scraggily beard. He motions with his rifle for me to follow, and leads the way around the hut to the six-wheeled Ural transport truck, which is blowing clouds of smoke as the driver in the oriole cap, his pipe clenched in his teeth, runs the engine just above an idle.

Yusup follows me into the rear compartment. Matthews is already there, sitting on the metal bench close to the cab. Charlie is next to him. The open flap of the canopy lets in a ray of light that falls on her left arm and illuminates the edge of a bloody bandage peeking from beneath her coat. Matthews nods a greeting to me and slowly blinks, keeping his eyes closed for an extra heartbeat, long enough to bury a confirmation in the gesture.

Yusup takes station on the bench between me and the back flap. He shouts instructions at the driver and the Ural begins to rut and rock on its descent toward Tindi. Nobody says a word for an hour as we switch back and forth in the night. Ahead through the windshield I see the lights of the village below and then, closer, the darkness is broken by streaks of yellow leaking between the wooden slats of a barn.

"The boy is not the only one who would have killed you," Yusup says suddenly in Russian, with an accent so heavy I have to concentrate to understand him. "Many of the men back there wanted to do it. One day not long ago, I would have done it myself."

"What's changed?"

He smacks his lips and uses his tongue to suck at the remains of his teeth. "I saw you in the *zindan,* years ago. Abreg talked to you all the time." He thumps his right fist into the left side of his chest. "He decided you are a man with a heart. That is why he let you live then, and now too, I think." He juts out his lower lip, considering his words. "He is a hard man to understand, sometimes."

Holding the spine of the canopy's support frame, he walks unsteadily up to the cab, where he squats on the deck near Matthews and Charlie and yells instructions to the driver through the hole cut into the cab. The driver steers to the side of the barn, next to a pile of mud and bricks that look like the stump of a broken molar—the remnants of the main house, apparently sheared to its foundation by a bomb blast—and kills the motor. Yusup directs us out into the night and herds us to the door of the barn. Then he stands for a moment, looking back down the path from which we just came as though he expects pursuit.

"Yes, he is a strange man, Abreg is," Yusup says, still watching in the direction of our tracks. "But he has lost his way, and the ones behind him are worse. They're not fighting for home and family. They'll destroy everything for the sake of their holy war."

"Abreg didn't save my life before. I was rescued before he finished with me."

The old man purses his lips together as though I am a simpleton who has failed to follow an easy lesson. "Abreg is the wrong man for these times. I know that." He works his jaw side to side while his eyes shift back and forth, following the switchbacks above us. "But you need to understand what really happened. For six months Abreg kept us from killing you. He only gave in when faced with outright rebellion. And then, lucky for you, Valya came."

"Valya? You know her?" And then I remember what she told me about her friends in the region. How one of them was close to Abreg.

Yusup draws his *kinzhal* and cuts my wrists free in one smooth motion. He pushes me into the door, his agile strength a surprise. It flies open, and I stumble into a cloud of smoke. I can't make out anything in the room. The ice in my hair and eyebrows begins to melt immediately, and cold rivulets run down my face.

Then, without warning, a body smacks into mine. I stagger back into the wall. My weary legs give out, and I slide down the wall and land hard on my butt while Valya covers my face with warm kisses, holding me tight. Through it all, however, I can still hear Yusup's voice, dry and crackling like the flames in the funeral pyre.

"Yes, I know her," he says. "I was there when she rescued you, one of the few who lived to remember the hell she brought with her."

chapter 52

I was out of my mind with pain that night. All the bones in my foot had already been mashed in the gearwheels of a 155-millimeter howitzer converted into a hand-operated mill being worked by the slow hand of a sadist. He smiled wetly as he cranked it back and forth. Each crackling turn sent lightning bolts of agony that exploded in my skull and twisted my body so violently that, the doctors told me later, both my tibia and fibula splintered apart from the torque. An emaciated old woman used a rag soaked in lighter fluid and tied to the end of a length of rebar to roast my body parts. Each time she was about to apply flame to flesh she would hum tunelessly to herself, the sound like dragging a saw blade across the strings of a violin.

No interrogation, no purpose except for the sport of it—and revenge. I was paying the price for my sins, and the sins of my country. Each of my screams was a long, slow brushstroke painting the world with pain.

The old woman's wrinkled face hovered over me like some unholy apparition, humming as she showed me the blue flame. She was inching it closer to my neck, her rheumy eyes bright with anticipation, when suddenly, as if someone had thrown a giant switch, an illumination flare cracked the darkness high above her, and then another in a retina-burning blaze, and within seconds the whole camp was a frenzy of shouts and gunfire.

The ring of people around me burst apart like a flock of startled birds, racing for cover, for weapons, for the safety of the mountains and the darkness. The ground shook from several detonations that rocked the homemade torture machine, jagging more agony up my leg. Another explosion deafened me. The geared vise rocked, teetered, then finally tipped, bringing its full weight to bear on my leg. Bones cracked, skin split, and my screams mingled with those of the wounded and the hoarse commands of the rebels trying to mount a defense.

Then, like the memory of an old dream, came hard voices bellowing in Russian and the familiar war whoops of my countrymen. Silhouettes flickered past a backdrop of roaring flames. Shouts of battle and stuttering gunfire melded with the marshal pounding of blood in my ears and the agonizing bolts of pain in my leg.

The flares died a sizzling death in the snow. Red and green tracers sliced the sky into geometric patterns interrupted by disembodied shadows running, screaming, falling as though the earth had dropped away beneath them. Another shattering blast shook the ground. I lay back, all the crazed images fading, my mind beginning to unplug.

A figure reared in the darkness, wearing a pearly cloak blowing wild in the wind, filling my vision, floating above me like a white bird against a terrible black sky. Suddenly, the darkness melted in the acetylene flash of another parachuted flare. I closed my eyes against the painful radiance, and when I opened them the soldier loomed again, backlit by the white-hot blare of light, a Kalashnikov raised high with both arms.

"Everybody dies!" Valya screamed.

Her words cut through the crash of battle and lofted to the heavens.

Some of the soldiers froze, turned to stare at her for a moment, and then rushed on.

"Everybody fucking dies!"

Then Valya dropped her rifle and collapsed to her knees beside me and cradled my head in her arms. Tracers etched multicolored lines in the sky above us as the sounds of battle swelled, punctuated by the screams of the dying. Beneath her hood, Valya's enormous eyes blazed with the unholy light of war.

"I'm here, my love. You're safe now, with me."

chapter 53

My memories of the night Valya rescued me, and the long months that came before it, have been shredded by time and by whatever mental anesthesia wipes away our worst moments of pain. I don't trust all the recollections, but that final image, the one of her cradling me in her arms, is one I hold dear.

This moment is almost as good. We're among people who are strangers to me, and the fire-lit mountain barn smells like goats and hay and overcooked mutton, but none of those things matter. Only Valya and her warm lips are important.

After a minute she pulls her face away from mine but stays on top of me with her hands on my shoulders. I hold her hair away from her cheeks, just looking at her, because words are hard right now. She laughs and says my name under her breath and squeezes me with her thighs.

"What are you doing here?" She brings her mouth closer to mine, as if to tell me a secret, and bites my lower lip, holding it lightly in her

278 / Brent Ghelfi

teeth. She bites harder and surges against me. Licks my captured lip, and then releases it, purring a laugh deep inside, more felt than heard. "I told you, I can take care of things here."

"I needed a vacation."

She sticks out her tongue at me. "Come on," she says. Standing, she pulls me to my feet.

The inside of the barn is a big square without a single partition. A sputtering lantern and a small fire vented through a hole in the roof provide the only light. A lopsided cart with a broken wheel cants in the far corner next to a pile of hay. Five people are huddled in blankets around the fire. Two of them are women. All of them have weapons. They are studiously ignoring Valya and me, trying to give us a measure of privacy.

Charlie has joined them near the flames. She's on her haunches, picking at her bandages. Matthews and Yusup stand talking near the lantern by the door. I'm too far away to make out any of the words.

"These are some of my friends," Valya says. "I'll introduce you later." She shoves a pile of blankets into my arms and pushes me toward the door. Matthews tracks her with his eyes, and as we pass by he says to me in English, "You don't deserve her, Volk," and Valya laughs gaily and says with her lilting accent, "I also tell him the same thing."

She leads the way up a slope until we're on a ledge made of granite. A hollow has formed in the stone from centuries of snowmelt, and the curved nook is soft with sifted loam and moist leaves, upon which we arrange the blankets and sit shoulder to shoulder pressed against each other. Together we look out over the village below and the dark shapes of the mountains all around us.

The winter air crackles beneath an electric dome of sky. Cragged peaks and spiked trees and the capped spire of the minaret are lit by a phosphorescent spray of stars cradled in a crescent moon. Starlight falls on the curve of Valya's cheek, a glowing fragment that implies the beauty of her features in their entirety. The sweet scent of pine rides the wash of air flowing in the valley between the towering peaks, giving off a low moan like a breath blown softly into a bottle. I feel as though we are being watched by the night as we rediscover all the things that I thought were gone forever.

✳

Later, as the constellations wheel above us, I tell her everything that has happened, covering the old ground as well as the new just in case she's able to see something I might have missed. She says she's terribly sorry for Alla and I say I know. She asks me what I thought about while I was in the Lubyanka hole, and I tell her that I remembered my time in Chechnya, and she nods and says she thinks about it all the time, too.

"We would do things differently now," she says.

"It's nice to think so, but I'm not so sure. We are what we are, and in that place and time . . ."

Lying next to me, she shakes her head against my shoulder. "I don't believe that. We're all capable of change."

The flash drive shines with a silvery light when I hold it above us. "This is Starye Atagi. I wonder how we would feel after seeing it for ourselves."

She takes it from me and turns it in her hands. "So much and so little," she says. "What good is it to the General?"

"I think he plans to alter it. Change the faces. Replace them with real people, all of whom will swear they were paid to act out those scenes. Then release it himself. You understand?"

She nods. "Like Lenin said, a lie told often enough will become the truth. And this will be even better: a lie with pictures."

The digitally altered masterpiece will confuse everything. Computer-generated art tied with a bow of plausibility. Look at this. See what we uncovered, see the propaganda put out by the enemies of Russia. Then, after they tell their story, the "actors" will begin to die, one by one, each death blamed on the separatists who supposedly hired them to make the fraudulent video. Anyone who tries to prove that Melnik's video is real won't be able to make a case; they won't be able to show that any of the men in it were ever anywhere near Starye Atagi, let alone serving together in a flying detachment of the interior ministry. Like the incident at Ryazan, the original video, or even the phony one, will probably become an iconic touchstone for conspiracy theorists, who will unwittingly cloud the issue even more, but the Kremlin will have the only thing it really needs: deniability.

"Maybe those men deserve Abreg's punishment," I say quietly.

An owl passes beneath the stars, a fleeting black standard.

"Who is he to judge?" she says.

"I know. I think the same thing." I turn on my side to face her. "But then I wonder, if not him, who? And what would I do if you were killed that way?"

My question tumbles away into the night like water falling tier by tier down a long slope. She doesn't need to answer because we both know that I would never stop looking for revenge until I was dead.

"That's the problem, Alexei. Where does it end?"

"Maybe it never does. When has there not been conquest and subjugation? What country or culture isn't a product of those things? Look at your *teip*, Valya. Are you Russian or Chechen?"

"I am inescapably both."

The owl is gone from the sky, but from somewhere in the valley below comes its eerie cry.

"Khanzad has Galina," I say.

"He also has the egg. He wants a meeting with you. To negotiate, he says."

"You've talked to him?"

"I was with him less than four hours ago, in the village. We were well armed, so he didn't try anything, but I don't think he intended to take me hostage anyway. He's made a better deal."

"What does he want from me?"

"He wants you to take the egg back to Moscow. And he says he'll talk to you about something to throw in for Galina, a tip for him, he said."

"What did they give him?"

"Who can tell Khanzad's lies from the truth? He *says* the Kremlin will appoint him as one of three key administrators to work in Chechnya's puppet government, in charge of a committee that will have oversight into the rebuilding of the country."

The first major project will be reconstructing Chechnya's infrastructure of oil refineries and pipelines—one of the primary goals of the newly constructed ownership group of Kombi-Oil. The scale of the corruption on such public works will rival the river of dirty money already flowing in Moscow.

"I know," Valya says, reading the direction of my thoughts. "I thought the same thing when you told me about Kombi-Oil. They'll be able to pull Khanzad's strings whenever they want. He's perfect for them."

"So I'm just the goddamned courier."

She doesn't answer.

"I'm not going to play that game."

"No," she says. "I didn't think you would."

chapter 54

Early in the afternoon of the following day I steer the six-wheeled Ural to the outskirts of the village. Valya is on the ripped vinyl seat beside me, Yusup next to her against the window. Just as before, the roar of the engine draws a crowd of curious onlookers, some of whom follow us after we park and set out on foot through winding streets and tiered rows of buildings made mostly of brick and wood. Valya knows the way and she strides ahead with her confident step, rolling in the same way I do, but her limp is far more pronounced. She hasn't had as much time to adjust to life with a prosthetic foot.

We arrive at a stone building with an ornately carved door. Inside is an antechamber hung with several coats. Two men armed with Kalashnikovs stand on either side of a curtained entryway, both wearing blue business suits with white shirts and red ties. One of them covers us while the other pats us down without enthusiasm and finds no weapons. The guards treat Yusup with disdain because he appears old and frail. He stays behind while Valya and I pass through the portiere into a restaurant with tables covered in white cloth set with glass candleholders.

Khanzad sits at the far table, flanked by two more of his men, their Kalashnikovs leaning against the wall next to them, the restaurant empty except for the five of us and a waiter nervously smoothing the front of his stained apron. A bottle of red wine and a round loaf of bread have been placed in front of Khanzad. He has light skin beneath a full black beard plaited into a fork and decorated with gold beads. His suit, black with chalky stripes, fits him well and he wears it comfortably. He's built like a circus strongman, but dressed this way he seems more like a middle-aged Western businessman. I've seen pictures of him in an unbuttoned camouflage jacket, his hairy chest crossed by bandoliers like the boy on the pony, and in those clothes he looks more like the brigand he is. The false Chechen adapts to his environment with chameleon-like efficiency.

"Sit," he says expansively, spreading his arms over the table. His invitation is meant to include Valya, something rarely done here, and like the wine it is intended, I think, to reflect a sophisticated air.

We sit as the waiter pours from a fresh bottle and Khanzad makes a show of tasting it. He raises his eyebrows and lifts the glass to demonstrate how good it is, and the waiter pours for Valya and me.

"You see, Volk, I told you I wouldn't harm her. Who could possibly do injury to Valya Novaskaya, the jewel of the Caucasus? Here, a toast to new friends."

"We're here for Galina and the egg," I say.

His urbane demeanor slips briefly before he is able to replace his mask. "First things first. Let's drink, eat, relax. Men like us have lots to talk about, Volk. Think of the opportunities we have before us."

"I'm not a man like you, Khanzad." *I suffer from doubts; I wonder about the choices I've made and the things I've done.* "I don't whore myself to the highest bidder."

His friendly cover drops away. "Don't talk to me that way. I'd rather make this easy, but I don't have to. You're here on a short string.

Who do you want me to call? General Nemstov? Maxim? Constantine?" He drags out the names, sneering, his lips turned into ugly red slashes against the blackness of his beard. "They need me more than they need you."

"He's right, Alexei," Valya says, feigning concern. "Let's make this as simple as we can."

Khanzad salutes her with his glass. "Ah! A good negotiator always seeks a peaceful solution. To unity *and* prosperity." He lifts his glass and takes a drink, smacking his lips like Yusup when he finishes. "Okay, now we're friends! Bring out the egg, then we can eat and talk about old times, eh, Volk?"

After one of his men leaves through a door in the back, Khanzad pulls back his forehead to aim the prongs of his beard at me. "Do you have any idea how much money there is to be made here? You're so well-connected and so . . . well, stupid! No, no, I didn't mean that the way it sounded."

The top of the bar to our right holds two empty bottles the same shape and color as the one on our table. Khanzad has already made a full day of it.

"I'm just saying, all these people try to throw money at you. They all want you on their side." He frowns. "I don't get it."

"Now they're all throwing money at you," Valya says brightly, and this cheers him.

"Yes! Go ahead and be a martyr, Volk. Who am I to stop you?"

He takes another drink, but then his frown reappears, I suppose because he's still unable to understand how someone might look upon the world differently than he does. He rips off a chunk of apricot-stuffed bread and crams it into his mouth. While he's still chewing the man who left earlier returns with a lacquered box, black, inlaid with gold lines in a design I can't make out. He sets the box on the table and backs away. Khanzad caresses the smooth finish and pulls it closer to him.

"You and your fucking egg! You're just like the General. No charge, he tells me!" Khanzad slumps in his chair for a moment, contemplating, but this part of his bargain has already been sealed, apparently. He growls, waving his hand in disgust. "You think I care about the egg? Have it, for all I care."

"Where's the girl?"

"Ah, little Galina," Khanzad says, taking another bite. "She's upstairs. Alive. Still worth something." His grin reveals a sliver of apricot stuck between two teeth. "How much will her family pay?"

I would be surprised if Khanzad really intends to bargain for Galina's release. The money she would fetch is a pittance compared to what he thinks he will soon receive. I suspect he's just milking the moment, cruelly stretching things out simply because he believes he can. Valya catches my eye. The time has come. Cupped in her hand beneath the table I see the knife that was hidden in her prosthesis. She's holding it upside down with the blade running along her forearm.

The antechamber behind us erupts in gunfire, just as Yusup steps through the curtains, holding a Kalashnikov. He blinks once, getting his bearings, then cuts loose. The guard nearest me takes the initial burst in the chest. He flies backward as though jerked by invisible strings. Valya throws her knife into the second bodyguard. It sucks into his hanging belly and disappears when he covers the handle with his hands. Two more of Valya's comrades step into the room behind Yusup, searching for targets, but the only man left is Khanzad. The others are down and the waiter is gone. Matthews comes into the room, holding his Beretta at his side, taking in the tableau with one sweep of his eyes.

Khanzad notices him immediately, starts to say something, then stands suddenly. He has to put his palms onto the table to steady himself. "You'll die for this, Volk," he grates. "I have fifty men in this village."

It is an empty threat. The false Chechen hasn't inspired any loyalty. All he has bought with his money and his promises was the feckless insincerity of the *kontraktniki,* the contract soldiers who believe in nothing. But even if there were that many men who would fight for him, they would make no difference to me.

I stand. Take the half-full bottle of wine by the neck and smash the fat end against the side of his face. It shatters, sprouting liquid ribbons of wine and blood. He grunts wetly and spins to his knees, his head in his hands, making a sound like a dog barking under water. I toss aside the table to clear the space between us. Slam my knee under his chin and ride him down, pulling his arms out of the way, blendering the shattered end of the bottle into his face . . .

And then I let the bottle slip out of my grasp. My hands are red and slick. So are his as he tries to hold filleted pieces of flesh in place. Crooked lines of blood are seeping through his fingers, sliding down his thick wrists. The room tilts and wobbles as I come to my feet. They're all staring. Valya. Yusup. Matthews. The two men from the barn. At me, and at Khanzad gurgling on the wooden floor, his blood destined to leave a permanent stain floating beneath the surface of the wood, similar to the one left in the warehouse concrete by Melnik, one of the many victims of his perfidy.

"Are you back?" Valya says.

I jerk a tablecloth free and use it to wipe my hands.

She orders the two fighters to stand guard outside the building, then steps to my side, looking down at the false Chechen dispassionately.

"You should end this here."

She's right. Khanzad's days as a duplicitous broker of misery are done, but he still has the money and the contacts to hire out my murder in a slew of unpredictable ways. I can't live my life with a knife that sharp at my back.

I pick up the Kalashnikov of one of the fallen bodyguards, liking the familiar way it feels in my hands and the weight of it in my arms. For the first time in months I'm not assailed by doubts. I'm sure about Khanzad. I *am* fit to judge him. Matthews starts to say something, but then he closes his mouth and clasps his hands behind his back. Except for Khanzad's wet burbles, everything is quiet and still. I fire three rounds in rapid succession. His powerful body jerks as each bullet strikes, and then his hands fall away from the ribboned remains of his face and he is still.

"You were going to say something, Matthews?" I say, roughly, waving the gun smoke away from my eyes. "Spare him, maybe? Something that sounds noble but is really just self-indulgent and useless?"

"I was going to suggest that you keep him alive until we were sure we had the girl," he says mildly.

I sling the rifle and lead the way through the kitchen. The stairs are in the back, concrete covered in blistered red paint. One flight up is a tight hallway, two rooms on each side, none of the doors locked. Inside the farthest room is a metal-frame bed covered with a bare mattress. Galina is on the bed, mouth gagged, hands and feet bound and then roped to the frame. As we enter she closes her eyes so tightly her face seems to form a fist and she begins to thrash desperately.

She's wearing a loose brown dress. She's so thin it looks as though a stick figure is struggling beneath the folds of cotton. She's covered in dirt, her hair unwashed and tangled. Her left eye is black beneath a thick scratch that starts above her eyebrow and disappears under the gag, a twisted blue bandana wet with her saliva. Valya rushes to her side, removes the gag, and begins stroking her cheeks, talking quietly into her ear while Yusup and Mathews gently untie the ropes. At the sound of Valya's soothing voice Galina opens her eyes. Hazel, wide, terrorized. The coquettish girl who threw a smile over her shoulder at the camera is gone forever.

✗

Valya scoots close to me during the drive back to the barn. "What happens when you get back to Moscow?"

"I'll be debriefed. I'll give Constantine and the General the video and the egg. They can decide what to do with them. Galina . . . I'll give Galina to Barokov so he can take her back to her family."

Her gaze feels hot against my cheek. "Let it go, Alexei. We did all we could. Now it's up to her and the people who love her."

I check the rearview mirror. Galina is asleep on one of the metal benches, wrapped in a blanket with her head on Yusup's lap. The old man carried her through the streets, rejecting offers of help, and now he's holding the upright barrel of his rifle in one hand with his free arm wrapped protectively across her waist. In sleep her face is peaceful, unlined, soft enough to give me hope for her. The others, including Matthews, are on the opposite bench, not talking.

I look back into Valya's smoky eyes, filled with their familiar confidence, but more assured than I remember. I realize that she has changed, too; already experienced beyond her years, she has fulfilled the promise suggested by the noblest moments of her youth.

"What happens after you're debriefed?" she says.

"Then they'll have less than twenty-four hours to decide what to do. After that, the transmitter is no good. Is Yusup up to it?"

She glances into the rear compartment. "Yes. He's committed. Not because he thinks Abreg needs to die, but because the others do. He's right. The new leaders are far worse—bad enough that if he won't do it, I will."

My mouth is suddenly dry. I steer around a plume of dirt and rock washed onto the trail.

"What?" she says.

Even through the tang of gun smoke she smells good, clean, like warm vanilla. Valya is not innocent, but she *is* guiltless, a distinction that makes all the sense in the world to me.

"I won't do it unless you promise to be nowhere near that transmitter."

She leans her back against my shoulder, her legs stretched out on the bench seat toward the passenger door. "How far away is safe?"

"Five kilometers."

She laughs. "Seriously."

"I am being serious. Promise me you'll be at least that far away."

She stares pensively out the window, watching the starlings swoop into the deep purple gulf between two towering ridges.

"I promise," she says finally in a quiet voice.

When she turns back around to face me a few minutes later, her brows have drawn together. She rests her chin on my shoulder. "What happens after this?" she says, and I belatedly realize that this is the question she has been asking all along—the one that really matters the most to both of us.

"We'll have to do our best as we go."

"Yes," she says, and her dazzling smile appears. "*We* will."

chapter 55

Matthews, Charlie, Galina, and I ride in the back of the Ural while our skinny driver with his pipe clenched in his teeth negotiates the trail away from Tindi and back to Grozny's Khankala base. This time we travel by the most direct route, no guide in a tall Astrakhan hat misdirecting us to crazed, looping trails. Charlie takes an interest in Galina, and for most of the trip the two of them talk in low tones in a mixture of English and Russian. For a few kilometers I entertain the dream that they'll both recover. From Khankala we hop a transport plane directly to Moscow, bumping and rocking through a storm that buffets the aircraft like a paper kite.

The pilot radios ahead, so Inspector Barokov is waiting for Galina at the Zhukovsky air base when we land. He catches my eye and nods his thanks, but we don't have time to exchange words before I'm hustled off. He'll take her to a civilian hospital for evaluation and treatment of her physical injuries, after which he'll close his file and Galina and her family will be left to cope, or not, as best they can.

Matthews and I are debriefed separately. Two of Constantine's men listen to my story, then ask me to repeat it while they pepper me with questions, going back and forth over the same ground like they're rolling dough. When they've gotten all they can out of me I'm deposited in a windowless office, empty except for a metal desk and chair, and left to wait. But there's no drama in the waiting, because I already know the outcome. There are many good reasons why Abreg should die, and one bad one: Constantine needs to cover his tracks.

Less than an hour later I'm taken to an elaborate conference room. Constantine and Matthews are already there. Thin black microphones stick up from the honey maple table. All the video-conferencing screens are blank, the cameras lifeless. The people who make decisions like this one don't want to be seen, but I have no doubt that they are listening in Washington and the Kremlin.

"We get one shot at this," Constantine says. He thrusts out his chin. "The signal is set to transmit at four P.M. Our man on the ground will make sure the target is within range." He looks at me. "That is correct, Volk?"

"Yes."

Constantine raises his hand to his throat in his unconscious gesture and thrusts his chin forward. "Mr. Matthews, do your people agree?"

Matthews straightens in his chair. He looks at me, then away, and I see that he has an earpiece drilled into his ear just before he cups his hand around it, his eyebrows raised in twin question marks. Constantine fidgets, clearly unhappy that he hasn't gotten an immediate answer.

After nearly a minute, Matthews takes his hand away from his ear. "We approve."

"You'll need to leave in six hours," Constantine says hoarsely, pretending nothing delayed the answer. He's talking to both of us, although I'm sure he wishes he didn't have to include me. He'd rather send one of his own men to do the dirty work. But he has no choice. The General, me, and the anonymous tech on the General's staff who programmed the GLONASS transmitter are the only people in the world

292 / Brent Ghelfi

who know the frequency of the signal, and the General, to his credit, apparently hasn't budged on this one.

"No mistakes, Volk," Constantine rasps.

Thirty minutes later, after another ride in a Mi-24 helicopter, the General's aide shaped like a question mark leads me down the long hallway toward his headquarters.

"Colonel, wait!"

Golko huffs up behind us, clutching his hat in one hand and his notepad in the other. His left arm is still heavily bandaged. When he draws close he seems to lose track of what he wanted to say. Flushing, he stammers, "I, uh, I just wanted to tell you I'm glad you're all right. I showed you the map, and then . . . well, I stopped hearing from you." He looks nervously at the aide. "Then I heard you went south. I was a little worried, that's all."

I clap his rubbery right shoulder. "Maybe we'll work together again someday, Lieutenant."

His blue eyes open wide. "Isn't there going to be a debriefing?" He angles his gaze toward the lacquered black box under my arm, then quickly starts paging through his notepad. "I have lots of questions. I—"

I nod to the aide and she resumes along the hallway. When we reach the transition to the steps down, I turn around. Golko is still rooted in place, studying his notes. His shirt is untucked over the pillow of his belly and a lank of black hair has fallen over his forehead. He looks up when he notices that I've stopped.

"Thanks, Golko."

"Yes, sir," he says, and salutes.

The General is at his desk reading a transcription of my interrogation. He probably has a similar transcript of Matthews's statement, parts of it undoubtedly blacked out by the Americans. When he sets his reports aside I hand him the egg in its lacquered box.

He removes it slowly, a pearly globe that weighs heavy in his hands, and carefully works the tiny catch to open it. The inside is lined in brushed gold, ingeniously fitted over a golden hen. He lifts the hen admiringly and holds it up to the light. The encrusted diamonds radiate, sparkling rays of white laced with scarlet from the red-diamond eyes. The General's hands are large for his body, sinewy and knotted in contrast to the smooth perfection of the egg and its finely worked contents. When he has finished his inspection he repacks the egg into its box and gives it to his aide. She shuffles off with careful steps.

"What about the pendant?"

"I'm keeping it for now. When she is old enough to understand the nature of the gift, I'm going to give it to Galina."

His eyes glaze and flatten into their reptilian stare, but it bounces off me and eventually he looks over at his monitor. "Do you want to watch the video before it's edited? Or would you prefer to see both versions when they hit the Internet?" He says this in a lighter tone, trying to ease the tension between us.

I tell him no. The streaming pictures already in my mind are more than I can bear.

He nods and settles back in his chair. "We've identified your man," he says, gesturing toward a file on his desk. "Another Saudi, evil to his core like the Black Arab was. They must have a factory there."

I open the file and find myself staring into the Wahhabi's obsidian eyes, burning their all-consuming hatred above his biblical beard. Behind the photo are two dozen pages detailing his known activities and associates.

"He's staying close to Abreg now," I say. "He's trying to take command."

"Good. Maybe we'll get two for one."

chapter 56

I awaken in a cold sweat. Palm the Sig.

Someone is pounding on the closed door of my cramped room in the basement of Vadim's Café.

Vadim says through the door, "Visitor upstairs. A cop."

My chronometer glows just past eight A.M. I have an hour before I leave for the air base to meet the four o'clock deadline. I throw on clothes and head up to the restaurant.

Barokov occupies a table near the front window. Beyond him a morning fog seethes down the street like artillery smoke. He catches my eye when I walk in, and I motion for him to join me at a table that Vadim is clearing in a back corner, partially hidden by the wall that separates the main dining area from the bathroom.

The ruddy inspector eases into a wooden chair with a cloth-covered cushion while I take a seat in one made of metal and red vinyl. He sets two thick folders on the tabletop next to an open jar of pickles. The front flap of the top folder is covered with his handwritten notes and doodles. Swimming among them somewhere is the address for the apartment Semerko used in Makhachkala and my phone number. It feels as if I put them there a long time ago.

"I'm here to thank you, Colonel," he says. "The life Galina has left is better than no life at all."

Vadim brings a kettle of tea and pours two cups. I take a scalding sip, then cradle the mug in my hands, wondering if they will ever feel warm again.

Barokov puts his index finger on the files. "There are still lots of things here I don't understand."

"Isn't it enough that she's alive?"

"Yes, of course. I suppose it's straightforward enough. She was abducted by a young man she knew from her neighborhood, he took her far away, and you went there and brought her back. It's just that I still need to know where he is. I need to make him for Tanya, and it would be nice to close Galina's case with more certainty."

"Semerko Torgov is embers and ashes, Inspector. What you have now is all you're ever going to have."

"He was cremated?"

Vadim places a steaming plate of eggs, ham, and toast in front of me and I begin to eat.

Barokov runs his hand over the top of his files, a thoughtful look on his ruddy features. "We still don't know who killed Alla Anfimova," he says, riffling the edges of the paper.

"Filip Lachek."

"Yes, that's what you said. But I've got nothing to go on. Asking questions about that guy is like trying to break through the Kremlin walls with my fists."

The police will never find Lachek. According to Constantine, whom I trust not at all, Lachek has vanished like windblown vapor, probably to Southeast Asia, his old stomping grounds. The General, Maxim, and the whole pack from my lupine network in the region are all sniffing the ground for him.

Barokov picks up a saltshaker. Puts it down again, then twists the pickle jar so hard some of the water slops out. My plate is emptying quickly. I'll have to leave soon, and Barokov is taking a long time to get to the real reason for his visit. Finally, he raps the table with his knuckles and leans closer.

"What about the AMERCO building?" he says harshly. "Nearly sixty people died, Volk. Sixty! Scores more were maimed."

"Chechen terrorists."

He leans back and sighs. He stretches his face, lifting his brows first, then opening his mouth as far as it will go. When he looks at me again, he starts to say something, but his mouth forms the word without sound: *Ryazan.*

I push away the pottered plate, stand, and drop my napkin on the table. Absently finger one of the scabs on my neck, the one Charlie ripped open, slow to heal. I remember thinking a few days ago in his office that I liked Barokov from the first, even before I crawled onto the beam in the roaring hearth of the AMERCO building.

"Sometimes your kind of justice eludes us, Inspector," I say, and then I have to walk away without acknowledging the wounded look in his eyes.

✷

Maxim calls me as I'm on my way to the base in a black BMW that came with its own driver, a major no less.

"Maybe it's time for a change for you," he says abruptly. "I think we should keep working together."

"What have you found out about Lachek?"

He chuckles, low and deep. "Always the same. Always your agenda. Okay. Lachek was in Hong Kong, but we think he took the ferry to Macao. I have people there who can help you."

I might need logistical help. But the wet work will be all mine.

Sometimes Maxim seems to have a sixth sense that tells him what I'm thinking. "You're a hard man, Volk," he says.

chapter 57

On the outskirts of the Budennovsk air base sits an obscure hangar that houses several battered Mi-8 transport helicopters and the scarred fuselage of an Su-25 attack plane that has been scavenged for parts. Below, in a hardened bunker, is a top-secret command-and-control center.

Only five steps by ten, the room is crowded with consoles holding keyboards and panels banked with switches and blinking lights. Three terminals line one side of the room, manned by technicians responsible for data exploitation, system management, and communications. They're staring at high-definition monitors, keying data, talking into headsets.

The pilot and payload operator workstations are on the other side of the room. The pilot manipulates a joystick and squints at a screen blasting what look like video-game images with numbers scrolling down the side, but this isn't a game. She's flying a drone, a Yak-130, patrolling at three thousand meters above a range of mountains that appear on another monitor looking like a white, brown, and green blanket left crumpled on the floor. Clinging to the side of the tallest mountainous clump is a village recognizable by the spire and polished-steel dome of its minaret.

The last monitor, mounted high on the wall so that it is visible to everyone, including Matthews and me standing at the back of the room, shows the same scene in computer-generated, black-and-white graphics. My chronometer beeps 4 P.M., and just as it does a pulsing dot appears, centered on the screen to the east of the village.

The throbbing dot represents the silicone-based GLONASS transmitter that was embedded beneath the skin of Charlie's slashed forearm, removed, and given to Yusup. It's sending a signal on the frequency I disclosed less than an hour ago, worried to the very end that Constantine might try to take the decision away from me. The red dot means that Yusup and Valya believe the signal pinpoints the location of Abreg—and his bearded Wahhabi fighter. If not, they would have destroyed the transmitter.

The commander of the operations center, a major general who wears so much makeup that her face appears painted, spent the last hour telling Matthews and me tedious facts about the coordination of the operation and the signals bouncing from the transmitter to the satellite, the drone, and the command center in a complex electronic dance. She is proud of the technology at her command. State-of-the-art computer systems, integrated software, PlayStation-like controls, and precision-guided munitions are more real to her than ruptured flesh and vaporized blood and charred bones—all those things that will occur at the other end of the air-to-surface tactical missile the drone is set to fire on my command.

"Check," says one of the techs, confirming that the coordinates are locked.

"Check," says another one, flicking the switches to arm the missile, which the major general has informed me is a Kh-35U packed with 145 kilograms of explosives.

Matthews stands off to one side, hands deep in his pockets. He's not looking at me, just staring reflectively at the video-game console while the major general cups one hand over her earpiece and listens intently. Apparently, she can barely hear the whispery, pained rasp on the other end of the line in the distant Kremlin.

I don't need to hear his voice to be certain the answer is still a go. Constantine, the ageless Cold Warrior, worships at the altar of geopolitical power, and cementing the polygamous marriage of Russia, China, and America with oil is his grand achievement. Abreg represents instability in a region Constantine has now decided should no longer be unstable. Abreg also represents a loose end, because I think it is likely that Constantine conspired with the mountain fighter to thwart efforts to unify the Chechen tribes. Abreg will probably be dead before he knows it, but he made a deal with a winged serpent.

A moment later the major general nods and says, "Affirmative." She removes her headset and looks at me, her painted face lit by the electronic glow of the monitors. "All parties have authorized the strike. We now have four minutes before the signal terminates."

The images on the multiple screens shift as the drone positions over the target. The glowing dot pulses rhythmically. One of the techs murmurs something into her headset. Matthews clears his throat, but it is not an impatient sound, more like something is lodged there. I stand perfectly still.

The flowery rhetoric we use to defend such decisions—a preemptive strike against nuclear terror, the execution of an international war criminal—fails to capture the essence of what we do. The people of the North Caucasus would have been granted their independence long ago and this fight would never have been joined except for those things that animate all conquest—God, glory, and gold. Black gold in this case.

The things done this day—this decision, this violent act—will cease to exist as soon as we leave the room. Neither this group of technicians nor their commander knows or cares who is on the receiving end of the missile.

"Three minutes left," a disembodied voice says.

And as she says the words my conversation with Abreg, the one he brought up during our frigid horseback ride in the mountains, blooms fully in my mind. I feel as if I am there again, back in the pit, all but dead from starvation and pain.

Lots of Cargo 200 in your wake, Volkovoy.

That was what he said three days ago, but he had said the same thing to me years before, standing at the edge of the *zindan*, impossible to see without slitting my eyes against the light that wrapped him in a glowing penumbra.

I don't think I responded to his comment about Cargo 200.

"Can you hear me, Volkovoy? They want to break you, and I can't stop them any longer."

My head drooped until my chin found the sunken hollow of my chest. I was indifferent in the way that only a beaten man can be. Abreg kept talking, though, almost as if he was having a dialogue with someone hidden under his cloak.

"This isn't me, Volkovoy. You—you are what you are. I'm not fit to judge you. But I know myself. I know who I am. And I am not supposed to be here!"

The sharp change in his tone roused me. I looked up to see him suspended in the light, swaying back and forth as if he was struggling to escape. But the effort to hold my head up became too much, and once again my chin fell to my chest.

"Volkovoy! Listen to me! You made the world into this hell. This is your creation. Russia razed this land and tried to wipe away its people. Don't lecture me about who is evil and who is not."

I can't recall delivering a lecture on good and evil. I don't believe I ever did, although I may have said something along those lines in a delirium of pain. More likely, he wasn't talking to me at all; he was answering the insufferable voice in his head, completing half of the dialogue with his soul, because then his tone changed again, riding a wave of resignation as he addressed me directly.

"If you can hear me, look up. Look at me one more time."

His words were more of a plea than command, his tone so strange that I did what he asked. Still caught in the nimbus of light, wavering and indistinct, he spread his arms in a gesture of absolution, or so I think now, looking back on it through the lens of time.

"Can you see me, Volkovoy? Can you see this thing that tortures soldiers and sets fire to hospitals and blows up school buildings filled with children? This is not me. This is not *me*! Your people have made this thing. And I hate it as much as you do. Do you understand? I hate it too!"

And the strange thing is that, now, irretrievable years later, I do understand him as something more than a propagandist's caricature of a monster. I can see Abreg as he used to be—a journalist, a husband, a father watching joy light the eyes of his son when the magician made the elephant disappear—and I can see him as the man he came to be, a man trapped in a horror beyond imagining, drowning in the evil all around him.

"Two minutes, Colonel," the major general says, angling her head toward a lighted button on the console.

I picture a warm room. Blankets covering the walls, bottles glowing in the light from the candles, smoke from the potbellied stove drifting the air. Abreg and the twins and the Wahhabi fighter are there. And somewhere nearby is Yusup, sucking with his tongue on the last of his teeth, stoic in the face of what he knows is about to come.

I let my mind drift over mountainous ridges, riding the cold air beneath the crescent moon on mythically long wings, swooping down and through purplish valleys all the way to a barn leaking yellow slashes of light. Inside is Valya, talking in her intense way, leaned slightly forward, lips parted, eyes fired like molten pewter, just as they were one night years ago when we huddled behind a parapet wall on the roof of a bombed-out Grozny building and she told me to spare the life of a captured separatist, an unlikely, hopeful poet.

You can't kill this one, she said. *It would make you evil.*

Valya, the refugee child of Allah's mountains, saved more than one life that night. She rescued me from the man I would have become, and now I can see his distorted shadow reared alongside Abreg, shuddering in the firelight.

"One minute, Colonel!"

"You don't have to do this, Volk," Matthews says suddenly, surprising me. His voice is loud even against the background chatter of clacking keys and whispered directives.

I walk slowly to stand at the shoulder of the pilot. My body blocks the light behind me, and the change in contrast seems to sharpen the display on the overhead screen, the one that shows the lines and shades of a world of darkness, a world where color has been banished forever. The image will jostle when the missile is launched, I know, first from the sudden drop in weight, then with the blowback from the thrust of the rocket. And then it will steady again as the technician corrects the drone's course and adjusts the main camera to record the white eruption—a star of death exploding like a supernova over an ice-covered shack that overlooks a village spilled down the side of a mountain.

For reasons that I am just beginning to understand, Matthews doesn't want Abreg to die, at least not here, not now. Matthews, the American, believes in free will. He thinks the world can be changed on a whim. But I am Russian, a captive of history. So I press the button to launch the missile.

chapter 58

"Who the hell knows the right thing anymore?" Matthews buckles his shoulder harness and savagely jerks the straps tight. "The world's a complicated place."

We are alone in the cavernous cargo area of an Ilyushin cargo plane, less than an hour after we received confirmation that the missile hit its target. Jet engines scream as the pilot turns the nose, throttles up, and powers down the runway toward Moscow. I have to shout to be heard.

"How long, the Americans and Abreg?"

He grimaces, but I don't think he'll try to deny anything. We're past that now. He waits until we're airborne and the noise drops before answering.

"Two years. He contacted us. We provided the technology to help him stay out of sight of your drones. He gave us information about you guys—local flavor we couldn't get otherwise." Matthews leans forward so that his gaze meets mine. "You can understand why we did it, can't you? It's not like the Kremlin isn't working the Iranians."

"Abreg made a side deal with Constantine."

"Yeah, we figured that out." Matthews settles back into his chair and wipes something nonexistent off his sleeve. "I liked him, Volk," he says bleakly. "I'm not saying he was innocent. I know he had a lot of blood on his hands. But I respected the man."

The pilot banks the plane into a slow turn, still climbing. I'm not sure what I'm going to do after we land in Moscow. Sleep for a long time. Maybe move back into the loft. Go east and find Lachek. Then decide what's next.

Matthews bounces his heels on the metal deck and pulls uncomfortably at his harness. "Men like us do what we're told. No questions. But we do it because we believe in something bigger, not because some asshole politician tells us so. Right?"

Defend the motherland, secure our southern flank, protect the innocents—those things don't resonate the way they used to. I never thought I would have to defend Russia against an onslaught from within. I never considered that our purpose in Chechnya might be something other than security. And who are the innocents? Children like Galina, of course, but Semerko was still a boy when he was marched into war, his just one more pair in a long line of bloodstained boots. When did he change from victim to victimizer?

I don't know what to think about Abreg. He crossed a terrible divide and found himself in a place he wasn't meant to be. He was not innocent, certainly not that, but somewhere in his forgotten past weren't he and those he loved worthy of protection?

acknowledgments

Sarah Knight, my editor and literary confidante, devoted herself to this novel with skill, patience, and grace. She is a shining star. The team at Holt, including John Sterling, Maggie Richards, Patrick Clark, Richard Rhorer, Emily Belford, Jason Liebman, Dana Trombley, and Rita Quintas, along with many others, has supported me in every way possible. I'm grateful for all they've done.

Scott Hoffman, my agent and advocate, kept the faith and always has my back.

Barbara Peters, bookseller extraordinaire, has been a tireless champion.

Paul Thayer worked his usual magic. Ron Rinaldi pored through an early draft of the manuscript and made dozens of trenchant comments. Mark Sands, Ph.D., Commander, U.S. Navy, provided invaluable insights into Russia's GLONASS, drone, and missile technology. Bob Ghelfi, M.D., Lee Ludden, Jessica Barranco, and Bill Doolittle answered countless questions. Jake Ghelfi and Brock Ghelfi were endlessly patient.

James Sallis applied his gimlet eye to several chapters of the novel; better still, he offered his unique blend of criticism and counsel, wisdom and wit. Others who read parts of the manuscript and provided many helpful suggestions are: Jerry Butler, Gigi Connelly, Kate Cross, Stephen Green, Kim Giunta, Chris Hazeltine, Stephen Laramore, Marylee MacDonald, Rita Marko, Amy Nichols, Kurt Reichenbaugh, E. J. Runyon, Shane Shellenbarger, and Joe Weidinger.

I owe special thanks to the people in Russia who have helped me in innumerable ways, particularly the four who have been indispensable: Valentina, Galina, Sergei, and Viktor—*Ya vam byeskonyechno blagodaren.* For anyone interested in reading more about Russia's wars in the "small corner of hell" that is Chechnya I recommend the books of Anna Politkovskaya, who paid the ultimate price for her courage.

As always, Lisa Ghelfi was my first reader (making notes on pages still hot off the printer), and my best friend and partner through everything. So talented, so capable . . .

Read on for an excerpt from

The Venona Cable

Now available in hardcover from Henry Holt and Company

Copyright © 2009 by Brent Ghelfi

PART I

Source No. 19: unidentified highly placed asset
who at the time of the Trident conference in 1943
reported to the KGB on a conversation with
Roosevelt and Churchill.

—John Earl Haynes and Harvey Klehr,
Venona: Decoding Soviet Espionage in America

I'm trapped, nearly out of time.

I have to *think*.

But I can't trust my judgment. Perceptions blurred, memories distorted and incomplete. No sleep for thirty-six hours, a punch behind the ear with the butt of a Glock, and a sickening tumble down the embankment of one of L.A.'s ubiquitous freeways have taken their toll. I landed in a drainage basin beneath an overpass, where a crawl of sixty meters through a nearby culvert saved my life. The tunnel led to the other side of the expressway. From there I hot-wired an ancient Datsun pickup, abandoned it ten miles later in a mall parking lot, then walked here, to a run-down motel near the airport.

I figure I bought an hour. Two if I'm lucky.

My cell phone is gone, but that doesn't matter, not anymore. The only person I trust is Valya, and she is half a world away. I'm on my own, hunted by the police and by American intelligence agencies. My adversaries could be from any of half a dozen organizations. What I don't know is who is pulling the strings. If I can't figure that out soon, I'll be dead.

Somehow I need to wrest answers from the document on the stained bedspread in front of me. Two pages, winged open at the folds, crumpled and smudged from much handling. Labeled VENONA, ~~TOP SECRET~~ it is a decrypted Soviet cable, originally sent from New York to Moscow on 29 May 1943.

No matter how many times I look at it, revelation fails to come.

I lean forward, elbows on my knees. My suit is mud-streaked, torn at the knees. A subcompact Beretta rests in my lap, only four rounds left in the magazine. It smells of burnt powder and gun oil. Opposite the bed, the door is locked and chained. A creaky wooden chair, the twin of the one I'm sitting on, is wedged beneath the knob. Next to the door is a window, the blinds closed as tight as they'll go but still admitting slits of electric yellow light that stripe the carpet and one corner of the bed where the glow cast by the feeble overhead bulb fails to reach.

I don't know how the Americans will handle a situation like this. Their methods in this country are restricted "by law and convention," as a British double agent once famously put it, but the usual rules won't apply in this case. In their position I would clear the area and launch a grenade or pump several hundred rounds through the window rather than risk any people in an assault.

My trembling hands are all that remains of the adrenaline rush brought on by the near miss on the freeway ramp. I clamp them together to steady myself. I need to concentrate in the little time I have left.

The decrypted cable in front of me is marked "3rd Reissue." Each reissue meant that more parts of the cable had been deciphered by the code-breakers at Arlington Hall's Venona Project or their successors in the NSA. This one was dated "10/9/74." More than thirty years after the original cable was sent. But less than two months before my father defected in a Soviet spy plane carrying reconnaissance equipment so advanced for its time that the Americans were desperate to have it.

Through the motel's paper-thin wall I hear a family moving their luggage into the room next door. A baby cries. A boy complains that he's hungry, and his father gruffly tells him to shut up. Jet engines scream overhead as another plane approaches the runway. Hoping the family will leave soon—dinner, a movie, anything—I reposition myself on the hard edge of the chair and bow over the papers again.

The decrypted cable is titled *"19" REPORTS ON DISCUSSIONS WITH "KAPITAN," "KABAN" AND "ZAMESTITEL" ON THE SECOND FRONT.* According to footnotes prepared by the Venona analysts, "19" was an "unidentified cover designation." "Kapitan" was Franklin D. Roosevelt. "Kaban," Russian for "boar," was Winston Churchill. "Zamestitel," the Russian word for "deputy," is believed to have been either Roosevelt aide Harry Hopkins or Vice President Wallace.

Before leaving Moscow—how long ago was that, four days, five?—I was briefed by a former KGB field operative, an aged Cold War veteran named Isadora, who described the Soviet encryption process to me. There in the glade near her dacha, her gaze flitting from one spot to another but rarely meeting mine, she told me how the Soviets' wall of secrecy was breached. Wartime madness, Soviet mistakes. "Point to what ever reason you like," she said. "Venona was still a singular counterintelligence achievement."

The phone in my room rings. One, two, three jangling peals before it goes silent. Nobody knows I am here. Nobody. I draw a deep breath, then another, casting through my memories of the past two weeks for answers. Starting with Everett Walker, a renowned Hollywood filmmaker and cinematographer found dead in my Moscow warehouse with the Venona cable hidden in his possessions, photographically shrunken to a microdot. He had come to Moscow looking for me, the son of Soviet defector Stepan Volkovoy.

Why?

I rub my eyes, picturing my father shivering in the cold cockpit as American interceptors escorted him toward a secret base above the Arctic Circle. What was he thinking at that moment, thousands of meters above the ice, guiding the enormous plane lower, ever lower, approaching—what? Foreign riches? Duty? Fate, I suppose. Either way, traitor or patriot, he was descending toward his new life.

My hand comes away from my eyes smeared with blood. A red trail stains the crinkled whiteness of the cable as I pull it closer, determined to see it anew, to find the clue I believe must be hiding among the words.

The Venona decrypts helped the Americans and British identify hundreds of Soviet spies—among them Julius Rosenberg, Kim Philby, and Alger Hiss—many of them placed at the highest levels of their governments. But despite the American and British successes, they never discovered the identity of 19. They never learned the name of this Soviet source.

A lesson I learned during a training course on counterespionage at Balashikha-2 springs to mind—the paradoxical truth that the more valuable an agent, the more reason to fear deception. If Source 19 was able to get this close to Roosevelt and Churchill at this most critical stage of World War II, he was as valuable as any agent the Soviets had, and therefore the most dangerous one to both the Soviets and the Americans. All of which should be simply a historical footnote, but it's not, because somebody protecting 19's identity wants me dead.

Think!

The KGB assigned cover names to its agents. Julius Rosenberg was "Antennae," then later was known as "Liberal." Alger Hiss was "Ales." The GRU—the Soviet military intelligence agency—often used numeric cover names. Everyone knows this, including all the people who have speculated about the identity of Source 19 for decades. But I know more. I know that GRU Captain Oleg Bassoff has been sniffing around Moscow, rooting through old files, pressuring former agents, and pushing me and others for answers. Does that mean 19 was a GRU source? Why would it matter anymore?

The certainty that nothing can be known or trusted entirely has been drilled into me by training and experience. Truth is elusive, and never more so than in the world of espionage, where patterns are concealed within webs of disinformation and misdirection. Somehow I need to see past the distorted mirrors of deception and time. I need to start at the beginning, make the connections between what I know and what I can infer, find the relationships. My life depends on whether I can solve the puzzle.

What started me along the path to this squalid room? *Your father was a traitor.* A man named Filip Lachek said that four months ago, when he held me in a torture chamber in the bowels of the Lubyanka. He said it again ten days ago, just before I killed him on a foggy night in Macao. That was the moment, I decide, when the past erupted into the present. That was when I changed from predator to prey.

I settle back into the creaking hardness of the motel chair, cup my face in my hands, and drag them downward, stretching sandpapery skin, pulling my eyes wide open. Another jet passes overhead, followed by a roll of thunder and hissing sheets of rain. The color of the thin blades of light between the blinds has changed with the weather. The parallel slashes are bone-white now, strobing as fitful gusts blow from the floor-mounted air vent.

A figure darkens the window.

My hand drops to the butt of the Beretta.

PART II

There is a man, there is a problem. No man, no problem.

—Joseph Stalin

I pursued Lachek for more than four months. Or maybe it is better to say I followed a trail of whispers and innuendo. He was rumored to be in Jakarta, Phuket, and as far north as Beijing, but I could never find any sign of him when I went to look. "Wasted days," Valya said of those trips, worried that my obsession with revenge was causing me to lose touch with what was truly important. "The General has work for you in Moscow, Tbilisi, London. How much longer is everyone supposed to wait while you chase a ghost?"

True enough, although I think her comment about the General reflected her impatience, not his, because he never questioned me during that time. But I didn't listen to her.

My life-and-death game with Lachek began when I killed his son during what I thought was a terrorist attack. I didn't intend to kill him, just to get him out of the way while I subdued two terrorists holed up in a burning building. But a blow to the head with the flat of a gun barrel speaks for itself.

Later I discovered that Lachek and others had staged the explosion of the offices of an American oil company to simulate a terrorist bombing, trying to frighten American investors and inflame passions against Chechen separatists in a bid to take over oil routes. He lost his bid and fled to Southeast Asia, but only after he raped and murdered my friend and business partner, Alla.

Then word leaked to one of my sources that China's Ministry of State Security's counterintelligence section, known as Sixth Bureau, had located him in Macao. I jumped on a commercial flight to Hong Kong, rode the jetfoil ferry to Macao's Outer Harbor, and spent two fruitless days patrolling cobbled streets with their names etched in blue enamel tiles—exotic leftovers from the days of Portuguese colonialism.

Lachek should have been hard to miss. Tall, cadaverous, thinning white hair combed back in oily strands. He would stand out even among all the tourists. But I trawled hotels, theaters, nightclubs, restaurants, bars, Internet cafés, food markets, and a giant shopping mall without a hit.

I showed his picture to chambermaids, waiters, street vendors, beggars. Cabbies smoking dark cigarillos as they leaned against dented fenders, waiting for the next fare. A lounging shopgirl, who jutted her hip, ticked a shiny red nail on the photo, and batted lashes long as butterfly wings as she slowly shook her head no. I trolled the Jockey Club while the thoroughbreds barreled around the turns at Taipa racetrack. Cruised among the flashing lights and burbling machines in the casinos, bumping shoulders with gamblers, junkies, painted hookers.

No sign of him.

Valya phoned me on my last night in Macao. I was done in, ready to call it another useless trip, trudging through a back alley so narrow a driver had to fold back the side mirrors of his delivery truck to squeeze through. Past the kitchen of a noodle shop, its recessed rear door propped partway open, leaking steam and the clamor of pots and shouted Cantonese. On the other side of the alley stood three rows of boxlike housing units that looked like metal shipping containers stacked beside and on top of one another. Wet clumps of fog absorbed the orange light cast by a bulb caged in metal over the delivery door of the restaurant.

"No luck?" Valya said.

"Nothing. The man is everywhere and nowhere."

"I went by the warehouse today. You don't have anyone watching the place, do you?"

"Not since Alla . . ."

I leaned my back against a wall made of sooty brick and propped my left heel behind me to relieve the pressure on my prosthesis. Alla ran my operations with dictatorial efficiency. She was so omnipresent that closing everything down had seemed inevitable after she died.

"Why?" I said.

"I went there to look for Vadim. One of the cooks told me he'd gone to get something at the warehouse."

Two people turned into the alley and strolled my way, shoulder to shoulder, holding hands. Another figure rounded the corner behind them, weaving, probably drunk.

"Three men were there," Valya said. "One out front talked on a cell phone while two others searched for something on the side nearest the river."

The couple turned into a gap between two buildings. Just before they disappeared, his hand dropped to her bottom and she slapped it away, giggling. The third figure resolved itself into an old man, jerking and swaying with an uneven gait. He appeared to be having difficulty finding purchase on the slick cobblestones.

"Police?"

"Probably."

"Did they see you?"

"You're joking, right?"

The old man drew even with me. Tall and thin, head down, one hand buried in his pocket, the other brushing the wall on the far side of the alley for balance. The upturned collar of his coat hid his face but left the top of his head exposed, revealing white strands of hair. He moved spasmodically, stooped, loosely placing one foot in front of the other before he stiffened his spine for the next step. That was what did it. His spastic movements triggered recognition.

"Got him," I said into the cell phone, then dropped it into my pocket, gathered a head of steam in five long steps, and smashed into Lachek like a battering ram.

Lachek slammed ass first onto the broken asphalt of the alley with me on top of him. Before he had a chance to take a breath, I elbowed him to the side of his head. Pistoned my knee into his groin. Hoisted him off the ground and drove him backward into the brick wall, all of my weight behind my shoulder. Ribs cracked as he hit with an explosive grunt. I held him there for long enough to see that he was done, then let him drop to the gutter, where he lay curled, clutching his midsection and groaning.

The delivery door of the noodle shop swung all the way open, casting a shaft of light into the alleyway. A Chinese cook stared without expression at us. He tucked his unlit cigarette behind his ear and looked off into the orange glow above the roofline of the building. Then he deliberately wiped his hands on his apron, turned away, and eased the door closed behind him.

I jammed the barrel of my Sig under Lachek's nose while I frisked him. Bony shoulders and hips, ribs that felt like broom handles. He cried out when I jostled one of the broken ones to find a chrome-plated Makarov in a shoulder holster and a nasty switchblade in a belt sheath. I transferred them to the pocket of my leather jacket. Found two keys on a ring in his pants pocket.

The twin headlights of a car swept into the alley, lit the scene, threw long shadows.

"Volk," Lachek said matter-of-factly while I watched the car reverse out of the alley. I had to assume the driver was dialing the police on his cell phone. Meaning I didn't have much time.

Without bothering to look directly at Lachek, I slashed the barrel of the Sig across his face. Skin split as his head snapped back. Blood welled between his fingers, and he pedaled his feet against the asphalt trying to escape another blow.

"Where are you staying?" I said.

Still holding his face, he aimed his chin toward a flight of metal stairs crawling up the side of the stacked housing units. "Second floor."

I pulled him to his feet and frog-marched him ahead and up the stairs, grinding the barrel of the Sig into his lower back. He stumbled when we reached the landing, so I lifted him by the neck in a stranglehold and drove him up the last flight and along a breezeway.

"Here," he wheezed outside a door numbered 243B. I twisted the key in the lock, then shoved him through the doorway as it swung open, holding his body in front of mine, aiming the Sig around the room under his arm.

Nobody in sight. I kicked the door closed with my heel, clouted Lachek in the back of the head to make sure he wouldn't get ideas about hideaway guns and knives, and rushed to recon the flat as he lay dazed on the floor.

In the back was a bedroom. Unmade bed, scattered clothes, two dirty syringes, the whole mess bathed in green neon from a sign outside the window advertising some energy drink. The window looked onto a steel-and-glass commercial mid-rise surrounded by a ramshackle collection of older buildings.

The combination dining room and kitchenette held a folding table, a built-in stovetop and oven combo, and a rust-stained sink. The door to the right opened onto a bathroom barely big enough to turn around in.

No bodyguard, no nurse, no maid.

Lachek had money. Not as much as he once had. Much of his wealth had been stripped away, along with all of his power and prestige, when the General and his group chased him out of Russia. But still, more money than most people could accumulate in several lifetimes. He didn't have to live this way. This was a choice.

I went back to where he lay sprawled in the front room. Half-eaten cartons of food, periodicals, and discarded clothes littered the floor, everything coated with the sour stink of neglect and decay. No pictures or plants or personal touches anywhere.

As I waited for Lachek to regain his senses I flipped through the newspapers and magazines. The *South China Morning Post*, the *International Herald Tribune*, the *Vladivostok News*, *Time* magazine's international edition, *The Economist*—some of them dated as far back as February. Lachek hadn't been traveling every corner of Southeast Asia during the last four months. He had been here the entire time, holed up amid the squalor and the putrid smell of spoiled food and dirty socks. Waiting to die, judging by the look of him.

He stirred. Fluttered his eyelids. Drew his knees to his chest and held his bloody cheek in his hands, making a whimpering sound. Looking at him, I finally understood how he had been able to evade me for so many months. I'd been searching for the wrong man. The towering operative with a face like the blade of an ax and rabidly bright eyes was gone, replaced by this empty husk.

After another minute or so his hands dropped from his face. He stared around the room, looking lost for a few seconds before he saw me. I watched the memory come back to him. He started to say something, stopped, and looked around again. Then his expression changed as a different kind of understanding dawned. He was seeing himself through my eyes.

"Cancer," he said. "You can't do anything worse to me."

I started to correct him, then didn't. I had come here intending to destroy him. Make it last for days, I'd told myself. But now that the moment was upon me, I no longer had the taste for it. Nothing could bring Alla back to life. Killing Lachek would give me no more satisfaction than stomping a cockroach.

"Do it," he wheezed. He tried to sit up, then cried out and fell back, clutching his rib cage. "Do what you came here to do, just get it over with."

I stood and exchanged my Sig for his Makarov. Racked the slide. "You're vermin, Lachek. I'm not going to waste time pulling the wings off a fly."

"Fuck you."

His gaze followed the barrel as I raised my arm. But no fear showed on his face. Instead, his lips curled in the shape of a smile.

"Major Stepan Volkovoy," he said, dragging out each syllable.

"What?"

The Lachek I remembered blossomed back to life. Vicious, all curdled malevolence, a wild, gleeful light in his eyes. "Your father was a traitor. A pig."

My finger tightened on the trigger.

"He defected. Stole our most valuable spy plane and gave it to the Americans."

I never knew my father. As far as I had been able to learn, he disappeared not long after my mother died as I clawed out of the womb. As an air force officer, he could have been killed in any one of dozens of Cold War theaters or exiled to one of many Soviet detention camps.

I firmed my grip on the Makarov, ignoring Lachek's demented eyes, my thoughts turned inward. I had gone through a period of several years during which I'd search the archives for news of my father whenever I was on leave or had spare time. Even during rehab while I was learning how to walk again I made calls and requested records, swimming upstream against a torrent of Soviet and post-Soviet falsifications.

The name S. Volkovoy appeared among the records of the political prisoners of a camp in Kolyma during the winter of 1979, but Volkovoy is a common name, and the reference led nowhere. The idea that my father might have betrayed his country and left his son to live an orphan's hellish existence . . .

"A defector, Volk."

Where not covered in blood Lachek's skin was parchment-dry, his hair oiled and ropey across this skull. Snot seeped from his nose, but he didn't seem to notice. He twisted his glistening red lips, visibly glad to have one last chance to injure somebody.

"He goes down in history as one of the vilest pigs our military ever produced. And it's not over. I've made sure of that. All of you are going to pay. Tell your precious General I said that. All of your worst secrets will come back from the dead when you least expect."

I knew the right thing to do if I wanted to learn more. Burn him, cut him, pistol-whip him. Tear every scrap of information from his ruptured flesh—whispered words from a former colleague in the KGB or one of his long-ago informants, or perhaps a connection he had made between the lines of one of his magazines. Who knows? But at that moment I didn't have the stomach to be in the same room with him any longer. I thought that anything else he said would be either a hateful lie or a truth I couldn't stand to hear.

Something in my bearing or expression forewarned him, gave him the chance to sink his fangs one last time. "Wait until you see what's coming. You, the General, Bassoff, all of you will pay. Wait and see," he said again, just before I crammed the barrel between his teeth and squeezed the trigger.